SHUTTLE RISING

TO RENDEZVOUS WITH A RUMOR

To
Tom Dod
with fond
memories
of Nasa

Charles Boyle

SHUTTLE RISING

TO RENDEZVOUS WITH A RUMOR

Charles Boyle

TridenT
PUBLISHING

Shuttle Rising by Charles Boyle

Published by Trident Publishing

1837 Cove Point Rd.

Annapolis, Maryland 21401-1009

www.whalebook.net

Cover illustration by David Lau, www.geocities.com/dclwin
Page Layout by John Culleton, Able Indexers and Typesetters
www.wexfordpress.com

Publishers Cataloging in Publication Data
Boyle, Charles P.
Shuttle Rising: To Rendezvous with a Rumor / Charles Boyle. p. cm.
ISBN 0-9657214-5-0

1. Science fiction. 2. Love stories. 3. Space flight–Fiction. 4. Space travelers–Fiction.
5. Astronauts–Fiction. 6. Space and time–Fiction. I. Title.

PS3552.0919 S5
813.54–dc22 2005902031

First Edition First Printing
Printed in the United States of America
10 09 08 07 06   1 2 3 4 5 6 7 8 9 10

Dedicated to the women of space

Acknowledgments

Help, guidance and support came from many sources over the years. I'm grateful to all who gave early encouragement, including Tom Clancy, and especially Hugh Downs and Frank Sietzen of the National Space Society.

My sincere appreciation goes to Astronaut Bryan O'Connor for his invaluable review, and to Astronauts Don Peterson, Story Musgrave, Charles Bolden, and Sally Ride for helpful comments and influence.

I'm indebted for facts, history and data to the Office of Public Affairs at Goddard Space Flight Center, Marshall Space Flight Center, Kennedy Space Center and NASA Headquarters.

For advice on aviation, I thank fighter pilot Jim Elliott, carrier Air Boss Jack Hoch, and Chris Stephanides–who flew the Atlantic alone, single engine, twice.

To the many technicians, engineers and scientists who advised, I'm grateful. Any inaccuracies will be mine.

I deeply appreciate the many reviews by Ed Buckley, Conrad Boyle, Vicki Jacobs, Bob Hutchison, Arnold Tannenbaum, Don Dement, Ruly Knox, Walter Sullivan, Mike Maher, Art Jenssen, Hans Steen, Pat O'Connell, Ken Jacobs, and Keith Walters. A special thanks goes to Brittany Boyle for the cover concept of life reaching out.

And, to my wife, Joan, thanks for your long-lasting patience.

Shuttle Rising

Part 1: SIGNAL AND MESSAGE — 11

Part 2: THE COMMANDER — 33

Part 3: CONFLICT AT THE UN — 53

Part 4: MISSION TO IVAN — 71

Part 5: RIPOSTE — 123

Part 6: REVENANT ONE — 163

Part 7: YLENA — 217

Part 8: THE SHANGRI-LA EFFECT — 291

Epilogue 1 — 334

Epilogue 2 — 335

Epilogue 3 — 336

PART I

SIGNAL AND MESSAGE

1

He spied on foreign agents and diplomats, and on their rulers, in ships, planes, limousines or beds. Mike Benson penetrated privacy routinely as Technical Director of the Central Intelligence Bureau. The man did his stealthy work proudly, his ethics singing harmony with his country's need to know.

His youngest sister, a medical nun, was unimpressed. She thought him a bureaucratic Peeping Tom and said so.

"Unfair, Peggy. Your own Bible shows my work is as worthy as yours. The good guys always had to spy or die. Look it up. They infiltrated. They sent out scouts. Why is spying right for them but wrong for me?"

"We're not at war, Big Brother."

"Wrong, little sis. Our enemies nowadays are a new breed. They're always active, so we're always at war."

"Nobody's army is after us."

"My dear sister, today's enemies sneak in. They down our planes, destroy our buildings and kill our people. But, in the forgiving gospel of St. Peggy, you want us to live by an 11th Commandment that says, *Thou shalt not listen in on thine enemy.* Now, tell me, why didn't any of the Big Ten ban spying?"

"No room on the Tablets."

He smiled, shaking his head at her innocence. Despite some contrary rumors, he *did* have a sense of humor. In addition, he had a hunter's instincts, endless patience, science skills, and electronic ingenuity. He also had a new peeve, started by an excited female voice in a phone call.

"I found a signal!"

"Intelligible?"

"Yes and no."

"How can that be?"

"It's in Morse code but it made no sense."

"Anna, think! Morse code means it's from us. People. Why should we care?"

"We can't account for any source."

"Are you pulling my leg?"

"Absolutely not. It's got us baffled."

"Try to decipher it?"

"No need. All it says is the letters 'u-s-c-o-m,' and nothing else."

"Does your Director know?"

"Yes. I told everyone. Now, we're all at work on it."

"Why didn't he notify me?"

"I guess it's his attitude toward your agency."

"I understand. I may not be welcome, but I'm coming down, anyway."

"How soon, Michael? Sorry. How soon, Dr. Benson?"

"Late this afternoon."

He cradled his phone, musing. The implications of her discovery grew. Anna Schutz, a doctoral candidate in astronomy from Purdue University, had detected a mysterious signal from a listening scan of the night sky. Could her discovery match his hopes, or did the use of Morse code rule that out? Gotta get down there and make sure! As he hung up, a thought mocked him. His fist slammed down like a gavel.

"Damn!" He struck the wincing desk again.

"Hypocrite!" Benson's demeanor, frank and blunt, also acted inward, making him confront himself. "It's not just the signal, is it?" he accused aloud in the empty office. He didn't like the answer. *She's part of the reason for making the trip.* Refusing such incitement, he began dialing her number to cancel. His hand slowed at this cowardice, and he stopped, recalling his visit to her remote observatory.

Anna had been his assigned student escort. First, she showed him the workings of the auditorium where he would lecture. Then, she toured him through the labs and around the antennae. Finally, she led him, a winded hiker, to her favorite ledge near the rim of the valley that sheltered the observatory.

"Enjoy the view," she said and began to spread a picnic lunch in silence.

Turning from his crawling view of roots and rock, he gaped. The grandeur of peaks, meadows, forests and sky spoke to his soul. He sagged against the cliff face, awed and humbled by the glory. His breath left in a long sough, as though deflating him to insignificance. Staring, breathless, he felt a seeping calm whose peace said he was not trivial, but a treasured part of the vast majesty.

He flinched when a hustling cloud, skimming the rim, dived as if to carry him off in puffed cotton. Instead, it dispersed into bright wisps in swirling wind. He snapped awake.

"Wow!"

"Like it up here, Dr. Benson?"

"Spectacular. It tells me I live too much indoors."

"I'm fortunate. Astronomers have it both ways. I live indoors to study the outdoors."

He stared at the sky as if drawing insights from its light. She broke in.

"Lunch!"

They feasted on sliced apples, peanut butter sandwiches, bananas, and stream water. They found childhood bonds in life on prairie farms and an early love of science.

Lost in talk of life, nature, hopes, and work, they startled at an alarm. She turned it off, stood and said, "Today, my job is also timekeeper. Off we go. You're to speak in three hours."

A sturdier cloud swooped. It hit with a twisting down draft and swamped them in shadowy fog. In the darkness, she gripped him.

"Down, quick. Don't move. You might go off the ledge."

Kneeling, they hugged stable in the sudden wind. She released him as they slowly emerged from swirling light. Her hair sparkled with droplets combed from the cloud. He stood staring, stunned and stirred by young beauty, as she turned to hike down.

Anna stayed distant in the blandishing throng of students before his lecture. But, later, on the crowded benches, in the give-and-take of student papers, she sat squeezed against him. No monk, he accepted the sensations. At the reception afterwards, she again drew near, now as a caterer. Pressed close by the crowd, she slowly refilled his wineglass. Her low voice breathed in his ear, "When will I see you again?"

Later, in pajamas and fussing about aimlessly, he resisted memories of Anna on the mountain. He sternly dismissed even the possibility of amorous risk, and went to bed. But he spent the dark hours groaning with yearning in restless sleep. He confronted his swollen obsession with a morning shower of mountain water. It did not help. Chilled, quivering, and concerned now to the point of worry, he focused for support on his triple safeguards: *personal control, agency rules, and marriage vows.* They would guarantee against impropriety in these caressing summer nights of the hushed southern mountains. They would. Yes, they would. Right? Certainly! No urge could vanquish that trio and tarnish him or his agency.

Yet, seriously unnerved and seeking insurance, he used a work pretext to leave a day early. Flying home, he was furious for doubting his restraint, for not believing in himself.

Now, phone in hand, a shiny new thought struck his mind. It brought a startled reality that made him abandon the phone call.

"Oh, you vain bastard," he mumbled. He shook his lowered head and smiled knowingly. Running for home hadn't been necessary at all. He had failed to recognize a fourth safeguard against foolishness: Anna, that warm, bright, talented, and graceful creature, couldn't possibly regard him, at his age, as an object of interest.

He was wrong. He was actually an object of desire.

<hr>
2
<hr>

Anna Schutz worked as a student volunteer with the records, computers, and giant antenna of a project called Watch on Other Worlds' Intelligence. The impish students pronounced the project "WOWEE," and often wrote WOWI with an exclamation point. Because it lived on a pittance budget from a university consortium, it needed the near-free labor of young scholars. In return, WOWI offered them access to mountains of data the students mined in hopes of finding topics for their doctoral theses.

Friends said, "Anna, you're ruining your career!" They enjoyed occasional visits to WOWI, but always ridiculed her search for high IQ cosmic aliens.

One said, "Anna, your guys have been trying for thirty years to find an electronic needle in a haystack of static. Get out of this dead end. They've found no evidence, not even a hint."

"They haven't yet," she fired back, "but the math is with us. What are the odds that we're the only intelligence in a universe with billions of planets? Get serious. And remember the sign you saw coming in."

The big sign at WOWI's gate said, *"Absence of evidence is not evidence of absence."*

Benson had a simple personal reason for visiting the WOWI site in its remote West Virginia valley: the possibility of listening in on a conversation between galaxies, the ultimate in eavesdropping! He knew that the fun would vanish if intelligible signals arrived. His job would take over. He could not assume that aliens would be friendly.

He had asked scientists, administrators and students to phone him should a signal appear. Some told him they'd have nothing to do with his damned security agency. Benson's physics doctorate meant nothing to those who saw him as part of an enemy that classified information and limited the free communication of research discoveries.

Not so with Anna Schutz, a red-white-and-blue All-American girl. Impressed with the capability, authority and personal power of the Technical Director of the CIB, Anna felt duty bound to notify him of anything unusual. She overflowed with as much patriotism as an Iowa farm family could instill, and with as much respect for her physical needs as the stockbreeding lessons of that farm could teach. She understood about coming into heat and the need for satisfaction. She saw it as nature's dictate, with denial unnatural. However, satisfaction could not be random. Anna lived the breeder's creed: use the best for mating. Benson qualified as a prize bull of her own species. She'd felt instinctive attraction when they met. He'd proven friendly, but remote. Then he'd gone. The moment she discovered the puzzling radio signal, she knew it would bring him back.

After the call, Benson shed appointments like an outbound ship drops hawsers. Packing, he remembered his night return from the last trip to WOWI. In a fortunate coincidence, his timing matched a peak of passion as Martha gave him a "welcome home" that started at the door and diverted his unsought lust into love. She viewed that night as a conjugal milestone, and sometimes reminded him. He, however, tried to forget it and its spur, Anna. Now, preparing to return, he faced the dilemma: vigorous middle age would again meet nubile youth, perhaps willing. The phone voice had embraced him like a warm coil.

Practical, he strode quickly to the medical office and got *the* prescription without any questions. The doctor knew the nature of some agents' assignments. Later, her brow would furrow as she reflected on the mature Benson as a customer. Normally, she issued the aptly named Dedenoll to young agents, bucks whose duties required emotional control. *Circus coming down,* she sometimes thought on dispensing the drug, guaranteed to ground tent poles for a week.

Back in his office, Benson saluted Martha's picture, took the tablet, threw a kiss in the same movement, and headed for Andrews Air Force Base. There he climbed alone into an agency plane and flew southwest to the mystery of "uscom."

Meanwhile, Anna's technicians were tiring of false starts and change-orders on the presentation being cobbled for Benson.

"What the hell's gotten into her? Somebody oughta tell Miss Perfection this ain't for a Congressional hearing."

Marie Ardenne shushed them with a frown and a crossthroat finger. Anna's mentor and confidante, she took a folding chair to Anna's desk and sat down.

"Un petit oiseau m'a dit," she said.

"What? I don't . . . " Anna knew only English.

"I said, 'A little bird told me.' "

"Told you what?"

"You are disconcerted today."

"So, it shows? Not good. Not good at all."

"Perhaps I can help."

"Oh, I wish you were another kind of doctor."

"Tell me."

" I'm coming unglued — fantasizing over somebody."

"Could it be Dr. Benson?" said the seer from Paris.

"How could you know he . . . ?"

"He stirs me, also. He is a prize."

"Like one of my prize bulls. And that's how I want him."

"This is a small fraternity. Be discreet."

3

In a bubbling "boiler room" of computers, sandwiches and activity, Benson worked with Anna and a score of project-oriented students who puzzled and debated over "uscom." They talked about chance, technical sources for the signal, stellar civilizations, and the possibilities for practical jokes. At one point Benson suspected Anna of hoaxing him. After all, he was in a crowd that might enjoy pulling his CIB tail. Sensing the scrutiny, and fearful of rejection, she worked for hours writing software to detect previous signals in the records. It impressed and relaxed him.

Student teams tested the software on several months of available data and found only the original signal. Benson began to suspect WOWI staff members of running a spoof. He imagined a small group gleefully watching the result. When he told Anna his belief of a prank, she disagreed.

"Then it must," he said, "be a bounce from the ionosphere."

"Too many variables," said Anna, and refreshed him on physics he'd forgotten. Her voice sounded odd. Looking up from her charts, he realized why. Her words were echoing flatly off the concrete walls of an almost empty room. Tired students had trickled away.

"I guess everybody's exhausted. We should go to bed, too." She gave him a key, and took his hand. "Come. I'll show you where you'll sleep tonight. Your baggage is there."

With passion battling fatigue, she led him cautiously in thin fog over rough ground through the green darkness of close trees toward the fuzzy light of a VIP cottage.

"Sorry," she said whenever she stumbled, jerking him off balance. Her coordination whittled by weariness, she fell once. He toppled slowly onto her, cushioned. He rolled off.

"You okay?"

"Just groggy," she said.

He rose to a knee, then up. He helped raise her and she leaned against him with a sob.

"I'm so stupid! I never even thought to bring a flashlight."

"You had too many things to think about today," he said. He gave a comforting hug and disengaged. "Let me go first."

"No. I really do know this way. Let's single file, and we'll go slower. Hold me from behind." She guided his hands to her hips. She walked confidently, as though to prove a point.

When she tripped, he could not control her fall. He sensed a shadowy toppling and then heard the sickening thump of skull on rock.

He felt no bleeding. He left the breathing body and, in a near crawl, got to the clearing. A phone call brought lights and rescuers.

When Anna awoke to bleary eyes and a head of pain, she saw Benson talking with her mother. When their joy subsided she heard the story of fractured skull and days of coma. With recovery predicted, Benson left.

"Jesus answered our supplications!"

"I'm glad, Mom."

"Let us pray together in thanks."

They did. There was no escape. Mom was in charge again. Their farm, at the buckle of the state's Bible Belt, had been a furnace of faith and revivalism. In the long days of stabilizing and healing, her mother's sectarian recitations resurrected Anna's childhood.

Her mother's voice now began each day with, "Today's readings will be from ... " and ended each with, " ... I pray the Lord my soul to take."

The old, familiar voice went on and on with the old, familiar readings from the Testaments. Their relentless, hypnotic Message penetrated, and by some mystical chemistry Anna's fresh hearing of the ancient verities took root in crevices of youthful rejection. Faith sprouted.

"I wish to be baptized," announced Anna one morning.

Her mother made it happen by noon, as her triumph of "Born again!" rendered her speechless with joy.

Anna's conversion had not come as in St. Paul's flash. Instead, it had seeped in, a brightening light. She could see now only in the black and white of evil and purity.

"I am a sinner," she declared privately to the minister. "I coveted a woman's husband, and tempted him, and lusted like a barnyard animal."

"You are now a child of God. Do not look back."

But the arrival of an unquestioning faith brought its companions, shame and hope. Grasping the concept of sin for the first time, Anna recoiled into a personal symbolism. Her fall in the forest became "The Fall" in the Garden. And she was Eve. On the endless tape of her mind a message rolled: "Lead him not into temptation." In the guilt of her enlightenment, she sought grace and forgiveness. She chose service to Benson as an absolving penance, vowing a personal research of "uscom" as her atonement.

---------------------------------- **4** ----------------------------------

The signal nibbled at the edges of his mind for weeks. Impatient, Benson ordered all CIB listening posts worldwide into a computer search for the letters "uscom" in radio data recorded on the Fourth of July. The zero results revived his suspicion of a subtle hoax by a WOWI staffer. His fretting persisted until "uscom" in Morse code tapped in his head for most hours of most days. It caused an unpleasant summer. He became cranky and impatient, always the consequence when a man with a hunch can't prove it.

Over time, the tapping subsided and his mind turned to other matters. The world turned for almost a year, one in which Anna wrote him several very formal letters. They described her continuing search for the message, and the decline of other students' interest. Then, on the Fourth of July, near noon, an excited Anna Schutz called him at home. Benson had to calm her to get the message. Then he had to calm himself.

"It's come again, Dr. Benson. The same signal!" she said, elated, vindicated, and fulfilled. She had searched every day for a year, doing her penance of service to this man.

Benson often lived out of a "bug out" bag, packed with essentials only, that waited in his office closet for unexpected trips. Gripped by the "uscom" mystery, he tossed the bag into the plane, filed a flight plan, and headed again for the valley. His eerie ecstasy about the message alternated with anger that he might be the butt of a hoax. He laughed, recalling a comic who said an inner voice was warning him not to trust his intuition.

Anna's patience and effort had triumphed through dogged use of her computer program every day in an eleven-month hunt. She convinced Benson that no one had tampered with the incoming data stream. "This is an actual transmission!" Once again, it had said, "uscom." Once again, it said nothing more. And, once again, it spoke on the Fourth of July.

Anna could conceive of no coincidence of weather that would allow even the most determined prankster to bounce the ionosphere successfully two years in a row. The giant antenna pointed straight up to space from the bottom of a bowl-shaped valley. No stray signals could leak in. A spurious transmission would have to come from a plane flying directly over the site.

"Flying a plane overhead would take time and money. The students have little of either," she said. "The staff isn't frivolous or imaginative enough. And what prankster would bury the signal in a cosmic data stream so vast that only chance would bring the message to anybody's attention? This is not a hoax."

When they met and worked together, she did not look at him directly, and her conversation always centered on the mystery signal. He wondered if the injury had affected her mind or personality. He would never know that remorse had triggered her relentless, successful search and its astounding and dangerous consequences.

Armed with two signals a year apart, Benson took his quest up the chain of command. He started bluntly with the WOWI Site Director.

"Dr. Zelig, we've got a mystery on our hands and I hope we can cooperate. Can you assign some students to search for more signals in data from earlier years?"

"No, sir. There is no one to spare for such a job."

"Well, how about checking for just the Fourth of July each year?"

"There is no one to spare for such a job."

"Come on, Franz, I'll pay for the work. We're dealing with a legitimate, repetitive enigma. It'll be worth the time and money to check it out."

"There is no one to spare for work that is not extra-terrestrial."

"We won't know that until we know its source."

"Its source is undoubtedly students or faculty playing a prank. Probably on you."

"Why would they do that?"

"Just to give you a hard time would be reason enough, Dr. Benson. You know, sir, that my people are scientists, and they have a built-in hostility to any organization, *any organization,* that tends to restrain open communications in scientific activity."

Benson stormed within but he spoke with passion about the merits of inter-agency cooperation until the director interrupted to say, "Ah, but WOWI is not a federal agency!"

Benson trotted out the patriotism arguments but couldn't move the man. The director kept asking for any evidence of national security issues. Stymied, Benson threatened White House intervention.

Anna had never seen authority figures in bureaucratic combat. In bewilderment, she excused herself and left the room, making Benson see himself through her eyes: a senior official getting out of control. He fell silent, focused his thoughts, apologized for his temper, and ended the meeting.

He found her standing outside the building. "Sorry, Anna. I didn't mean to upset you in there. We butt heads all the time in Washington."

"It's okay."

"Well, his decision isn't okay. The guy's impossible. He says that the whole 'uscom' business is probably some of his people pulling my leg."

"I've looked carefully. There's no way to fake that signal. However, I will not be offended if you believe him. After all, who am I to refute him?"

"But you think he's wrong."

"Very much so." She explained her reasoning. Her technical explanations made sense to him. She concluded that the signal could have entered the data only by transmission from the sky, a sky whose radar history said nothing had flown anywhere near the site for months. Benson thanked her and said goodnight.

Walking back to the laboratory, alone, he mused about Anna's influence as the diligent digger whose sparks light the way for others. Her flight from the room shocked him back to what he did best, analysis. Summing up his thoughts, he concluded: the signals couldn't be a hoax, they seemed to come a year apart, they came on the same day each time, they came from above, and they could not have been an accidental reflection from the ionosphere.

He recalled Anna's comment about how unlikely it would be for anyone to send up a local plane once a year just to fly over this remote place. Even the high-flying airliners didn't pass anywhere near. So what could it...?

He started to smile. "Dummy," he said, and took out his cell phone.

5

Benson had suddenly realized that other groups also watched the sky. He had forgotten about the Sky Perimeter Command. Their people stood radar guard against unauthorized vehicles entering U.S. air space. They tracked everything in the sky, including all objects in space. He felt stupid for not thinking of them earlier. A phone call got immediate and enthusiastic cooperation by bringing some excitement into work that his friend Art Cooper described as "Big long chunks of deadly dull."

Art served as the colonel in charge of intelligence and tracking operations. He worked in a place he called "the funny mountain," because it had been hollowed out. Huge caverns, blasted and drilled out of the rock, held computers and displays to interpret torrents of data pouring in from non-stop, sky-scanning sensors. Its design made the mountain base an underground city-fortress, ready to withstand all but a direct nuclear missile hit, and perhaps even that.

It took almost an Act of God to allow entry of anyone not on the duty roster. But in this business Benson sat at the right hand of the Father, always welcome. An electric cart, swift and silent, swooshed him through craggy tunnels with blast-cushioning switchbacks every hundred feet or so.

The driver broke silence when the cart swept into a vaulting chamber and stopped. "Lift's to your right," he said.

What looked like a concrete pillar holding up the roof turned out to be an elevator shaft. A ride to the sole stop took Benson to the unlit balcony office of Art Cooper.

Art called, "Over here!" Benson crept through the gloom toward his old friend. Art, blowing into a cup of coffee, crouched over a tripod telescope pointed at the window. He moved back from the eye piece saying, "Your turn."

Squinting, Benson brought into focus an eye-filling female at a console on the main floor.

"Distracting," he said.

"Yes," said Art, "but remember, living indoors requires substitute scenery."

Art's forehead soared above keen, piercing eyes. Behind it lived the odd, gifted brain that kept him employed. He held his job by sheer merit and did it with confident energy. The system needed his skills as science wizard, gifted manager, and technical sleuth. To get them, it accepted his quirky, capricious humor and malapropisms. Once, about a computer failure, he remarked, "Well, there's no use crying over sour grapes." Pushing a safety design, he pontificated, "A stitch in time gathers no moss."

Knowing the dominance values of controlled eccentricity, Benson marveled at the utter confidence of Art's behavior, but he couldn't distinguish ploy from personality despite years of friendship. Cooper always delivered his lines deadpan, making strangers exchange glances, wondering about competence. They needn't have worried; Cooper took his job seriously. As usual, he had done his homework. He turned on a few projectors, and some very rough sketches of three odd looking spacecraft appeared on the wall screen.

"Bottom line," Cooper said," is that one of these is doing the transmitting. Guess which one."

Two of the spacecraft were American, both in near-polar orbit so that each revolution let them see a new north-to-south swath of the earth rotating below. Benson saw an earth resources observer, a weather satellite and a Soviet vessel, all ancient and dead. Prompting the game along, Benson hung his head.

"I give up, Art. Lead me like a child."

"Am I being unfair?"

"Right," said Benson, "and you're wasting time, too."

Art's explanation came fast. "On the Fourth of July last year, two of these three satellites passed over the WOWI site in the same time frame: one Soviet, the other ours. The same thing happened a year later, but now our second satellite was paired with the Russian."

A triumphant Cooper asked, "See who went over West Virginia in the same few minutes for two years in a row?"

"Got a theory?"

Art smiled. "The Russky is calling somebody," he said, "and I don't know who, how, or why. I think there's a timer set to go off only once a year, and only over the continental U.S., and only in the hydrogen wavelength. That satellite's from the twentieth century and has never been visited, so whatever lets it do these things is the old, original equipment. But you know what? Back then, nobody knew how to trigger specific time-and-location broadcasting. You know what else? Nobody listened in the hydrogen frequency until Frank Drake started doing it in 1961. So who the hell were they signaling? When did it start and why? How can it be possible? They had no technology back then that could do this. I have a headache. And that's strange, too, because normally you're just a pain in the ass."

6

With grim pleasure, Benson unleashed White House pressure on the WOWI director. It began with a phone call from the President's Chief of Staff to the Chairman of the university consortium that funded WOWI. The professor listened and nodded; she understood politics. She wanted no high level enemies in Washington. She prepared a royal invitation for the observatory to cooperate, and she delivered it in silken phrases in a phone call of sweet reasonableness. The "or else" hints in that call produced an agreement by WOWI to collaborate, but in no way did it change the principled attitude of Franz Zelig. Benson gave him credit for that.

The order to cooperate had humbled and embittered the man. He sat tense, hostile, and silent through the litany of requirements that Benson and Cooper described to him. He never asked a question. At the end of Benson's explanation the bristling director said, "I understand." Without another word, he took the pages of instructions from Benson and held the door of his office open for them to leave.

Outside, Cooper said, "Now I know why the Irish had a song about a big stick. How did it go? Something like 'the same auld shillelagh me father brought from Ireland'?"

Benson smiled and supplied the refrain, "Many's the time he used it on me to make me understand!"

With Anna Schutz again in charge, the voluminous search effort began.

Her team scanned old data for the "uscom" signal, starting as far back as the records existed.

While Anna and her team labored, Benson flew Cooper to CIB Headquarters. There they prowled RECON, the computer program that reconnoitered imagery files. Their search produced a recent photo of an ancient Soviet satellite. The picture, shot by a photographer documenting spacecraft models in a Russian space museum, showed a satellite with a cylindrical body. One end had the appearance of an onion-shaped dome from a Russian Orthodox church. The other end carried a bulky ablative shield to dissipate the heat of reentry. At several places antennae stuck out.

"Not impressive by today's standards," Benson said, "but the world's best back then."

Other photos of the satellite, taken by the best ground-based telescopes of the mid 1900's, appeared grainy and fuzzy. But comparisons of old and new photos implied the same vessel, consistently.

Two other kinds of consistency got their attention a week later, surfacing in a breathless phone call from Anna Schutz. Her team, in searching 30 years of WOWI's data, had found the mysterious signal recorded every year. The second consistency said that "uscom" always appeared on the Fourth of July, and on no other day.

---------------------------------- 7 ----------------------------------

Cooper nicknamed the mysterious broadcaster "Ivan." They studied Ivan's design, its evolution from predecessors, and the technical and political circumstances that prevailed at its launch. In those days, the Soviets were scoring "first-in-history" achievements one after another. This, Cooper knew, had been a contrived sequence of triumphs intended to show the world the superiority of a socialist society.

Capable of orbiting great weight, the Soviets rushed rockets into the sky. A magazine editor of the day summed it up: "They're straining to create history. After all, things can be pioneered only once. This is their chance, but it doesn't seem right to run such risks with people." He criticized the Vostok flight of Valentina Tereshkova, the first woman in space, because he felt she had been sent unprepared, just for a line in the record books.

Some European radio amateurs in the early days of Soviet space flight claimed they heard messages from victims, space-stranded Soviet cosmonauts. Starting with the Sputnik flight, these radio "hams," and assorted space enthusiasts, monitored Soviet radio frequencies all hours of every day. Some reported hearing cryptic farewells, perhaps from cosmonauts marooned in orbit.

Continentale, the Italian news agency, published four names and the dates of their loss, for the years 1957 through 1959 alone. Newsweek magazine quoted confirming sources. The Soviet practice of total secrecy fueled the rumors. The West "knew" of many failures, but the USSR never admitted any. When a launch fell short of its obvious intent, the Kremlin would declare that its performance had been its goal. The socialist system confessed no shortcomings. An irritated American rocketeer described their practice: "They shoot an arrow, find where it landed, and draw the target around it."

The Soviets denied putting their people at risk, and they vigorously disclaimed any deaths in orbit. They became outraged at such charges. But the rumors would not die, and critics could point to Soviet satellites, apparently man-rated, that stayed in orbit. As the years went by, nature's toll left fewer suspect satellites in the sky to wonder about. As their orbits degraded, the suspect spacecraft fell to earth, obliterated in the consuming fire of friction upon reentering the atmosphere. In a closed society, evidence that vanishes can be denied forever.

Suspicious accusers insisted radio failure alone could have marooned a man. "Remember," one explained, "they fly their guys monkey-mode." Reentry commands were kept entirely in the hands of ground controllers.

As another put it, "Can you conceive of their system allowing one man — all alone, mind you — to fly over other countries and have the power to choose where he could land? Imagine plopping down in America with the latest Soviet technology. What a great way to defect! So they controlled the whole thing from the ground, and some guys who thought they'd be heroes ended up very dead."

Benson did not reject this reasoning. He knew Soviet fighter planes had always flown with limited fuel; this prevented runaways. Even so, some pilots had dashed to freedom. He remembered interrogating one runaway from Vladivostok who had glided his fighter plane the last few miles to a landing in Japan.

The Ivan spacecraft turned out to be one-of-a-kind. Although larger than the Vostok series in which Yuri Gagarin became the first human in space, Ivan was smaller than the two-man Voskhod series that followed. Ivan had been launched in the transition period between the two, as though impatience reigned. *Perhaps*, thought Benson, *someone couldn't wait for Voskhod to pass its tests.* After launch, Ivan had all the earmarks of a manned flight. It received and sent encrypted telemetry and, although its codes had never been broken, the patterns resembled those used in earlier, manned flights.

"How do you like the thought," mused Cooper, "that it's a Vostok and a half — an old one beefed up for some kind of record?"

Benson shrugged. "All we know is that they never did it again and there's never been an explanation. But I can guess. My guess is that somebody was aboard and that something went wrong. As for the 'uscom' message, who knows?"

They parted, but with an agreement to meet or phone quarterly to shake the topic again for new insights. Three months later, Benson phoned to describe how he had begun to use new young minds and their hungry ambitions on the message.

"I talk in private to every college 'fresh-out' we hire and I swear each to secrecy. Then I ask help in finding what 'uscom' might mean. These kids really work at it. They're giving me ballooned acronyms and stuff from international slang, dead languages, and pornography. Some of it's hilarious, Art. I'll bring you some notes. We can both use a laugh. God, these young minds . . . !"

The comment proved prescient, because a young mind, very young, would be the one to see "uscom's" meaning — a mind in his own family.

8

One night, Benson worked at home. He knew this, he told himself, because of the homework. It wasn't his own homework, and that made him grateful. He felt weary, very weary, and thought, *Lucky me that it's not beyond kindergarten.*

With Martha at class, Benson owned the evening. He had the refreshing task of hearing Mark read. The boy was a joy, precocious and imaginative. Little escaped him. Whatever caught his attention got sustained consideration. He probed every page. Questions. Questions. Benson sometimes gave him an answer. Other times he said, "You tell me," just to watch the flying chips of creativity. Time also flew that night. The boy in his lap dozed off first. Martha woke them two hours later, and a groggy father gamely tried to put a refreshed boy to bed for the night.

Mark's idolizing of his father didn't bother Martha. She saw her husband as a good role model for the boy and she encouraged Mark's habit of collecting Benson memorabilia. Mark's bedroom held photo albums, newspaper articles, yearbooks, and hung diplomas — anything related to his father. The hoarding bedeviled Benson. It didn't bother Martha.

"Don't worry about it, Michael. You're not a fetish. It's all due to your traveling. This isn't unhealthful behavior. It's just that he misses you. He'll adjust."

But Benson worried; and he held Mark to a quota of pictures of Dad in high school, in college, in sports, in the Air Force. On the walls and mirrors hung taped postcards that Benson had sent from travel. Magazines brought home from airlines lay about.

Mark filled the long absences with fantasizing and with tangible evidence of his father. On occasion he got hold of something prohibited. One lay on his bed, a crumpled yellow sheet from one of Benson's recent meetings. It had no notes, but did have Benson's impatient doodles from a session of boring rehash. Trained to leave nothing behind, he had put it into his coat pocket. At home, he had thrown it into the collecting can for shredder waste in his study. It was clear that Mark had been prowling. Some of the sheet's markings said "uscom," many times. Benson picked it up, ready to chastise Mark about security.

Mark, watching, sat up eagerly and said, "Dad, who wants the United States to come?"

9

"Hire that kid!" said Cooper, exuberant. "He's smarter than half your half-assed analysts."

The boy's question exposed a new path into the Ivan fog. Benson hesitated at first to tell even Cooper of the child's insight. He knew how U.S. President Jimmy Carter had been ridiculed for publicly quoting his teenaged daughter's views on nuclear arms. Cooper wangled the story out of him and called the reluctance to credit Mark "1000 percent wrong." That loosened things up.

Benson, relieved, said, "OK. Thanks. So, it might be an opening. Want to work on this lead together? Where can we meet?"

Cooper refused to meet without Mark. "At your house, of course. I want the kid in on it! You and I don't have the imagination for the job."

They spent the next afternoon playing games with Mark, tapping an uninhibited mind full of space cartoons from movies, television, and comic books, plus the playacting scenarios of boys his age. Atop it all stood his sweeping imagination. The men told him of the satellite and its strange message. They asked for stories on what it might mean. They gave him free rein. Tales tumbled out in a swift run to breathlessness, a big suck of air, and another headlong verbal rush. Mark told of monsters or machines taking over, or of invaders from stars. Years later, Benson would feel his skin crawl with recollection of the random divinations of his child.

At one point Cooper asked, "Mark, what would you do if you got this message?"

"I'd tell them OK."

"OK?!"

"Yes."

"Why?"

"It's an invitation."

"What!"

"Mommy says you have to answer an invitation."

When the afternoon ended, Cooper picked him up for a big hug. Then, holding him face to face, he stared long into the immense unknown in the endless depths of a child's eyes. "Who are you in there?"

After the boy's head dropped in slumber, they reviewed the tape of his fantasies until they reached two conclusions. They decided that neither man would ever mention a child's involvement. They decided also to respond to Ivan's "invitation." But how? They faced unknown technical and code problems. Benson's analysts had suggestions. One said, "Why not send its own message right back to it?" They decided to recommend WOWI for the job because it could both transmit and receive on the hydrogen frequency. The sullen director took the task and made Anna Schutz the project leader.

But the director himself phoned Benson three days later. He shouted apologies for his past behavior and continued incoherent until Benson calmed him. In a breaking and erratic voice the director tried to explain the experiment and its results.

"We broadcast 'uscom' on each Ivan pass. We can't believe what happened!" the man babbled. "We sent 'uscom' again and again, sometimes singly and sometimes in fast bursts. And every time we sent the message up we got a response back down at once. I mean *immediately.* And this isn't the Fourth of July!"

"What kind of response?"

The man's coherence broke down again, but Benson began to understand. The team always got an intelligible response; they got one word; and it never changed. Puzzling. Electrifying. The word stood firmly, clearly, in the data: "Freedom."

──────────────── 10 ────────────────

Benson now faced seeming tons of scenarios to explain the mysteries of the Ivan spacecraft. With his staff and Cooper, he explored them ad nauseam. Weeks of work failed to trigger Ivan into saying anything new. It could hear only "uscom" and could say only "freedom." One experiment deepened the mystery. Even a small, portable unit transmitting to Ivan from the observatory site could get it to respond. Benson sent them to various parts of the world, but they could trigger Ivan only in the northeast United States.

"As though Ivan's only supposed to talk to Washington," said Cooper.

Conclusions were slow in coming. After long weeks of speculating and experimenting, Benson had compiled a few. He believed with all his heart that Ivan had been a manned flight and that it had gone wrong. It moved in an elliptical orbit the Soviets had never used before the Ivan launch, or for many years after. That orbit accounted for Ivan's existence today. Its launch gone awry, the satellite ended up too high, and friction with the upper atmosphere wasn't enough to drag it to reentry.

The signals perplexed him. Perhaps a dissident cosmonaut had been aboard, one who wanted freedom. Maybe he had broadcast for the United States to come and get him. But that didn't make sense. Neither Russia nor America, in those days, had done even a practice rendezvous in space, never mind performing a rescue. Equipment for docking with and entering each other's vessels had emerged much later, after great effort. And yet, this idea — what Cooper called "the defecting cosmonaut theory" — seemed the most rational of the explanations.

"Which proves," said Cooper, "how really bad our bad ideas really are."

One day a vision came to Cooper. He imagined a cosmonaut who did not believe in the readiness of his ship, but who felt unable to refuse due to pride, patriotism, or concern for his future. American astronauts, by contrast, never hesitated to speak up. He recalled America's first orbiter, John Glenn, telling the press his apprehensions about flying a machine "built by the lowest bidder." He remembered how Gus Grissom had disagreed with the designers and hung a lemon sign on the Apollo capsule that shortly afterwards killed him and his crew during ground tests.

Cooper could, therefore, see the imagined cosmonaut going ahead and doing his job, just as astronauts do, but staying silent. He imagined a cosmonaut, one with the instincts of a counterpunching boxer, who thought, *"If they're using me unfairly, I want the world to know."*

Benson thought Cooper might be right, but he believed it unlikely that one man could have the necessary combination of personality and skills: a cold-blooded planner, a vindictive citizen, a superb actor, a consummate magician, and a multiskilled technician.

"You realize what that idea implies, of course!" he told Cooper. "The guy would have had to conceal his fear and disagreement, prepare his plot under their noses, develop some remarkable equipment, and then get it aboard without their knowledge. He would also have needed the gift of prophecy. First, to predict that Americans would someday listen in the hydrogen band. Second, that we would hear him and figure out what he wanted. Third, that we'd have the ability to go up there and get whatever embarrassing information he wants made known."

"Mike. Listen. All that's behind us. Remember, this guy chose the United States as his audience. He's talking to us! To us!"

"I know. I know! We and we alone are being sent signals — for a purpose — by somebody who thought out a process — for a purpose. This is no message in a drifting bottle! This is like an envelope addressed, 'In the event of my death.' Your scenario may bring us the closest we'll ever get to the truth without flying up there to inspect that thing. And I have two thoughts about that. First, we ought to go up. Second, it may be a trap."

PART 2

THE COMMANDER

—————————————— 11 ——————————————

He turned a little under the straps, shifting slowly. He hoped his motion would not be detected; he wanted to steal a look at her. She lay strapped next to him, at the same odd angle, waiting silently in her own tilted chair. His concerned, fleeting glance revealed a cheekbone streak of glistening sweat.

A wilting of the renowned personal cool? Possible. Even understandable, the way this is going.

"Are you as hot as I am?"

"Probably," she said.

"The suit?" he ventured.

"No. Just pissed. Why can't they predict better?"

"Hang in there," he buoyed. "I still think we'll go today." This woman distracted him, and so did the conflicting signals his sources sent about her. But now, deep in his tipped chair, Commander Adam MacGregor had to turn his mind from her to his tiresome and threatening problem. He focused straight up through the space shuttle's cockpit windows at a wintry Florida sky of cinder-gray clouds scudding by in endless supply to feed a chain of frigid, boring days.

Feeling vaguely cheated, the tourists who'd anticipated a sunshine launch had long since run for warmth. Others, however, in bright yellow slickers, still dotted the viewing stand. Affectionately known as the "science-aficionados," they stood hunched in their die-hard groups chattering unquenchable hopes for a "go."

Far more than they, Adam longed to hear the countdown resume, yearned to hear the flat voice say, at last, "Constitution, you are go for launch." His well tuned crew needed to hear it too, before the gloomy train of dim, chill days eroded their spirits and dulled the razor edge of skills. Each dawn they suited up and prayed for launch. But the great clamps held their ship like anchors as the earth-bound hours dragged on and the dreary run of "cold-and-hold" days piled up ominously.

Adam put no stock in omens, but all the superstitions of the astronaut corps dwelt in his bones. He believed that when all goes well, someone usually experiments. Again and again, he had seen design or equipment changes yield damage or disaster, all the while being promoted as improvements. Yet, as a former test pilot he realized that promising ideas had to be tried and modified until they worked. He knew that he wouldn't be an astronaut today but for those who had pushed their dream, a ship of space. He knew that change might kill him, but that without change we will not see progress. He knew how to live with the ambivalence.

Adam enjoyed a wry near-poem about his odd dichotomy. A favorite of astronauts, the parody said:

> *Roses are red, and violets are blue,*
> *I'm a schizophrenic, and so are I.*

The ironic little trope matched his mood about flying this particular spaceship, one of the second-generation space shuttles. Its assets listed like the TV car ads: faster, bigger, stronger, smarter, safer. He questioned the last of these, and with cause, as he lay strapped into a shuttle "improved" by a thrust upgrade. Constitution sat atop the untried engines designed for the next advance, the revolutionary third-generation shuttle, still a year from maiden flight. Unhappy about flying today's test-bed, he considered its engine refit a forced fit. And yet, this marriage of old and new might click.

The mission boasted another marriage: Adam and his unexpected crew. Another forced fit, the newcomers replaced his prime crew, now in hospital beds from tainted food. Adam's curiosity about the pilot, Major Ellen Mehler, U.S. Air Force, didn't stem from any question about her capability. As pilot for five missions on second-generation shuttles, she arrived with kudos from commanders Adam respected. She arrived, also, in a cloud of gossip that intrigued him, as did the conflicts inherent in the gossip. He could not accept this decisive and chilly professional as the libertine described by believable outsiders. Only outsiders, mind you. No stories about her ever came from inside the agency.

Ellen Mehler avoided insiders, instantly quashing attempts at familiarity with an icy formality. Maybe, Adam mused, two different people live in that big suit; but he could see just one, an all-business astronaut. He liked it that way. Still, he wondered. And, in the wondering, the unbidden question came: what would it be like with that rumored other? His head gave a hard, involuntary shake, jolting loose the images of tumbling tans on tangled pink. *Damn!* A wall breached. Here, of all places! He jammed the visions into a guarded cranny of his mind.

"You OK?" she asked.

"Yes, Major, thank you," he said, his wall rebuilt.

Adam had felt an immediate bond with the other member of the crew, Dr. Dave Tanzier, Mission Specialist. In a way, Adam and Ellen served as Dave's chauffeurs, truck drivers for delivery of the scientist and his astronomy instrument. The eager and very bright young scientist brimmed with training for the care and feeding of the science payload sitting in the cargo bay. A novel telescope, it went by the nickname "Fax," short for its imposing official title, the Facility for Advanced X-ray Studies. Before putting it overboard, Dave would check every aspect of operation to make it ready for use in its circular orbit of 400 nautical miles.

Fax marked the latest in the long series of specialized telescopes called The Great Observatories, begun in the previous century by NASA, America's original space organization. At sixty tons, this huge instrument, designed to study stellar X-rays, proved too heavy for a second-generation shuttle to lift into orbit. The intended launcher, a new and more powerful shuttle now being built, lagged far behind schedule. That delay incensed thousands of astronomers, students, and support staff in the global research team awaiting the new telescope. Their political pressure drove the space flight agency into mating the powerful new engines with the current shuttle, making an earlier launch possible. Maybe today.

Adam admired Dave's calm acceptance of yet another session of pre-breathing pure oxygen in full suit. It prevented the sickness of decompression, a condition that can cripple or kill. "Diver's bends," as it's known, happens when nitrogen gas starts bubbling out of blood if the water or air pressure on a person's body drops sharply. Dave realized that some accident or failure might cause the cabin to lose air pressure in the vacuum of space. And so, although he found pre-breathing in full suit inconvenient, lengthy, and uncomfortable, he endured it without complaint. He wanted no bubbles in his brain or spinal cord causing paralysis and convulsions. He wanted nothing to threaten *his* telescope.

Management did not require the pre-breathing process for launch, but MacGregor did. Adam remembered the three Russian cosmonauts found dead in their parachuted return vehicle on the barren Siberian steppes. *Some homecoming!* Their capsule had accidentally vented to the outside during reentry, plunging the cabin into vacuum. Adam wanted no such failure to kill anyone in his crews. Other spaceship commanders simply flew to orbit like airline pilots, with nobody suited up to function in sudden vacuum. Adam's managers saw no harm in his procedure, and they let him have his way.

When Adam first announced his requirement he said, "Tanzier, this is the law according to MacGregor."

Dave replied, "The law is my shepherd," and got a smile out of the somber Adam. A joyful scientist, Dave's enthusiasm helped weld the new team. He ignored discomfort, dreaming only of getting that telescope into the sky. He welcomed MacGregor's legendary reputation for anticipating emergencies; it delighted him as insurance for science.

—————————————————— **12** ——————————————————

Adam proved right; launch was approved. The thunder began and the ground trembled. Mythology paled as humans again rose from the earth on a pillar of fire. Heavy from the acceleration, they pressed hard into the seats. They bore the pressure easily, feeling half that of the centrifuge where speed could prevent lifting a hand to operate controls.

As the shuttle cleared the tower, control of the mission switched from the launch director in Florida to the flight director in Houston. With the nickname, "Flight," this person would be their controller until the "wheels stop" report after landing.

Climbing out of Florida, they sped toward Africa as Ellen confirmed the automatic throttling back of the main engines to ease the ship through maximum dynamic pressure at the speed of sound. Twenty seconds later, with the stress behind, the ship throttled up to 100%, striving for 25 times the speed of sound to enter orbit.

Minutes after launch the booster rockets of solid fuel burned out. Now dead weight, the empty motor casings automatically jettisoned from their perches on the giant liquid-fuel tank. Once clear of the shuttle and each other, their gimbaled helicopter blades telescoped to full length. Like angled pencils they flew home to soft landings and reloading.

"Constitution, this is Houston," said a flat voice from ground control, "You are negative return."

"Roger, Houston," Adam replied, "Negative return."

Until this milestone, the shuttle could have glided back to a landing at the launch site. From here on, however, any engine failure would force tougher choices. One required limping across the ocean in a *trans-Atlantic abort,* with landing options at emergency runways in Spain or Africa. Another option, *abort-once-around,* meant circling the globe to land at a California site, avoiding the cost of shipping a shuttle home from overseas.

A final option, *abort-to-orbit,* called for getting high enough to reach a sustainable orbit, even though it might be lower than the mission intended. This happened once, in 1985, when an engine shut itself down on the shuttle Challenger. The ship went into a less desirable orbit, but the cost of getting into space made it wise to keep her in the sky and do as much useful science as possible.

All went well as Constitution climbed a nominal track to orbit. Adam assigned the actual flying to Ellen. He regarded the title of Pilot seriously, unlike Commanders who wanted their own hands on the controls. His practice proved wise, leaving him more flexible when the first emergency struck the ship. Engine Two exploded silently in the vacuum of space, and the high-pressure fireball rammed the astronauts deep into their seats.

They blinked in dismay and frustration at the sudden alarm lights of a lost engine shutting itself down.

However, with the two remaining engines, it would be easy to reach a landing site. That prospect died when shrapnel apparently tore into nearby high-pressure pipes, sending jets of hydrogen and oxygen into the furnace of rocket exhaust.

Adam could not see the inferno behind him, but his sizzling heat sensors said his aft end was blazing like the rampaging hydrogen fire of the 1937 Hindenburg zeppelin holocaust. He knew it would soon destroy his two good engines and perhaps his giant rudder. Heart pounding, adrenaline pumping, he switched into the automatic behavior acquired by test pilots from crises and the countless disaster drills in flight simulators.

"Override 1 and 3!" he ordered, racing to block automatic shutdown.

Swift and sure, Ellen avoided fuel cutoff. The engines roared on at full throttle as Adam, seizing on a desperate idea, abandoned the ship's routine path to orbit.

"Flight," he told Houston, "I am going for height. My call."

"Roger, Constitution," said Flight, locked on the drama. "Proceed on commander's judgment."

They clawed up the sky for every foot he could nurse from the melting engines. Furious that his ship might be doomed, Adam hadn't stopped to think of personal risk. He and Ellen, trained to utilize crisis adrenaline, used it now. In a rush of heightened reflexes, memory and concentration, they automatically shut out fear and worked with urgent calm.

Dave, from a much different past, choked on a hammering heart. He did his best, trying to read the trembling emergency sheets. His temples pounded in a furious rhythm as cold sweat blurred his eyes and his mind crinkled with guilt. Why hadn't he paid more attention in the emergency training? Atop a spine of ice, his eyes plodded the dense text, seeking competence. He heard a quavering, mumbling voice, and knew he was hearing himself sounding out the words like a child. He read on, stammering in shame because Houston would know what wetness was short-circuiting his body monitors. Sickening in fear and embarrassment, he fought not to vomit inside his quaking helmet.

When Adam again ran through Constitution's options, it confirmed his choice of action. He might have a chance at saving the precious telescope and its ten years of money, dreams, sweat, and talent. He winced when the pressure against his back ceased, and Ellen confirmed zero acceleration. It meant that all his main engines, finally destroyed, no longer gave him thrust. The shuttle would now coast, rising up the hill of gravity, but slowing its climb until the inevitable turnaround.

Ellen, knowing her physics, said, "I'm dropping the ET."

He nodded. She discarded the external tank and its now useless fuel to avoid pushing those masses around in the crucial moves ahead. Their one remaining source of fuel waited in the shuttle's tanks. It would fire their only significant propulsion, the puny thrusters of the Orbital Maneuvering System they called the OMS.

When Ellen blew the explosive bolts the castoff tank swept in a long arc for earth. Falling from their low height, some flaming parts would survive and strike the ocean. Air friction burned up tanks completely when they jettisoned at the greater height and speed of a normal launch. It would not happen today. Adam prayed for empty sea-lanes below, as he added a new peril for mariners.

They turned to the vital task of testing their ship's ability to fly. The orbital maneuvering system proved undamaged, but the reaction control system had taken hits. One of two aft-facing, primary thrusters in the starboard pod reported ruined. *I can live with that,* thought Adam.

Less harmful was the loss of one of two vernier engines in the port side aft pod. These helped provide the fine rotational adjustment needed in station keeping, a maneuver Adam didn't anticipate on this flight. When he checked the giant, split rudder and the inner and outer elevons, he found them unharmed. He appreciated this miracle, suspecting it due to shielding against shrapnel by closely bunched main engines.

In the twenty striving minutes since launch they had achieved more than the height and speed needed for a trans-Atlantic abort. If only one engine failed, this possibility began as early as two minutes into flight. In that case, thrust from the other two would take them across the ocean. But the shuttle had entered uncharted territory when all three engines died, and when Adam had steepened his flight to run for height in his radical plan to save the telescope.

Thinking in the jargon of his trade, he knew he could not AOA, abort-once-around, and he could not ATO, abort-to-orbit. A quirky corner of his mind made the wry translation of ATO into "abort-to-ocean."

Not on my watch! he vowed. He knew his exact position over the Atlantic, using data from the multiple satellites of the Global Positioning System. Sucking up information from all displays, he and Ellen did a horseback estimate of whether they could glide the miles to the African shore.

Adam grimaced at their reckoning. "Shy by a hundred!" Ellen reached for the checklist. She had the job of preparing the rescue pod for ejection and crew escape.

———————————— 13 ————————————

The flat voice said, "Constitution, Houston. We read all engines out. Confirm." The flight director, though burning with questions, had delayed calling, not breaking the crew's emergency focus any earlier.

Adam summarized their predicament.

"Understood, Constitution. You are 'contingency abort.' "

Adam balked at the idea although he met the requirement of all engines disabled. *Not just yet!* he told himself.

"Contingency abort" meant a steep dive, with a wrenching pull-up at about 20,000 feet. There, they'd eject the cockpit section and the floatable module would parachute the crew to safety. A few small thrusters gave the escape pod a little control for steering around obstacles at touchdown.

In a surprise announcement, he said, "Houston, we can still save something out of this mess. We're high enough to open the bay doors without wind damage, so I'm going to put Fax over the side. If we can get her to point about right, we'll burn her to nominal orbit. If not, we'll try parking."

His comment implied a desperate, ingenious strategy. Houston concluded that Adam would gamble on saving the observatory before diving in a contingency abort. Ellen, meanwhile, fired both thrusters of the orbital maneuvering system, normally used for large vector changes once in orbit. Their impulse, though only one-sixtieth the thrust of the main engines, helped maintain the shuttle's slowing climb.

The telescope was held in place by remotely controlled clamps. At its base sat a thruster called the Payload Assist Module. This attached rocket would boost the payload to its higher orbit, after the shuttle took it as high as possible and set it free in space. Heart pounding, fighting fear and nausea, a recovering Dave prayed over his own options, "Oh, Lord, at least park it."

His heavenly petition called for the little PAM rocket to push the seven billion dollar telescope into a temporary, preserving orbit, in a desperate hope that it could wait there for retrieval.

Normally, the shuttle would back off to a safe distance before sending the signal to ignite the booster rocket. From there, they would make a last minute check of the payload's systems and orientation. On this flight, they didn't have time to back away before firing the booster rocket. Dave knew it might not simply "light off;" rockets sometimes blew up.

Chilled at this prospect, Dave groped carefully down his blurred check-off list for opening the bay doors. He would put the telescope overboard, and then close those doors tightly for the shuttle's screaming trip down through earth's atmosphere. If he didn't get the closure aerodynamically smooth, the doors would be torn off, threatening to tumble and destroy the shuttle in the frictional fire of reentry. Dave took his place at the aft crew station window where he could see the cargo bay. He readied the huge grappling arm for moving the now weightless 60-ton telescope from the bay. He would move its mass overboard, point it at a proper angle for launch, let go, and let Ellen know to back away.

------------------------------ 14 ------------------------------

Exhilarated by Adam's daring idea, Houston relaxed and backed him. The shuttle's drive for altitude had changed all the rules. Skill, luck and quick action might save Fax. After that, Houston would concentrate on helping to save the crew; they had no hope for the shuttle. The USS Constitution faced a watery grave.

Adam told Houston he had enough altitude to open the cargo bay doors without wind damage.

"Constitution, Houston. We think you're right, but I want you belly first before you open the doors."

"Roger, Flight. We're turning her now."

Flight had thrown in a hedge on Adam's bet. He wanted the fragile doors leeward for protection as the shuttle sped through any little remnants of atmosphere.

Dave, overcoming fear by action, started cranking the doors open before Ellen got Constitution belly-forward.

"Dave. Stop. Wait my count. Five, four, three, two, steadied up. OK. Open."

"Swinging wide. Here go the clamps," said Dave, as he released the anchors holding Fax.

Adam hovered aft, mute, engrossed in Dave's work, and nursed a next-step secret hope. *Will we have time to make it happen?* Everything depended on Dave's skill. Adam held his breath as he watched the scientist's long training take hold and subdue the man's fear and panic. With smooth, rapid control, Dave locked the grappling arm around the clamping knob of the telescope's frame and lifted the payload out of the cargo bay.

Admiring Dave's economy of motion, Adam watched him hold Fax well clear of the shuttle, point it along the flight path toward its own intended orbit, delicately let go, park the arm, and turn to close the bay doors.

"Move off," Adam called. "Clean. No jitters."

Ellen inched them away from the telescope with small thrusts of her reaction control system's tiny rockets. She directed their exhaust to avoid contaminating the telescope's optics or huffing Fax into random motion. If she made it move, and it began to point awry, it would have little chance for a parking orbit.

With no time to spare, quelling training and instinct, Adam ignored the rule to move far away before firing the telescope's booster rocket. He knew that being too close might let the residue of rocket exhaust coat and obscure his windows. Too close meant also that a rocket explosion could pepper the shuttle with shrapnel holes, releasing the life-giving cabin air. He worried that his full-suit demand might be about to pay off.

"Crank us 180," he said. "Belly to Fax."

Ellen cranked the ship around, blocking their sight of the great telescope.

"Dave, we'll fire from here. Stand by for ignition."

Deciding to take his chances on giving Fax an immediate blastoff, Adam had to ignore its proximity. Sending the telescope on its way at once would free the shuttle to start the next part of his cobbled plan. When Dave radioed the ignition signal, none of them could see or hear if the rocket fired. Perhaps there had been no ignition, and they would have to try a blind firing again. In an anxious, hopeful hush, they waited priceless moments. They waited for Houston to tell them.

While the minutes passed at half speed, Adam asked Houston for a calculation.

"Flight, how close to Africa can I get from here?"

Meanwhile, he and Ellen did their own estimates again. They came up with 80 miles. Houston came in at 140 miles. Adam wore a knowing smile. They waited in silence as time chipped at their odds.

Flight's jubilant voice broke the silence. "Constitution, Houston. Fax is nominal for a parking orbit. Congratulations! It looks like a save. You are *still* contingency abort."

Adam clipped, "Roger, Houston." Now he could leave. His plan for survival required the disposal of Fax. Without its huge mass, Constitution's modest engines would push them over more miles of ocean. Houston's computers hadn't thought of lightening ship, a factor always part of the equation in Adam's head.

Racing time and gravity, Ellen pointed the shuttle east for Africa under full thrust of the OMS and every aft-facing rocket in the reaction control system.

15

Adam announced, "Houston, I want personal time with the meteorologist."

This just might work. His mind rummaged lore from years of Naval Academy sailing races while he considered the consequences of losing a shuttle. It meant much more than kissing good-bye to a three billion dollar investment. He knew it also meant new experiments couldn't fly for years, waiting for a replacement carrier to be built. In the squeeze of fewer chances to fly, some promising experiments would never fly at all. He thought of that bitter pill for talented scientists who might have worked a decade on one project, as many had done on Fax. Even worse, the launch shortage might scare off new, young talent from starting a career in space research. He thought, too, of the cut in his own chances to flee into the sky.

"Constitution, we have meteorologist Don Ordlee ready."

"Ordlee, we need your help! Big time! How close are we to the jet stream? I need to know its speed, height, thickness, width, length, and where it's headed. And I need to know as fast as you can deliver!"

"Yes, sir, I'll get right on it .... " He trailed off in puzzlement. Then, in dazed admiration, the smile of an enlightened conspirator dawned on his earnest face.

"I see it! I see it! Elegant!" gasped Ordlee, his mind kindling with the audacity of Adam's intention. The calculations from Mission Control said the shuttle could not make a landfall. Adam, however, intended to pit flying skill against the computer prediction. He intended to squeeze out extra distance by getting into the jet stream and using it as a tail wind. Alive with adrenaline, and aflame with his key role, Ordlee went to work, recalling history as he ran down the corridor to his facts.

Startled pilots of World War II discovered the wind called the jet stream when their high-flying aircraft slowed or moved rearwards over the earth. The Luftwaffe learned of its existence after several of their stripped-down, unarmed, high altitude observation planes hadn't enough fuel to fly home after scouting the British fleet in the Mediterranean. Flying far higher than antiaircraft guns or pursuit planes could reach, they had stumbled upon the unknown jet stream and exhausted their fuel in running against it. The Americans first encountered the mysterious winds high over the Japanese home islands. Entire bombing raids had to abort. Laboring against the stream, they used up too much fuel to reach their targets and still fly home.

Adam pinned his hopes on a particular jet, a low latitude, high altitude river of wind called the Subtropical Jet Stream. Pushed south by another, the Polar Jet Stream, it had meandered far, bringing to Florida the arctic chill of this morning. Without his shivering at dawn, he might never have thought of grasping this straw. Blowing from west to east, the subtropical jet passes into the Atlantic. Adam knew it didn't die at sea, but continued fitfully around the world at winter speeds that can exceed 300 knots. Riding the jet stream would mean covering distance like a raft in a swift river.

The navigation blessings of GPS, the Global Positioning System, would let Ordlee know, at any moment, the latitude, longitude, altitude, speed and path of the USS Constitution. He had similar data on the jet stream itself from CLAWS — the Climate, Atmospheric, and Winds Satellite, whose instruments watched the Atlantic and the bordering lands continuously from its aerie in geostationary orbit.

Ordlee's upper air charts placed the jet stream core only twenty miles north of the shuttle's track. Elated, he broadcast his gift of data to the crew. His job, now, would be to steer them into the stream and guide them to stay within it for as long as possible. He saw that, far ahead, its path veered away from the emergency-landing site. The shuttle would cover that distance in minutes, as it plunged on at eight thousand miles an hour. It might be a short ride, but it would be crucial.

Ordlee knew he would have to manage a smart tradeoff among speed, height, and direction to get maximum flying time. At some point, he would have to turn the shuttle, having drained the jet stream of all the help it could give. He knew Ellen would power hard with the maneuvering engines within the great tailwind, trying hard to fly under power.

He understood Ellen had a very heavy glider on her hands, a "sink rate" absurdly low. A sailplane can proceed forty feet for every foot it drops. Pilots call this relationship "L over D," using the ratio to express lift-over-drag. Commercial airliners can glide about fifteen feet for one foot of drop, whenever they have to land unpowered. The USS Constitution, a 110-ton glider, enjoyed a ratio of five to one, not very good for a smooth landing. But, at high altitude, the shuttle's delta shaped wings gave a much better ratio than in the lower atmosphere. Ellen would use that fact to stay aloft longer, to fly within the jet stream, powering hard for distance.

Buoyed by Ordlee's news, Adam told Houston to alert air traffic controllers to prepare for an emergency landing. He began working on the flight plan. As the shuttle fell in a suborbital trajectory toward Africa, Ellen banked northeast to the hurtling river of air that might save them.

16

Ordlee was back, excited and ready. "Constitution, Ordlee here."

"Yeah, Don. What have you got?"

"Commander, good news! The jet stream is topping out at 45,000 feet. It's twenty miles wide, two miles deep, and blowing at 280 knots straight for Dakar."

"Ordlee, that's not good news, that's great news! Good man. Now, let's use it. I need you to get us right in the middle of that thing and hold us there for as long as we can ride it."

"I'll wrap it around you, Commander."

Adam was headed for the westernmost point of Africa. If the jet's direction held, it could give Constitution a great boost toward the commercial runways on the coast of Senegal at Yoff Airfield. The jet stream, notorious for meandering, would force Ordlee to work every quirk as he wafted them to shore.

Ellen nursed her remaining fuel for its job of propelling Constitution within the core of the jet stream. She focused on eking out all the pathetic little lift she could get from the stubby wings to maximize flying time in the stream.

During a routine reentry of a shuttle, she would pitch its nose up to an angle of attack near forty degrees to take the braking heat of the atmosphere on the belly thermal tiles. This time, fiercely hoarding speed, she wished for no braking at all. Roaring through the first traces of air at about four hundred thousand feet, Ellen flew with minimal pitchup.

She tweaked her glide angle as Adam called out the temperatures of reentry friction. He was risking a burn-through of the shuttle's skin that would let superheated gases into Constitution. Like the original shuttles, it wore insulating tiles against the furnace of reentry friction. Some tiles would be lost, a predictable outcome of reentry, but he had to take the risk. It made him remember the shuttle Columbia, and he shuddered. In 2003, scorching gases penetrated and weakened its left wing, breaking up the ship and killing its crew of seven. He moaned at that loss but brightened a little at the thought of future astronauts flying the third-generation shuttle with its amazing all-metal fuselage.

Houston reported suddenly, "Constitution, we have you 700 miles out of Yoff Field, at Mach 12, 165,000 feet. Energy management shows improvement, but you will still end up shy of landfall. Estimate: 30 miles. You are still authorized to eject."

Adam acknowledged, but ignored, intent on hunting for the jet stream. Once inside, they would not only have a tail wind, but would meet less air resistance because the shuttle would be traveling with the stream. That should let him milk a few more precious miles from his time in the air.

Ordlee dropped them into the jet stream at 44,000 feet. He guided Constitution left or right, keeping it centered in the hurtling core. Adam bent and twisted unknowingly, lending body english to the maneuvers. With all of its aft-facing thrusters firing, Constitution speeded up from gliding and began flying.

Ellen played the orientation rockets to keep the ship centered in the stream for the full twenty minutes that Ordlee allowed. Then, as their racing tailwind began its bend away to the northeast, he called them out for a banking turn at the last possible moment. He had done his job well. They had gained almost 130 miles toward Africa from riding the jet stream.

Ellen bored ahead with continuous, maximum thrust from their little engines until the fuel ran out. Adam would never have consumed all fuel while in orbit, but would hoard it for the final reverse firing to slow the shuttle for return to earth. He saw another difference about this approach. Ellen would do none of the banking, air-drag turns she normally used for dumping energy and reducing speed during a routine landing. *Not on this run!* he thought.

And what a run! They swept straight in from the sea, on a glide path seven times steeper than a commercial jet landing with power. Startled fishermen heard the twin sonic booms and cringed under a howling shadow, a flying whale trying not to beach. The huge craft cleared the coastal road and strained for the runway.

Adam groaned, "Oh, man, we're short!" He could see the airport, and the sparkling surface of the huge, surrounding ponds. A commercial venture, their owners periodically flooded them with ocean water, allowed evaporation time, and mined the salt residue.

Constitution would sink here, with corrosion and ruin its fate. He imagined the devastation to mechanisms, computers, and electronics. After all their risk and efforts, he had found nothing but a different way to destroy his shuttle and probably kill his crew.

At long last, the danger of death on this mission loomed large. Even if Ellen could pull off a non-fatal ditching, Adam expected harm at least. The specter of horrendous injuries stared back at him. Just one watery dip of a wingtip would whirl them into a tumbling breakup. Until now, he had somehow postponed any thoughts of being killed. The old saw about being too busy to think about dying seemed to be true on this flight.

Adam knew scores of cases where the sheer professionalism of pilots kept them at the controls, trying to prevent disaster. He had heard their voices on the black boxes, talking in calm analysis of events and efforts right to the end. Similar behavior showed in pilots from all cultures. Another common feature, a constant puzzle to psychiatrists, is the usual final statement, the last words. In whatever their national language, the pilots reflexively said a dispassionate, "Ah, shit!" just before crashing. What would each of his crew be saying today? He felt guilty that Dave should die. David did not belong to the sky, but to a life on the ground. *The ground!!*

Salvation jumped out at him, yelling "ground effect!" It hollered the message from flight school memories of touch-and-go landing drills, with his plane floating along the runway, resisting touchdown.

"Pancake!" Adam cried. Ellen understood. When an aircraft gets close to the earth in landing, its wings squash a large volume of air against the ground; this forces it back up, prolonging flight. The behavior is very strong with a delta wing. As Ellen made the shuttle drop faster than ideal for landing, it obeyed the laws of physics, settled into "ground effect," and hovered while hurtling. Hope also rose and hovered, then subsided. "Not enough!" she cried.

Adam could see it, too. The prolonged flight time would get them only half way across the vast watery expanse. He prayed that the shuttle's enormous mass and speed would let them coast into ditching, would carry them splashing, spraying and wallowing to shallow water, maybe even to a beaching. He could see it happening.

He could also see an enormous bow wave holding them back. They wouldn't make the shallows.

"It's over, skipper," said Ellen. "Sorry. Great try — great try. Great flying with you guys! Hang on! Here we go!"

"Skipper," she had called him. It swirled in his head. During ultimate danger, the mind churns and digs for survival clues. Its desperate scans can reach to childhood. And childhood memories gave Adam another answer.

"Ellen!" he called, loud enough to break through her fierce final focus. "Ellen! Skip us in! Skip! Skip us in!"

She executed the idea at once. It seemed so right, so based in something bright and happy, that it got automatic acceptance. That subconscious something came from summer camp, where she won little awards and ribbons playing "ducks and drakes." Her memory held those shining moments when her skill united with the flat lake surface to skip her stone farther than any other kid's. Today, she would skip on a grand scale, giving up forward momentum to get some upward thrust. Done wrong, it would kill them. Done right, who knew? In desperation, she attempted the unproven maneuver.

"*Tricky–tricky–tricky*," she murmured, bringing Constitution skimming toward the glassy water with a best-judgment angle. *We may break apart. The bay — the bay . . . "*

She worried that the ship would snap somewhere along the cargo bay. Its long, open structure had no cross members, and most of its girders were the partial hoops of the bay door structure. Their cargo bay resembled those of Great Lakes ore freighters, with no bulkheads down the cavernous length. Here ships snapped in storms, sinking fast.

The USS Constitution hit at a useful angle and nothing snapped. The shuttle's skip contact gave it a huge bounce, higher than Ellen believed possible. After all, she'd never ridden, in scale, on one of her scaled stones. The upward jolt sent their heads into their necks, compressed their spines, and bulged their eyes. Dave sat in a crash protection huddle. Even so, the high-g forces of the bounce drained his brain and he blacked out, hanging limp. Training and reflexes saved Adam and Ellen. She cleared a sudden double vision by batting her forehead with the palm of her hand. Groggy, but aware, she felt her hopes rise.

"Maybe! Maybe! Maybe . . . " she intoned, like an auctioneer stretching time. "Maybe" they could make it to the runway. But no, she saw that they would come down just past the beach, onto grasping scrub.

Adam still had the wheels up. Ellen pictured their landing: a tail-drag through dirt, a flat-bellied slam onto the runway, a sparking scrape down the concrete and an engulfing fire.

Ellen abruptly aborted the flight. She acted on the memory of one beautiful childhood moment with an ideal stone. Her skilled throw gave it six skips before it dug in and sank. Reliving that awesome moment, she put Constitution down early for a second thump on the water. She knew that the huge shuttle still had enormous forward momentum, and she gambled on using the water for one last redirection of energy. She had often watched her track team's high jumpers redirect. The best of them couldn't clear a four-foot bar from a standstill, but could soar over a seven-foot bar by redirecting their mass and speed.

They braced themselves for the whack of her second skip and they suffered less. Adam popped the landing gear on the bounce, using the high-speed deploy — boosted by a prayer. The second skip got them past the pond. The shuttle screamed forward over an incredible, crucial, margin of 100 feet. With the belly tiles almost kissing the numbers at runway start, the landing gear locked. Tires screeching, they came down harder than he had ever landed. The tires didn't blow, nor did the landing gear buckle. The USS Constitution plopped onto concrete and rolled away from the clutching sea at two hundred knots, toward snaring sand at the end of a runway too short.

─────────────────── 17 ───────────────────

Ellen popped the drag chute, praying it had survived the fire. No luck. Trapped behind its warped door, it didn't deploy. She braked hard, grating out encouragement to the computerized anti-skid system. She flared the gigantic split rudder for more braking. She killed more energy by risky side-to-side steering.

All her efforts failed. The shuttle ran off the end of the runway and pounded along in the safety zone's hard, rough dirt. One by one, the six tires blew out, and the ship hurtled on with their thumping drag. That drag helped. The pounding slowed and the shuttle stopped, just shy of the sand that waited to buckle the nose wheel strut.

Adam sat immobile, worn and exultant. He had brought in his ship. Over the ages the goals of mariners were to weather the storm, save the crew, and deliver the owner's cargo. In this new ocean he had matched that tradition. He felt happier about saving the shuttle than about saving its payload. After all, they could build another Fax from its old design.

Building the next-step shuttle, however, required a step into the unknown. He had just proved it. He had used the engines of the third-generation shuttle and found them defective. Now, he and his crew could hand them over to the keen-eyed hunters who would find the flaws and then the cures. After that, the new shuttle, that metal-hulled beauty in his future, might fly without killing its crew. Maybe, too, there would be no mysterious failure, with the new shuttle down at sea, leaving only speculation as to the cause of a $3 billion loss for his country. He and his crew had brought home a priceless package of burned and twisted facts.

Outside, hazy in the swirling dust, ambulances and fire trucks caught up and circled. As the sound of sirens leaked through to Houston, an anxious flight director held his breath while also holding off further premature cheers from engineers who believed the shuttle's data as it poured onto screens.

The crew of the USS Constitution, the people with the most to cheer about, did not. Instead, shushed by a sweating but smiling Adam, they listened as he reported their "wheels stop" status in a monotone parody of the first words from the moon.

"Houston. It's a tranquil base here. The seagull has landed."

From an ocean away, uproarious boos and groans burst back at him for warping Neil Armstrong's announcement of the historic lunar landing. Adam lowered Houston's clamorous volume, and began ticking off the check list actions for shutting down. Later, reporting out, he said, "Houston, I see our Marines gathering 'round, so we're going to inspect the outside, find the Ambassador, and clear Customs. See you soon."

He released his belt and rose. Standing in a theatrical pose, he lifted his helmet with great ceremony. Pointing to his gleaming bald head, he said, "You guys better rub this for good luck. You just used up your lifetime supply!"

Released by his unexpected raillery, they erupted in the bright joy of deliverance. They pounced on him, hugging, cheering, and convulsing with the laughter of sudden immunity and abrupt success. Adam blinked in amazement at the flashing smile and tight, dancing spins of a whooping Major Ellen Mehler. *There are indeed two people in that big suit!* He took his urge to find out for sure and resolutely placed it outside his shell. Two people of controlled refrigeration would be going their separate ways. His resolve would quash any roused passions. So would the routine way of life in his career; a career of moving on without looking back; a career in which teams gather, perform and disperse after life-dependent intimacy. Yet, on this man for whom control of emotions meant not to have any, a smile grew as he watched Dave's antics.

The gamboling scientist jigged and clogged and beat rhythms on his thighs. He whirled like a dervish, and it didn't matter that his knuckles hit close walls. Dave, an emotional medley, sang with the happy sobs that follow total laughter. His telescope sat waiting in the sky. Revering Adam for that save, Dave marveled at the vibrant spirit and flaming will of this caring martinet, the "lean mean dean" of the astronaut corps, a man whose agonizing history should have destroyed him. Dave knew the stories; knew what had turned Adam's bright red top into that shiny pate; knew of the man's searing tragedy and its unique creation — this dynamic, monastic personality with a near-spiritual dedication to space. He wiped away grateful, joyous tears and followed the leader out to the sunshine of Africa.

PART 3

CONFLICT AT THE UN

18

People who will one day enter our lives are out there today, somewhere, living their own long preparations. Each will enter differently, perhaps forced on us, perhaps not. It may be as sudden as a collision or as paced as a pregnancy. They will enter because of actions or decisions, sometimes our own, but often those of people in power. Diplomats of America and Russia proved this truth as they clashed on an issue and sent the currents of many lives swirling together in a whirlpool of wills. Mike Benson's life was one, and Carla Truzski's, another.

Carla carried an affectionate title, "The Grand Old Lady of Negotiations." Cavorting now with her team, she called out in English, "What's the best part of arms reduction talks?"

Responding in Russian, her interpreter called out the standard answer, "Writing the joint communiqué!"

Then Carla put the question in Russian and got the same answer in English.

"Amazing!" Carla cried. "Both sides agree. It's time to go home. Let's get the hell out of here."

Her teammates on the Arms Reduction Commission knew this Truzski trademark. It typified her personal, quirky kind of cheerleading for restoring morale during the grinding days and nights of bargaining. She, on the other hand, never seemed to need rejuvenation. She had been recruited many times from the Georgetown University faculty over the decades to serve on one arms commission after another. This year, in an appointment considered overdue by some hard-liners, she headed the American delegation.

Carla served as one of the few threads of continuity on the American side. The Communists, by contrast, fielded the same group of tough professionals again and again. Every last one of them respected her. When first told of this, Carla had said, wryly, "Well, naturally. They're all males. I probably remind those boys of their grandmothers."

Her father, a fiery young Polish artillery expert, had played a major role in the stunning defeat of the Red Army in the Battle of Warsaw in 1920. Captured in the 1939 Soviet invasion, he puzzled over the way they took revenge; they used him. They treated him with respect, shipped him to Vladivostok, and pressed him into service as an artillery instructor. Theoretically a civilian, he was theoretically promoted: they called him

"Colonel." After Nazi Germany attacked the USSR, he became enthusiastic in his training of the Red Army. He made their officers into precision artillerymen, hoping to help prolong the struggle on the Eastern Front into an abrading war of attrition that would bleed both vile regimes to exhaustion. He bided his time.

His status allowed the freedom of local travel. When he heard of the Soviet massacre of thousands of Polish officers in the Katyn Forest, he recognized his "freedom" under their patronage as precarious. Using his local-travel privileges he escaped, stowing away on a Swedish freighter bound for Tokyo where Japanese customs agents turned him over to Military Intelligence. A short interrogation proved he had refused to continue aiding the enemy of their German ally. Release followed, and he survived as a teacher of languages and sometime translator. He spent ten years in this role, enduring scarcity, marrying, working, surviving the war, and saving money. Carla, born in the mid-1950's, turned eight years old when the family migrated to Canada, and then to the United States.

The gene mix from a Prussian Pole and a rebellious Japanese aristocrat proved potent. Carla's talents were enhanced by the pace and scope of an exacting private education that fostered tenacity, thoroughness, order, memory, and discipline. However, she left rote learning, compelled by the complexity of written Japanese, while young enough to avoid stifling her creativity. She grew up a prodigy of language and logic, amassing several degrees by the age of 24. Until his death at 93, her father designed and planned her overseas travels. He never accompanied her into East European countries, fearing capture. But, he made sure that she went there, and often, throughout her teens and twenties.

She realized much later that he had programmed her to grow up a free spirit (" ... with the wind in your blood!"), so she would suffer from the confinement of body and mind during visits in those lands. She came to understand what he believed a Pole should feel toward Russian demagogues: a passionate distrust. She could express this strong emotion like a poet. It often carried Americans on to cheering endorsement when she hammered away at the Communist leadership with her arms-control challenges.

Carla anguished over the renewed need for arms reduction work. She knew that humanity had almost succeeded in making nuclear weapons obsolete, had nearly rolled into a new world vision on the momentum of reforms sparked by the breakaway Russian leaders Gorbachev and Yeltsin. Carla had supported the possibilities like a beggar. She'd gone from country to country, pleading for financial and material aid to Russia. She'd pushed for the U.S. and the UN to send experts and consultants to fertilize economics and politics in the new Russia. She'd watched, breathless with hope, as the reforms met alternating successes and setbacks.

On television and in print, in speeches and interviews, Carla warned the world of the outcomes possible in the dangerous social and political mess of the disintegrating USSR. She lectured and wrote of the need for the world's democracies to provide on-site political education teams, vital in her view for creating a multi-party electorate with its checks and balances. The democracies did not act.

Yet the entire political commissar system and structure had been available and ready for conversion, ready for a different evangelistic work. She watched in dismay as disorder led to martial law. Premier Dmitri Yemetov justified what he called the Russian equivalent of the American Civil War. While he quoted Lincoln on preserving the union, his troops bombed and burned. Slaughter and starvation succeeded in subjugating many of the original republics into a reborn tyranny now named the United Communist States, the UCS.

Carla's alternating horror and hope in the years of civil conflict and rebellions led her into and out of depression. She agonized as the transition into messy democracy slowed down, stalled, and died. When Fortress Russia emerged — a high tech, militarized tyranny, a communist fascism — she wept. To her mind, inadequate Western foresight and action had dashed humanity's high hopes and stifled an incredible opportunity. She also knew that the worst scenario imaginable had surfaced: recidivism with a vengeance.

19

Although Carla had stamina, her UCS counterparts seemed inexhaustible. True bureaucrats, they functioned patiently across an entire career, sometimes dawdling for months to win a small point. They appeared to feel no anxiety to reach agreement and under no pressure to return to other pursuits. Arms negotiations always seemed stalemated until the Americans felt the need to make headway and conceded some point or other.

She marveled at the depth of understanding in the anonymous comment, "The Americans play poker; the Russians play chess." The two sides didn't even meet for the same purpose. It suited UCS plans to be seen on the world stage of arms limitation talks, with every move designed to drag out the spotlighted role of peace-seeker for its propaganda value in Europe.

Their strategy portrayed their country as a misunderstood and friendly neighbor. Europeans might then no longer feel a protective need for the European Community Defense Organization, and that could diminish its cohesion and power.

Carla puzzled over the short memories of some European leaders. It took little for them to start an impetuous campaign for imprudent disarmament. She shook her head in sad memory of the shock some leaders had received when Iraq overran Kuwait. In her experience, dictators with a preponderance of power tended to push their neighbors around. History told that story over and again.

Carla, wanting a breakthrough, had devised a plan for putting world pressure on the Communists. She presented it to the President of the United States, Simon Sisco, before his summit meeting with Premier Dmitri Yemetov. He went to the Geneva meeting with a very large bomb to drop into the proceedings. It consisted of one paragraph on one sheet of paper.

20

The usual procedures prevailed in Geneva. Lower level diplomats floated proposals and counter proposals on arms reductions. All media gushed the technical terms, making the public boggle over multiple warheads, movable launchers, fixed-site launchers, throw-weight power, tactical missiles, strategic missiles, anti-missile missiles, hunter-killer satellites, and over-the-horizon radar.

The stupefying array went on to include rail guns, particle beam weapons, laser beams, fighting-mirrors, long-range bombers, submarine launchers, megatonnage in the arsenals, first-strike weapons, what to count, and what not to count. The overwhelming volumes of data, tables, charts, and statistics on the stuff of death deadened the mind.

Into the dark and gloom, Simon Sisco flashed the bright light of Carla's proposal for an Open Lands Treaty. The Communists didn't caucus or even lean in whispered discussion at the table. He had their frozen attention. But, within seconds after Sisco finished, Yemetov vehemently rejected Carla's proposal. His behavior reminded her of an early Soviet leader, Nikita Khrushchev, who removed his shoe at the United Nations and pounded it like a gavel in his shouted speech.

In words of fire, Sisco countered, "Here we see the naked differences in our societies. I have invited you into trust and sunshine, but you choose in its place distrust, darkness, and concealment. You refuse even a trial period. You make it certain that what we all dread will occur again and again. Our peoples face nuclear annihilation whenever equipment fails, or instructions are misunderstood, or fanatics get out of control. We are all hostage to accidents, misinterpretations, and terrorists. The offer of the United States can change this; but you say no. You refuse! You refuse despite the suitcase blast in London and the container ship destruction of Haifa. You refuse even though you cannot find the thirty five nuclear weapons that 'disappeared' into the breakaway republics of the USSR. This irrational behavior keeps the entire world at risk. It must end!"

His clarion message plunged to a near whisper. He went on in a more conciliatory, but menacing manner. "I realize," he growled, "that our negotiating offers are confidential until agreed upon. I will, therefore, make no public mention of your rejection. The joint public communiqué may say that our teams will continue their sessions."

He paused, staring across the table, his face stony, shocked firm by his rapid changes from naiveté, disbelief and revelation, to an eventual understanding. Carla saw him for the first time as a great, patient beast, rising at last to confront harassers. Parts of his character had met and locked.

Yemetov knew Sisco from a personality analysis that described an animated, cheerful, and optimistic American politician. It had not prepared him for the man's alarming behavior. Sisco radiated with the intensity of conviction and will. Pulsing with outraged menace, his blazing eyes moved in a scorching scan of his startled opponents. Though they braced and faced him without blinking, they felt those eyes probe their souls and gather strength. Inexplicably, Yemetov recalled two faces from a schoolbook. He saw the face of a Japanese boy, and then of that boy as the "Tiger of Malaya," in charge of an army besieging Singapore. Simon Sisco's face had made an eerie, similar transformation.

Absorbed in the passion of his own thundering, Yemetov had not noticed change occurring in the American. Now, through his settling vision, Yemetov felt himself facing a man either wearing makeup or transported to the present from thirty years in the future. Startling and unsettling, the transformation made him wonder. *Hypnosis? New technology?* He could not lean to an aide and comment. He had to return the gaze. It became a contest, a trial, and it accounted for his astonishing silence as the chilling voice went on.

"We are finished here. But the idea, which the United States has proposed, is not finished. It will be unfinished business until implemented, for so long as I draw breath. And it will not be concealed. This is the best hope for humanity, if we wish to assure humanity that it can have a future.

It affects all of the people of this planet. They deserve to have it explained, and they are entitled to discuss it freely. I shall take this message to the United Nations. We are finished here."

He leaned forward, and the seething voice, repeating the last thought, struck them like Siberia's winter wind. "Finished," he hissed.

He turned and left them. Three weeks later he strode to the podium of the General Assembly in New York.

21

President Sisco thanked the United Nations Secretary General and the delegates for convening an extraordinary session of the General Assembly at his request.

"I did not seek an emergency session," he began. "I did not want to cause alarm. Yet there is a sense of emergency in my message. The nuclear vaporization of Damascus by terrorists is only three years behind us. Our high goal of 'Never Again!' lies trampled. Our dreams of firm cooperation are coated with the slippery mud of committee maneuvering. And this, despite last year's miraculous failure of the nuclear trigger in the accidental launch of the Pakistani missile! This, despite the mystery of thirty five nuclear weapons that 'disappeared' into the new republics in the early breakup of the USSR, never to be seen again!

"Add to this the proven, continuing spread of such weapons and the means for their delivery! I will not again detail the problem. You know it well. Instead, I will propose a solution to remove this blight from our lives forever. To do this, the United States now makes a formal offer to dismantle and destroy all of its nuclear arsenal, delivery systems, materials stockpiles, research facilities and test sites. Everything!"

He paused, exulting within, soaring in spirit, tears stirring. The thing had been said. He would not turn back. He heard no applause, noise or movement. The chamber could have been empty. In the silence, Carla felt the thumbump of her heart. With the idea loose, her words had become his words. He had hardened into a tenderness for humanity, her own strange amalgam.

"We are not naive," the President went on. "The United States cannot do this alone. The world eliminated smallpox from this planet only when you pursued it to extinction in each of your countries. You stamped that sickness like a fire, and you left no spark to flare again. I call you now to stamp out the fire of a greater illness, a sickness of the soul, a contagion reversing our long climb from barbarism, a contagion subtly destroying our very instinct to live. It has warped our very nature, for now we knowingly nurture a terrifying new kind of spark, the spark of nuclear weapons. These will one day flare into the ultimate fire.

"I propose two steps. First, let us decide to eliminate these weapons. Then, let us forge a mechanism for making it happen. The decision-step for abolishing these weapons is obvious and straightforward. Simply cast your vote that every nation should destroy such weapons and then prove it did so by inviting the world to come and see. That's the easy part. It will be more difficult, however, to establish the mechanism for the free and open inspections. You must prepare a plan for phased reduction, overseen by experts from your countries. Your teams would be authorized to go anywhere, in any country, at any time, for verification. I hope they will be welcomed in every land, and acclaimed as your peacemakers, and as your agents for preserving the gift of life.

"Someday, there must come a generation in which believer and non-believer alike will ask, 'What kind of Creator would make a human race with self-destruction its destiny?' A generation that would ask such a question would also have an answer. They would conclude that time, and only time, should take humanity to its fate — its natural fate; that mankind must not incinerate its own children; that the light of life, perhaps unique to this planet, must not be snuffed out by life itself.

"And such a generation would act on its decisions. This may be that generation! You may be its instruments! You can be! I pray that you will lead us to reason, openness and trust. Give us hope. Lead us to sanity. For many of you in this room, your children and your children's children are on this planet already. In their name, and in that of all others whom you love, give this world a future!"

He could not go on. He sensed his dream making no impact. His words felt puny and useless. Overcome, he felt himself failed, inarticulate, ineffective, a dreamer. There had been no reaction. Before him, beyond his outstretched arms, sat the world, unresponding. He had gambled it all and they merely stared back at him, unmoving, unmoved. They sat rigid, seeming sullen in a frozen indifference. He stood transfixed in numb despair. Where now his flying optimism, his perpetual vigor? Believing himself an incongruous messiah, he did not realize he appeared powerful and compelling. He should have known, because he spoke for reason, truth, faith, and optimism; a proxy for life demanding its rights.

The Assembly sat stunned. No imagination had dreamed of this opportunity. What prayer had worked? No one had anticipated this man's offer, nor his agony, and the imperative of his vision. He stirred their darkest primal recesses and drew up hope from their turbid, roiling national pools of fear and suspicion. From here, they knew, they might press on to a gathering of wills seeking freedom from fear of the basest terror. But some knew also the nature of the tyrants who had sent them here, and it froze their souls. They shivered in the shadow of nightmare — torture, nuclear winter, glowing dust.

In the awesome stillness, Carla saw movement. The delegate from Zambia rose. She stood with head bowed, an act that called others to silent prayer. They arose at random, in individual decisions. Some just sat, faces in their hands. Silence prevailed. Even the television networks had gone silent, frozen to one scene.

The Secretary General knew that this rare moment in shared humanity could dissolve into deprecation. He sensed that soon some delegates would be tempted to demonstrate a serene objectivity by a public, obstreperous display of individuality. Each would parade his personal sophistication, proving he had not been caught up in anything so plebeian as mass reflection, brotherhood, piety, love, or whatever name people might later give the stirred emotions.

Driven by the egos in this chamber, the posturing could reach heights of harm. He had to prevent an unraveling or the Assembly would become ungovernable. He did not want his job made harder. He had never seen a consensus like this. He could build on it, could make it hold. He switched the microphone from the rapt, perplexed President to himself. Then, borrowing from the faith of others, he said, "Go in Peace." He said it in the nine languages he knew and half-knew, moving from one to the next in soothing, measured tones. The spell held.

Members began to move from the room, alert in a focused ease, as in a respite from toil. Many stayed on in a psychic compact of compassion. Carla felt cushioned in a refuge. The chamber had become a sanctuary. She thanked God for the canny Secretary General. Perhaps more than anyone else, he understood the enormity of what had been offered. He understood the nature of the offer, a courageous confrontation of the mindset for violence. Carla watched him seat the American President and stay with him. Neither spoke. No one bothered them.

Carla stayed a long while, marveling. She knew some political systems sent atheists to represent them here, but no person had so behaved. The mention of a Creator had been a bonding act, an enfoldment. A warm kinship flowed through her, puddling benevolently in her heart. She sighed, snug in the soothing silence, envisioning those she loved, and musing on those she would love in the years to come. She felt now there *could* be years to come. Faces drifted in a soft haze — friends, relatives, her smiling mother. People's features swam in and out of focus. Her dead father appeared, unsmiling. She saw him in battle dress, bearing arms. She shuddered at the omen. He had always been an oracle.

22

When the General Assembly convened again, it did so with the goal of acting on the President's proposals. First, each nation would vote on its intent to eliminate nuclear weapons and allow unlimited on-site inspection. Then there would be resolutions to propose the machinery for conducting the onsite verifications of disarmament. Many delegates had been called home for consultation and to draft policy positions. In the few remaining Communist countries, full delegations did not return. There had been swift and efficient purges by leaders alarmed over the public response to the President's offer. On television, they had seen the consensus of conscience. They knew its power. But they had not been present, and so they could not comprehend the transformation in those who had been there.

They considered the results a mass "hysterical inertia," in which even their most seasoned spokesmen had been mute. Some of these clever people explained they had kept deliberate silence so as not to impede any party line that Moscow would develop. In the main, these pleaders kept their posts. Others, not so clever, argued for the disarmament and inspection ideas of the American President. They vanished for reeducation or worse, regarded as missionaries for a dangerous doctrine.

Those who journeyed to the next UN session included people unpolluted by the American President's "seance," fanatical hard-liners who would vote as directed. Some others, considered purified, did not agree with what they had to do but kept that to themselves. Among them came some original delegates, professed as changed, but with personal convictions, hidden agendas, and the willingness to time their moves.

Carla spoke first, as emissary of the nation that initiated the subject. She reviewed the issues. She described the enthusiastic support that poured in from millions of people around the world in unprecedented numbers of letters, calls, and telegrams. Parades, speeches and demonstrations had erupted globally, even in Communist cities. Carla appealed to the UCS to join world opinion on the "Open Lands" proposal. Carla reminded them that their predecessors had rejected President Eisenhower's "Open Skies" proposal to let observation planes fly unhindered over each other's territory.

"And now," she said, "satellites perform the same function, and in far more detail than our earlier leaders would have believed possible. You know this very well, because you are observing us as often as we observe you. It has caused no harm to the UCS. In fact, it has produced a tremendous reduction in our mutual potential for possible misinterpretation and misunderstanding. This has been a great boon to peace. 'Open Skies' have become a reality. We must move now to 'Open Lands.' It is time to fling our doors wide to each other and behave as good neighbors on this planet. Last month in this chamber we trembled with the clear vision of our responsibility and of our power to shape the future. Today requires the noblest performance ever asked of this body. Today we can make history. Please! Let us not fail! I call upon you, each and every member nation, to cast out old suspicions and sensitivities and vote yes." As she finished, the cries of support turned from thunderous to sustained.

The new Communist representative spoke next. "My country knows the horrors of massive devastation. The Nazis warred against us with a viciousness unknown to any other modern nation. The lesson we learned guarantees our passion for peace. We place the protection of peace on a plane with our national honor. The American President has called for trust. We agree that mutual trust is fundamental to progress toward peace. We agree also with his proposal to disarm. We will do so. We will match the United States in a step-by-step reduction. Rocket for rocket! Bomb for bomb!"

In a standing ovation, the delegates drowned him in a frenzy of cheering acclaim. As the plaudits slackened, he continued.

"We are a sovereign state. We make agreements. We honor our agreements. We will help in the development of the formulas and timetables for the agreement to eliminate nuclear weapons. We will sign an agreement and adhere to it. We will trust the United States to do the same. Such trust is fundamental. Trust means we do not need to walk the sovereign land of the United States, seeking to police its adherence to terms it has pledged on its national honor. We would not so insult this great nation. The integrity of the United States is above question."

He turned to the American delegation and spoke with force: "You do not lie. We trust you, and we will believe what you tell us. We expect no less in return."

For Carla, the room began to tilt. She imagined sliding without control as this devious, insidious man began to tumble the delegates down the mountain of hope they had climbed.

He continued. "The idea of 'Open Lands' inspection would be an affront to every nation here. The very idea starts with the premise that we are each and every one dishonest, and that we must watch each other as though we are all thieves. This should not be acceptable to you, your leaders, or your people, just as it is not acceptable to the United Communist States." He returned to his table.

As the roaring fury of disappointment subsided, the gavel's command began to be heard over booing and shouts of rage. When a soundless animosity prevailed in the great chamber, the President of the Assembly began the voting process. The Communist Bloc proved not to be a block when Ukrainia voted; it voted yes. At once, every one of its members defected, requesting asylum. Pandemonium! The gavel broke through again. The voting resumed. The Kazakhstan delegate surprised the Assembly by voting yes. He started to leave his seat, but a countryman restrained him at gunpoint. Weapons could get into the assembly hall because diplomatic immunity exempted the members from search. Decades before, the leader of the Palestinian Liberation Organization, Yassar Arafat, although a guest, had once taken advantage of this privilege by wearing loaded side arms while addressing the General Assembly.

The President of the Assembly, tiring rapidly, pressed on grim and determined. Only the closest Communist allies voted no. And even in their ranks were members who took advantage of the tumult to dash forward to a security guard to defect. This presented the Secretary General with difficult problems, because the United Nations complex is an international zone with its own security forces. When defections occurred on American soil the United States and its laws had jurisdiction, but in this part of New York the UN prevailed.

The tallied vote delivered a staggering defeat for the United Communist States. True, this vote had no force of law. However, under the enormous moral pressure the Communists became social and political pariahs. The following day their delegate requested an emergency session of the General Assembly.

23

Carla had not anticipated the Communists' extreme reaction to the "Open Lands" proposal. She had underestimated the security paranoia of their leaders. The world had voted against the UCS, but it was making no difference. Their delegate was now at the podium, railing against those who would dare to threaten sovereign rights or to question his nation's integrity. He grew livid when denouncing those who accused the Communists of breaking agreements or of noncompliance with treaties. He bordered on logorrhea, perhaps from the tension of his next outrage.

"Capitalist newsmongers say that we have tested nuclear devices in violation of the test ban treaties. They say that we have built weapons and delivery systems beyond the numbers to which we agreed. Proof has never been provided to justify these accusations. Proof never will be, because the accusers lie. Until now, the government of the United States has used its journalistic lackeys to voice the accusations it did not dare to raise in public. Now it has at last shown its face — a face of hypocrisy and of animosity toward the United Communist States. In its devious attempt to embarrass and intimidate us into allowing spies onto our sacred soil, it has crassly played upon the most sincere and legitimate longings of all nations. This is global, callous behavior by a nation that has called us a callous society. Let me give you an example.

"You will all remember when America and its lackeys made scurrilous attacks on the pioneering achievements of the early Soviet space program. The American delegate insinuated we had lost cosmonauts in orbit and kept the loss a secret. This is another version of America's despicable innuendo that we have low regard for human life. The capitalist newspapers and commentators said we had lied for the fleeting prestige of appearing to have a flawless space program. Such an accusation is itself a lie. If such a tragedy had happened, do you think we would have hidden the sacrifices of our own heroes? The fact is this: the Union of Soviet Socialist Republics never lost a cosmonaut in orbit, nor has the United Communist States, their dutiful descendants!

"I will give you another example of our misnamed 'callous society.' In 1984, a Korean Airlines plane violated a sensitive sector of my country's air space while spying for the United States. You may have heard of Flight KA 007. It did not respond to challenges for identification. Our defense forces shot it down. The United States vilified us as a nation with a disregard for human life. Their campaign of lies ignored our long history of humanitarian actions. What other nation, every year, saves as many lives on the high seas as my nation? Our great merchant marine does business in every ocean, but we stop doing business as usual when people are in peril on the sea. We go to their aid!

"Nor did America mention that the Soviet Union — in that same year — was the only nation operating an unpaid search and rescue satellite system for the citizens of any nation whose aircraft had crashed or whose ships foundered. In that year, the efforts of the Soviet Union saved hundreds of lives. Could you call that uncaring? Hardly! But America would have you believe us callous and intransigent.

"And now they demand the right to inspect the United Communist

States on our own soil! What lies would grow from that? Next they will want inspection for what they call 'human rights,' an action that guarantees encouragement of criminal behavior and crimes against the state by our citizens. We will not let them export lawlessness to our nation. Do you not see what they intend? The proposal for which you voted is the thin edge of their wedge. The United States seeks involvement in our internal affairs. It intends to impose its ideas and systems on our society. The United Communist States will not permit such seeds of counterrevolutionary activity to be planted."

The tirade went on and on, haranguing the assembly with accumulated grievances. Carla knew that the man could not be expressing personal beliefs. She sensed the public debut of a new policy, one with implications bewildering and fearsome. The delegate spoke in a rambling diatribe, but even that might be deliberate. Carla wondered if his excessive vehemence intended an image of frightening unpredictability. She perceived his message and its angry delivery as parts of a strategy with a purpose not yet evident. She puzzled over his wide range of complaints and challenges. *Will he leave anything out?* It seemed as if nothing that had ever annoyed Communist officialdom would be omitted this day. He went on, relentless and unpredictable.

"American suspicions and accusations seem to know no bounds, nor limits of decency. We resent the accusations of deception, of concealment and of treaty violations. Our position on these matters is factual and secure; so much so that we challenge the United States to prove any accusation. Our challenge and offer is this: If even one imputation can be proven, we will come at once to this assembly and sign the repugnant 'Open Lands' agreement!

"And now, I repeat that we refute the American accusations, and we reject their proposals to plant spies in our midst. We call upon them to apologize for their insult to the integrity of the United Communist States. We will now leave this organization, which America has so tragically steered into animosity and suspicion towards my country. We will not return until the United States apologizes or presents evidence that we have not spoken the truth. That is the heart of this issue: the claim that we are untrustworthy and must be inspected.

"The United States will fail to prove us deceptive or untrustworthy, now or in the past, no matter how hard or long it may try. That means that we are prepared to leave this body forever. However, one other thing could bring us back. That would be an admission, by the United States, that there is no proof to any of the accusations I have mentioned. We would accept that admission as an apology for its affront to the reputation and integrity of my country. When the United States has done this, we may all once again join in the search for peace.

"Meanwhile, we view the accusations and proposals of the United States as provocations. We must now look to our defenses! We must do this because we regard the United States' procedures and proposals as part of a detrimental strategy of sinister intent toward Communist society. We feel no restraint now. We will resume underground nuclear testing within the month. In the spring, we will move our tactical atomic artillery into our allied countries to defend against imperialist forces being assembled along their borders with the training and financing of the United States. These are unfortunate steps, but they are necessary steps. The peace-loving peoples of the United Communist States now bid you farewell until the American provocateurs come to their senses and retract their accusations so that we may all meet here once again to continue the search for accord among all nations."

He grouped his papers, closed the folder, and left a dazed audience. Carla's earlier sensation of sliding resumed, now intensified by her unbidden memory of a catastrophe in a French village.

At a wedding reception, the overcrowded floor had collapsed under the dancers. It gave way at the center, swiftly sloping into the shape of a funnel. By a ghastly error, the hall had been built over an ancient well, unfilled and uncovered. On the tilted world of their polished floor, the tumbled dancers slithered in a frantic, uncontrolled slide to oblivion.

Carla trembled in abhorrence and nausea at the obscene comparison. Unlike the French disaster, the drama she watched today was no accident. Instead, here in this chamber, the redoubt and rallying point for civilization's aspirations, humanity's slide into deep, smothering darkness had begun with a push. Distressed and dismayed by lost opportunity, she envisioned all the dancers of all countries tipped in horrifying glissade toward a nuclear gorge.

24

Cooper, exultant on the phone, chortled.

"Did you hear what the Russkies said today at the UN?" he crowed.

"No," said Benson. After Cooper brought him up to date, Benson asked, "Tragedy makes you happy, Art?"

Art answered in gleeful sarcasm, "And you call yourself an analyst! The greatest opportunity we could ask for just flew in. Listen up, strategist!

Yemetov practically says that if we could prove they lost a cosmonaut, they'd come back and sign the treaty. Michael, if we play this right we could get a flight approved to go and look . . ."

Benson cut him off. "Stop! Don't even breathe that! Understand? Not a word! Understand? I'll see you this weekend. Think, but don't talk. And don't write anything down."

Benson hung up, thought awhile, punched his intercom, and told his aide, "Get me Carla Truzski at the UN."

The Ambassador, open-minded and flexible, agreed to see him. Clicking along on the evening train to New York, covering pages with a proposal, Benson put flesh on Cooper's skeletal idea. He greeted Carla with vigor in the morning.

"Join me," she called from the suite window. They looked out at the city in silence until she said, "Beautiful, but brutal."

He nodded. "So much of what we create is like that."

"Will we ever learn to do better?" she mused. Then, as the sun's edge slid past a building and lit up the room, she, too, brightened. Smiling, she said, "We're about to get too much of a good thing. Morning light becomes glare; it needs control."

She reached out, paused, and laughed, "I think there's a rule that says 'The first pull on the cord will always send the drapes the wrong way.' Here goes!" They went the wrong way.

"In my experience, this is more than chance."

He laughed, "All experience is chancy."

They settled into a long discussion. When it ended, he and Cooper had an ally.

The following week he went to see key people in Space Command, visited space shuttle factory executives, and interviewed key officials at rocket launch sites. Then he returned to Washington and began serious planning.

Within twelve days of Cooper's phone call, Carla ushered Benson into a private session. They stayed closeted with the Vice President for hours. At the end, neither woman had any more questions. Better yet, Benson thought, neither had any objections to his plan. In fact, their enthusiasm exceeded Cooper's, and both women took the plan to a private session with the President. The practical politician in Sisco quipped, "You're asking me to sanction a rendezvous with a rumor?"

"We see this action as a space debris cleanup sweep."

"Interesting," said Sisco. "I know some people who would see it as breaking and entering a tomb for body snatching."

––––––––––––––––––––––––––––––– 25 –––––––––––––––––––––––––––––––

The President gave the question to the National Issues Council and, in his simple management style, stayed out of the discussion. Simon Sisco usually confined experts for as long as it took the dust of debate to settle on a recommendation. If Sisco liked the outcome, he took action. If he didn't like it, each side had to summarize its case in a full group session where he'd listen and interrogate. Few could predict how he'd choose on an issue, and many predictors lost heavy-odds bets.

Tight security kept all media unaware of the vitriolic debate. Not even the furious losers leaked information, although two had considered sabotaging the project by whispering to certain reporters. The losers wanted nothing to do with theft of another country's spaceship. Their opponents shouted that salvage is not theft.

The last hope of the losers provided them some consolation: perhaps the mission would find a vacant Soviet satellite. After that, they would own the phrase, "I told you so." An empty spaceship would let the losers come off as well as if they had prevented the flight. They had tried so hard that the Vice President had been compelled to break the counselors' tie vote.

She justified her vote with an impassioned argument: "Don't be misled about the old USSR. Think of that society as you would a murderous family bloodline. Today's communists are the philosophical heirs of the rulers who shot down civilians in a strayed airliner. Their disregard for human life is well known. Does it include even the denial of heroism within their cosmonaut corps? I'd bet on it. We may have a chance to prove that to the world. If we're right, we can hammer away in public that their regime stays closed and shuttered so it can lie without being refuted.

"If we get hard evidence, it will show that the communists can't be believed or trusted. They'll be shamed into becoming more open, just to acquire some credibility. And we will press them hard on their own conditions for reconsidering the Open Lands Treaty. Think also about this: none of the technical lies and violations we might prove to the World Court could compare in impact or clarity to showing the world their dead cosmonaut. What could be as dramatic, as compelling? And, I remind you, their spacecraft is signaling to us for some reason. To us! Why? We cannot ignore that mystery. It gives us a second reason to investigate. So, you see why I must vote yes. OK, it's done. Let's say 'go' to the President."

When President Sisco agreed, he had no philosopher present to mark his turning point, his personal mutation. Simon Sisco would go on from this milestone to violate the law, deceive the press, lie to the UCS, and stonewall the Congress. A flawed idealist will do bad things for a good cause.

PART 4

MISSION TO IVAN

26

Frank Cole came bearing a name to the President. As head of Nastran, the National Space Transportation Agency, it was Frank's job to propose a space shuttle commander for "Mission Ivan."

"Who's your choice, Frank?"

"Commander MacGregor."

"Man or woman?"

"Sorry. A man. Adam MacGregor."

"Have I met him?"

"You've probably read about him. Your predecessor gave him the Distinguished Service Award."

"Doesn't ring a bell."

"He rang a lot of bells back then. Made an impossible save of a damaged shuttle."

"I remember that someone saved a shuttle. I forget how."

"With our first and only trans-Atlantic abort."

"Brief me."

"Well, shortly after launch a main engine exploded and damaged the other two. We knew MacGregor couldn't make it into orbit or even back to base. He faced a sure ditch and a sunk shuttle. We told him to eject and save the crew. But he overrode the shutdown system. He nursed two engines until they burned up. He got high enough to open the bay doors and fire the payload into a parking orbit. Then he maneuvered into the jet stream and coached the pilot through a glide to an African airport."

"Saving a three billion dollar spacecraft."

"Well, more, really."

"How so?"

"Well, for one, he also saved a multi-billion dollar telescope payload. For another, he handed us the shuttle itself for failure analysis. Seeing is the cheapest way to learn what needs fixing. That let us avoid scores of millions of dollars worth of speculating, testing, modeling, flight delays, investigation, accident reports, and congressional testimony. You name it. A mess."

"Why can't I recall this man?"

"Mr. President, he's the one you saw on film once and joked about looking the same with or without a helmet."

"The bald one!"

"That's the man, but he's ermine, now."

"Ermine?"

"Yeah. It grew back in, but the whitest white. Used to be red."

"Odd. How many other candidates did you consider?"

"Four."

"Do they have more experience?"

"Two do, in terms of having more flight time. But ten years' experience can sometimes mean having one year's experience ten times. That's not MacGregor. He's coped with far more flight glitches."

"Glitches? Another oddity. Hmmm. We have an odd man that odd things happen to. I know you're not superstitious, Frank, so I won't ask whether you think he's jinxed."

"You just asked by not asking."

"Well, I'm sure you wouldn't have chosen him if you thought the problems *his* fault. But would you say that on the telescope flight he disobeyed an order for crew ejection?"

"Not really. What we do from Mission Control is to give advice. It's strong advice, but it's still just advice, because we're not right at the scene. We can't fault him on any case of independence. His judgment is good, and he's versatile and inventive. And may I remind you, we may need those qualities on this mission."

"Please, Frank, you must realize that I'm not secondguessing you with these questions. I simply want to put myself at ease. I need a good feeling for who's up there doing the job."

"I understand."

"Fine. Now, what makes him so good?"

"He just plain knows more than anybody else. He studies all the time. He trains harder. He's dealt with more emergencies. He's a lot like you; his job totally absorbs him."

"Always been this way?"

"Damned near, but not quite. He became a real workaholic after he lost his family. That's when his hair fell out. He buried his grief in his work and stayed that way."

"Who did he lose?"

"Wife, two sons, a daughter."

"What happened?"

"He was at sea when his wife drove off a cliff."

"Suicide?"

"Nobody ever said so."

"Has he remarried?"

"No."

"Living with someone?"

"No. His friends fix him up with dates, but he never follows up. He pleads being busy. And he is busy. Keeps busy. Very busy."

"Given that unusual background, what's your opinion of his emotional stability?"

"Mr. President!"

"Well, I . . . "

"My opinion, sir, should be very evident! I brought you an eagle, damn it. Eagles don't flock. You find them one by one, and I brought you a good one. Now you're questioning my selection! Let me sum it up. Is he a top pilot? The best! Dedicated? Absolutely! Track record? He's a constant winner. Tough? He shaves with a blowtorch. Leadership? Like you wouldn't believe. His crews are his family. Now, if *you* wish to choose *my* mission commander, what does my job become? And what should I do about it?"

Sisco, who knew Frank Cole could triple his salary by returning to private industry, began a comforting smile of friendly, subtle mischief.

Cole had seen it before. "Hell," Cole muttered, shaking his head, mellowing, starting to laugh. He'd been had. Sisco had played him, learning his depth of belief.

Simon Sisco valued conviction. Cole's certainty ended any doubts. Based on all he had learned, Sisco wanted MacGregor, too. However, he had not learned the rest of the astronaut's history — a story that only Adam knew.

27

Adam's problems began when he met Maria in his third year at the Naval Academy. A late-emerging twin, she held the honor of last child in a string of eight girls. Her father, Dr. Hans Kroner, made a strategic decision after his wife died in childbirth. He sold his Philadelphia practice and moved his business to Annapolis in a strategic investment in taking his girls to market. "This is where the boys are," he confided to a colleague. A social throwback and a coldly calculating entrepreneur, he believed in arranged marriages, scorning what he called comparison-shopping in the bizarre bazaar of romance. He viewed courting as equivalent to drinking from a mirage.

Appalled by how his daughters' friends chose boyfriends, Kroner counseled his own children with logic.

"What do your silly friends know about the young men they meet? Basically, very little. No, no, don't fight my reasoning! It's right, and your juvenile friends are wrong. They are not doing *any* reasoning, or even thinking. Their way is much too random, maybe even dangerous. Clearly, you should focus on the midshipmen. They are known quantities. Otherwise, they don't get into the Academy. They're healthy, smart, ambitious, and emotionally stable. What more do you want, for starters? You have a chance to choose from the cream of the country. Most of the important questions in husband selection have already been answered for you, for God's sake! Trust me. People marry among those they know. It's that simple. All you have to do is socialize with people you can grow to know."

The good doctor supported his advice with opportunity, and he had the money to do things right. He made it interesting and easy for midshipmen to visit. His huge walkout basement game room or his expansive riverfront lawn let the good times roll in any weather. Adam was invited to one of the celebrated Sunday Open House events. It changed his life.

Maria was a clinger. As a child, she scrambled to sit in her father's lap and lay her head against his chest for hours while he would read, snooze or watch TV. Her father-fetish began to diminish in her teens. It vanished when she met Adam. She took to the mature midshipman like an imprinted duckling: silent, needful, watching, following everywhere. She endured dress parades, she swiveled at his tennis matches, she cheered at finish lines, and she consoled after exams. Her pervasive attention nourished his buds of affection.

Adam saw her as the ready, steady support and comfort a man needed in his assaults on the world. He saw her as base camp, partner, friend, and booster. The chemistry of time and companionship produced love, a grave risk for someone like Adam; he had the instincts of a one-man dog.

In public, Maria showed as a quiet, devoted, handholding prop. In private she hugged, wriggled and snuggled, causing raw torture. She had him cooking in the sexless cauldron of serious Catholicism. His nature required dedication, and he had been content in his commitments to his religion and his country. Now, however, he would fail one or the other, perhaps both. If he slept with this woman he loved, he would fail her and his faith. If he did not, he would fail his courses; sleepless nights guaranteed it. Before Maria, he had always been able to bridle his passions, applying Aristotle's philosophy: *"I count him braver who overcomes his desires, than him who conquers his enemies, for the hardest victory is the victory over self."*

The quote had hung on the back of his bedroom door through high school, helping to steel him against self-indulgence. He fought that by exhausting himself in sports. But the exercise only made him healthier, which made him hornier. Nature often came to the rescue during dreams, yielding a starching of sheets that left him relieved, but embarrassed and confused. He often had the heretical questions of why his religion did not require confession when nature did this to him; and why, since it would happen anyway, it forbade him to help. His determination and agony had grown from a long steeping in the practices of his faith. His impressionable young years coincided with the fervent public religious interest that burgeoned after the 2001 terrorist attacks on America. As morals, ethics, and standards reassumed their earlier social importance, they helped to shape his formidable will. And now, it threatened to crumble at Maria's shrine.

With the failure of his standards imminent, he sought guidance. His father understood, but had a startling, unacceptable solution: "Stop seeing her. She's not for you, anyway. If she truly cared about you, she'd keep her distance, knowing what it causes. And I don't believe there's real passion there. Either you're misreading her or she's faking. Yes, I mean faking! Women can do that. Men can't. We're either at attention or not. With women, it's different ... and at this stage in life you can be misled by your ego and your wishful thinking. She behaves like a cuddly cat, but I'll bet she's a cold fish. For your sake, I hope I'm wrong. But I'd drop her."

Adam had been stunned and offended by his blunt, analytical father. Lost, he groped for help. His confessor, offering the standard remedies of prayer and will power, had no advice that worked. In a desperate, frank session with Maria's father, Adam got better results. The far-seeing doctor provided the comfort of a prescription to calm his dreams and quell his swellings. It worked even in the close entwinement slow rhythms of the last melody of the Seven Seas Ring Dance. It got him through to graduation and the chapel wedding, complete with sword arch. That evening, Dr. Kroner sat smiling in his tuxedo as he drew a short, diagonal line across another one of eight vertical marks on the inside cover of his diary.

28

Within days of his marriage, Adam knew he did not have a wife of shyness and modesty, the qualities so evident in courtship. Instead, he had a wife with distaste for any ardor that went beyond embracing. Maria compounded his confusion by her continued desire for comforting physical contact. Although still a hugging honey, she shied from the next-step needs of his steaming skin. His lovemaking seemed a bother, something to be avoided or at best tolerated. Sex didn't provide the mutual joy that their faith preached. She could barely endure even its sounds. Its moist resonance scraped her mind like the screech of brakes. She matched the clap of flesh with a repellent silence. Her inert, remote disdain soon had Adam in anguish that their mating was nothing but a form of masturbation. He whispered, cajoled and pleaded on how he might please, but the statue wouldn't talk. An aloof, fretful, lumpish lay, Maria triggered in her confident achiever his first sense of inadequacy.

She refused to join a group of other young wives in living at his ship's overseas homeport. Adam attributed this to insecurity. After all, she had no experience of a roving life. She had grown up in the secure, predictable household of a small town professional. Adam, in contrast, offered a life of eruptive unpredictability. He thought of resigning from the Navy. Perhaps normal living would help them work things out, could help stop the growth of resentment and anger. He endured, hoping. Time passed.

The first birth, ten months after graduation, brought a daughter. The second, less than a year later, gave them twin boys. She had less need for him now, even as a cuddler. He learned this in a startling way. He arrived home on an unexpected leave to find she had bought a huge bed in which all four of his family slept bundled together. The house had no children's beds. Maria welcomed him aboard the big mattress to join them, but on condition that he avoid animal behavior.

Direct and practical, Adam had no tools for understanding her behavior, but he knew they both needed professional help. She laughed at his "ridiculous" recommendation for psychiatric counseling. She suggested, instead, that, given his lascivious nature, it would be fine with her if he used other women to meet his needs. He winced in disbelief at her stony debasement of his love. Across that night he wandered the house, stumbling blindly and moaning like a wounded animal. At about three o'clock, he shook her awake, demanding hoarsely why she had married him.

When she answered, her voice sounded matter of fact: "I need somebody to take care of me."

Knees melting, he slumped to the floor stricken. An insight of ghastly humor let him see the ludicrous irony of his fate and hopes. He had gone to her with an ardent, faithful love, and been met halfway by an enticer seeking a father replacement and a free lunch. Adam, the lover, had become Adam, the patsy. He wasn't Adam, the psychiatrist, able to see immaturity and dread. He could see only hidden motives and deception. Chills swept him, then fever. Struggling to breathe, in a sweat of pain and revulsion, he lurched to his feet, desperate to be away, fearing his rising rage. Staggering to another room, he sank in a stunned collapse onto their old bed and into a dazed agony and exhausted sleep.

In the morning, Adam awoke worn, but alert and grim. In icy control, he confronted her. He had resolved to try saving their union, even if only to give the children the feeling of a family. He and Maria had won the anxious lottery of their children's health, looks, and intelligence, but now they faced the risk of damaging them emotionally. He would fight to prevent it. He had brought them into the world and he would not abandon them. Perhaps he could be sustained by the total, uncritical, innocent love that flowed from his little ones.

Perhaps that would be enough. Perhaps he could endure an unrequited life on the rim of the volcano that had been his love for Maria, there patrolling the slowing bubbles and fading fires.

Perhaps, but impossible. How could he live such a fated nightmare? He saw the dilemma. A hostage to his vows, Adam's nature now pushed him into the martyrdom of wistful self-sacrifice. Of this, saints are made, mostly unsung legions of women. With befuddled memory he conjured a long-gone lecturer quoting Maugham: *"When he sacrifices himself, man for a moment is greater than God, for how can God, infinite and omnipotent, sacrifice himself? At best he can only sacrifice his only begotten son."*

Rejecting self-sacrifice, he confronted Maria in the morning. She knew how determined he could be, but she had never seen anything like his adamant, hollow-eyed intensity as he gave her two ultimatums. Before his return, she must get psychiatric help, and she must wean the children to their own beds. She listened in silent foreboding.

After he left, she took no action on either demand. She considered seeking a divorce and going home, but reality told her that the doctor would not take her back. Time passed. Adam's phone calls grew relentless about the need for her psychiatric care and their joint counseling that could give love a chance. He knew that love can not be compelled.

She believed herself not in need of help, but she realized that his problem-solving nature would never let their issues coast. As Adam's next leave drew near, her apprehension grew. She became anxious, fearing a confrontation worse than the last. Needing time to think, she decided to hide. Telling no one, she took the children and drove away at night, headed to a mountain resort. All died in a crash to the base of an overshot turn on the Blue Ridge Parkway.

29

When Adam collapsed, his fleet commander understood. The admiral had lost two young sons in a car crash. *But, my God! Three kids and the wife, too.* Yet, from his own recovery, he believed that time and work would heal even Adam's loss. He transferred Adam to shore duty, and wisely offered a goal, an open ended option to requalify as a carrier pilot.

When Adam's appetite and an interest in life began to return, he felt again the yearning to fly. He began his long march back with private flying lessons. They went well, and he began to recover in a rush. The admiral heard of his progress and called him in for a talk. It ended with a reason to live again, an OK for return to flight school and, maybe, his beloved carriers. He graduated.

Adam began to realize that no one knew anything about his tortuous, debilitating relationship with Maria. To his amazement, those emotional wounds had stayed invisible. Time and determination scarred them over. His powerful will let him focus on his responsibilities so that his performance never lagged. But he would always remember times early in his recovery that he lay in his bunk trembling, as after night landings on the carrier.

Before Maria died, his love for her had still been alive, but no longer robust. The pained, bewildered withdrawal guaranteed by repeated avoidance had begun. His amorous decline had started to show in the lonely nightmare called sleep. He would come awake, throbbing with desire; he would turn to her instinctively, and then wilt in the unwelcome submission. Enough chops with the hatchet of rejection will cut the strongest bond. Adam, hacked often, and tilted for a toppling snap, was nearing love's rupture. It can die in a flash, as it often is born.

He still believed he had been normal in his needs, hopes, and intentions as a husband. This helped to keep him sane, but it left him with deep doubts. What had been the defect, he wondered, in the nature of his love that it could cause the loss of his wife and children? He felt it had also caused the loss of love itself. Could he trust such emotion, if it ever came again? No, he concluded. He could not endure a repetition, not ever. And so he would have to impose a tight control on the genie of passion that marriage had unleashed.

He had a knack for standing back in personal appraisal, watching himself respond to danger, emotion, or circumstances. He did this now with the agony of failed love and his need to cope. He decided to lose himself and his problems in work. He would age into a skilled veteran, experienced and objective, a dispenser of wisdom, sexless as an oracle. With wry humor, he pictured enduring the life ahead. He would have to learn how.

―――――――――――――――― 30 ――――――――――――――――

In courtship and marriage, Adam qualified for Thoreau's observation, *"Most men live lives of quiet desperation."* Now, however, he lived a weird, painful freedom from care. He worked hard and cleverly, hoping to make the most of this second chance. He drew upon the mighty medicine of love, an earlier love: flying, his passion since childhood.

All the money from his teenage allowance and chores went for airplane rides and flying lessons. Frantic to be in the sky, he had soloed at the earliest possible moment. His father had arranged a chance to become the youngest official solo pilot in the Guinness Book of Records. Adam revved up on the runway at twilight, in the care of an inspiring instructor who had assembled qualified witnesses. It would be his birthday in minutes, when the new day began officially. That would bring him the legal age to fly. He roared down the runway and into the book by lifting wheels at precisely midnight, Greenwich Mean Time.

The prospect of flying again, shining at the end of his personal, stygian tunnel saved him. Thoughts of being once again in the sky led, lured, and dragged him into crawling and battling through to physical recovery and mental health. He embraced his recaptured life fully, but not fanatically. He had to show a counter image to one of all work and no play. Adam understood the importance of appearances, of the public balance required of leaders. He had a mantra for dealing with society, *"In it, but not of it."* And so, when grateful hostesses used him as the available man to fill out parties, he used the events to show a public social life.

The essence of romance novels hung in the air. Compassionate women saw Adam as a tragic figure. They ached in sympathy with the agony of a man in eternal grief for a great, lost love. His model of devotion for a woman honored and exalted them. They throbbed with noble yearnings to banish his loneliness, to fill his empty life, to heal his spirit. As healers, they had ancient knowledge: they knew that the cure for a broken heart is a new woman. For his sake, Adam would be taught to love again.

These women also had the historic duty of easing a bachelor's suffering by easing him into marriage. The spur of challenge adds to duty when the target is a wary specimen. The excitement grows if the bachelor is fearful or hostile. In rare cases, when the prey is considered resolute, the stakes rise to the equivalent of big game hunting. Spirited competition among the matchmakers began.

Some memorable women found themselves maneuvered into bewildering auditions on Adam's stage of courteous, unbreachable solitude.

Nothing ever resulted. Adam, hurting and cautious and fearful, intended not to make the same mistake again. He would not let another agenda-driven woman into his life. He knew that a perpetual calm never made a sailor, but he wanted no more emotional storms. He had to transcend sex, make it subordinate. He did this with a pitiless repression that sometimes failed and brought the prescription of his senior year back into use.

His concept of love spawned a creed that you can't be denied what you don't want. And he did not want sex, as such. In his blunt code, it had to be based in love. His code had been forged in religion, and he still believed in God, but he no longer loved God. His engrained view said that sex without love equaled mere lust and could not be considered. To Adam, love could encompass and transcend lust, but not vice versa. He believed the purpose of love is creative union in mutual consolation; but the purpose of lust is pleasure, power, or sensation in singular gratification. Adam did not believe in gratification, not even with flying. It, too, had to be part of something greater.

He became intense and focused, happiest when absorbed in work and risk, sublimating sex for achievement and adrenaline. He courted hazards, but with no disregard for life. He undertook danger analytically, making his risks a calculated exposure. His skydiving gave a good example. He did not pack his own chute; he left that to experts. But he had three hedges on his bet for surviving free fall: he always wore a reserve chute; a different person packed each of his chutes; and the signed dates of packing had to be days apart, thus avoiding packers who might have partied together the night before.

His ways drew comments. A fellow pilot said, "How can anybody have 'instinctive deliberation'? That's almost a contradiction. But he's got it, got it in spades, and it's often saved his ass in the sky."

His judgment, experience, knowledge and reflexes won him an assignment to the Navy's Test Pilot School. He finished first in his class. Then, two things arrived at once — the honor of an offer to join the flight faculty, and a letter from Nastran offering astronaut training.

———————————— 31 ————————————

Adam met Mike Benson and Carla Truzski during the selection process for commander of the Ivan mission. He didn't quite understand their roles, but he respected their insights and advice. His respect rose when he worked with them on the interview team that chose Tim Carver to be the space shuttle pilot. Carver had been ten years behind Adam at the Naval Academy. Both had been carrier-based aviators before astronaut training.

Adam had transferred to space flight a few years before Tim did. Adam had flown to orbit twice as pilot and four times as commander. Tim had piloted two space flights and he headed the list of next year's candidates to command a shuttle flight. Tim had experience in polar orbit flights, while Adam had never flown on a mission from north to south. Frank Cole, wanting polar orbit experience on the Ivan mission, had put Tim on the interview list. That made Darlene Carver a happy wife. She would not have to live with an impatient, grumpy astronaut waiting to fly again.

Tim and Adam bonded fast, even to the level of joint argument with the project leader against the intended modifications to the shuttle chosen for Mission Ivan.

"We don't need the mods you're dreaming up. Look, we fly these things all the time, and when Tim and I agree this one's ready to go, you can bet it is."

"Commander, I don't dream up these changes. I get told, and usually not why. You've got to bark up the hierarchy, but even that may not help because I hear that Cole himself is being overruled."

Adam seethed with impatience. He wanted to fly this third-generation beauty that made his heart pound anew each morning. Featuring an alloy skin, with no thermal tiles, she offered impressive improvements in power, safety, durability, comfort, utilities, communications, and stay-time on orbit.

Olympia had an innovative cargo bay, with doors that sealed airtight and allowed a shirtsleeve environment in the huge cargo compartment. Earlier shuttles had to keep the bay doors open so that panel radiators on the inner side of the doors could dump the excess heat of operations into space. Instead, Olympia used retractable heat pipes. The original space shuttles compared to Olympia like the early diesel submarines compare to today's nuclear leviathans.

The original NASA always referred to its several shuttles as comprising a "fleet," conjuring images of ships. The huge Olympia looked and played the part of a ship of space — namely, a freighter that lofted special cargoes to Space Station Freedom.

Benson heard about the astronauts' insistence on an early launch. He took them aside.

"You guys have got to stop. Family feuds get attention, and we don't want the press to get interested. It could kill the whole mission. Furthermore, the mods will be for your protection because we don't know how the Russians will react if they sniff out what we're up to. You're both going to start school on the mods beginning Monday. It'll make more sense to you then. Meanwhile, zip up."

Adam respected Benson's rationale for improving security and protection, so he accepted the installation of encryption equipment, decoys, defensive shields, and weaponry. All that stuff made sense only if you wanted ultimate insurance. The bosses of this flight seemed to prefer caution, so Adam went along. He found it hard to do, however, because Olympia would not be on a combat mission.

Frank Cole outlawed overtime at the launch pad. Overtime would have stirred the curiosity of the trade-journal reporters and brought them sniffing around. Whenever the routine pace rankled Adam, Carla calmed him with her impressive insights about political timing.

The split personality of Nastran made secrecy possible. In Cooper's words, the agency provided "truck service to orbit" for all U.S. needs. One of its divisions served commerce and science; the other, much more secure, handled military flights.

Far-flung factories made the "security" add-ons for Olympia and sent them as routine shipments to California for assembly. That helped continue the sense of normalcy at the launch site. Nastran's cost conscious bosses disciplined the due dates, believing that work will lag in areas where the highest overtime rates lie waiting.

As a cover story, Nastran described Olympia as a candidate for lofting a defense satellite. But secrecy has limits when an action or object is so large it can't be hidden. At such times, distraction can help. Cooper put the distraction strategy into mangled perspective, saying, "It's time for smoke and mirrors, with a pea under every shell."

Cole announced "training exercises" for improving launch proficiency. A series of shuttles went to the launch pad in practice rollouts and dry firings, all in open view and at a leisurely pace. Each shuttle stayed out several nights before return. Reporters conjectured on which vehicle would be chosen to carry the next "spy satellite."

Meanwhile, the new doors for Olympia's huge cargo bay arrived. When closed, their gaskets tested well, sealing airtight. Brackets with explosive bolts and power/signal plug-ins adorned the doors. Defense pods and weapons would be mounted on these, installed behind prying-eye curtains, and just before the night launch.

When Olympia's turn came to trundle to the pad, she seemed just one more horse being brought out of the stable for exercise. But she never returned to the readiness high bay. Her part in the dull, distracting, maneuvers of roll-out/roll-in ended one night later.

When Olympia flew, the world knew only of a routine launch to the south from California. Even the pad crews had seen little more than the familiar box-shaped instrument being put into the bay, just another Big Eye satellite bristling with defense observation sensors going on station.

32

"There are people you cannot trust with your money; so with your emotions."
Adam recalled writing that line on a distant campus in a distant time. Now, as he arced for the horizon and another high-speed dawn, he wondered why the thought had surfaced and how it related to Mission Ivan. He could see no connection between his thought and the slowly tumbling Soviet satellite ahead. Annoyed by the seeming irrelevance, he did his mnemonic trick and ran up the alphabet in a quick-tick listing of emotions from "anger" to "yearning." Not a clue. Doubling back, he hit "patriotism" and stopped.

Perhaps the long-stranded cosmonaut had offered, from love of country, to do the will of those in charge. Such trust had to be total in the early days, with every launch an experiment. Ivan must have wondered if the planners considered him expendable in their gamble for political impact.

No book contained his history. Nowhere did it say those who sent Ivan into space had used him, nor that the ship and systems had not been ready, but they had decided to fly him, even so. Nowhere did it say they had been forcing time, trying for another first for the record books.

What promises had they shouted to him in the hugs through the big suit? How had they felt when they could not bring him down? They had sent Ivan into space under ground control only. Passive. He went passive. And passive he stayed in the hush of failure. With heroic quiet, no one could write the wrong kind of history. Inquiries by the inevitable foreign trackers went unanswered. Ivan became a non-person, participating in a non-event. He became non-living in a non-known way — by needle, perhaps, or by pill — or perhaps in the slow retreat of anoxia.

Then, man and orbit hardened into giant, enduring loops of soaring, anonymous salute to his loves, his country and his leaders. Coveted by sun, earth and moon into a hurtling poise of wingless flight, he swept the void in eyeless vigil.

But now, damn it, there would be truth! Adam would bring him down. *It's decades late, but this pioneer will at last have honors and a proper burial.* He smiled a bitter smile at a heretical prospect: maybe Ivan had no one inside! Maybe the Soviets had not lied, and no cosmonauts had ever been lost in space. Who could know for sure, given how proof vanished?

Two similar Soviet craft had come down. Orbiting for years, pelted by an occasional molecule, they had slowed until the cumulative, decelerating drag of atmospheric friction clawed them from orbit to fiery reentry. Now, up ahead drifted the last of the three suspect vessels. Mission Ivan gave the only remaining chance to prove an international deception before the evidence vanished forever. Turning to Tim, Adam said, "Harvest time, Mr.

Carver!" He watched with satisfaction as Tim floated aft to open the cargo
bay doors and flex the grappling arm.

---------------------------------- **33** ----------------------------------

Everything so far pleased Adam. When Tim had put Big Eye overboard,
it worked just fine. Its omnivorous gaze watched a new part of earth rotating
into view on each cycle from pole to pole. Big Eye made a beautiful cover
for the Ivan mission; the press and public understood the routine of tight
secrecy that always surrounded the launch of a defense system spacecraft.
Adam and Tim had paced alongside the free-flying Big Eye for a while.
They tested it for function, in their legitimate, routine role of station
keeping and checkout. They then backed away and rested, continuing the
deception, and they waited for the time and orbital positions that would
foster the breakaway to an Ivan rendezvous.

On plan, they turned their huge mass of shuttle and external tank
toward Ivan's orbital path. On a routine flight, they would have discarded
the massive tank soon after launch. This time they kept it; they had
to. Only this could provide for the enormous fuel consumption needed
to power from the Big Eye orbit into Ivan's inclination. They made the
orbital-change burn in the Southern Hemisphere, using half of earth to
block a direct Moscow view.

That caused only a temporary screen, for they were being tracked from
"fishing trawlers" sprinkled along the ocean under their path. Bursting with
electronics, the trawlers relayed data to Russia via communications satellites
called Molniya. Spaced like beads in the sky, they traveled in elliptical
orbits, with the apogee high over Russia so they could stay in view for hours.
Russia's far northern latitude made "stationary" satellites over the equator
hover too close to the horizon, preventing reliable communications.

Despite a swift relay to Moscow, the orbit data would take time to be
processed, understood, and believed. That period, thought Adam, would
give him enough time to catch up, rendezvous, and capture. If he got
his prize, there would be screams from the Communists. He knew that
Benson, Carla, and the State Department had an arsenal of justifications
ready. Adam had been briefed on the arguments they would use. He
wondered if Carla's diplomacy group in the Ivan team would ever get
heard over the Communist protests. At least he, Adam, would give them
lots to tell the world if his target held a dead cosmonaut.

Ivan's unusual orbit had preserved the ship for many decades, after something had apparently gone wrong at launch. In the early days, the Soviets used circular orbits less than 200 miles high and highly inclined to the equator (*near-polar*) because of the high latitudes of their launch sites.

American flights from Florida went down the ocean alleyway between Africa and South America. That avoided the consequences of having a launch fail over populated countries. Florida-based launches normally produced low-inclination orbits, cutting the equator at about 30 degrees. But building the Westprong launch site on the farthest California shoreline made a near-polar orbit feasible for Nastran. With South America tucked eastward, there were no populated areas to endanger in case of an early failure in a launch straight south.

Ivan had gone wrong. Its rockets apparently ignored commands for shutdown, and kept on firing until exhausted. Piling vexation upon frustration for the Soviets, it boosted the ship into a great egg-shaped orbit. Ivan's apogee, or high point, became two thousand miles, and its perigee about 150 miles; this was not the circular, polar orbit the Soviets intended. If no part of a satellite's orbit ever enters the atmosphere, the spacecraft will, theoretically, stay up forever. Ivan's perigee, however, became low enough to cause minute frictional drag with the upper atmosphere. Over decades, this tiny air resistance caused the satellite to lose a little of its kinetic energy on every orbit. As a result, on each revolution, Ivan did not rise quite so high as the last time around. This made its apogee decrease on each orbit, bringing it closer to earth.

However, perigee stayed almost constant. Over time, apogee and perigee would become nearly identical, producing a low, circular orbit. Whenever that happens, a spacecraft's full orbit is occurring within the tenuous upper atmosphere. When air resistance acts over its entire path, the satellite's life is nearing an end. It will begin tumbling, digging into the atmosphere more and more, and will lose speed so that it falls out of orbit. Its high-speed plunge into the atmosphere produces enough frictional heat to cause fiery destruction. Little or nothing reaches the ground. Ivan would someday soon meet that fate.

The Communist trawlers in the Southern Hemisphere could detect Olympia only by interception of its encrypted communications. By contrast, Nastran had a much better view. The New Zealand observatory at Christchurch could illuminate both spacecraft with radar and could also distinguish their size profiles with its great optical telescope. Their captured images went through the security scrambling and unscrambling process before appearing on the screens and displays in the Washington command post.

Breaking the tension in that crowded room, Cooper quipped, "This is high drama."

The President countered, "It's right up there with the best."

Carla chuckled, delighted to see this resurgence of banter. The President seemed himself again.

34

When they began closing on the twinkling dot of Ivan ahead, Adam mumbled, "It's all done with mirrors," and Tim grunted agreement. Adam marveled anew at computer navigation. He recalled a line from science writer Arthur Clark, *"A sufficiently advanced technology is indistinguishable from magic."*

To this he said a slow, "Amen."

He cut the closing speed and settled into trailing at a fixed distance. Its fuel job done, he would now discard the giant external tank, larger than the shuttle itself. Of a new, lighter alloy, it saved thousands of pounds of liftoff weight, allowing fuel in their place. Also, a clever engineer had realized the new tank would resist cold embrittlement. This allowed technicians to chill it to a new low, sending Olympia up with slush fuel, not liquid. The combined benefit of weight saving and added fuel resulted in the extra thrust duration needed for the orbit change and chase to rendezvous with Ivan.

As Adam reached to jettison the nearly empty tank, some primal alarm stayed his hand. Suddenly asweat from the implications, he watched in astonishment as the hand withdrew and started instead to its next task. Respecting his instincts, he did not insist. To continue mated would be unwieldy, but the mission could proceed. His sense of impending danger had proven so right, so often, that flight directors called him "the clairvoyant."

He told Tim, "She's all yours, but keep the tank," and turned to review his instructions.

Tim did the flying. He played the thrusters as surely and swiftly as a teenager with a high-speed video game. Adam felt aged as he watched the reflexes on display. He often needed deliberate thought in order to make all his moves correct in accuracy, timing, duration, and power. Tim, however, moved the ship as an athlete moves his own body, with all calculations for a hundred variables made by some instantaneous, biological computer. He and the ship seemed to be just that — one body. As a fighter pilot, Tim had been known as a top gun. Adam, who had been one himself, both as test pilot and in flight combat training, could see why. These skills of youth had begun to leave him. They had not yet left Tim. It made Adam happy to have them aboard, realizing they might come in handy if the Communists threw stuff at Olympia.

Tim maneuvered, and Adam rested, as their mutual home spun slowly below. Watching this blue-black man in the blue-black setting of space, Adam mused on the anthropologist's view of human life. Originating in Africa, migrating over millennia, it eventually peopled earth with all the variations of modern humanity. It seemed fitting that Tim, clear son of those wanderers, should be part of the modern migration, pushing outward from the earth itself. What kind of human, Adam wondered, will evolve from 100,000 years of off-earth living? Will the people who choose to live in a weightless setting even need legs? The musing part of his mind cut out abruptly when Tim said, "Positioned."

They flew formation with Ivan, noting size, shape and points to grasp with the giant arm. They saw a cylinder, onion-shaped at one end and flat at the other. It carried a red star, the hammer and sickle insignia, and the letters CCCP on opposite sides. It had a man-sized hatch. The craft tumbled ponderously.

The numerous windows hinted at a need for looking out. The glass seemed tinted. Solar panels occupied most of every window. Even with binoculars they could see nothing inside. "Darkness of the tomb," said Tim. An ablation shield at the base, designed to dissipate reentry heat by vaporizing, protected an air bag shock absorber for softening ground impact in parachute return. Adam had intense admiration for the pioneers who flew these contraptions. Landing must have been worse, he thought, than the "controlled crash" of routine landing on an aircraft carrier. He knew that the chute had dragged some of the early Soviet spacecraft, landing in wind, over rocks and into ravines.

Once, a chute had stayed full and pulled like a mad horse, in a bruising cross-country nightmare. On the open steppes, where this could go on for miles, it threatened to batter the crew to death. Unaccountably, the impacts stopped, and a new motion began. They now endured the random tossing of stormy waves, having been dragged into a frigid lake where the chute at last collapsed.

They fought to smother seasickness, hope that their locator beacon still transmitted, and plan against two new lethal hazards: suffocation and hypothermia. Opening the hatch for air would mean water entry and swamping in the tossing waves. They felt the start of a creeping chill from the frigid grip of the icy water on their metal container. The electric heaters wouldn't operate after the pounding sleigh ride. Trying to keep warm by moving about would only consume air faster. And who knew when rescue would come?

The demands of an early director of cosmonaut training saved their lives. He insisted on survival skills that far exceeded those required of American astronauts. He had been a paratroop guerrilla, often inserted behind the Nazi army. He understood what nature could inflict, and what men could endure. Now, the long hours of cosmonaut practice on yoga control and the biofeedback machines paid off. The men knew how to will a drop in body temperature, heart rate, and metabolism, and enter trance. This version of suspended animation saved them.

The amphibious rescue truck had tracked their beacon through the whiteout. It pushed and battered across country, and then through waves and spume, to reach the capsule and tow it ashore. Adam, amid the comforts and spaciousness of the latest shuttle, wondered if he could have succeeded among those early space pioneers. *Oh, just do your damned job! To each his time. Maybe those guys couldn't handle today's navigation.*

He had orders to look inside Ivan. If he found it empty, he would shoot some photos, get away from the thing, and leave orbit. There had been heated debate on this sequence. Some engineers argued for the return of even an empty Ivan, for study. They wanted the mysterious mechanisms that controlled when and where it broadcast "uscom." They lost. The winners argued that the ingenious technology had no value except to a museum. Today's engineers knew full well how to produce power for decades, and how to use computers to time signals. Also, they knew how to send radio bursts above specific sites, as dictated by the strength and direction of the earth's magnetic field. Or they could do it by the scheduled alignment of designated stars, or by using the Global Positioning System. No problem, nowadays.

The winners accused the losers of wanting to go forward into the past. Adam's sympathies were against these smart asses. Though fascinated by the ancient technology, he wondered if some of it indeed waited to booby-trap him, as Benson speculated.

35

Through Adam's early orbits the trawlers' technicians were deceived. When Big Eye came alive and began some non-secure streams of data, they captured it all. However, Big Eye sent its actual spy data down elsewhere, in secure transmissions via bursts of tight laser beams to receivers in the continental U.S.. The trawlers' equipment couldn't distinguish a distance between the parallel flyers, Olympia and Big Eye. The operators saw the radio energy as coming from one point in the sky, not two. Benson's people had relied on this. The trawlers therefore never noticed when Adam sent one last message from Olympia and entered radio silence.

That final message was a short code to activate an electronic changeling bolted to Big Eye's flank. Cooper's idea, this device could transmit a run of prepared messages, duplicating Olympia's routine transmissions. Adam flew away under this cover, silent and undetected, hoping to gain many hours of secrecy. He got just a few.

American intelligence usually did a good job of keeping up with spying actions in Africa. But, in Angola, it did not detect a Communist innovation — an odd outcome, because the introduction of high-tech devices into Africa gets attention, and at least creates gossip and speculation. The Communists did their job cleverly, using the country's vast oil operations as a mask. In an oil tank storage depot, they added a few more tanks. These seemed standard in every way. The earlier Big Eye had even sent clear pictures of them. But one tank had something non-standard, a roof not fixed to the sides, but riding on their upper rim so that it could rotate. This roof could also slide open, like an observatory. In fact, a large telescope sloped skyward inside. This legitimate device pioneered a clever, new intelligence concept called "open concealment."

If the site went undetected, the telescope would give way to particle beam weapons for shooting down military satellites. If the Americans became aware and demanded explanation during the installation, they would be given invitations for a site inspection of an astronomical telescope as innocence prevailed. The international press would, of course, also be invited and encouraged to show the world the paranoia of America.

The Angolan telescope, in its first realistic exercise, followed the Big Eye deployment. It tracked well, keeping the two twinkling spots centered on the video screen. When Adam left for the Ivan orbit, the scope followed his bright, thrusting flame. The maneuver had no significance for the telescope operators, but it did for the wide-awake technicians in Moscow. A new team had just come on shift and settled into the work of analyzing data streams from Angola and the trawlers.

"The American shuttle has changed its orbit."

"What are you saying? They are servicing their Big Eye."

"Yesterday, yes. Today, there are two orbits."

"I suppose they finished sooner than we expected."

"That may be, but they are not landing. They are in another orbit plane."

"Double check your numbers. They don't have fuel to do that."

The technicians reran their calculations, confirming orbital path and parameters. Then they convinced the shift manager, who told the commissar on duty, who alerted her superior and the military. In half an hour, her boss arrived with a few peers, all looking grim, but inwardly delighted. And why not? They lived for this, their meat: deviation from the norm.

Schooled in suspicion, these paranoid, bureaucratic hacks dug for meaning in the bewildering jargon. First they scanned the Big Eye history, comparing the flight patterns of the satellite and the shuttle. Then they demanded confirmation of the shuttle's orbit deviation. They verified calculations, confirming there had been no retrofire by the American shuttle to slow down and re-enter. On request, Angola flashed them the videotape of Adam's rocket firing when he had kicked off to the new orbit. The heat of their frustration and anger matched his bright flare. Orbit analysts, driven hard, worked on the meager data out of Angola and gave them several orbit options open to Adam. They grilled the flight controllers about how the USSR had used such orbits, seeking a clue to what Adam might be doing. Computers buried them under mini-mountains of flight data history.

The tendrils of their anxious minds probed and groped, grasping facts and ideas, beating at them to shake loose an answer. They challenged each other to produce precedent and to speculate. They hammered around the charts and tables, scanned the printouts and sketched on easels and on walls. Some played "what if" games in teams, gathering frequently to report their brain storming, no matter how technically mundane or politically bizarre.

When they powered past the technology, the jargon, and the numbing data, they came to a gasping insight of Adam's mission. With emergency passwords they pierced the organizational canopy to tell the leaders. Within ninety minutes of Adam's separation from Big Eye, the Premier knew. He understood. Yemetov's fist came down. "Get Marshal Ogrov in here!"

36

Adam and Tim pondered booby traps.

"If we try to trigger something and it doesn't happen," said Tim, "it won't tell us for sure that things are safe. Age, cold, or radiation may have screwed up the works. In fact, it may test OK now, but blow up when we jiggle it aboard."

Adam realized this, but felt he had no choice. He would save time by bringing Ivan aboard without trying to trigger a trap, but that might kill them. He had been given a field commander's decision authority; everyone realized that time and circumstances would dictate needs.

"Prepare the LAD," he said.

"Aye, aye, skipper!" smiled Tim.

Cooper had coined "LAD" as shorthand for an improvised tool called the "Lead Ass Dummy." About 2500 pounds of shaped lead, it sat strapped to a Manned Maneuvering Unit. In the MMU, a flying seat, astronauts could fly from one spacecraft to another. Now, instead of an astronaut, the block of lead sat in the seat. Tim threw the switch to free the LAD's restraints. Snap locks pivoted open. Energizing the LAD's console, he began the complex radio burst combinations for force vectors that gave direction and speed.

The Lead Ass Dummy rose from its base, left the payload bay, and moved toward Ivan. Its mass and proximity, designed to get close to Ivan, substituted for a much larger and heavier object at a greater range. Adam kept Olympia well beyond that range, anxious even so that the LAD might trigger either a gravity switch or a proximity fuse. Its concentrated mass provided what Cooper called "a tufor," meaning "two for one." The LAD was capable of tripping either booby trap trigger.

"Just get in close, Tim. Circling won't be necessary with all her spinning. Start at the nose, and then ease in. Do your best with the tumbling."

Tim's best proved very good. He dodged Ivan's antennas, buzzing close from all directions.

"Unless Ivan's trigger also has a timer," Tim concluded, "I'd say we're OK. Job done. And, now, mon capitaine, if you have no objections, I'm going to bring our little LAD back aboard." They had been told not to spend time doing that, but Tim's waste-not want-not philosophy prevailed.

"The need for speed does not exceed my greed," Tim rhymed. "I know where I can sell this thing used." Swift and skilled, he had the job almost done as he and Adam finished talking. He settled the LAD into its rack, pivoting the snap locks to hook and hold.

"I say we forget the Beach Ball," said Tim, looking through the window at the metal sphere in the cargo bay. It consisted of two hemispheres held together with explosive bolts. Inside, vacuum-packed, flat-folded in layers, waited a silvery, thin-skinned balloon. After inflation, it would be 150 feet in diameter. A subliming powder dusted the folds of the balloon's insides. Tim was to drift the thing near Ivan and blow the explosive bolts by radio signal. The powder, vaporizing directly to gas, would inflate the unrestrained balloon. Its huge surface, treated for high reflection, would trigger any radar booby trap.

"What say, Commander?"

"Don't nag me. I'm thinking. Why shouldn't we use it?"

"The LAD's been up real close, and it triggered no radar. Plus, that tank we're carrying makes a pretty good reflector. Nothing's happened. I'd say the radar job's done."

Adam hesitated, so Tim went on, "Remember where we're going, skipper. We're headed for perigee. We'll get so low, that ball will go bye-bye."

Adam nodded, realizing that even the slightest air resistance would drag at the huge surface area of the inflated balloon. Because of its tiny mass, the balloon would be left behind. Higher in an orbit, of course, in the hard vacuum of space, feathers could keep pace with anvils. But not at Ivan's perigee.

Adam knew that, as fact; but Tim understood it without thought, as though somehow sensing the needs of life and survival in this strange setting. He anticipated. Early. His foresight now saved them from a procedural failure, loss of the Beach Ball, and time lost committing that failure. An impressed Adam began wondering who should be running this mission.

To himself, he said, *"Why am I so damned process-oriented?"*

To Tim he said, "Good catch! Nice thinking. So! Let's move in and lasso that thing."

37

Deep beneath the White House, the President had set up a command post. Cooper spoke of it as the "sub-basement's sub-basement." Designed for assured continuity of command in a crisis, it bulged with computers and communications gear. Every piece of equipment had a backup for its backup. The site had three independent sources of power, but little room for creature comforts. Cooper found the place so spartan he promptly dubbed it "Tenement One." Laughing, the President accepted the name.

"Moscow has activated the Hot Line, Mr. President," Benson announced. "They may realize what we're doing."

Technicians in Moscow sent test messages above and beyond the routine maintenance schedule. Their behavior announced importance: they were testing both the ground system and the satellite communications system simultaneously. They left nothing to chance, unlike the old days, when chance dominated decision-making.

Benson recalled reading of the Cuban Missile Crisis of 1962 when the U.S. and the USSR went to the brink of nuclear war. After that frightening event, both sides agreed on a terrestrial Hot Line and a radio link backup. He remembered that neither proved reliable, and for the most outlandish reasons. A Danish bulldozer operator had severed the line once, near Copenhagen. Later, a farmer in Finland plowed it up. On another occasion, a fire in a Baltimore manhole took it out of service.

He knew none of these were acts of sabotage, but they could have been. For greater reliability and security, both nations had set up a satellite system between the White House and the Kremlin to ensure opposing leaders could communicate their intentions or circumstances. Two parallel systems allowed secure transmission of printed messages. Benson had seen them in action during drills. One used Russian communications satellites, while the other went through Intelsat, a commercial international satellite system. The two technically incompatible systems required a Russian-designed ground station at Fort Detrick, MD, and a US-designed station near Moscow. This allowed the "technical nationality" of each system to be constant from sending point to receiving point. The messages were made secure by scramblers that sent outgoing messages as gibberish. An identical black box at the receiving end unscrambled them.

Proving itself well named, the Hot Line began to sizzle with Communist demands for information and explanation. Benson hoped to buy time by calling on the stable of lower-level officials he had gathered as verbal swordsmen for fencing with Russian questions or demands. His Task Team had prepared a set of delaying tactics. Cabinet officers stood ready to take turns at the teletype. They would work from prepared text, creatively impromptu in style, and neatly stacked for transmission.

The scenario called for using the President as late as possible in this game. Although present, he had the press thinking otherwise. Offering no photo opportunity, a presidential look-alike had been seen the day before, boarding Air Force One at Andrews Air Force Base, off to a Hawaiian vacation. Now, Tenement One told the Kremlin, he had been contacted in the air and he had decided to turn back at once, out of respect for their claims of an emergency. No, he would not talk from his aircraft, but only after arrival and a thorough briefing. Meanwhile, they said, a helicopter had been dispatched to lift the Vice President from her sloop, off the coast of Maine, and would rush her to Washington. In fact, the messages said, she would reach town before the President and be made available immediately upon arrival.

38

Adam kept the shuttle in position while Tim did his magic with the grappling arm. Ivan, massive and tumbling, proved a difficult package to subdue. The whip antennas could be avoided as they reeled by, but a sturdy boom stood in the way. It stuck out about 5 feet. At its end hung an instrument of some sort. A stubby antenna stuck out just a few feet away from the boom's base. Ivan did a wobbly imitation of rotating about that stub. If he grabbed that, as a substitute for the end of an axle, Tim thought, he could squeeze like a fist and brake the spin. But if the big boom struck the grappling arm, the damage would be irreparable in orbit. From studying the gross photos of Ivan, he had anticipated just a few negligible collisions with whip antennas.

Tim practiced off to the side. He kept the end clamp focused on a distant star while flexing the grappling arm at the elbow. Back and forth, back and forth, he flexed in rhythm with the drunken, rotary arrival and departure of the threatening boom. Finally, he built up a synchronized skill that would let him reach in past the boom, nuzzle over the stub antenna, and squeeze. He would move the grappler out of the way repeatedly, but would clamp and brake on each grab. This would go on until the united ships came to rest.

Tim suddenly went in and clamped. He began an avoidance ballet of the grappler and the boom. It worked again and again. Ivan slowed each time until it stopped spinning. "Bless those Canadians," Tim muttered. Canada had manufactured all the grappling arms since the early shuttles. It helped explain the country's world stature in commercial robotics.

Gently, Tim lowered Ivan into the cargo bay. The whip antennas bent as he nested the Ivan spacecraft flush with the bay floor.

"Big problem, Chief. That instrument boom won't break or bend. I'll have to suit up, go out there and saw the thing off or we won't be able to close the doors."

39

Arnold Tanner, Secretary of State, had been waiting near the teletype machines, reviewing his lines. At Moscow's request, he got on the line after an ostensible search, notification, and rush to the White House. He switched into diplomatese, trying to soothe the Communists' impatience by using non-stop procedural fatuities and disclaimers of his own technical competence. The messages shot back and forth as he put new questions, but conceded nothing.

Tanner jabbered on as the typist plied the keyboard and the Russians. "I hope you will forgive me, Minister, for finding it hard to even grasp the idea of your accusation. In the United States, what you are suggesting might be called hijacking. Sometimes you make it sound as though you are suggesting a kidnapping, although a kidnapper will usually hold persons, not things, for ransom. But hijacking means to steal something while it's in transit. Your old spacecraft is surely not in transit. The craft is a derelict. What in the world would we want with a derelict?

'Will you please explain why you are suggesting such a fantasy? What makes you think such a thing is happening? Why would anyone make such an effort? Oh, wait! I do see a reason. A country might wish to remove a derelict as a hazard to navigation. Now, that would be a good idea. There you would create a benefit for all spacefaring nations. The United States would be eager to cooperate with you on such missions. Shall we add this to the agenda for our July summit meeting?"

Then, continuing his flooding transmissions, Tanner trotted out his stable of spokesmen. The first song and dance came from the Presidential Science Advisor, and it spun out the derelict concept.

"Retrieval could provide significant technical gain!" He rambled on with an impassioned rationale for a joint study of the effects on spacecraft materials and electronics of long-time exposure to cosmic rays and other energetic particles. The results would, of course, become public knowledge for the benefit of all space-faring nations if the United States made a salvage recovery. In such cases, he said, the owning country would be invited to send science teams to take part in the studies and to take their rescued spacecraft home. He proposed that such actions could become routine, depending upon the availability of rescue craft. Perhaps this time, he said, someone had acted on this good idea, but we would not know for sure until the President arrived. He called it beyond belief that any salvage effort of a Soviet derelict would be occurring without the President's knowledge.

The outgoing teletype continued to chatter nonstop as the Attorney General stepped in and helped play out the string of time that the astronauts needed. He used "the salvage argument" which Benson asked him to prepare. It said that even if the accusation from Moscow turned out to be true, the law of the sea applied to the ocean of space. On these grounds, the defunct, derelict vessel stood abandoned by its owners and open to salvage by anyone. Far more important, however, it had become a hazard to navigation. If, indeed, Olympia planned to remove Ivan, the act could serve as a model for all space-faring nations to follow in removing hulks hazardous to space mariners.

In fact, he went on, the United States stood ready to offer this service in the United Nations for the good of all nations. Unlike maritime salvage, however, our view of space salvage did not contemplate keeping the vessel. They had historical value and therefore belonged in the museums of the launching countries. He speculated that one nation might someday salvage another's derelict spacecraft as an expression of goodwill. Why, they might even be dealing with such a gesture right now, as a friendly surprise! Only the president would know if that were happening.

When the Kremlin demanded communication with a space flight official, Frank Cole stepped in. As Director of Nastran, he explained that Big Eye didn't come under his jurisdiction. It belonged, he said, to the Defense Department. Therefore, could the matter await the arrival of the President? "Nobody here knows the answer to your question!" He passed the ball to another space official.

The Deep Space Exploration Director sent teletype greetings to his fellow scientists in the UCS. He thanked them for their contributions to the joint ventures both countries had conducted on missions to other planets. He followed this with a series of questions and a statement of plans for future cooperative flights. Moscow did not want to hear from him! They said so repeatedly, then vehemently. Benson wished for the good old days of one-way transmission at a time.

The Kremlin wanted information from another official, the Commander of Space Missions, Orbital Spacecraft. After a delay to "find" him, the usually laconic COSMOS began to tell Moscow volumes, focusing attention on Big Eye as not his responsibility, either, but that of the Defense Department. However, he went on to provide all the unclassified information available to him and blathered on with a long statement of policy and specifications, as the White House continued to bury Moscow in bureaucratic snow.

The Kremlin's requests for information suddenly turned into demands. Premier Yemetov wanted personal contact with the American President.

The teletype thundered, "I am at this end and I want him at that end!"

In response, he got this message in bursts: "The President is in flight, returning from Hawaii ... All secure outgoing circuits on Air Force One have failed ... Only an open voice channel remains ... The President has been briefed in code on that channel ... He will not speak of these matters over an open voice circuit ... He will be on the Hot Line in Washington in six hours." An immediate response began to come in. It arrived in an unhesitating blast.

"We reject your statements about derelicts and salvage. Your purposes are to set the precedent of piracy and of imperialist interference in the internal affairs of other nations. Our space vessels are both property and sovereign territory, an extension of the United Communist States. They may not be boarded, nor taken as salvage or prizes. We had anticipated this theft and acted to prevent it. A mine is hidden aboard. The mine can be triggered in several ways. Any attempt at tampering will cause our satellite and your shuttle to blow up. Also, if you try to steal it, there will be an explosion upon reentry due to atmospheric pressure. We will now tell the media of all nations about your provocative action and that we have warned you of the mine. The world will await your decision. The wrong decision will kill your astronauts. This discussion is concluded."

The line went dead.

40

Tim's plan had been to close the cargo bay doors, pressurize the bay, go out there, and lash Ivan down. That would have been quick. Closing the doors would seal the bay airtight and he would use the high-pressure tanks to create a near-sea-level pressure. The astronauts could then work in a "shirt-sleeve environment," as the human-engineering specialists termed it. The thick layers of door and bulkhead insulation in the bay would ward off the swift, lethal cold. But that damned boom on Ivan prevented closing the bay doors.

Adam realized he could close the doors part way, like powerful opposing jaws, to hold Ivan in place. That would let him maneuver Olympia in space. But for reentry, the doors would have to be locked shut to make the smooth aerodynamic surfaces he would need in high-speed flight down through the atmosphere.

Tim would be compelled to work in the vacuum of space. Even with a power saw to cut off the boom, he'd be clumsy in his suit, consuming precious time. During the lost hours, the ship would pass through perigee at least once and be slowed by upper atmosphere friction. It might even begin to tumble. They needed to move the shuttle to a higher perigee, and soon. The work had gone so well that Adam had been on the verge of sending a coded signal to indicate success and imminent reentry.

With a coded buzz, the high-speed fax machine started reeling out a priority message. Adam drifted over and read what Tenement One had to say about the Russian warning of a bomb. "Oh, shit!" he mumbled, "The damned thing may go off in our laps."

Tim heard a fulminating oath and loud thump. The exasperated Adam, undone by accumulated tension and fatigue, had sworn aloud and pounded his fist on the console in flash frustration. When Tim turned at the sounds, he saw Adam floating away—a huge, slow pinwheel—in reaction to the powerful blow.

———————————————— 41 ————————————————

The threat of a mine aboard Ivan jolted Tenement One from its posture of amiable, cooperative dissembling. The President stood. He held up a wastebasket.

"Ladies and Gentlemen," he said, "We must decide if Yemetov is lying. I want each of you to print 'lie' or 'truth' on a sheet of paper, fold it and drop it in this basket. Do it fast. I want your gut reaction. We'll hear your reasoning later."

He placed the wastebasket on the table. In a moment the silence ended, broken by the hushed zip of sheets ripped from pads. *Hmmm. No hesitations.* Everyone knew where he stood on this issue. People walked to the basket and voted.

The President removed each sheet. He placed 'lies' to the left and 'truths' to the right. He counted a tie.

"This won't be easy," he said, "but it must be quick." He turned to the Secretary of State, saying, "Arnold, did you vote 'truth'?" Tanner nodded. "OK, I want you to take the truth-people to a far corner now and summarize their reasons."

Benson convened the lie-people in the opposite corner for the same drill. The President took chalk and wrote the time on the board. He turned and faced them. "Your analysis is crucial. I will return in fifteen minutes to hear your reasoning." He left the room.

———————————————— 42 ————————————————

Tim's dad had once told him, "You'll get a job because they think you're ready. You'll take the job because you know you can do it. So the job is easy; it's the politics that'll kill you."

Tim remembered this as he saw his Commander cushion a collision with the far wall. Adam, facing away, did not see the disbelief and concern on the pilot's shocked features. Tim worried about a leader cracking up.

Space flight had no leeway for poor judgment or unpredictable emotions. Either failing would further risk an already risky mission. *What to say? What to do?* Tim's leadership instincts flared, urging him to take charge. His diplomacy doused the flare. He had learned well the politics of dealing with varied skippers. He had served under tyrants, hermits, politicians, and egoholics who drank deeply of themselves. What weird variety did he now have on his hands?

He could not show concern; he could not offer help; he could not ask what went wrong. But he could use a talent he had developed and honed into a skill he called, "Coaching From Below." He would use it to initiate action. He would ask for permission to suit up. Perhaps a reminder of authority and responsibility might reestablish normalcy. He opened his mouth to talk, but went silent as loud, gasping sobs burst from a wracked Adam, bending in spasms. Alarmed, Tim flew to offer help. Bracing to torque, he turned the quivering Adam and confronted a contorting visage of bared teeth, slit eyes and giant tears.

Tim let go of Adam and drifted back a few feet. He hung in midair, perplexed, staring at his convulsing, demented leader. Fear came; the cold, startling apprehension of being alone in the presence of the deranged. Then, in a dawning, Tim lost control in relieved awareness. He had been hearing a strong man in therapy. He had been hearing the sanity of unrestrained, prodigious laughter. Risible and irresistible, it swept him from tension into hilarity in a roaring, jovial release. In shrieking paroxysms they pawed at each other, hung on each other, till a final quiet found them spent, gasping.

Tim, time-tossed, thought of childhood visits to his father's family. "Granpa" had an old Victrola he used for playing an ancient phonograph record from the mid-1900s. He called it "The Laughing Record." It had no words or music. It began with one man chuckling and a woman tittering. It mounted to laughter as others joined in, sequencing into mirth that escalated toward hysteria. Before the end, it had the whole family howling and whooping in gales of merriment. On every visit Tim's family had been subjected to Granpa's Record. When Tim, proud of his determination and discipline, had tried to keep a straight face he failed, starting in stone but ending in jello.

"Good," his grandfather would say, "They ain't got you yet, son! Stay loose."

Seeing *Adam* as loose amazed and enlightened Tim. His all-business commander — he of the no-nonsense reputation — seemed not only human, but hearty human. Tim felt the growing attachment for his skipper turn from formal bond to personal weld until he realized he would run almost any risk for this complex, focused man. And Tim knew, too, with feeling and understanding that Adam would go in harm's way for him. He knew it despite a statement attributed to Adam, *"Every life is a solo flight."* That must have been out of context, mulled Tim, for he'd seen that this rumored self-sufficient warrior needed, wanted, and valued a wingman.

"You forgot Newton!" laughed Tim.

Amid low sighs and after-laughs, Adam rumbled, "Yeah. Right. And they spent a fortune teaching me."

In his frustration he had overlooked Newton's Law that an action will produce an equal and opposite reaction. He paid the price of forgetting with a stupid flip across the cabin.

"I'll tell you, Tim," said Adam. "I haven't been so damned frustrated in years! But now, I feel terrific. I needed that, I guess."

He looked at Tim. "Lucky for us, bucko, we weren't on the air. If Houston had ever heard us, we'd be sent to the funny farm. Now, bear with me. I'll be OK in a minute. First, let's mop up."

They stalked the floating tears, capturing them in terry cloth. Capillary action works just fine in low gravity.

43

The President strode in, "Truth people first! Arnold, you're on."

Tanner began an unorthodox briefing. He placed the back of his flip pad easel toward the audience, and stood a little way behind it, so that only he could see any of the 12-page hash of arguments that his hurried group had surfaced and scribbled. He would try to read from the hodgepodge of ideas overwritten, amended or struck. He had to work from a mess, a new experience. He'd been a corporate attorney, accustomed to speaking from thorough briefs, and from well researched charts from the art department. Urgently needing order, he had color-numbered the consensus items in the jumble.

"Mr. President," he groped, "we think it's important to consider geopolitics at the time of Ivan's launch. Back when the USSR wooed the nonaligned nations, it posed as a country of technical infallibility, due to the superiority of the socialist system. Rather than allow the appearance of failure, the Soviets lied routinely. Remember their behavior and denials when parts of their nuclear-powered satellite fell on Canada? Their mentality could not admit to failure. Since then, they have apparently shot down several of their own satellites that we know did not perform well. And they have exploded at least one, so we know there is precedent for having put a bomb aboard. We submit that the Soviets had this mentality at the time of the Ivan launch. We conclude that the Ivan satellite does indeed carry a bomb."

He paused, expecting comment. The President's right hand moved in fast circular motions. Tanner kept rolling.

"Second, they have always adamantly denied losing a cosmonaut in orbit. Now, if we are about to return a dead cosmonaut to earth, they will not stand for it. Their national honor is on the line. Remember, too, that if we are successful, world opinion will turn against them. The pressure will rise for their return to the UN and the topic of Open Lands. They have too much at stake. They will detonate the bomb."

He spoke with conviction, gathering momentum, drawing upon a vast experience in emotional courtroom summations, and using his rich tool of a voice to sculpt opinion. "Third," he asserted, "they will explode the bomb for another reason: to hammer their point of national sovereignty. The satellite is theirs. They reject anyone's inspection of this inherited, orbiting piece of the USSR, just as they reject inspection of the UCS itself under the Open Lands proposal. They will have a cosmic stage on which to show how serious they are on the Open Lands issue. Blowing that bomb, especially if it kills our astronauts, will show an implacable resolve. The UN will wilt and remove Open Lands from debate."

The President had stopped his rolling signal; he listened intently. Tanner began soaring. Confidence slipped over him like a second skin.

"Fourth," he boomed, "they will blame us as trespassers, even thieves. They will trumpet our disregard for human life, saying we would not phone them back to get the facts that could save our astronauts, saying we sacrificed those brave men in order to steal technical secrets of their great space program."

Then Tanner got personal. "Fifth," he whispered, and then went on in slow staccato. "Does the President see a gain great enough to risk our astronauts' lives? And, finally, sixth, does he see enough gain to offset the possible loss of a multi-billion dollar shuttle?"

Tanner's deliberate, whispered delivery had created a breathless, listening silence. In court, he'd often found this hushed technique led juries to reflection in the quiet aftermath, adding impact to his arguments. He used it now as the capstone to a strong and well-presented case. The President killed that prospect with a prompt, loud question, "What does your group say, Mike?"

44

Mission Control contained a mole. An electronic service technician, Byron Desault, came on shift for the first time in the Ivan mission. This man had not been bought or blackmailed into becoming a spy. No. He had a loftier motivation, that of ideologue. He preferred socialism to callous capitalism, partly because the damnable free enterprise system had let his mother die when money for dialysis treatments ran out.

During a visit to Houston by the Russian science attache', Desault left a message and phone number at the desk of the woman's hotel. A week later, he'd been contacted. He offered his services. He would accept no money, but would live frugally, work hard, acquire responsibility, gain access, and wait to be useful.

Moscow had tested him a few times, requesting classified materials. He delivered. When commended, he felt gratified. It gave his life meaning, on an historical scale. He felt himself the hidden force that could affect the course of nations. The Communists saw him as a zealot; possibly reliable, and of minimum value. They left him buried deep in an area of modest priority and sporadic importance to their interests.

The Russians sometimes tested him further, asking that he use judgment to select and relay significant information. He told them of the oxygen tank explosion on Ares-B, one of the tandem Mars-bound expeditionary ships, hours before the American public knew. Useful, they concluded, but not vital information. He also passed them helpful, but not important, data on U.S. space shuttles; and occasionally he gave further insight into defense satellites. Now, facing a crisis, his handler activated and briefed him on an implausible project: an unlawful American attempt to steal a Soviet spacecraft. They needed Byron's freedom of movement in Mission Control to discover events and plans. Recognized at last!

He moved about in his routine, performing tests and maintenance. He paid special attention to action near Ken Hemming, the Chief of Flight Directors; he observed screens, noted messages, and listened. He was soon rewarded.

He heard Adam's voice, "Houston; Olympia here."

The Flight Communicator responded, "Olympia; Houston."

Adam said, "Houston, I'm pregnant."

Several cheers rang out; some people understood. Byron, puzzled, did not know it meant they had the Soviet craft in the bay.

Adam went on, "Standby for text." A moment later, Adam's decoded message poured out of the laser printer in English. It described his inability to close the bay doors; announced there'd be an unpredictable period for sawing off the boom; proclaimed his intent to use the doors as a giant clamp to restrain and stabilize Ivan; and requested permission, time, and duration for a rocket burn to raise his orbit's perigee out of the dragging atmosphere.

Ken Hemming's job, Chief of Flight Directors, is a democratic dictatorship, with lots of experts available for advice. "Flight" confers, debates, discusses and ponders; but, finally, he must decide alone. Byron and other communications specialists set about helping Hemming patch together a conference call linking him with bosses in the big room and with specialists in nearby computer carrels and anterooms. Hemming asked how could they increase Olympia's speed without lashing Ivan down tight in the payload bay. This new and unpredictable payload might shift and do serious damage. Questions flew. They dealt with shuttle thrust, Ivan's estimated mass, inertial forces, strength of the aft cross girder, and allowable shuttle acceleration rate. Physicists and structural engineers worried the issues.

A second problem involved orbital mechanics, the province of the flight dynamicists, a mixed bag of mathematicians, computer programmers, aerospace engineers and physicists.

As the jargon flew, Byron gained an overview of the situation. The American shuttle had indeed seized a Soviet satellite but needed time to trim it to fit the payload bay for a return to earth and a complete theft. Within an hour of Adam's request to make an orbit change, the approval and detailed instructions sped to the shuttle. In another twenty minutes, Byron, on his lunch break, spoke on a public phone with his contact. Ten minutes later, a woman in an office in Virginia finished writing what he'd said and sealed an envelope. She rode the Metro to a commercial center just inside the District of Columbia. One of the city's kamikaze bicycle couriers sped her message to the UCS Embassy. In two hours Moscow had it.

———————————————— 45 ————————————————

Benson spoke from his seat, working from a sheaf of notes gleaned from the brainstorming lie-people.

"Mr. President, our historians say at least three Soviet manned flights became stranded in orbit. The Russians deny that it ever happened. Two of the suspects slowed and fell from orbit and burned up in the atmosphere. My group thinks it's significant that Moscow did not blow them up. Nor have they done it with Ivan. To us this means they never had a policy of placing bombs aboard. Stranded cosmonauts had other options for ending life."

Benson rose and paced about. "Why," he said, "would they omit such bombs? For several reasons. First, they did not need bombs to hide failure. Their cosmonauts were dedicated and disciplined enough to die quietly. Second, the Soviets didn't want to litter space with shrapnel that could puncture future spacecraft.

"Next, do you remember their first successful human flight? Yuri Gagarin kept yelling, 'I am Eagle, I am Eagle!' The whole world heard this Hero of the Soviet Union."

Benson stopped at the chalkboard and drew the earth, an orbital path, and a dotted trajectory for reentry.

"You all know what Yemetov said on the Hot Line. He said the bomb could be triggered by barometric pressure and blow up at some point on this reentry path. My team rejects the idea that Heroes of the Soviet Union would be blown up on the way home. It would be an absolute propaganda disaster.

"You can argue that cosmonauts could disconnect a bomb before reentry, but my team argues that the Soviets would never take that chance. The disconnect switch might not work. In addition, suppose the crew became disabled in some way and could not disconnect, and had to be brought home by remote control? Remember, too, that the explosives back then were not very stable and might have detonated from jarring, launch vibration, or reentry shock. I think it's clear why my team believes that the Soviets would have — forgive the expression — 'banned the bomb.'"

He took the chalk and wrote, "We anticipated this theft and acted to prevent it. A mine is aboard." He spun on Tanner, saying, "Arnold, that's what Yemetov said on the Hot Line. I'd like you to make believe you're on our team, here among the lie-people. Then, tell us how you would conclude, from his own words, that Yemetov lied?"

The Secretary of State would not be drawn in. He waved Benson off, saying, "Come now, Mike; you know that diplomats never accuse each other of lying. This is your argument. You make it."

The President broke in, "Cut this out! Mike, state your case."

"OK, sorry. My point is this: Yemetov lied about anticipating a theft, and therefore he lied about acting to prevent it. How do we know? Because when they launched Ivan, the Soviet Union reigned as the greatest space power in the world, yet even they could not rendezvous in orbit with another spacecraft. They could not even pull up alongside and destroy it, never mind capture one and take it home. And we were even worse off. At that time, the Soviets laughed at us in public because all we could launch was a satellite so small that Khrushchev called it 'a grapefruit.' So what does Yemetov mean when he says they anticipated the theft? Nothing. He made it up! His advisers are so rattled they're not thinking straight, and they got him to say this foolish thing."

Benson went to the board again, traced down the reentry path and chalked in the letter X near earth.

"This," he said, "is the blast point. Letting the blast happen is the easiest thing that Moscow could do. It would solve all their problems. Just by saying nothing, by not giving us a so-called warning, by letting us fly home, they could get rid of Ivan and our shuttle in one big bomb blast. We'd have no recourse to courts or public opinion. We'd have lost our evidence. We'd have lost our shuttle. We'd look like cosmic thieves getting our just desserts. Our space program would be set back by years, and by $5 billion. Plus we'd spend the rest of your administration up on the Hill trying to explain to Congress what happened. Why isn't the Kremlin letting all those goodies happen?"

He paused for effect. Turning slowly, the hub of eyes and thought, he faced Sisco and said, "Because, Mr. President, there is no bomb aboard Ivan."

He returned to his place, and stood, hammering his points home. "Let me sum up. First: from early Soviet propaganda requirements, we know they would not place bombs on manned spacecraft. Second: from their actual practice on manned flights, we know they never did use bombs. Third: from the technology capabilities at the time of Ivan's launch we know they could not trust any device to do their bidding. Conclusion? Yemetov is lying."

After a moment of quiet, he added: "But Yemetov's lie, and all the other Kremlin behavior, is telling us something basic: Ivan is very important to them. Why?" He looked hard at Tanner. "My team says there can be only one conclusion: Because there's a body on board." He sat down.

The President spoke at once, as he had after the Secretary of State's summary, again choking off residual impact.

"I'm thankful to both teams. You've done me a great service. I wish now to reflect on what you've both told me. You'll have my decision within the hour." He turned and left the room.

46

Sealed in his space suit, Tim made good use of his pressure-adjustment time. He read numbers aloud from a printed message from Houston, while

Adam, in earphones, listened and fed the figures into the rocket system's computer. Flight had authorized a prudent series of orbit-adjustment burns to determine their effect on Ivan's stability.

"They gave you some leeway, skipper."

"Yeah, but it's just crap from the gradual-goose manual. I think we could have done one long, low-thrust burn. That wouldn't make Ivan shift around. Where can it go, for God's sake? Straight back. But that's no problem because you've got it snug up against the rear cross girder. And that baby's strong. I'm tempted to just boost us, Tim, to just go ahead on our own decision. But there's a book. 'They' wrote the book. 'They' want you to go by the book. Or 'they' will throw the book at you. Then, maybe, 'they' won't let you fly any more! And I like it up here."

He had earlier helped Tim into a flexible suit to begin the process of purging nitrogen from the blood. Going outside meant that Tim would be switching to 100% oxygen. He would also be dropping from the cabin's sea-level pressure of 14.7 pounds per square inch, going down to the space suit's pressure of 4 psi. The lower pressure prevented the suit from ballooning stiff in the vacuum of space and restricting movement. But at that lower pressure, nitrogen could bubble out of Tim's bloodstream to cause the painful, sometimes deadly, "bends" that scuba divers experience in moving too rapidly from depth to the lower pressure at the water's surface.

They had no complications with the rocket bursts. After a few trials, Houston realized how stably Tim had anchored Ivan, and Hemming gave Adam autonomy on how to rocket to the height he wanted. The mission had been delayed, but now, at last, settled into the new orbit, Adam did not have to worry about the possible problems of grazing the atmosphere. Instead, he could focus on making Ivan secure and getting the cargo bay doors closed. Adam inspected Tim a final time, helped him into the air lock, handed in the tools, sealed the door, and vented the lock to vacuum.

Tim radioed formally, "No suit leaks, Commander." He now enjoyed addressing Adam that way. He, who had earlier imagined losing a mad shipmate, had gained a friend. But, it couldn't be presumed upon. Using Adam's title emphasized that Tim acknowledged continuity of the hierarchy, and it subtly entrenched the mission's business tone.

Tim plugged in the chain saw, trailed the power cord, floated off to Ivan, positioned himself with bungee cords, gave the saw some wary trials and began to amputate the boom.

Encountering very tough metal, Tim began to worry about blade failure. He mumbled encouragement to the saw blade, "Come on, baby. Just a little more. Don't fail me, baby." He hoped for success because of embarrassment; he'd forgotten to take along spare blades. A snapped or dulled blade would mean time lost in the getting and replacing. He had almost cut through the boom when the blade stalled. It would not respond to trials of the trigger. Suddenly, it did, making the blade break and fly off, whipping and slashing. Miraculously, it passed through the small clearance between the doors, gone to join the scores of thousands of debris items circling earth in constant threat of smashing into spacecraft at thousands of miles an hour.

Tim breathed a grateful sigh that the broken blade had missed all targets in the bay, including his suit, and caused no damage. He wondered if his luck would hold, if he could snap off the boom. He asked Adam to relax the doors' grip on the boom. Crouched, with feet braced against door ribs, he began rocking Ivan's boom to fatigue the metal. It fatigued him instead, and he rested often.

He soon got a rhythm going. The metal began to yield, began to move more easily, and to heat up from the internal friction of flexing. Suddenly it gave way, falling flat against Ivan's shell.

Adam had been watching from the window. "Great," he said, "but don't let that thing touch your suit. It's hot and sharp. Lash it down. Fine. Fine. That's good. Now watch the clearances. I'm going to close up."

The great concave doors moved together, met and locked. Tim reported that the stub's ragged end cleared the doors by three inches.

"Good, good, good," said Adam. "Now, let's finish the lashdown and we'll inspect that thing. I'll pressure up the bay and come out to help you."

All indicators showed the doors' closure firm enough to hold the bay airtight. He began the pressure buildup. As it reached mountain top levels, he donned a warm jacket and gloves and passed through the air lock. In the chill, thin air he labored, moving and working faster than the bulky Tim.

Work done, Adam said, "OK. Let's try to see what's inside. If this thing is empty, we can put it back overboard."

They put their faces to all windows, peering hard, trying to see through the areas around the solar cells. Even the beam of a flashlight could not illuminate the inside.

"It's like night driving in fog," said Tim. "This feels like headlights reflecting off mist."

Adam, impatient, said, "We'll have to break in."

From the bay's tool locker Tim got a hammer and a roll of sticky packing tape. He taped the window thoroughly to prevent glass particles from flying about when smashed with the hammer.

"Wait!" Adam cried, as Tim raised the hammer. "That seems so much like fog in there, that I wonder if it's gas. We don't want to let gas out! How can we check?"

They talked it over and decided to apply heat. Tim rigged a bright lamp and shined it on a window for a few minutes.

"Bingo!" he said. They could see a swirling movement as the internal atmosphere warmed and began to circulate slowly.

"Damn," said Adam. "We can't let that gas out. We don't know what it is."

Tim agreed, saying, "Looks like we have to take this baby home."

They looped cables over Ivan and drew them taut with turnbuckles. The air pressure in the bay continued to build. It would stop at less than one atmosphere, at less than that of Mexico City. Back on earth, the President's teams debated the truth about a barometric-triggered bomb. The astronauts knew nothing of that' part of the bomb threat. In the shuttle bay, the Soviet ship interpreted the gradual pressure increase as a normal parachute descent from orbit.

47

The President returned to Tenement One, brisk and purposeful.

"I have made a decision. I thank you again for your help. I do not believe there is a bomb. The mission is to proceed. Houston says they've succeeded in closing the doors and are now securing Ivan. I do not want those men distracted by further talk about a bomb. However, Moscow did threaten to tell the press that they warned us about a bomb. Therefore, I want you all to suggest appropriate public statements for our own press release in response to whatever the Kremlin may announce."

At this point, Frank Cole, the Nastran Administrator, reentered the room, visibly upset. He conferred with the White House Chief of Staff who interrupted the proceedings.

"Excuse me, Mr. President," Ron Engle said, "Frank has an important development."

The space boss spoke, "Houston has reported an impact or an explosion on the shuttle. On-board sensors registered sudden vibration and structural oscillation, with severity greatest in the cargo bay area. We have no voice contact with the crew. Tim Carver has been injured. He was suited up, so we got his vital signs. His heart rate and blood pressure spiked just at the time of the explosion sound. The flight surgeon says Tim's temperature, pulse, and blood pressure are now low, but steady, and that Tim is unconscious due to injury.

"Our flight telemetry readings say all systems are undamaged with one exception: the starboard fiber optics wiring for elevon operation; that appears to be ruptured. Reentry and landing are still possible, but risky.

The elevon controls will now function only through the alternate wiring path along the port side. The crew may be able to fix that. There's no fire, but the automatic air sampler shows contaminants typical of the discharge from firearms. The crew doesn't respond to our voice communications, so we are sending them hard copy messages, asking them to explain what's happening. Also, the flight director is continuing to make voice calls on the wake-up frequency. We've had no response in ten minutes of trying. If the crew comes up on the voice circuit, we will patch the conversation here and you'll hear it live."

48

Byron Desault's latest message had Premier Yemetov enraged and frustrated. "They are calling our bluff," he said. "They are ignoring our warning that there is a bomb aboard. They are going ahead with the theft."

Ten of the thirteen Politburo members sat with him. He had more than a quorum for the momentous decision looming.

Yemetov went on, "They have taken Falcon aboard and found that it won't fit inside. They are cutting pieces off to make it the right size. Only because the metal is hard do we have the time for this meeting. Comrades, the American action would be outrageous under any circumstances, but this is unacceptable! You know what is at stake in this case. They must be stopped. I want your vote that they be stopped."

He polled the group and got a unanimous vote. He played on their anger and fear.

"The vital question," he went on, "is how to stop them. The method must be certain. But we have a secondary concern. We must seek world endorsement of our action. That means we must develop an argument for our action, to mark it as reasonable.

"It's clear that the Americans will not be deterred by any threat. Their President has become aggressive and unpredictable as the result of a major personality change. Nothing short of force will suffice. Marshal Ogrov has proposed that we shoot down the shuttle. I concur. I believe it to be our only remaining option. The Marshal will explain our attack arsenal, what he intends to do, and when. Tell us your plan, Marshall Ogrov!"

When the briefing ended, they approved the plan and Marshal Ogrov hustled away to prepare his attack. Intense discussion on propaganda strategy spawned two statements: one for the press, the other to the American President.

The Minister for Industry said, "Congratulations, Comrade Kopelev," addressing the party theoretician who had conceived and written the statements. "This turns their own arguments against them! It's a beautiful suppository for the American President. It puts his arguments where they belong. I love it."

What he loved went sizzling over the Hot Line with the opening statement, "The following message is from Marshal Ogrov."

In Washington, a furious declaration unfolded on one of the command post's large screens.

"I am the Supreme Commander of the armed forces of the United Communist States. I am warning you that my country is about to begin a battle exercise. It will be conducted under a basic law of the sea as applied to the ocean of space. We know the location of our space vessel, the Falcon, and we will treat it as we choose. We have chosen to destroy it. We will bombard it as we would be free to fire upon and sink one of our own ships in target practice under the law of the sea. It is your obligation to stand clear of our target area in space as you would at sea. You are now being given that notification. We will begin firing upon our spacecraft today, at 1300 hours, Moscow time. All international media will be told that, for humanitarian reasons, your astronauts are being given one hour to leave the vicinity of our property and target. Our discussions are concluded."

The line went dead again.

49

A great strength of the early NASA lay in its practice of asking, "What if...?" followed by a risk possibility. NASA posed the question in design, in engineering, in planning, and in operations, as a way to anticipate and obviate undesired, harmful events. It pervaded all thought for years following the Apollo 1 fire of 1967 that killed three astronauts during a ground test. It peaked with a religious intensity after the loss of seven astronauts in 1986 when the shuttle Challenger broke up during launch. "What if...?" became a fixation after the metal rain of 2003 when seven astronauts perished within a meteor in the reentry breakup of shuttle Columbia.

One engineer, explaining its values, said, "Assume you're responsible for highways in the Rocky Mountains. You say, 'What if — a truck loses its brakes going down hill?' To cope with that possibility, you build frequent, short, side roads that run steeply uphill, tapering to sand. That'll let the runaway driver steer off the road, and dump his kinetic energy into lifting the truck uphill and plowing through sand. Furthermore, bogging down in the sand will prevent rollback. If you don't do that kind of thinking, you dump an emergency on some poor bastard who may not be prepared to handle it. It's better to anticipate things like that and design them away."

The imaginative precautions did not transfer as a bone marrow philosophy to Nastran, the new agency. Cautious questioning did not get asked for every step of bringing Ivan to earth. The urgency of the mission added haste to the blind spot. Even the Kremlin's rejected threat of a barometric bomb triggered no one to think of any other effects that might result from Ivan's return to atmospheric pressure.

The old Soviet craft knew its job. Its sensors detected the increase in air pressure in the cargo bay. To Ivan this meant one thing: descent through the atmosphere. It prepared for touchdown. Adam, high and forward in the bay, whirled as he heard an explosion. He saw the drogue of Ivan's parachute eject and tangle in the cross-bay girder. Explosive squibs had fired, triggered by the higher air pressure.

"What the hell?" shouted Tim, his view blocked. He did not see the parachute. Nor did he recognize that Ivan had begun its next program: cushion the cosmonaut against the impact of hitting earth. The Ivan design had a huge parachute, a frangible couch, and a shock-absorbing air bag cushion located behind the heat shield on its base. More explosive squibs fired. A blasting whoosh of compressed air rammed the heat shield forward. The landing cushion bag had inflated behind it. Tim, floating past Ivan's base, saw the mass of ablative material lurch at him. Like a giant fist, the heat shield hit his total body from the side.

By luck, the device had reached its limit of movement, stretched the restraining bag, and slowed. A full force blow would have been fatal. Flung forward unconscious, Tim smashed into the rear wall of the cabin. *Hit twice,* thought Adam, *and more to come!* Tim's limp body could now carom randomly about the bay. Adam knew the consequences. Tim's lolling head would make every collision a whiplash threat to his neck; edges of structures would break bones and snap him about; pointed objects would spear him. Tim, rebounding from the cabin's flat wall, hurtled back toward the heat shield. The oscillating shield, sending tremors through the shuttle, prepared to play handball with Tim as the ball.

Without an encumbering suit, a nimble Adam dived across the bay to intersect and deflect Tim. Their collision sent them off, united, on a third path, to crash into the thick insulation blankets on the walls. In a cushioned ricochet, they flew more slowly toward the opposite wall. Adam steered the direction of rebounds and absorbed the shocks of impact by "landing" feet first, knees bent.

When they halted, he floated Tim's limp body through the air lock and into the cabin. Parking Tim in mid air, he raised Mission Control.

"Houston, this is Ivan. We have a casualty."

An immediate answer said, "Houston here. Yes, we know. The doc's been watching the instruments. He'll take over now."

A new voice came on, "This is Surgeon. Tell me what happened." Adam ran through it, occasionally stopping to take questions as he stripped Tim and described the visible injuries. The reassuring medical voice from Houston changed, shouting a demand.

"Flight, I want high magnification TV!"

Hemming debated whether to say yes. Could Moscow unscramble Olympia's enhanced broadcast and see the crew's condition? He had trouble swallowing this security bubble, but decided that Tim's life outweighed the silence.

"Olympia, use the high resolution color cam," he ordered.

As directed by the flight surgeon, Adam turned Tim's body this way or that and moved parts toward or away from the camera eye for optimum focus and clarity. He checked limbs for breaks and tested for range of motion. He felt for the threadlike beat of Tim's pulse. The remote diagnosis ended. Adam, armed with the medical kit, followed instructions and treated the floating Tim. He thought it ironic that the cold, unblinking eye watching him had such a warm, tender bedside manner. In a chilling sweat of fear and anguish, he asked for Tim's prognosis. A harder voice intruded.

"Olympia, Houston. We read an alarm, a circuit interrupt to elevon control, starboard side. Ivan may have broken fiber optics."

Adam investigated and reported back. "Houston, Olympia. I can't see any break, but it may be out of sight behind Ivan. Should I move Ivan and look? Your call."

50

The President got more than Frank Cole offered. Instead of merely hearing the voices of Houston and Ivan, the command post group got a TV view of Adam treating Tim. Worry followed compassion as they saw only one man still functioning on a damaged shuttle about to be attacked.

To cope with the threat, Sisco formed a crisis management team of the Nastran chief, the boss of Space Command, the Secretary of State, the Chairman of the Joint Chiefs, the Director of the Johnson Space Center, and Benson. Only Ken Hemming wouldn't be privy to all conversation and information; he had flight operations to worry about. However, in frequent updates, the President spoke to him by phone.

"Ken, Moscow says they'll bombard Ivan within the hour. I believe them. I also believe such a desperate act means it's vital to them that we don't see what's inside. That means it contains what we suspect and we must do everything possible to land it. I don't want to be run off after getting this far. You and the crew may have to fight your ship. You know what Olympia can do. You know the defenses we put aboard. I've got a team here that'll get you anything else you may need. What *we* need right now are your opinions. I have some questions. First, can Olympia land without repairing the elevon damage? Second, if not, can Adam fix it? Third, how long might that take?"

In a laconic, controlled, machinelike drawl, the response clipped off.

"Mr. President, the answers are, first, yes, one man could land, but with extreme risk; second, maybe he can fix it; and, third, I can't estimate repair time until I see what's broken. That means Ivan must be moved away from where the heat shield banged around, so we can see what damage it did. I can send Adam right back to do that. But reaching a decision will take most of that hour you mentioned. Our time might be up before we got started on repair itself."

The team conferred and began to bang out ideas. As one defense they could buy time by dodging from orbit to orbit, hoping to confuse missiles sent to hit Olympia. Other defenses would use equipment in the pods mounted on the outside of the shuttle's doors. Some of these could launch decoys to mask Olympia. Others could explode directed-fragment bombs in the path of incoming rockets. All plans hoped to exhaust the Communist inventory, based on the assumption that they had a limited number of anti-satellite missiles due to a treaty ban. Given the Russian threat, the ban had not worked. Some missiles had apparently been saved or later manufactured. But how many? And what kind?

"I'm just sorry," said the President, "that we didn't deploy the SDI. It was meant for a situation like this."

He referred to a space-based weapons system, the Strategic Defense Initiative, intended to shoot down hostile missiles. Its theme was, "Hit a bullet with a bullet."

"May I suggest another approach?" asked Hemming.

"Of course," said the President.

"Well, sir, we based all of our preflight plans for fighting on a full crew. I don't think any one man can carry out these plans well enough. I'd like to avoid even the slightest chance of more damage from a hit. The smallest problem could keep us from getting that ship back to earth. So

I'm wondering if maybe we can arrange things so they shoot only at Ivan, not Olympia. Can I spell out my idea? Is this a secure line?"

"It's ultra secure," said the President.

"Suppose," Flight went on, "we just open up Ivan, *remove the contents* for return to earth, put Ivan over the side, and move Olympia far away for uninterrupted repairs? We can tell the Kremlin we're returning their craft to orbit. They can probably verify it's Ivan with their biggest telescope. If they want to fire on Ivan, so be it."

The Secretary of State leaped at the idea. "They'd welcome the opportunity. It would make it unnecessary for them to open fire while we're there. It would also help them avoid letting the world know they've violated the ban on anti-satellite missiles. This plan might work if they don't see through our strategy."

The President demurred, saying, "Arnold, Ken has an ingenious idea. But that would leave us with the contents and not the package. What would we do to prove our point, embalm the contents for display at the UN?"

Benson jumped in. "Mr. President, I agree with the flight director. Since we now find that we can't see into Ivan, we're forced to open it in advance, anyway, just in case there are no contents. We can't risk convening the media for a public opening of an empty vessel. We've got to open it first. But once we open it privately, Moscow can claim that we did it in secret and then fabricated the contents. Our way around this problem is to do a continuing filming of the entire process. We can publicly present the film record and any dead cosmonaut simultaneously. People will know that the broadcast is not a fabrication."

A solemn Sisco said, "Frankly, I'm not prepared for this. I assumed that we'd look in the window and either find Ivan occupied and bring it home or else find it empty and leave it behind. I guess we had no way of predicting we wouldn't be able to see in. However, what matters now is that we've invested heavily, and we seem to have a trophy. Also, Ken's idea shows a way to survive. I'm for his idea. But how do we break into Ivan?"

Hemming spoke for Adam, "He'll tape a window and smash it. If he can't reach in to open the hatch door, he'll just have to torch the door hinges."

The President gave his approval. "You tell Adam," he said, "to break in there. He can pick the best way to break in."

Ken had just finished saying, "Thank you, Mr. President," when the group heard him called into urgent conversation. They heard him asking muffled questions of an excited person. A moment later, Ken's voice came back.

"Mr. President. Our readings show another impact or minor explosion has just occurred in the payload bay. We record firearm contaminants again. Adam is going back to investigate. I've ordered him to turn on the bay's TV cameras. You'll have a picture in a moment."

The big TV screen still showed Tim floating unconscious, but tied to prevent drifting. He had no open wounds or visible bleeding. His image faded and the cargo bay appeared.

51

"We're looking at concussion," said the flight surgeon.

Adam, distressed, asked, "Will he come out of this? Will he be all right?"

He got a guarded answer. "Every case is different. He may be in a coma and stay that way. He may regain consciousness and be impaired in some manner. Or he may wake up with a headache but be totally functional. The only thing we do know is this: being battered does not improve people."

The wry comment gave no solace to Adam. "What can I do to help him?"

He got a clinical answer. "You've already done everything I'd have done, and you did it well. He's stabilized. Just be sure that he doesn't get bumped anymore. So string him up very carefully and leave him alone."

Adam proposed a barbecue suspension. The doctor agreed. Adam made a topknot of Tim's dreadlocks and tied a string from this to a cleat on one wall. Then, as an offset, he tied a line from Tim's ankles to the opposite wall. He put Tim in a near-fetal position before setting the string lengths. This would prevent Tim from inadvertently pulling loose, as might happen if he were tied while stretched full length, but should later crouch. Adam tested the range of Tim's amplitude on the string in case he should begin to flail about. Even when any thrashing straightened him full length, Tim would not strike any nearby surface, assuming the strings held.

Then Adam added some insurance, with a touch that got the doctor's applause. He ran a line from a wall anchor, passed it through Tim's jockey shorts and tied it fast on the opposite wall. He passed one more line through Tim's drawers and secured each end far from those of the first line.

"With this rig, Doc, if he flails his arms and rips off his hair knot, he's still restrained."

In response, he got the question, "Good idea, Navy, but why two more lines instead of just one more?"

The mathematician surfaced in Adam. "I strung him like a bead on the narrow point of a hyperbola. On a single string he might get to either end. But this way he can't get far from the middle."

Adam called for Hemming, "Listen, Flight, I'm going back to strap down that heat shield. It's finally stopped banging around. There's nothing more I can do now for Tim." As he finished speaking, he heard sudden noises through the open air lock. First came sounds like several near-simultaneous gunshots, followed at once by a metallic bang-clang. Olympia shuddered slightly, sensitive to all vibrations.

"What was that?" called Hemming.

Adam in motion called, "I'm going back to see!"

Ken yelled, "Olympia! I want zoom TV in the bay!"

Adam turned it on and then passed into the vast enclosure. He knew how seductively easy it is to move about in orbit where a person can exhale and float away. But that kind of movement would be random. It takes skill to land where you want after pushing off for a destination. Some astronauts in Skylab, America's first space station, said they could fly its entire length accurately in a ninety foot glide. Adam had more than that distance available in the unoccupied cargo bay. He had practiced coasting it many times.

Now, with the bay partially occupied, he pushed off for a shorter flight, soaring fifty feet from the air lock exit to Ivan's base. On his angle of flight he could not see the cause of the bang-clang noise. Somewhere behind the heat shield, the noise slowed and diminished. Adam cushioned his encounter with the face of the shield and then floated up. As his eyes rose over the shield's edge he reacted as to an ambush. Movement! His fists clenched the shield's edge and he pushed back, ducking to make the heat shield his own shield. Heart cannonading, he moved to another quadrant for a quick peek around the barrier. Now he saw clearly what his peripheral vision had detected, the thing that had triggered his dive for cover. Ivan's door, no longer locked, swung on its hinges, rebounding and clanging in open-shut-open arcs.

In vacuum, the door would have swung for a long time. Here, it fanned air with each swing. Watching, Adam reasoned out the action. Ivan's reentry program had waited a reasonable period, allowing time for parachute landing; it then fired explosive bolts to blow the door for exit. Now, as if to mesmerize, the cycling door veiled and unveiled the chamber's somber shadows. A hazy atmosphere, redolent of an unremembered flower, wafted past, fanned by the door.

Why had he come without a lamp? He stared, eyes adjusting to the dim, ephemeral light and shadows within. A deeper shadow in the trembling dusk took and lost form, an amorphous, shifting something. He hovered, hesitant in apprehension as clammy prickles swept his skin in spasms to a full frame shudder. Then came another, as the wraith seemed to move in an unveiling. It loomed, withdrew, and then loomed again. *God! Is something moving in there?* He eased sideways, removing his own shadow from the scene. The diaphanous specter congealed in the lighter, eerie gloom, into the dark contour of a seated form.

52

The zoom camera, adjusting to follow him, gave the watchers in Tenement One a semi-silent movie of Adam's ducking for cover behind the heat shield. They heard his sharp intake of air and they watched his cautious scouting movements. Then they heard the controlled, flat speech of the combat pilot.

"Houston," said the voice from space, "Ivan is here. Really here."

Ken replied with quick understanding, "All right! Congratulations. Excellent. Brief me."

A phlegmatic personality, mission focused, Hemming limited even this moment of triumph to a workaday excitement.

Adam explained the explosive opening of the hatch door and what he could see.

Hemming interrupted, ordering him to back off, "We show unidentified contaminants in your air, perhaps from Ivan's cabin. Get away from there and into a mask. Get one on Tim, too."

Adam reentered the shuttle cabin, masked himself and Tim, turned on another bay TV camera and stole toward Ivan. One hand held a lamp, the other gripped a hatchet's helve at midpoint for close quarters use.

The team in the command post understood the meaning of command. They stayed out of the action, remaining silent onlookers as Hemming directed the historic scene in the bizarre, complex milieu. The new TV camera let them see the hatch door, now stilled and wide open. The movement Adam thought he had imagined appeared again, visible to all through the hatch door. Through the lingering vapors, Adam's lamp showed a somber human silhouette swaying in slow arcs. Rapt in caution, Adam approached, one hand wielding the lamp and the other the hatchet.

"Houston," he breathed, "our friend is settling down. I guess he got set to rocking when the door began to fan. Listen, Flight, there's something else in here. I can't make it out. We've had too many surprises, so I'm going for a blower to clear the smog and check this out."

He turned and plunged into a swift, skillful glide as he spoke. Hemming gave crisp instructions to return with a local TV camera to document the scene.

Tenement One had matched the flight director's restraint. Instead of cheers, commotion or glee, the group showed only grim satisfaction. President Sisco paced with determined intensity, hands at chest, slowly striking fist into palm, eyes burning above an austere, confident smile. A failed manned flight, denied by the Communists, had been proven, and a great uncertainty had ended.

The President closed the microphone to Houston and broke the command post's silence. "We're forgetting the time. We have what we wanted. I've decided to adopt the flight director's strategy."

He turned to the Secretary of State, "Arnold, we've got to cope with whatever Premier Yemetov announces. The media will be down our throats any minute. I'd like you to huddle with the press secretary and Frank. Come up with a statement that explains our actions. You know — removing space derelicts, practicing for emergency rescues — whatever. Pick one or create one. Let me see it the minute you're ready."

Turning to Ron Engle he ordered, "Tell Moscow right now that their spacecraft is being placed back into space, that we have been damaged and that we are withdrawing to another orbit to effect repairs. Don't give any reason why we bothered with that satellite in the first place; and don't apologize for anything."

The Chief of Staff hurried off to the Hot Line, already too late.

53

Armed with a battery-driven blower, Adam leapt the gap to Ivan. He trailed a fiber optic cable for the helmet-mounted TV camera. Positioning his hand lamp, he worked in its beam to blow the obscuring mist from the cabin. A massive sadness crept over him as the view cleared. He saw the dead promise of dead youth. A handsome man, perhaps in his late twenties, materialized from the somber contour that had been so unnerving. He wore no helmet on his ancient space suit, and no glove on his right hand, the near one, with its arm blown snug against the body. The body itself leaned away from the fan's blast. It leaned sideways toward the something Adam had earlier reported, now obscured by the denseness of the fan-packed haze.

Adam wondered how the body could be flexible enough to lean. The lap restraint, clamped tight, should have held upright any sitting, frozen mass of this size and shape. He realized it did not look frozen. He hesitated to touch, apprehensive again. *Too many unknowns.* His legendary instinct for danger shook in full alarm. Then he admitted something that had been knocking at the back of his mind: an embarrassment. He sensed that it could grow into shame. He could not poke, or prod, or further violate this ancient youth in his cosmic shrine. He had already desecrated the tomb. *No. The door blew open. I did not break in.*

He pushed away from the hatch, confused. *Did I get a whiff of that gas?* His reasoned, trained self had vanished into remorse at just the wrong time. *Stay objective!!*

He set his mind to duty and returned to Ivan's door. By observation, not touch, he deduced an unfrozen body. How could that be possible after even an hour of the ultimate cold of space? He stopped the fan, intent on a closer examination. The body moved eerily toward the door, and Adam dodged off in a reflex. He shook his head. *Damn. Physics again.* The body had rebounded when Adam turned off the fan. *Definitely not frozen.* A large hypodermic needle protruded from the forearm. Adam concentrated on blowing out the remaining gas. In a swirl of clearance, he saw a bulge in the inner gloom. It clarified into the bulk of another human form, seated beside the first. A damp horripilation swept him in an ice-wind shiver. An incredulous gasp broke the strenuous pattern of breathing and grunts being broadcast to earth.

Hemming came in at once, concerned and informal: "What? What happened?"

Adam, on a very prominent stage, fought for composure. "Wait one," he said, and directed the gaze of his helmet vidicam for his audience. He swallowed hard and leaned well into the craft, avoiding contact with the man's body. He dispersed the miasma with his blower. He could now see the man's far arm leading inward, toward a second seat. Its hand, wearing no glove, held the bare hand of another person. With light and fan, Adam worked to pierce the haze that hugged the second form.

The wisps of fogging haze moved, blown to thinning, and Adam saw the second form materialize. He saw a smaller hand, with long fingers. Swaying in the fan's breeze, pivoting on its point, deep in the forearm flesh, stuck a large hypodermic needle. Adam winced at the sight. Why had they decided to die like this? A gun would have done the job faster. But, he realized, it would create a mess, making a horror of the capsule and the last minutes and memory of the second person to die. A poison pill made a lot more sense.

What had they said to one another about being stranded? How had they dealt with the knowledge of no rescue? Of finality? He struggled with the desolate sense of loss that strikes adults when a young person self-destructs. He felt betrayed. *How dared they do such a thing?* And he felt foolish, then angry, for even thinking such a question. Empty and disconsolate, he stared at them, lamenting the truncated lives of these brave pioneers. The nodding hypodermic needle caught his eye. The arm, somewhat small in girth, unhaired, had little muscular definition. A great disquiet swept him. It accelerated to dismay on a harrowing thought: *No! Back then? That couldn't be! A female?! Never!*

Finding one person had been a jolt. Finding two had been a shock. This third prospect stunned him. *Confirm! Confirm!* The features would tell. He aimed the fan at the figure's head. It wore no helmet. Long auburn hair streamed away from a woman's face. Adam sobbed. Tears blurred his eyes. He flung his head to whip them floating off. In his cleared vision he saw lovers in death.

The tragedy lumped his throat and cramped his heart. Then, in a dawning reprieve, an awesome fear crept his mind. These two looked like no dead he had ever seen. They looked immortal, bodies vacant temporarily. He had heard about the astral body, where the self comes and goes. Surely, this couple had achieved it, perhaps by a permanence of love, a reliability in eternity, a commitment past death. In the mirror of his thinking he began to see his own great emptiness, deep yearnings, denied needs. He saw, too, why the thought had flooded him: he wanted it to be so, for himself and for every aching, lonely soul in the world.

The two, leaning toward each other, interrupted in their private and eternal clasp, swayed mutely in the moving air. The closed eyes dwelled in features of infinite calm. Waxlike. Yet each face had a hint of remembered animation. Adam gazed in wonder at this serene couple, each with the countenance of innocence; each with the endearing, unlined face of young youth. They swayed as though nodding to confirm that yes, there is a peace nearing bliss. Adam smiled weakly at them from a mind of happy sorrow.

Part 5

RIPOSTE

54

Marshal Ogrov had been too young for the heroic struggle against the Nazis. A savage, energetic, and ambitious man, he had been compelled to seek his battles wherever Soviet political intervention made it possible. The scent of combat had led him to Angola and Ethiopia. There he had often discarded his advisory role, rushing into the combat. His political superiors chided, but without penalty, realizing that he might survive his dangers. Survivors of a different kind, they knew how to adjust to a blazing energy, talent and ferocity like his that might some day, perhaps soon, eclipse them.

His military superiors saw in him the embodiment of what they had been in their youth in the Great Patriotic War against the Third Reich. For political purposes, in the presence of bureaucratic officials, they counseled Ogrov to restraint, but each understood his explanation, "I must learn my trade. I am a soldier. It may be a banality, comrades, but this is the only war we have." Ogrov had envied the Americans their combat years in Vietnam, as their armed forces acquired skills and experience that might be used against him some day. When the USSR invaded Afghanistan he volunteered at once.

In what Ogrov regarded as proof of incompetence among the generals, he, a veteran of guerrilla combat, got assigned to head the tank command. He controlled the cities and plains, every day. But much fighting took place at night or in the valleys and mountains. Frustrated in his passion to encounter and annihilate the enemy, Ogrov used every political connection he could muster for a transfer to special forces combat. He succeeded.

Assigned to search-and-destroy operations, he planned and often led them with stunning results. He stayed in the field, declining leave, learning his trade, and using every weapon, tactic, practice or deception that could destroy the enemy. He did not fight by any rules. He had once been scrupulous about battling by the rules, the stringent rules of wrestling, his sport. Unlike boxing, which he despised, wrestling did not incapacitate or harm; it subdued.

Wrestling in international meets, he became convinced that a bias existed among the judges from other countries against Soviet athletes. He began to see his mat opponents not as competitors, but as enemies. Wrestling became personal combat. To overcome prejudice by any judge, anywhere, he developed a personal creed of "no decisions." He would deprive the judges of the opportunity to award points in making their subjective decisions as to who won. He could do this because in wrestling, final victory goes to the athlete who can pin and hold the other man's shoulders to the mat for the referee's count. A pin is always a win. He vowed that he would always wrestle to pin, not to win by points. Then there could be no question about victory. He wrestled with relentless fury to overwhelm totally. The strategy served him well in sports.

He made it his philosophy in the military, combining it with cunning and ruthlessness. Now, confronting the Americans in a climax to his career, he would apply his philosophy to the destruction of Olympia. *Full strength,* he thought. *Now. Before they can fly from orbit.*

He did not know that a damaged Olympia would continue to cycle by in the sky on its own orbital shooting gallery. He believed he would have but one chance to smash his target. Even now, the Americans might be counting down to retrofire their rockets and leave orbit! He worried about the sorry state of quality control in the UCS factories. Unreliable warheads and detonators continued to come off the assembly lines. Like flash bulbs, they could not be tested without being destroyed. He swore aloud at being forced into an enormous gamble.

He could not risk the equivalent of rifle shots at this quarry. Single shots might fail or miss. He did not need the missile equivalent of a rifle, but of a missile shotgun. That kind of weapon would guarantee that some of his ammunition would strike and destroy the enemy. He could see such a weapon in his mind's eye. The image encouraged him in his gamble. It matched the philosophy and strategy that had never failed him in combat: overwhelming firepower and total decimation. He embraced this as the answer to his slipping opportunity! He would salvo the full inventory of his most sophisticated missiles from the small, clandestine stockpile. Nothing could escape that blanket barrage. He ordered the bombardment.

55

Before rendezvous, bantering in his best Scottish burr, Adam said to Tim, "We're going to take ourselves into MacGregor's orbit, laddie; it's a wee version of Halley's." He referred to the gigantic elliptical path of Halley's comet. About every 76 years the comet can be seen coming toward the sun. It spends half that time climbing out to its apogee, slowing as it goes. After 38 years, the gravitational pull of the sun stops the comet's escape and reverses its course. Then begins the plunge back. The comet moves faster and faster as it falls closer to the sun, reaching a peak speed as it whips around that foci at perigee, its closest distance, and starts the long trek out again. It will do this routinely, lighting up like a blazing ball on nearing the sun. A distant day will come when the sun's recurring heat has vaporized the comet's icy elements in forming its tail, and reduced it to a nonvolatile core. Then it will follow the old path as a new entity, as a dark rock, an unlikely asteroid, forever on a predictable path.

Earth gripped Ivan and Olympia in a similar, but smaller and flatter ellipse. That orbital configuration gave Marshal Ogrov a problem. At perigee, Ivan swept close to earth, not much over a hundred miles high. Any object so close should make a good target, but Ivan did not, because of its great speed. One swift pass and then it would be gone. Gone over the horizon. Gone out of sight until earth turned for more hours and showed it again, smaller and farther away in its long climb to apogee.

Marshal Ogrov thought of these things and it gave him pause. Ivan would soon be nearing its low point. *Perhaps my one and only chance to kill it.* The wily Americans might sweep down from orbit at any minute. His instincts prompted him to commit all his Komar missiles. In the past, when Ogrov had applied total resources, he had thought himself prudent.

Now, however, he felt profligate and that made him rethink his decision. But, as he reflected on the interplay of variables such as time, height, speed, earth pull, sun pull, atmospheric drag, solar wind pressure, force vectors, and other complex aspects of celestial mechanics, he became even more convinced that he'd have but one shot at his quarry. He ended up reaffirmed, more convinced than ever of the rightness of his decision to send all his hounds together after this space fox.

56

All in Tenement One gaped in disbelief and anxious fright. Through the vidicam on Adam's helmet they saw what he saw. They heard the soft sounds from the hard commander, sounds that spoke their own feelings. A swell of universal grief had washed through every watcher at the sight of the dead young couple. No matter that these ancient youngsters came from an enemy's military loins. They represented the precious young striving for the precious future. And they had snuffed themselves out like candles.

The watchers expected to find "a cosmonaut," a man. That version of a dead male aviator would not have shocked or saddened men hardened to the random carnage of flight and battle. A dead man would have evoked merely a silent respect and admiration for the lifeless pioneer. But now, the watchers encountered an enervating sadness and emptiness. Some should have known that their melancholy masked a yearning for what might have been, a woman who would venture with her man as this one had done. Tenement One held some stern men who had sacrificed home life to their careers. And some of the wives had walked off. But here they saw a different kind of woman: one who would try with you and die with you.

Not so for Benson. He had such a woman, and his reaction had a different aspect, the subtle aspect of pity for what must have been Ivan's shame. Benson saw himself in Ivan's role, stranded in the spacecraft with her, preparing to watch her die in this alien place. He could not save her. He had failed her. Now he had to kill her. Had Ivan indeed suffered through these thoughts? He cringed.

A firm voice restored reality. "Olympia, Houston."

"Go ahead, Houston."

The specific instructions rattled forth. Ken, a natural leader, wanted things done because they had to be done, but also for action to buoy the only functioning crewmember.

"Close Ivan's door and tape it," he said. He knew that the door could be locked only from the inside.

"Your visitors are strapped in and should reenter OK. The air filters will clean things up in a few minutes and we'll let you out of that mask. Get rid of the TV helmet. We'll follow you on the other cameras. Our biggest problem is to fix the elevon damage and get you out of orbit. Put a come-along on that heat shield and move it aside so we can see the damage and whether you can repair it. Pop the pelican hooks so you can move your cargo. Don't worry about leaving the cargo unanchored; we're bargaining to put your prize over the side, anyway. It may be the price of getting people not to shoot at you."

Adam blinked. "Put it back in orbit!?"

Ken came right back, "Correct. The package may have to go back. But gifts stay. Repeat. The gifts stay. Let's get things ready."

Adam, grasping the intent, went to work. In his strange environment of minimal gravity, Adam moved the Soviet spacecraft. Although huge, it weighed nothing. However, he couldn't move it without overcoming the inertia of its mass. When Adam cranked the come-along cable, Ivan began to move. Once in motion, it could float across the payload bay and punch a hole in the opposite wall. He countered that danger with a restraining line, using friction in the rope loops for drag control. Like capillary action, friction works just fine in orbit. A drilled product of the Navy, Adam belayed all lines. He talked as he labored.

"When does the shooting start?" Ken soothed him. "It may never start. They gave us an hour's warning about 45 minutes ago. But we've told them on the Hot Line we're putting the payload back into space and asked for time to move away. We expect an answer any minute. I'll alert you if anything changes." He did not have long to wait.

57

The Chief of Staff burst into the command post, breathless. Sweat beads sat across his forehead.

"Mr. President," he panted, "they do not respond to the Hot Line. Our technicians say the other end has been shut down. We've placed your message on constant, automatic transmit. However, Sir, I don't think we should wait for the line to be reactivated. I recommend that we at once use other ways to get through."

The President, conscious of the short time remaining in Ogrov's threat, placed an urgent call to the Embassy for Ambassador Grigory Taksis. Luck prevailed, and Sisco got through. Although well informed, Taksis had not been told about the Hot Line shutdown.

"I agree, Mr. President," he said. "We must not wait. The line may be broken and repairs may be lengthy. We must convey your decision promptly. I'm sure that it will allow my Premier to halt the justified reaction of our military to your trespassing. My Premier will understand your decision to retreat and apologize. Please tell me the words you wish to use in your submission to my Premier and I will write them down so that there is no mistake in communicating to him. I compliment you on the exceptional courage you have shown in making this inevitable decision. I will transmit your message at once by every means I have. Please begin."

Sisco gaped at the man's sanctimonious language. The speech of fetial professionals like Taksis, whom Sisco considered striped-pants dandies, could cut like velvet knives. The Ambassador used speech as a psychological weapon. The infuriated Sisco almost choked, but he held silence and recovered his composure. He marveled at the paradox of this man's ability to be obsequious and arrogant at the same time. He had insulted the American President in the very sentence used to compliment him, all the while manipulating him into a nearly word-by-word pleading. Stifling a grudging admiration of this daring toady, the President swallowed hard. *Do what you have to do.* He did, with his act tempered by the knowledge that duplicity could work both ways. The Communists would soon learn what he had up his gambler's sleeves. In a clipped and acerbic response, he promised that the Russian spacecraft would be put overboard within the hour, and that Olympia would leave. He asked that the shuttle not be fired upon. Taksis promised an immediate call to Moscow.

Sisco made a call to Houston. With avuncular affection, he spoke to the key person in the crucial maneuvers looming, the flight director. Sisco briefed Hemming on the Hot Line problem and on the desperate effort to reach and influence Moscow.

"Ken, I want you and Adam to do whatever it takes to defend your vessel. You are in charge. I will be here with Dr. Cole to help in any way we can."

Sisco had the good sense to stay out of the action. He had learned well the mistakes of an earlier president in trying to fight the Vietnam War from an office in Washington. Angry, ancient generals still reminisced about micromanagement and the theft of field authority.

"But I want you to get some rest. You've been at this since the beginning," said the President. "I don't want you going into the next phase tired. It wouldn't be fair to you."

Touched by the kindness and consideration, Ken said, "No problem, Mr. President. We get long tours like this quite often and I've learned to nap at the drop of a hint. We have cots and quiet rooms nearby. The guys have been great in letting me get plenty of rest. I've got a superb flight director for each shift, so there's always somebody good on duty while I'm away. But now, sir, I must get Commander MacGregor back to the cockpit. Please excuse me."

Ken stopped Adam from working in the payload bay and got him into the pilot's seat for another review of how to defend against a missile attack.

58

It's true in the military or the theater that a key deficiency will never show itself during the dry runs. When Marshal Ogrov's rocket soldiers went into action they proved that truth again. The men had never fired their latest-version missiles because Ogrov feared detection. Under the treaty, they were forbidden to have such weapons. They did all their training in simulators. Now, facing the real thing, a subtle uneasiness filled each man. Like any deficiency of each part in a machine, every man's inadequacy multiplied serially toward an accumulating margin of error for the group.

Ogrov knew that a squad could contract the buck fever that afflicts some first-time deer hunters. He would not let this squad freeze on the trigger.

However, the Marshal made the mistake of personalizing the enemy. Each man had been ordered to kill arrogant astronauts in the act of stealing a Russian spacecraft. The squad knew that Falcon had failed in orbit, probably due to some aspect of poor quality. It had been left there for decades, awaiting the destruction of uncontrolled reentry. The thoughts moved within every one of them. Stealing space junk? Could there be a mistake? What if the Americans were in its vicinity by accident? If they'd been warned of impending attack, why hadn't they separated from the target? Was their ship damaged? Why was it necessary for these defenseless men to be blown to bits? It would be like shooting fish in a barrel.

But it wouldn't be fish; they'd be killing the American counterparts of their own brave cosmonauts. The comparison increased each man's doubts and questions, because cosmonauts are majestic heroes in Russia. Also, the adage applied that adversaries are not necessarily enemies. Despite the wavering light and shadows of his uncertainty, each man moved automatically to his duties. Their automatism diminished thought, and that affected preparation. In this lay hope for Adam and Tim.

The flight guidance officer's job includes putting target data into two sets of computers. The first, a ground-based system, would adjust azimuth and elevation, pointing the missiles properly. The second would fly as the onboard guidance system of each missile. The squad needed speed, precision and critical timing for the equivalent of hitting one rifle bullet with another. An ideal shot for the Komar weapon required a near-vertical intercept. Ogrov had a straight-for-the-jugular killer.

The flight guidance officer took the data printout from the tracking team's outbox. He fed the computers the parameters of Ivan's famous orbit and adjusted for time. Here, too, Ogrov had a problem of quality control. Several people watched the process, but no one caught the error.

59

Cooper had been keeping his key people briefed on events as they occurred. His top man, John Evans, had authority to talk with Cooper in the command post. Now he used it, because he had a theory. It grew out of a hobby: Evans, a student of military history, had a special interest in the psychology of military leaders. His grandfather had inspired and fanned this interest. The old man had apparently been good at relating the psyche of generals and admirals to their strategies and tactics.

He claimed to have predicted the end run by General MacArthur to a massive landing over the mud flats at Inchon; it came close to trapping the invading North Korean army at the southern end of the country. He also knew about the ignored German colonel who predicted where General Patton would assault Sicily, based on analysis of Patton's admiration for ancient Greek invaders.

Evans himself predicted how the Soviet invasion of Afghanistan would be fought. He read the European papers, especially the French, for thorough, continuing knowledge of events in the field. He knew of and followed Marshal Ogrov's career and performance. Also, knowing the Afghans, he predicted how the war would end. The Soviet warrior's remote leaders, he knew, would succumb before the Afghan warrior's ancient intransigence in battle. As Hitler had ignored what happened to Napoleon in Russia, so the Soviets had ignored the British experience in Afghanistan.

Yet, Evans felt, the historical pattern had been there for all to see. He saw it in the merciless, adamantine raids, attacks, and ambushes of the Afghans against Soviet units and individuals, including collaborators. In city or countryside, the Soviets had no respite or safety, day or night. Kipling advised, in his poem "To The Young British Soldier":

> *When you're wounded and left on Afghanistan's plains,*
> *And the women come out to cut up what remains,*
> *Jest roll to your rifle and blow out your brains*
> *An' go to your Gawd like a soldier.*

They came for trophies, and for parts not tanned.

Ogrov slaughtered such people by firepower. Evans predicted that the Marshal would now be true to form. Ogrov would confront the enemy with all he had. Evans expected a thundering salvo, fired on the perigee loop. Ogrov would want the target at closest range. Perigee would soon occur. No other time would be as attractive to the Communist commander. Firing earlier would not do, because Ogrov would not fire at the small area of an oncoming target. He would want more of a lingering broadside shot. Firing later would be even less desirable because Ogrov's rockets would be trying to overtake a small and departing bull's-eye. Finally, Ogrov could not know when Olympia might suddenly depart from orbit, leaving him with no target at all. He had to act soon.

Evans said all these things. Impressed, Cooper brought the Nastran Administrator into the sidebar conversation. Frank Cole questioned, listened and thought. Then, he got the President's agreement to take the ideas right to the flight director. Ever the practical realist, Hemming absorbed the theories about Ogrov's fighting style, and he kept in mind that perigee would occur over Russia just as the grace hour ended.

─────────────────────────── 60 ───────────────────────────

Diane Chang, medical doctor, worked in the middle of a rather lonely shift with her burned patient. The rest of the crew floated nearby in sleep confinement bags. Her patient gave a low, pitiful whimper. A drugged young dog, it floated in intensive care — strung in mid air from muzzle and tail. It had nearly burned to death in a Miami auto crash, but some kindly veterinarians had rushed the sedated animal to the Kennedy Space Center, courtesy of Civil Air Patrol pilots, just in time for a supply flight to Space Station Freedom.

A flight director accepted the dog into Nastran's "Moment of Opportunity" program for burn treatment research, and fired it off to orbit. Diane marveled at the speed of healing in orbit, a process hampered on earth by body weight crushing traumatized skin against bed sheets. None of that problem here, she mused. She loved the joyful energy of toy boxers. She would play with this one some day, she hoped. She continued applying the trial medications.

A strange voice distracted her, saying, "Freedom, this is Houston."

"Houston, this is Diane. Please keep your voice down. People are sleeping here."

Ken Hemming groaned within. He had used the President's prestige and Frank Cole's intervention to get Sam Meyers, Freedom's Flight Director, to contravene all plans and schedules for the station. Meyers had agreed to patch him through to Freedom and break the sleep period. Now, in this emergency, Hemming felt shushed as if his mother had answered the phone. It would have been funny under other circumstances.

"Please wake up your commander. This is an emergency."

Another voice cut in, "Dr. Chang, this is Sam Meyers. You may listen in, but we need Hank right now. Please get him."

Tension may be a form of radiant energy, because all of the crew felt a strange *something* discomfit their slumber. They crept up from sleep as the briefing of commander Hank Rodan went on, crisp and technical. Some of the crew, understanding the nature of the problem, began setting up infrared sensors without being told. In Freedom's coming nighttime pass over Russia, they would watch for the flashes and fire of rockets launched at Olympia. By coincidence, Freedom would cross the shuttle's orbit as Olympia passed through perigee. Hank estimated that the two spacecraft would be in mutual line of sight for less than ten minutes. He prayed that his sensors would see no missile heat and that he wouldn't have to sound an alarm.

Ken Hemming took no chances. He gave Hank Rodan two direct, scrambled voice pathways to Olympia. One went down to earth and up, passing through a ground antenna in a Middle East country; the other went to an equatorial communications satellite, a part of "teedriss," the Tracking and Data Relay Satellite System. It had reduced the need for large ground antennas around the world. TDRSS could "see" both of the crewed craft, and could relay messages between them. Ken instructed the Space Station Freedom crew to warn Olympia the instant they detected Russian launches. He auditioned a swift conversation between Hank and Adam, letting them talk on secure circuits. Silence followed on the starry stage. The waiting began.

61

Adam wanted to see for himself. Fighter pilots believe in eyeball testimony. They must be trained intensively to suspend personal beliefs and put their trust in radar and other sensors. He wanted to watch the UCS for signs of rocket firings. He found a way. And his way had another benefit. He stood Olympia on her nose as he swept in to perigee. This not only let him look out the front windows, but it gave a smaller, head-on target for oncoming missiles. He became sorry that he'd kept the external tank. That thing made him a bigger target than he wanted to be. Should he blow it off? If he dumped the tank and accelerated away, his timing might be wrong, so that his rocket thrust would show a heat target just as Ogrov launched his missiles. Adam scanned what he could see of the dark, vast land below. The lights of some cities shone through breaks in the overcast. He sighed and kept his hands on special triggers.

Ken had briefed him on the expected attack style and on the probability of an early strike. Neither man would rely on the hiccups of Hot Line communication to achieve a diplomats' decision in time to call off the attack. *Hell, given the mood they're in, the Communists might want to blast the shuttle whether we did or didn't put Ivan back in orbit.* An idealist when a student, Adam had lived through the great hope of the Soviet Bloc thaw in the 1990s, cheering as its satellite republics disengaged to become nations. Later, he had seen the savage control reapplied by Moscow.

That memory helped Adam stay alert against this merciless enemy. He wished he could have the added eyes of his battered pilot, strung up behind him like meat. Adam's eyeballs proved inferior to Hank's instruments. Before Adam even realized that there were new, bright lights below, the infrared sensors on Space Station Freedom reported a series of flashes. They saw each one as a single point of heat that bloomed into a mass of flame. The sensors, knowing the temperature, knew the origin. Nothing but rocket blasts would reach such heat so fast. There had been twenty-one nearly simultaneous ignitions. Ogrov's fusillade climbed the night sky.

Hank Rodan's shout came over the speaker, "Olympia! They're firing at you!"

In Tenement One, Cooper offered a silent thanks for the insight and prescience of John Evans. He had not only predicted the use of a salvo, but that it would occur before the hour of grace had expired. It had given Adam and Ken time to ready a particular kind of defense.

---------------------------------- 62 ----------------------------------

The Komar missile, unknown in the West, could home on a target by radar, or by the target's heat, or by any radiation transmissions. Whichever sensor got the stronger signal would control.

Adam, contrary to all his training, did not acknowledge Hank's shouted warning. Adam's combat clairvoyance dictated absolute silence in the face of this enemy. He could never have explained why. Instinct, again. His lack of response qualified as a breach of military communications protocol. But the breach proved that it's possible to make the right mistake. Otherwise, the Komar sensors would have detected the energy of his voice signal and turned toward it as the controlling guide. Then, upon closer approach, radar would have found and locked onto Olympia.

Hank yelled his warning again and again, fearful of not getting through. He saw the missiles' swift climb as he shouted. Neither he nor anyone on the ground realized the danger his warnings created for Space Station Freedom. Fortunately, the space station passed at such a distance from the straight-up Komar path that its signal did not turn the whole barrage his way. But, in the random quality of Russian production, the sensitivity of one sensor on one Komar exceeded that of all others in the salvo. That missile veered out of the pack, heading for what it heard, Space Station

Freedom. Hank saw the fiery turn. His voice dropped from warning shouts to awed, rapid whispers of "Oh, shit!"

Stoic Hemming held his breath and his silence. He wondered why Olympia didn't acknowledge, but he could do nothing about it. He had given both spacecraft all the facts and guidance he could provide. If circuits had gone bad, he had no time to fix them. If Adam had heard, Adam would act. A similar silence gripped the group in Tenement One, back to their policy of quiet observation.

Silence prevailed also in Adam's part of the sky. The electronic hush saved him. He did not know this, of course. He did know that he had to divert the missiles. The mathematics of celestial mechanics would steer them into his path. The Komars' radar would acquire him and correct any slight error in the flight calculations. The rockets, thrusting at 200 miles a minute, would drive the warheads through him in about 40 seconds. Upon hearing Hank's warning shout, Adam triggered two hot puffers.

Compressed air launched the puffers, each a gourd-shaped decoy device about the size of a phone booth. Adam fired them downward and forward of his path to make them visible sooner. In 20 seconds the halves of the puffer's clamshell covering would blow apart, releasing a folded sphere of plastic film. This would puff up into a balloon with a radar reflective surface.

Benson's people had added a distraction in addition to radar scattering: each of the tumbling clamshell halves would ignite a blazing thermite torch. The four hot spots, plus the enormous balloons' radar echoes might lure the missiles away. The puffers were state-of-the-art equipment, but their timers triggered nothing. Adam winced as they sailed on, buttoned up, to add more junk satellites to the sky.

The single Komar heading for Space Station Freedom worked well. Its radar acquired the huge mass of the station. It had eighty miles to go before reaching its target. Although its rocket had burned out after the turn, the dark menace would coast to collision. Tiny vector jets directed it to stay true to target. Two things happened as the Komar sped to intersect.

First, its radar began to see several targets, then a dozen, as the missile streaked for the station — a gigantic tinkertoy with appendages in all directions. What target to choose? Should it be the power-generating solar panels stuck off on long structures? The dormitories and laboratories attached to the long keel? The free floating factories flying formation? What? While the radar computer juggled the overload of information it became indecisive.

At that moment, the second event occurred. An ocean temperature sensor on Freedom began a transmission to dump accumulated data. The

Komar locked onto the power of the proximate radio signal, and, overriding its radar, steered for the broadcast source.

When the Komar hit, the explosion destroyed the end of a tower for the radio antenna. The blast itself proved harmless, for the void had no air to compress and transmit the blow. Shrapnel behaved otherwise. Pieces cut power lines, ripped structures, and punctured modules, starting fires that died without air. One punctured module held people. Unhurt, they scrambled away from the jagged metal sticking through their wall. As air hissed out to the vacuum of space, they fled into adjacent compartments. Hank thanked God that his power center and communications heart had survived.

63

Adam, staring with disbelief, twisted and turned to put body english on his decoys. He saw them shrink and vanish, inoperable. *Damn and double damn!* He railed at the crap coming out of the factories. He would die because of their failure. Then, piling amazement upon disbelief, he watched Ogrev's flaming salvo bore onward, heading for an encounter with a ghost. What looked like the full fusillade passed below him by fifty miles and, flaming out one by one, disappeared into darkness. He counted twenty burns winking out. Any one of them would have destroyed Olympia. What incredible thing had happened?

A scenario began to write itself in his mind. Someone in Ogrov's ranks had programmed the missiles for Ivan's orbit. Not the one Ivan now flew, tucked aboard Olympia, but the original orbit in which Adam had rendezvoused for the capture. Had the aim error been deliberate? Or had there been some mistake in thinking, caused by focus on hitting Ivan as the gunners knew of it? Either way, he gave thanks. The miss confirmed his conviction that combat, like nature, is full of random events.

He got more confirmation when the radio came alive with excited reports from Space Station Freedom. For some reason, a missile had turned toward the station. He watched with binoculars, and he listened all through the approach, explosion, and damage control. Fantastic! That target had been almost a hundred miles away. He wondered how any nation's missiles could be that unpredictable. Or had the Kremlin broadened the conflict with a direct attack? Ken Hemming supplied the answer. He interrogated Adam on what had occurred, and then concluded that the radio calls of warning from Space Station Freedom had attracted one of the missiles.

"As I see it," he said, "you'd have been hit with all the other warheads if you had broadcast even a thank-you to Hank. Not only that, but if your decoys had worked, that barrage would have turned your way. Who knows how many missiles would have chosen you? Benson says those babies must be something new in the arsenal and they're quirky as hell."

Then, philosophizing for what may have been the first time in his life, Ken said, "You know, if we'd done no defense at all, you'd have come to no harm at all! What's that you used to say? 'Life is random'? Is that it?"

"That's close enough. Now give me a few minutes to visit the head, and I'll get back to that heat shield damage."

He entered the enclosure, prepared himself, aligned his orifices with the narrow slot, sealed his rear to the chamber and started the airflow that guided waste into his collection container. Unlike the bathroom on earth, its spacecraft counterpart is not a place of dwelling and meditation. Done, he secured the equipment, deeming it less complex than that on submarines. Passing near the unconscious Tim, he drifted up to the flight deck's front windows and gazed in wistful awe at the rolling earth. Home. One entity. Beautiful. It made him wonder why so few poets wrote about such beauty or of the venture of humans into space. He whispered a few lines from Archibald MacLeish about the first lunar landing,

" ... *over us on these silent beaches the bright Earth, presence among us.*"

He seemed to hear whispering other than his own. He listened. It came again, almost inaudible. It said, "Help."

---------------------------------- 64 ----------------------------------

Byron Desault tried hard to stay in the midst of the action. He even volunteered to work overtime on menial jobs and at unpopular hours. However, he got no takers, so he spent sixteen hours out of touch with Olympia's situation. The tight security prevented learning anything about the mission while off duty, even in his efforts to pump information out of fellow workers from other shifts. They volunteered nothing; he backed off to avoid arousing suspicion. Finally, he phoned to tell his Virginia contact of the situation and his frustration. Despite strenuous questioning, he learned nothing from her about UCS activity and he came to believe her claim that Moscow compartmented all information.

Now, back on duty at last in the Control Center, he found it deep into planning Olympia's defense and repair. Listening and watching, he gradually pieced together what had happened. With shock, he learned of

Tim's coma, the broken elevon control, the missile damage to Space Station Freedom, and the complete miss of the salvo against Olympia. Like the flight director, he could barely believe the probable reason for the miss: the Russian computers had been fed the wrong orbital information.

He paced the silent rest room, mumbling, "Beautiful! Wonderful! Hot damn!" He enjoyed his great good fortune and began scheming his next move. Olympia had not been destroyed. Not destroyed! Now, he, Byron Desault, would be the only person able to tell the Kremlin that Olympia merely suffered damage. Better yet, he'd be able to tell them that it would have to stay in orbit, probably for days of repair, giving Moscow more opportunities to hit the target. Next time there'd be better marksmanship and its success would be due to his intelligence gathering. On his lunch break he made for the phone.

65

Marshal Ogrov held his revolver rock steady, the muzzle just inches from the man's eye socket. The man closed his eyes and spoke without permission.

"Comrade Marshal Ogrov . . . "

"You are no comrade of mine!"

The man continued, eyes still closed, "Respected Marshal, I deserve to die. I have answered all your questions and it is clear that the fault is mine. I blame no one but myself. I cannot explain my error and will invent no excuses. However, there is no one you could find in all of our country who would try harder to destroy that ship. Let me do so on the next orbit. I beg you to let me redeem myself."

"Too late. You fool. You are about to die because there may be no 'next orbit.' They may land! Due to you! You! You idiot! You have lost us our only certain chance. Open your eyes and see what's coming."

Ogrov clamped a hand behind the man's head and yanked it forward against the gun. Chipping teeth, he forced the man's mouth open with the gun barrel and shoved the muzzle against the soft palate. Blood ran down the gun barrel and over his clenched fingers. As he began squeezing the trigger, one of his horrified staff began shouting.

"Houston! Houston! A message from our man in Houston. Marshal Ogrov! Houston! For you! For you!"

The desperate cries got Ogrov's attention in time to stop the murder. The destruction of Olympia had become his passion. The killing of this fool would not distract him. He cushioned the hammer and set the gun on safety.

Ogrov read and reread the sweet music in the message from Byron Desault. A damaged Olympia could not land! Stuck in orbit. He dashed back to where the flight guidance officer nursed his bleeding lips. "You have your chance!" he cried out to Nikolai Gerasimov. "Let's see just how good you are. I'm giving give you a sitting duck."

Radar in Turkey first spotted the rocket heat of Ogrov's missile rising from beyond the Urals. Then the Big Eye satellite in polar orbit saw it, and so did the Owl spacecraft in geostationary orbit. The combined tracking data agreed: something had been sent to chase Olympia in her current orbit.

66

Tim, awakening dazed, felt himself stripped, trussed and hung like skinned game in a hunting camp. Every part ached. He could see his bruises. He'd been battered, he knew, but did not recall how or why. A feeling of strangeness about his surroundings roused him to vigilance. Making no noise, he undid the hair knot, freeing his upper body. Floating, he bent and untied the ankle knot. Reaching over his head, he pulled himself along a restraining line toward its tiedown point on the wall. He came to a halt, stopped by the divergence of other lines passing through his shorts. They veered off to distant points on the same wall. Not comprehending the impasse, he struggled to continue moving.

Weak to begin with, he soon tired and hung bewildered on Adam's hyperbolic rig. There seemed no way out. He faced the other way and pulled himself along a line toward the opposite wall. He jammed again as the lines diverged. Vexed and groggy, he missed the solution of undressing to get free. The simple restraints seemed to him a Gordian Knot. He thought of chewing loose, then lost that idea. His inability to get free told of injury beyond the physical. Enervated by tussling with the restraints, he yielded and hung on the ropes in crumpled levitation.

In the silent ship he heard only routine machinery. Dimly, he heard the toilet being used. Who could that be? Then he heard a banging about as someone passed on to the flight deck. He heard coughing. He knew that cough! A friend. Someone to untangle him from this damned spider's snare. He called out, but got no sound from a thick tongue and dry throat. He called again, getting nothing; like nose-blowing without a honk. He tried to make sound like a dog's bark. He got out a low, curt grunt of "Help!" The volume equaled a trumpet blast, hurting his ears. On the flight deck it arrived as a whisper. Adam heard it and sped to him in swift glides. Adam, the stranger.

––––––––––––––––––––– 67 –––––––––––––––––––––

Congress felt stonewalled. Their sources in the government agencies fed them only bits and pieces about the space story. A bipartisan delegation from the House and Senate, united in their anxiety, stormed in to see the White House Chief of Staff, loudly demanding a meeting with the President.

Daniel Russell, the majority leader of the Senate, shook his white mane and thundered, "There's no damned way around it, Engle. You tell Sisco to get his ass in here or I will go to the sidewalk."

Engle wished the antique senator would take his retirement. But "senile" didn't apply to this phenomenon, old in wisdom and years, but young in vigor. At 82, Russell contended like an athlete of 50. He stayed young, he claimed, through tough exercise, living his health motto: "Live forever, or die trying." He had one other motto, this one for politics: "Raise hell, and never give up."

Time and patience helped him to get his way in major legislation. He returned year after year on an issue, battering away at the opposition. He jostled like an orca, which will ram a whale's head until the exhausted creature allows its delicious tongue to be eaten.

Russell prevailed by delivering on his threats. He had often "gone to the sidewalk." It meant he would enter a total fast, as Mahatma Ghandi used to do, and he would live outdoors on a city street near the Capitol until he collapsed. It always made international headlines, and no president wanted to be the insensitive bully who killed him. The curbside interviews from an ancient, perishing senator, soaked and forlorn in chilling rain, broadcast to the world, gave his opinions great circulation. His tactics made him the embarrassment and pride of the Senate.

The House majority leader, Theodore Nelson, half Russell's age, got left behind in a walk, but not in a talk. Known as "Triple Tongue Teddy" for his speedy speech, he made even court reporters ask for catch-up time. He had an enormous following in and out of his Bronx district, partly due to his swift intellect and partly to the entertainment attraction of his machine gun speech. Stores sold a disc game, called "What Did He Say?" On it, players heard him answering interview questions. The disc ran at normal speed for questions, but had to run at slow speed for his answers.

Whenever Nelson spoke on TV, the nation tuned in. During one of his rushing responses he had coined the term "Repator" for a member of the House of Representatives. Explaining it later, he said, "You don't hear 'senator' and 'senatrix,' do you? That house doesn't say stuff like 'Will the gentlelady from Florida yield?' Phony chivalry. Archaic. We need just one simple title like the Senate has! Don't waste my time. I like it. The people like it. Don't call me anything else."

Knowing Russell and Nelson as formidable men with enormous followings, Sisco appeared quickly with oil for their troubled waters. After swearing them to secrecy, he told them everything. Afterwards, he invited them to join the Crisis Team.

In immediate reaction, Nelson let fly with a lecture on the separation of powers, climaxing with, "You know the drill, Simon! It's your job to run the show and ours to hang you if it goes wrong!"

Unable to keep up, the contemplative Sisco smiled in distress and said, "Ted, I never had a course in rapid listening. Could you give it to me at least andante instead of allegro?"

Pausing between words, Nelson said, "Play your tapes, Mr. President."

Russell moved in. "Simon," he said, "You're a very bold man. The goal seems worth the cost and risk, so I hope you succeed. However, you know what Teddy said. We're out of this. But I want you to keep us informed; unofficially, of course. We will do our best to cool things on the Hill."

Sisco knew they could. The Congress had become a coherent body, disciplined under strong leaders during the depression crisis. Returning to Capitol Hill, Russell and Nelson spread the word, asking for trust on a national security matter. Respecting these leaders, the Congress subsided.

Not so the public and the special interest groups! They made it almost impossible for Sisco to contain the story. Thousands of eyes beyond the Russian borders had seen the missiles rising.

"Like reverse meteors," reported one paper, "they burst upward and sped into the night, only to die away one by one. Kremlin officials refuse to acknowledge the event, and have even refused to look at pictures of the incredible fireworks."

Hundreds of people had taken pictures from cities, towns, ships, and a few aircraft. Every form of media bought and displayed them. TV stations used footage from scores of alert hobbyists. Commentators harkened back to the Chernobyl nuclear plant disaster and the initial Soviet denials. Fears of an impending catastrophe ran unbridled, and people demanded information. In spasms of investigative reporting, the media clamored for facts from their governments.

The governments knew that missiles had been fired from the "abandoned" Rocket Defense Test Center east of the Ural Mountains. But why? At what? And why in such numbers? Any country that questioned its Communist ambassador met evasions.

Aroused by possibilities of duplicity, the leaders of some nations thought back on Chernobyl and soon followed their own citizens into mild paranoia. Norway requested a meeting of the UN Security Council.

Reporters besieged Stepka Yakunin, the UCS Minister of Information. Breaking away from a family emergency in Leningrad, she rushed for Moscow to calm her frantic deputy. Premier Yemetov, she learned, had stopped release of the story agreed upon: an ultimatum to the Americans, with a deadline to stop their space theft. She knew Dmitri well enough to storm into his presence. Hell hath no fury like a bureaucrat scorned.

"Comrade Yemetov," she demanded, rippling with rage, "Why did you change the rules you gave me, and the instructions I gave to my people? Why did you not tell me? Why did you leave me unprepared to face the capitalist news jackals?"

"I changed my mind."

68

Seething in Washington, Grigory Taksis waited for a response from Moscow. Why did they not confirm that Yemetov had received his message? *Why am I being ignored?* In wicked satisfaction, he soothed his hurt feelings with the memory of the American president gulping down humble pie, pleading for time, and scrambling to get out of the hole he had dug for himself. Then he frowned with the realization that Sisco had made no apology. That memory rubbed him raw.

Anxiety galloped in again. What if his message had not been received in time? Why did the Politburo suddenly get so interested in that damned old satellite? A serious business this, not like downing a fighter plane whose crew might bail out and survive. A hit on the shuttle would mean killing astronaut demigods, not to mention the loss of a $5 billion machine. Given the strange behavior of the American president lately, the man might counterattack in some dangerous manner, triggering a tit-for-tat escalation. Something like that could get out of hand.

He began to sweat. Mere moments counted greatly in crisis communications. Yet he had delayed to tantalize and humiliate the president. Although his dislike for Sisco ran deep, Taksis had the diplomat's skill of hiding such emotion. It did not mean he understood his feelings. He did not recognize envy as the basis for his dislike, but a few moments on an analyst's couch would have had it waving like a flag. He resented the man's success, popularity, and power. He felt that it hadn't been earned. Sisco had been born into a wealthy family. He seemed the closest copy of President John Kennedy that could be imagined. The finest schools. Influence. Name recognition. What would Sisco be today had he been born into the wretched city and family of Grigory Taksis?

The Ambassador had fought his way up. He often thanked the imaginary God for the existence of the Communist Party. It had been the means for salvaging his life. Its national, dredging searches for brains and talent had provided an outlet for the brilliant, crippled slum child. He knew how society, even current society, felt about massive deformity. The ancient Spartans would have placed him on a hill outside the city to die of exposure or as a predator's meal. Without doubt, he owed the Party everything. He would be willing to die on behalf of the system that had plucked him up. His soul winced sore at any prospect of its decline.

At diplomatic soirees he would say, "You are right. We are a planned society. But you are a random society. You have no goal or purpose but consumption. Therefore, you cannot control what happens to you."

He believed his dogma. He expected another global capitalist crash and depression. He implored his superiors to prepare for that time.

"We must start training up leaders in those countries now. The last time we were not ready."

In the economic chaos, every capitalist country had its riotous, undisciplined hordes. The newly poor, blaming political leaders, assassinated them by the hundreds. Unfortunately, socialist communism had not been ready with replacement leaders, nor with plans for a swift assumption of world control.

Indeed, it faced the menace of world anarchy. In the massive turmoil, erratic political eruptions ignored law and treaties. Some countries invaded others, seeking loot, assets, or to settle old scores. Invaded nations only suspected of having nuclear weapons came forth as owners, with a willingness to shoot. The madness spread beyond the battlefield, vaporizing several cities.

Only then did the chill prospect of obliterating humanity frighten the fanatical. The use of atomic weapons ceased as if by decree. However, Taksis knew, the weapons still existed in hidden inventories. No one knew the quantity, power, locations, or ease of delivery. It would be madness for a nation to disarm in the face of all that hidden horror. He praised his country for resisting total disarmament. Many nations had nuclear devices so compact that they could ship, by trunk or crate, a bomb big enough to destroy most of a large city. Soon, perhaps they would be small enough to carry into a country by suitcase. The U.S., with its leaky borders, had more to worry about than anyone else, but his own beloved Russia would become vulnerable.

Taksis preached to the Kremlin that Russia must retain nuclear weapons and publicize its intent to retaliate. Also, he proposed training and positioning moles to take command in the confusion of the next disrupting depression. Byron Desault was an example. This man had proven valuable already. Taksis had plans for him. But they might never be used if the American president continued with his recent mad behavior. Ambassador Taksis feared that a prologue to war had begun, and he found himself mumbling an atheistic version of prayer.

69

Neither rumors nor bits and pieces of the story explained the mysterious doings in the sky. Reporters got speculation when they interviewed scientists. University astronomers were not willing to be quoted because the government funded much of their science. Politically savvy, they did not want to get crosswise with their benefactor. But they knew what they knew: Olympia had left orbit. They had searched for her in the twinkling orbit of Big Eye and found nothing. Yet, no one knew of a landing.

Amateur astronomers, by contrast, spoke without restraint. Publicity seldom descends upon these obscure people in their arcane pursuits, so it was not surprising when egos emerged to gush fact and speculation. Yes, some said, Olympia was gone, but she could have landed without fanfare. Others disputed the possibility of a landing, pointing out that the identifying twin sonic booms of a shuttle reentering had not been heard near either American landing strip. The public would have known; the sonic booms caused buildings to sway and tickle seismographs. No, they said, Olympia is actually missing.

Also intriguing, some said, is that another spacecraft, an ancient Soviet vessel, seems to be missing from its decaying orbit. Its flickering presence is no more. How could it have fallen without its flaming reentry being reported from somewhere? After all, half the earth is always in darkness. Yes, storm clouds or overcast could have concealed its fiery arc. But let's move on, they said, because even more mysterious things are happening. A huge cylindrical shape has been sighted in a high inclination orbit. It is not the result of any known launch.

"Could that mean," asked one broadcast interviewer, "that it might have been orbited by a nation which has a launch capability we don't know about?"

The astronomer hedged, "I can't say that's impossible, but it's unheard of for any nation to go from a condition of no capability to one of vast capability. Word would have leaked out. Observation satellites would have seen the launch facilities being built. The launch itself would have been a blazing display that could not have gone unnoticed."

When the call-in portion of this broadcast began, the first caller, speaking from the fringe of rationality, set off fireworks of his own.

"Of course we saw no launch! We all know why. That thing is not from earth. We have visitors. It's obvious that the thing spooked the Russians and they attacked it, but the aliens used a force field to deflect the missiles. Who do you people think you're fooling? We're not idiots. And what is earth going to do when the visitors start shooting back?"

The thought flew around the world within the hour. Telephone networks overloaded as citizens called police and media for information and called each other for reassurance. The fact that earthlings routinely engage in space travel made it easy to believe that "others" could do so. For many, aliens hovered above.

70

Adam's laughter and bantering joy at Tim's revival got no response. Hard eyes surveyed him coldly. Tim sent no sign of recognition, no request for care, no words at all. Adam knew that Tim had called for help, but he apparently expected someone else to show up. *Does he even know where he is?*

Adam literally hovered over his patient, wiping from Tim what appeared to be a perspiration of anxiety. Tim watched with suspicion, his mental alertness evident and growing along with obvious apprehension.

Adam decided against hallucinations, seeing Tim as disoriented at least, amnesiac at most. He wondered if Tim would benefit from a reminder of some recent history. Swabbing Tim gently, he told their story.

He emphasized the accident, telling Tim, "You got hammered by the heat shield, young fella. That's why you're a little confused."

Adam got no indication that Tim heard him, nor did he see a reduction in the captive-animal suspicion in those eyes. Adam switched to simple declarative statements. "You are Tim Carver," he said, again and again.

He reviewed Tim's history, repeatedly reminding him of name and affiliations. Tim continued detached, as though on nepenthe, but without its pleasures.

Discouraged at last, Adam donned the nose cone microphone hood. The thing had been a great success in helping keep a ship silent when crewmembers needed sleep. It would keep Tim from hearing a conversation with Houston. The indefatigable Ken Hemming responded. After two sentences, Ken interrupted.

"Go wake the flight surgeon," he ordered someone nearby, and then he turned back to the conversation with Adam.

Byron Desault, always willing, and seemingly always available, heard and obeyed. He trotted to the room marked "Siesta Sanctum," pushed past a portal marked "Snore Door," and woke Dr. Bill Nanterre. The doctor had stayed on duty, committing himself to caring for Tim. As Chief Flight Surgeon, he intended no handoff of this patient to anyone else. He believed in the medical truth that most problems originate at the interfaces between organizations or people. Here, where information and understanding must pass from one organism to the other is the breeding ground of confusion. In his experience, clearly stated instructions always produced multiple interpretations. Nanterre had even made up a little poem about the interface malady just to keep himself reminded of guarding against consequences.

To a toneless tune he hummed,

"Things go wrong in lots of places, but mainly at the interfaces."

He knew and liked Tim Carver. He vowed that with this friend and patient, there would be no misunderstandings. No vital facts would be lost because no one would be allowed to replace him as primary caregiver. He would guard against fatigue, sleeping as often as possible.

The penalties for miscommunication, misunderstanding and missing facts had been seared into his early soul. The child of a marriage already shaky, Nanterre, in tears, witnessed the event that toppled it. His spotless mother had finished spring cleaning the house and taken him shopping. His father, moved to provide a helping hand, proceeded to clean the winter's cold ashes from the fireplace. Unknown to him, his wife had removed the vacuum's bag, found no replacement, closed the cleaner, added "vac bags" to her shopping list and left. Busy, facing into the huge fireplace, Dad had not noticed the vacuum behind him spewing fine ash, soot, and odor into all the airing rooms and closets. Each hostile parent blamed the other, finally parting company as a good conclusion to a bad marriage. Because of the incidents and silences that cost him a father, Nanterre's peers and nurses lived with his obsession for total communication and documentation.

Nanterre listened intently to Adam's account of Tim's behavior, asked lots of questions, and then issued instructions for Adam to wire Tim with biomedical sensors. Tim offered no resistance, but followed every move with his eyes, sometimes staring into the TV cameras Adam had rigged. Tim took some water through a straw, showing no appreciation or interest. Adam fitted him with the communications hood. Tim struggled in alarm when the nose cone microphone settled over his face, as though fearful of being gassed. Nanterre's soothing but authoritative voice calmed him. Then the doctor personally resumed the reviewing and reassuring that Adam had tried earlier. Again and again, insistently, he called for Tim to make eye-blinking responses to questions. The reconditioning of a warrior's reflexes had begun. It would end with startling results.

71

Art Cooper talked again with his man, John Evans, calling to thank him for the suggestions about the Ogrov attack.

"Nothing struck Olympia," he said. He did not mention that the result would have been the same without Evans's warning. Art knew how to motivate people. He knew, too, that this adventure might be far from over and that he might need more insight and advice from Evans. The need began right then, during the conversation. Evans interrupted to report on the new launch from beyond the Ural Mountains. Radar profiles showed a large missile, apparently with a satellite payload at the front end. It had been aimed into the plane of Olympia's current orbit.

The mystery missile now flew in a lower orbit than Olympia's and therefore traveled faster to offset a stronger gravitational pull. Such speed allowed it to race more rapidly around the globe, letting it catch up to rendezvous with the shuttle. That could have any of several goals: first, observe and transmit what it sees; second, get close and explode; and finally, both of these. It might, Evans said, be one of the blowup machines the Soviets had used long ago in military practice. They would approach and destroy their own dead or dying satellites.

Cooper arranged for direct, secure conversation between Evans and the flight director. Adam, freed from tending Tim, listened in on the talk. What he heard changed his plans; he would postpone looking at the payload bay damage. Right now, it seemed, he had to get ready for another attack, one of an unknown nature. He turned his mammoth combination of shuttle and tank to point the cockpit windows toward the pursuing rocket. He could see its long tail of flame far below him as it came out of earth's night side. With binoculars he followed it to a position nearly under him, and then he watched it rising toward him. It behaved as if someone were aboard and steering.

The thing came drifting closer. Adam had seen it shed some rocket stages as their fuel burned out. What remained might become his nemesis. It looked like a ship's torpedo and seemed about the same size. Oddly, it came toward him broadside. Why would that be so? The binoculars let him see a TV camera eye mounted midway down its length. *Aha, that's why!* He reported this to Houston. Evans heard it, elated. He talked to Cooper on a separate line, saying, "The description fits a flyer the Soviets called 'Cyclops.' It's very early technology. We may be lucky. If they're going back this far in the inventory, it may mean they used up everything newer and better. Adam may be able to outmaneuver the thing. The bad news is they may have lots of them and may throw them at him until he's out of maneuvering fuel. I'm just surprised that they didn't send up two at a time and come at him from both sides."

Although somewhat ponderous, the Cyclops had attitude control and local maneuverability. Someone steered it from the ground, basing maneuvers on what could be seen with the mid-mount TV eye. Adam kept Olympia sideways to the threat. Twice it moved to get around to his back, and he rotated tank and shuttle to prevent that advantage. He had set TV cameras to watch it from the pilot's side window so that Houston could help track its action.

Experts from Space Command studied the TV scene intensively and sent Adam an analysis. Cyclops had been designed for inspection and destruction of fixed orbit spacecraft. It specialized in leisurely attack on Soviet practice targets. It had no radio control detonation, due to fear that espionage might compromise the code. Designed for coming alongside, it would turn to crash head on. The impact would trigger the warhead at its prow. A crude early device intended to blow up static quarry, Cyclops had its TV camera in the side, instead of the nose, to make production less costly.

Space Command hoped to jam Cyclops' TV broadcasting with powerful transmitters on the ground. They told Adam to search for its strong, nearby frequency. His seeker scanned and soon found the carrier. He told the experts the frequency and relaxed a bit on hearing their promise to start jamming in a half hour. Not sure that jamming would work, they asked Adam to report from Cyclops' behavior if jamming made it blind.

They told him, "We think the gunner will line you up steadily for a good while and then turn ninety degrees to ram you with the warhead."

Adam decided to test the idea. He allowed the earthbased gunner to get Cyclops into position. Out the ceiling windows he could see the thing take the bait and start to turn prematurely. *The gunner is anxious!* He had to outthink him. He did not know that beside the man sat Marshal Ogrov, also watching Olympia on the gunner's TV screen, and holding the big revolver in his lap. In this dogfight, the remote control gunner also faced death.

Adam knew now why he had instinctively kept the giant fuel tank. He would make the tank the target if he could. He would try to place it between the shuttle and the space torpedo. Sweating heavily from the gamble, Adam did a short countdown from the time he lost sight of Cyclops, and then he acted. Carefully, he spun the unwieldy united tank and shuttle, met the swing with opposing blasts, and steadied up at 180 degrees from where he had been. The big tank would now take the impact. It did not come. The gunner, understandably nervous, had decided to turn back for a confirming peek. He spun sideways for that last look and found the enormous wall of the tank facing him. *Quickly! Quickly! Delay will alert this clever astronaut.*

He at once flew the Cyclops around the lower end of the tank and came up behind Adam.

72

"We are very much alike," Premier Yemetov told his Minister of Information. He spoke with head forward and down, his gaze strained through bushy brows while his hands slowly bobbed in the palms-facing gesture of sincere proselytizing.

"We are 'people-people.' We are not 'technology-people.' You and I make things happen through human beings, not machines. Ogrov is the opposite. He loves machines. He thinks he can depend upon them. He is wrong. Machines are impartial, like nature. They have no conscience, no perseverance, and no loyalty. They are whores. Ogrov hugged all his shiny missiles and sent them out to hustle for him and they let him down. They did not let me down, because I had no expectations. That is why I changed my mind about announcing an ultimatum. You, of all people, Stepka Yakunin, know that if you fail to deliver on the threat in an ultimatum, you lose credibility."

Her mouth still worked in anger.

He laughed, "Calm yourself. Would you rather be facing the reporters now to explain why your nation couldn't shoot the bird on the merry-go-round, or to explain why all those roman candles went off last night?"

She considered before answering. "The latter," she said.

He smiled again.

She shouted, "Don't patronize me! You can make any damned changes you want, but I insist that you tell me before you tell my subordinates!"

He gave her the point.

"I don't want to play any more games," she said. "You know what you want me to say. So tell me! Don't ask me to stand here and make up something to tell the reporters when you already know what you want."

He relented. "You're right. I already know some things you don't yet know. For example, the American shuttle is damaged and can't land."

"How do you know that!?"

"You know I don't discuss sources. But believe me, it's true. Also, one of the two astronauts is injured and unconscious. We don't know why."

Eager now, she began formulating the public story. "I see a way to tell this . . . " she began.

"No. No. Let me tell you what's been developed so far. Then think it through and see if you agree. Here is our story. We will say that our technology discovered the Americans in the act of thievery, that it listened to them, and that it learned their unreliable equipment has broken down and stranded them in orbit. We will say that we respect the brave men aboard but we have contempt for the leaders who sent them to steal. Last night, as the American astronauts passed over our country, we launched a space salute to these brave men who may die in orbit because of the schemes of their politicians. That salute may also be considered a warning salvo to their leaders. Finally, on behalf of those men, abandoned by the schemers who sent them, we will send our own cosmonauts to bring them home safely. The Americans do not have the ability to reach those men in time to save them."

He paused. "Sound good to you?"

"Yes. But can you get to them?"

"Who knows? Remember what I just said about machines. All I can tell you is that cosmonauts should rendezvous with the shuttle in thirty six hours. They'll ask to be invited aboard. If that's denied, they'll break in. The American crew will be returned to earth and sent home. By effecting rescue in this new ocean, we will then claim salvage rights. Our manned flight experts are convinced that our cosmonauts can fly the American shuttle to a landing. That assumes we can repair it up there. If we can't, we'll slow it down, saying we're clearing the skies of derelicts and we'll let it burn up on reentry. Since our spacecraft is inside, we'll solve two problems at once. But, if we can land their shuttle, we get our spacecraft back. Either way, we win."

Unconvinced, she said, "Suppose the Americans repair fast enough to get away before our cosmonauts arrive?"

He became irritable, "You and I agreed we prefer to rely on people, right? So I'm relying on the information from our informant that one man cannot repair and land that shuttle. However, should that happen, I will not let the shuttle land intact with Falcon inside. Several of our submarines are taking position off each American coast. Both American landing sites are conveniently near seaside. Our submarines will be waiting to shoot the shuttle down as soon as it appears in the sky.

"At that time, of course, it is an easier target than an aircraft. You see, the shuttle is at that point only a glider. It cannot even maneuver to save itself. In addition, it will be a raging hot target for our heat-seeking missiles. The entire bottom becomes thousands of degrees hot from friction. To cover the shooting, we will say that Falcon's barometric bomb exploded. We will say that the Americans ignored our public and private warnings. Now, what do you think?"

"I will put finishing touches on the story to release it within the hour. I like the planning, the cover, the contingency arrangements, the . . . "

She went silent in reaction to an urgent knocking on the door. He called permission to enter. The door flew open. His appointment secretary hurried in with the smiling, jubilant, political officer assigned to Marshal Ogrov's staff.

The secretary said, "Forgive me, but I'm sure you'll want to hear his message at once!"

The man clicked to attention, saluted and fairly shouted in his enthusiasm, "Marshal Ogrov sends you his compliments, Comrade Premier, and reports that he has destroyed the American shuttle. He got a direct hit! The whole sky lit up. I saw it! It was beautiful!"

Yemetov controlled his trembling rage. In a low, drained voice he said, "Thank you, Colonel. Please give the Marshal my congratulations. Dismissed."

The commissar's smile faded. He saluted, wheeled uncertainly and exited with the secretary.

She asked, "What is going on?"

He kicked the desk. "That madman! That absolute rutting bull! Nothing stops him. He doesn't know when to quit. We consoled him about his attack going wrong and told him we'd take another, better, approach based on new information. The crazy bastard found more missiles somewhere and kept shooting!"

He groaned ruefully. "He didn't even hear what we told him! I should have listened to Taksis. One day he pointed to Ogrov's head and said, 'The ears have walls.' Now I understand what he meant, but it isn't funny. I don't know whether to hang Ogrov or give him a medal. Damn. Damn. In a war a man like that is worth ten regiments. One man like that could save a nation. But what do you do with the likes of him between wars?"

"Good question. But I have a better one. What do we tell the press between crises?"

73

Adam waited for the impact of the warhead. It would blow apart the giant fuel tank attached to Olympia. That would split open both the hydrogen and oxygen sections on the opposite side from the shuttle. It would rock the shuttle about, but at least Olympia would be protected from shrapnel. He did not expect pieces of metal to pierce his side of the tank. If he could only survive this Cyclops, any other torpedoes sent up might be nullified by the jamming broadcasts of the counter electronics experts. Then, at last, he could settle down to repairing the ship and flying home.

Nothing happened. He had expected an almost immediate explosion. All seemed quiet and normal in the ship, except . . . something. Something nagged. A chill trickled over him. Senses tingling, he looked around. Great God! He saw the frequency seeker rippling with the strong signal of Cyclops. He did not know much about TV transmission, but his instincts said that such strong reception could not happen unless Cyclops hovered on his side of the tank. That must be why the attack had not come! Immediately, with the awareness of the fighter pilot, he knew that the gunner had gone under and behind him.

Here sat Ogrov's duck, startled by a movement in the weeds into a heart pounding need to scramble for the sky and distance. Pilots have little thought at such moments. Everything is response, exploding in an adrenaline burst of insight, training, judgment, and reflexes. He blazed through steps and sequence. Fingers flew, hands pulled, feet pressed. The controls seemed to understand the urgency. Nothing failed or stalled. Like a woodpecker startled from a tree trunk, Olympia jumped free of the tank and suddenly soared up its length. Clearing the top, it did a front flip as Adam desperately tried to swing his stern up out of the way of shrapnel.

The momentum carried the inverted shuttle over the top and away on the far side just as the warhead blew up in the odd manner of a space explosion, totally silent. Adam knew it had occurred, knew from the brilliant light inside a blazing, ballooning fireball that pushed and enveloped the slowly receding Olympia. The color of the light fluctuated as the pressured hydrogen and oxygen, escaping their ruptured tanks, mixed randomly into flaming flashes.

Adam, having thrown the shuttle's tail up in the flip over the tank top, fought to keep that attitude, holding the shuttle's heat-resistant bottom toward the fire.

A great thump shook the ship. The ejecting gases had moved the huge tank in the direction the shuttle took. Like a giant, blasted turtle shell, the tank moved in slow, flaming, erratic pursuit and had slowly closed the gap. The ponderous nudge sent Olympia ricocheting out of the fireball. Adam spun ship and faced the dying arcs and jets of flame. He immediately moved as close as possible to the un-split side of the tank. He studied its slight tumbling and carefully set Olympia to the same motion. They wheeled in a slow, synchronized, untouching dance. Many telescopes would be turned his way after that enlightening explosion and he wanted their images to give the impression of a single hulk. A pose of death and destruction, if good enough, might forestall the Communists from sending up another Cyclops, even if just for inspection. Another attack would be too much.

He mumbled aloud, "We'd never live through it." The "we" startled him into a sudden remembrance of Tim. Semiconscious, and still trussed, Tim had probably been whipped about badly, had probably smashed into things. Adam headed for the lower deck.

74

The President had the same problem as the Premier: what to tell the reporters. Sisco's problem grew more acute because the United States, an open society, violated its basic principles with every delay of full disclosure. He pondered the problem with Ron Engle. He trusted the judgment of the chief of staff because the man had an incredible insight into public opinion.

Engle's father, a bridge construction foreman, had taken his family wherever he found work. Engle had become especially adept at adjustment. He learned the skills of being accepted among strangers, making them friends, and keeping friendships after moving on. He had majored in journalism, transferring among state colleges to further his reach into the diverse parts of America. He worked on many papers in many states after graduation, starting as a community news reporter. Decades later, he remained welcome in hundreds of homes all across the country.

His people-skills, the essence of management skills, led him naturally to editorships, power, money, and the eventual ownership of a major newspaper chain. His papers hummed with harmony and efficiency with him at the helm. He understood America and its people. He had predicted the outcome of the last four presidential elections. He had never been wrong on an election for the House of Representatives. He had been wrong several times for the Senate.

"The Senate's mystical in ways the others aren't," he laughed. "People don't feel close to their senators, don't really know what they want from them. It leads to random choices sometimes."

Because he understood, inspired, and managed people so well, he had been asked to become Chief of Staff. Those talents now made him repeatedly suggest adding the Secretary of State to the discussion.

The President kept ignoring the hints. "Yes," he would say, "We've got to get Arnold's views on this." He meant what he said, but he wanted a national view before coloring it with an international view. He got it.

"This new development," Ron said, "is increasing the pressure. Folks have an open mind about alien visitors. They don't believe in flying saucers, but they also don't believe government studies that say there are none. It's schizophrenic, and that's not a big problem. But we've got to keep it from becoming paranoia. That could happen.

"Folks know that any visitor who can get here when we can't get there is more powerful than we are. Anything or anybody more powerful is threatening. Hollywood doesn't often show us any friendly aliens, so we've been raised to be apprehensive. The Kremlin isn't talking and we aren't talking, so the press is speculating. It's now popular wisdom that the Communists fired at the thing. People believe it. Moscow won't deny it. The evidence exists and is being run and rerun in every form of communication.

"There's anxiety that the thing is going to start firing back. Big scares of this type produce suicides. This one's going to get very big unless we act soon. We've got small crowds outside already, demanding information. I've doubled all shifts of the guard force and have a few companies of Marines on standby at Quantico. I don't want any panicky crowds pushing down the fences. The thing is going to build unless we issue a press release about what's going on. I do not advise a presidential press conference, just a press release."

Before the President could question Ron further, the press secretary burst in and strode directly to a TV set, saying as he went, "Forgive the interruption, Mr. President, but you must see this." He turned to a commercial station. The screen showed a telescopic view of a large dot twinkling across the sky. The announcer described it as the space object shot at by the United Communist States, saying, "We will show you another replay of the results of their attack on the unknown object." The screen's dark background lit up in the flash and fiery aftermath of explosion.

At once, the press secretary said, "Olympia is safe, Mr. President. They hit only the tank. We would all like you to come back to the Command Center."

75

Moscow got a press release out first. It told the story of a lengthy Soviet satellite experiment of extreme scientific importance. They compared their satellite with an American spacecraft, the Long Duration Exposure Facility. It had been retrieved for study after six years in orbit and returned to earth by the U.S. Shuttle Columbia back in 1990.

Using the same technique, the Americans had tried to pilfer a Soviet science satellite. The attempt to defile years of research qualified as a crime against science, a disreputable low in the noble cause of space exploration. The United States had tried, on the space frontier, to commit history's first case of cosmic sneak thievery. This, of course, might be expected from a nation that had committed grand larceny on its earlier frontier, taking the land of the American Indian by treachery or force. However, this time the United States did not get away with deceit and theft. The technology and alertness of the UCS had caught, exposed, and routed them.

The vigilant defenders, after detecting the American trespass, had engaged in patient negotiations before issuing an ultimatum. During those talks, the Americans had used ruse and lie to deny their true purpose while pursuing their audacious crime. The enormous Kremlin press release at this point referred to its appendix. Here, verbatim, they quoted the extensive dissembling communications used by the Americans to cover or justify their highjacking operation.

The press statement told how the UCS, in a compassionate gesture to the astronauts, had given a one-hour warning of its intent to defend its property. They had warned the Americans to push the old Soviet satellite into orbit, sending it free and distant from the shuttle. This had not been done by the time the hour of reprieve ended. In a further humanitarian gesture, the UCS had fired a warning salvo, the space equivalent of a shot across the bow. It fired at night to create visible evidence to the world of Moscow's forbearance under this incredible provocation. Naturally, those token missiles had not been armed.

However, that blank salvo did the trick. The political provocateurs in the White House and the Pentagon got the message. The Americans placed the old satellite back in orbit and flew away. Unfortunately, the Russian experiments had been handled and damaged enough to make them useless. The old satellite had therefore been used for target practice.

The American shuttle could not land with its huge fuel tank attached, so this had apparently been left behind as Olympia departed the scene. Apparently, the American tank had a deficiency that caused it to explode. However, its timely destruction relieved public anxiety that saw the new huge bulk in the sky as an alien presence.

The Minister of Information did not flinch from holding a press conference to coincide with the press release. She handled all questions adroitly, and some nonchalantly.

To a question asking the current whereabouts of Olympia, Stepka Yakunin quipped, "Probably in hiding somewhere, where they belong, after this shameful attempt at piracy. I suggest you ask the Americans."

—————————————— 76 ——————————————

Mike Benson wrestled with second thoughts about the entire operation. The risks now outweighed recognizable benefits, and Moscow had escalated beyond predictable confrontation. *The President must be wondering why he ever agreed to snatch Ivan.*

He saw one bright spot: the incipient panic about UFOs had died away. American TV, with administration encouragement, had given top billing to the Kremlin press conference, alleviating the alien invasion question. The apprehensive, chanting mob of citizens at the White House fence had gone away. Noisy hordes of reporters took their place. Elsewhere, TV anchors, commentators, and news analysts clamored for an American answer to the Russian accusations.

Fully briefed on the attack of the space torpedo, the President fervidly lauded Hemming, Cooper, and Evans, and he controlled an urge to canonize Adam. He inquired after Tim's health and got the good news of no further injury. Tim did not get slammed against the walls or equipment. When Olympia began to back off the tank, Tim's inertia made him move on the suspension lines. His exceptional balance responded, despite his dazed and weakened state.

Anticipating danger, his subconscious took instinctive, protective action: Tim crossed the lines and began rotating. This large-scale braiding took the slack out of his lines and reduced his amplitude of swing. The shuttle made its moves around him. Inertia kept him motionless until the lines jerked and tried to fling him somewhere. Rope friction and his grip prevented unraveling. He struck nothing. But now, spent by the effort, he hung limp on the lines.

The President waited for word on Olympia's repair needs. He settled down to watch the TV feeds from Olympia and Houston, confer with staff members, ask questions, and make notes. He was trying to prepare something to tell the American people. But what? He wouldn't lie and he couldn't yet announce the truth. Occasionally, he gave some handwritten sheets to his speechwriter; the man would exit and return with typed drafts.

No one bothered the President as he reflected on his options. He gazed absently at the scenes from Olympia where TV monitored areas of the ship, as in routine security scans of banks. With electronic rigor, they silently switched in slow cycle from one camera to another. Abstractedly, he saw the sequence of air lock, Adam on the flight deck, Tim in the mid deck, the cargo bay, the zoom on Ivan, and around again. And then again. Hypnotic.

Something caught his eye. A movement. New scene. He waited through the cycle, interested and puzzled. Once again, on the zoom lens. Again, a movement. It seemed to be a quick jiggle of Ivan's door. New scene. Nothing. Around again. Once more, Ivan's door. It appeared to suddenly move against the tape and then subside. New scene. Around again. Ivan again. No movement. Around again. Ivan again. In a coincidence of timing, the tape strips on Ivan's door snapped taut, then relaxed. *Am I hallucinating?* He called to Hemming, asking to dwell on Ivan. Nothing.

"Hold there, please. I thought I saw something." Nothing. Then they both saw movement. The blade of a hunting knife appeared in the slit of the slightly open door. It began to saw away the metallized tape.

"Dear Jesus!" said Simon Sisco.

77

With Tim in the flight surgeon's care, Adam turned to other essentials. He moved Olympia close to the ruptured tank. He intended to hide behind the hulk, to give any watchers the impression of one object in the sky, not two. The closer he got, the better the deception. He kept jetting closer, wanting eventual contact, but planning not to bump. Contact should happen soon, he knew, and it would happen more gently than he could do it. It would happen naturally, since every object exerts a gravitational force on every other object. These two huge masses, when very close, should ultimately float into contact.

He moved within inches and waited for union. The wait became boring. He recalled his last industrial flight, when he flew the shuttle in formation with a manufacturer's bowl-shaped crystal growth furnace. The bowl created an ultra vacuum by flying with the bottom first, like a shield, thus avoiding contamination from collision with stray atoms wandering around in the vacuum of space. The furnace made crystals of super purity and uniformity because of the bowl-shield and because the free-flyer had none of the shuttle's vibrations. Constant laser ranging showed then that the furnace never drifted closer to the shuttle, but that situation was different: the gap was greater.

Impatient, Adam decided that the attractive force was too tiny. He jetted Olympia gently into contact with the tank and held pressure, forestalling a rebound. Tank and ship met like giant hands entering prayer.

Got to find a way to latch on, he thought, sifting ideas for staying united, while hiding the shuttle behind the tank. They had to move as one. The blast had nearly flattened the tank. It was now far larger than its original profile. The shuttle's wings might stick out beyond its new boundaries, but not by much. Now, he had only frictional drag to use as the controlling force in moving the tank. If he moved Olympia too suddenly, he'd lift away, or slip across the tank's surface instead of moving tank and shuttle in unison. He saw a way to guard against this.

At a few places, some flaps of metal bent back enough to touch the tank's outside surface. But other flaps had less arch. Deftly, he tucked a wing under one flap. Even more delicately, he wedged ahead, as into a jam cleat, until he got a non-bruise grip. He slowly cranked the combined mass around so that the tank faced earth. The tank hid most of Olympia. Then he prepared to do his "moon trick." At least that's what he'd have called it if he had Tim to talk to.

It meant that he would try to duplicate the moon's behavior of always keeping the same face toward Earth. As with the moon's unseen backside, Adam wanted to be the backside of this union. He tapped a few keystrokes into the flight control computer. A program came alive, one designed to keep the shuttle's belly pointed toward the center of Earth. The result was like one person circling another and always facing inward.

Hmmmm. No talent required. Satisfied, he took a deep breath and started back to the job of finding and repairing the elevon damage. A voice interrupted.

"Olympia, Houston. Come in at once!"

He reported, "Houston, Olympia here."

Ken was like swift ice. "Adam. Emergency! Repeat. *Emergency.* Go at once to the air lock and seal it at both ends. Go at once. Acknowledge."

Adam shouted acknowledgment while literally flying through the deck opening and into the air lock to its far door, taking a few banging bruises along the way. While closing the outer door, he heard a heavy thump in the cargo bay and then a familiar bang. It sounded like the clanging sound that Ivan's door made when it swung full open against its stops. Trusting Hemming's orders, he did not take time to investigate. He did as ordered, as rapidly as he could, and he latched the door shut. Backing out of the air lock, he closed and latched the inner door. He reported both doors sealed.

"Good," said the flight chief. "Now, this is a little spooky, but I'm not kidding, so listen up and bear with me. While the President was watching your TV monitors, he noticed something trying to batter Ivan's door open. From the inside."

"You guys are drinking from the same bottle of . . . "

"Listen up, Commander! THE MAN called it to our attention, so we looked. We saw a knife sawing away the sealing tape. From the inside, I mean. The door has swung open. Nothing is visible in Ivan. Bring it up on your screen and we'll watch things together. Do not, I repeat, *do not* go near the bay windows. Watch only on your TV screen. Acknowledge that order, please."

Adam did, eyes fixed on the monitor that showed wisps of haze wafting erratically from Ivan.

78

Ogrov danced, hugged, cheered, and sang. He pressed the dazed flight guidance officer along with him into a cavorting mazurka.

"Gerasimov! Gerasimov!" he sang, calling the man by name for the first time.

For the minutes that this went on, the onlookers swung nervously between a restless stirring and rhythmic, clapping laughter they found hard to sustain. They did not enjoy their classic dilemma: when the king laughs, the joke is funny.

"You are a man!" shouted Ogrov. "You stood up to me! You fought on after losing! And you are an interplanetary marksman, first class!"

After effusive handshaking and praise, the Marshal began to subside and get back to basics.

"Gerasimov, you've had a hard day. But I'd like you to put another Cyclops up there so I can see what's left of your target."

Ogrov's aide entered the room in excitement and interrupted, "Excuse me, Comrade Marshal! Premier Yemetov has sent his congratulations and asks that you come to Moscow immediately."

Still ebullient, Ogrov gave his dazed marksman a last hug, stepped back, snapped to attention and saluted him. Saluted him! It stunned the audience.

"Good-bye, my friend." He turned and left. The men crowded around Gerasimov in consolation and relief. He had killed in a fight he did not want. They knew he would rather have killed Ogrov. He had no interest in launching another Cyclops to look at his kill. Let some one else do Ogrov's body counts! No one questioned his decision. He left to find a dentist, wishing that he could send Ogrov the bill.

PART 6

REVENANT ONE

79

Andrei Borodin stirred. He yawned. He stretched. Pain sprang from the movement. Pain in his forearm. In the strange, dim light he saw the cause. Something stuck into his flesh flopped as he moved, grinding deep and making him wince. He held it steady, raising arm and object to the light. He saw a large hypodermic needle. Memory began flooding back. He himself had stuck that in. Why? When? He removed it. It slipped from his grasp and floated slowly away. The thing floated! *I'm hallucinating. Where the hell am I?*

He turned to a window. Brightness outside let him see from his dark chamber. He seemed to be inside a container that sat inside a huge cylinder. He cupped his hands around his eyes and looked out intently. Ahead, he could see the upper part of a sort of wall, like a ship's bulkhead. It had two glass areas that made him think of large portholes. He turned away from the cheerful light outside and looked about in the gloom. He saw a person sitting immobile next to him.

By sight and touch, he inspected his surroundings. He found himself in a small machine with a few dials and controls. Somehow, it did not seem alien. In fact, he felt it to be rather familiar. Maddeningly, he believed he should know about this machine.

A hatch-type door curved in the wall at his right. He spun its control wheel and saw spoke-type bolts move into slots, locking him in! He reversed spin, unlocking the door. It had been open in the first place, he realized. He pushed the door. It resisted spongily. He pushed harder. It gave farther, but held. He decided to ram it open and began to leave his seat. A harness held him. His hand, moving automatically, found and sprang the release. That startled him. How had he known what to do and how to do it?

The familiarity amid the confusion rattled him further and he moved to batter the door. The movement set him to floating! Just as the needle had floated! He felt the dry, bilious, compression of throat and chest that foretold nausea. He would feel better if he could only get out of this coffin! Maneuvering into a back-braced position, he kicked the door with both feet. It yielded farther. Shift. Brace. Kick the door again. Repeat. Simon Sisco saw it happening.

Finally, he had enough yield to see light around the door rim. At a few points, something blocked the door-crack's light. He checked for the reason, and his fingers felt a flat, flexible band that taped the door shut.

He would cut it. He snapped open a hinged locker and reached in. His hand found the knife. He began sawing the tape. It was tough material, but it yielded slowly to the sharp knife. How had he known where to find the knife?

Clouds of memory swept and burst upon him. He cried out. He remembered this machine! He recalled it darkening about him. His coffin! Gasping and sobbing, he stopped slicing, frantic to get out. He braced, and kicked, and snapped the tape. The door burst open and crashed, clanging, against its stops. An instant later he heard a similar sound, a hatch door slamming. It came from the direction of the wall ahead. An echo?

He wanted to leap out, out into the bright light, to escape this box of death. Discipline competed with instinct, stopping him. Training compelled him to control himself, to make sense of his incredible surroundings, to conquer the fearful recollection of dying. *Who am I? Why am I here?* He had to scout this setting. Trembling with willpower and revulsion, he stayed in the shrouded cabin. Taking the seat cushion, he began waving it to sweep away the haze. He would explore in here; then he would explore the cylinder.

80

The President ordered all but essential workers out of Mission Control and Tenement One. He imposed tight censorship on the drama in the payload bay. The ban would prove porous because technicians have ways of tapping in. Hemming awoke the shift flight directors on site and ordered others to come in from home. He sent supervisors to roam the building on security checks. Workers dutifully displayed blank screens, but some slyly recorded, driven by the sudden secrecy in a normally open agency. The technical grapevine began to buzz.

The drama unfolded slowly. Ivan's swinging door damped to a stop. Mist puffed out of the capsule sporadically. Minutes went by. The President, already adjusting, looked more composed than anyone in the group. New arrivals, catching up in hushed questions and answers, slowly traded their tolerant smiles and cynicism for a skin-crawling apprehension. Jaws agape, ears athump with pounding blood, they saw with bulging eyes a deepening shadow in the gloom of Ivan's doorway. The frights of childhood dreams caromed and volleyed in their skulls as movement took a blurred shape. Then, emerging from the shadowy lair into light, inching cautiously like a sensing tentacle, came verification of intelligence and humanity and civilization. Moving slowly from side to side, poised to deliver death, appeared a human hand with a revolver.

81

Byron Desault eagerly watched the news broadcasts proclaiming the Kremlin's explanation of the giant explosion in the sky. He knew better than to believe the official line. Olympia destroyed! Destroyed through him! He, and he alone, had given Moscow the information about its damage and being stuck in orbit. He had proven his value and reliability at last, after years of deep cover and little appreciation.

Now, back in Mission Control to start his shift, he staggered in dismay to see Adam being congratulated by the President for saving the shuttle. Survived! Alive! It was incredible. Byron slipped away to a switching closet, connected equipment and began recording a disc. He watched his tiny TV screen as he captured the action of Ivan's door opening. Then came a more important scene, one that struck him speechless and trembling. He saw a man float cautiously out of Ivan's hatch and look about, moving a gun and his gaze about warily.

The man wore a zippered flight suit with a large locking collar for a total helmet, and he looked like an animated photo of a cosmonaut from an old encyclopedia. Already dazed by Olympia's survival, Byron's brain overloaded with the implications of a third person on the shuttle. Stupefied, he huddled on the floor in a corner, methodically replaying his disc. Fear, shame and perverse ambition somehow restored thought. He realized that the whole space center would be secured drum tight as soon as the key managers overcame their shock. Byron believed his new information was far more urgent than the last message to Moscow. He had to get these new facts out before the base buttoned up. He had an advantage. Mission Control had been cleared of most personnel. The flight director was totally absorbed. Byron would not be missed if he phoned his contact right now. He knew how to sneak the disc out later on, to provide proof of his message. He would, in fact, insist on taking it to Washington to deliver personally to Ambassador Taksis.

Feeding coins into the booth phone, Byron panted like a stressed runner. Sweat ran in thin streams. His contact spoke. He said a code word and hung up. She called him back, puzzled by his incoherence. She asked him, often, to repeat himself. His voice rose in excited impatience. When she asked if he'd been drinking, he yelled at her. Volume seldom persuades, and she laughed at his resurrection story. She taunted him to bring the spurious disc to Washington. When Byron escalated to shouting, it caught Susan Hoffen's attention.

Susan had been chatting away in the women's rest room, on the other side of the wall with the phone. Byron's tirade seeped through. It seemed to include threats. That stirred Susan's professional interest. She shushed the other women to silence and put an ear to the wall. With her hushing hand damping further chatter, she heard invective and profanity, along with gender insults. Some key words spelled security breach. Susan Hoffen, guard force sergeant, dropped the phone and began to run. On rounding the corner, she found the long corridor empty. The lone phone booth stood vacant, but she knew that voice.

82

Ken Hemming had been raised on science fiction, reading everything of quality from Jules Verne on. The grand contagion came from his father, a man of vigorous imagination. As a child, Dad had been shocked into cosmic awareness in the late 1930's by his own father. The two had been listening to a radio broadcast that reported aliens from Mars landing in New Jersey. The "news account" turned out to be a drama based on "The War of the Worlds," by H.G. Wells. Ken's grandfather listened a while, shut off the radio and said, quietly, "Time for us to go."

He provisioned for survival, and drove the family from Scotch Plains, NJ, to the family cabin in the Pocono Mountains. Here, he intended to hole up and fight the invaders in protective terrain. He kept the radio turned off because he believed it would tell the aliens his location. Several days of gunnery practice bothered the distant neighbors and they complained to the state police. A trooper who came in to investigate happened to have some recent newspapers in his patrol car. Grandpa read carefully about the misunderstood broadcast, noticing that some people had panicked into suicide. He derided them to the trooper as spineless people who would not fight back. Then, he drove the family home, predicting, "They'll come. If not now, someday!"

Grandfather lived long enough to see Armstrong and Aldrin walk on the moon. From a wheel chair, he rapped his cane on the TV face and said, "See. It was possible. And it'll get to be routine." His foresight had a strong and lasting effect on the family. Ken, a skilled and practical aerospace engineer, the son and grandson of visionaries, was also an active futurist and a reader of science fiction. It stood him in good stead. He took the arrival of Andrei Borodin in stride, calmly devising ways to disarm the man and begin questions about his obvious hibernation.

---------------------------------- 83 ----------------------------------

Arnold Tanner ogled the screen, with the very lining of his brain in pain as though ablaze. In awe and disbelief he watched the biblical equivalent of resurrection. He faced a hoax or a miracle, or a delusion. Always conscious of appearances, he had rammed his trembling hands deep into pockets. He had been educated in the law, a training that looks to the past, in a preparation of precedents. But he had no precedents for what he now saw. Added to his unimaginative nature, a training in precedents handicapped him for the 21st century.

A fastidious man, enamored of archaisms, the Secretary of State was repeatedly amazed by the indelicate, disrupting world of technology. It constantly rushed him into the future. The people of medicine, electronics, computers, and space research routinely astonished him with their actions and results. His experience had no prototype for a return from the dead. Even to consider such a thing fell into the realm of spiritualism and superstition, beliefs he rejected. It fell, also, into the realm of horror and terror, both of which gripped him.

He had, however, learned the essence of political life. He knew how to adapt. Anticipating that his teeth would begin to chatter, he felt prematurely humiliated. Almost moaning at the thought of that embarrassment, he fought for his sanity and appearance. In his business, image was vital. It mattered nothing to him that everyone in the room might be rooted in fear. Unlike others, he was a leader. At least he would be, if he could only get this situation to make sense. For the moment, he needed someone to follow, someone to stabilize chaos. Behaving like a general in a swamping lifeboat, he recruited a technical sailor.

Preempting everyone in the command post, Arnold Tanner called to the person on Screen One, "Ken, explain what's happening."

It was a masterstroke in the practice of form over substance. The question calmed most in the room, their astonishment and fear yielding to that suspenseful moment before the magician's trick is explained.

Intensely concentrating, Hemming did not respond. With eyes locked on Andrei, he wrote furiously on a clipboard, automatically jump-spacing downward to prevent overwriting. Unlike Tanner, he presented an image of trained competence.

A voice got through to him. It said, "Ken, this is the President. Come in, please."

84

Memories of the past popped into Andrei Borodin's mind. He recalled sounds, bothersome and unnerving, sometimes of rolling thunder, sometimes sobs. He sorted mental images, stringing them into a jerky, gap-laden, foggy movie of memory. He had ridden in that capsule. Trapped in there, he had died there. In his hurtling steel mausoleum, he'd been buried unseen in plain view of the whole world, failed and dead.

He was life, ejected from the world amid smoke, flame, and thunder into barren, silent wastes. He represented the cell of humanity. It would one day proliferate in this barren, uncultivated void, the future home of his species. That is what the leaders told him. They had a long- range plan. He was the vanguard, the symbol. No. Wrong. He hadn't gone alone. She had gone with him.

It seemed to be a reasonable idea at the start. These two fliers would represent life and the ability to make life. To the rest of the world, the symbolism would be unmistakable. People from the socialist system would inherit the heavens and all therein. His countrymen would be inspired. But on his way to the high ground of the future, the woman had changed from a training companion to a cherishment.

At first, he stayed remote and aloof. This evolved into a respect for her qualifications. Then began a tolerant politeness. He progressed through an active courtesy, a distracting affection, and finally, a groaning passion.

What their trainers noticed most was his obsessive protectiveness. The dangers of space flight meant nothing to him. He had, however, vowed no harm would come to this blithesome, talented spirit who had committed so eagerly to great risk. And he had failed.

Now he floated in a giant, bright, silver cylinder. Passions and memories moved and shuddered in mind and frame. In surges of disoriented emotion, he thought about himself.

Where am I? What am I? He felt like a dreamer who dreamed about himself dreaming. *This must be a dream.* No, he reasoned, it couldn't be. He must be in a type of heaven. After all, he moved like an angel, though volant without wings. Would they be issued soon?

With or without wings, life — or, more accurately, this afterlife — felt wonderful. It made distraction easy and concentration difficult. Smiling, he pocketed the gun and played in the air. Twisting, turning and spinning for pure joy, he abandoned himself to aerial frolic and gymnastics. The contortions stirred his insides. Rumblings began. Gas built pressure. He stopped the acrobatics, instantly again suspicious and wary. He drew the gun. It might be needed. He now understood his status: one does not pass wind in the afterlife.

Spinning frequently and suddenly, to see what might be watching him, or even stalking, he moved in floating paranoia. He inspected the cylindrical world forward of his spacecraft. His ship's name suddenly came to him: Falcon. In a close scrutiny, he looped Falcon several times, stirring up more memories of launch and mission. He looked closely at the buckled stub antenna. Sawn through. Why?

Truth illuminated his technical mind. The boom had been cut in order to fit into the cylinder. He probed the long cleavage in the cylinder's insulation above the cut antenna. He felt rubber. It was cool. Prying the overlapping insulation pads apart, he saw a longitudinal joint of rubber facing rubber. He pushed his gun into the joint, leveraging his way. His hand entered, chilling as it went. Air began to rush out of the pliant opening. He jerked his hand back, striving for answers.

Free-floating meant weightlessness. The rush of air meant lower external pressure, perhaps vacuum. This had to be the environment of space! Falcon had been cut to fit into this cylinder. The idea swamped his imagination. No space vehicle could be large enough to contain his ship! *Find out. Trace the seam.* He moved aft, finding more rubber. At the end, at a bulkhead of sorts, more rubber faces abutted, making a circumferential seam. He tracked the arc to its base, a hinge. Choking on the implication, he banged and bumped his way to a point on the opposite side. He clawed the insulation away. He found more floating hinges, designed for the fore and aft movement of thermal expansion of giant doors.

On earth, he would have sat down stunned. Here, he merely drifted limp in body and mind. Visions of a great cosmic ship flickered in and out of his mind's eye. He imagined the action. The ship, with its great jaws agape, had overtaken Falcon and flicked out a tongue. Like a frog snapping a fly from the air, it had pulled Falcon into its maw and closed jaws. Falcon's antenna stuck out of the rubbery lips. Chain teeth oscillated and sawed into the metal boom while a giant tongue levered it flat. Then the maw closed. *I'm a Jonah.*

But this mechanical whale had to be conceived and built by something alive. A great intelligence might be aboard, perhaps behind that flat wall. He hung inert, studying the forward bulkhead. At one side of its base he saw what looked like a hatch-type door, and near that a glass rectangle. Higher up he saw two other glass rectangles, but they seemed darker. Cautiously, pulling himself along the insulation, as though creeping toward a foe, he moved to look into what might be a window.

85

Ron Engle believed that every job he ever held was really the same job: communicator. He had managed and led thousands of people. He knew that managing and leading are two different things. A manager has followers assigned to him and may, to the simple mind, look like a leader. But both functions have one thing in common, the resolution of misunderstandings. He saw such a situation shaping up.

Leaning over to the Secretary of State he said, "Who is your best Russian interpreter?"

Tanner needed nothing more. He simply said, "Right. Thanks." He wrote a note headed "Urgent."

It gave a name and phone number and then a second choice. He handed it to Engle, who passed it with instructions to the Marine colonel in charge of security, saying, "Find him, Mike. Brief him and get him here pronto."

Returning, Engle heard Hemming responding to the President. "Sir. I believe we are witnessing a revival from suspended animation. That may sound like science fiction, but we seem to be living in science fiction today. I propose that we manage the situation as an awakening from a long sleep. We must put ourselves in Ivan's shoes. We must recognize that he is a time traveler and treat him carefully. He is armed and may react aggressively to further emotional shock. His behavior so far indicates that he's disoriented, impulsive and irrational. We must welcome him, encourage him, and educate him. First, we must calm him. I intend to pipe music to him from a Radio Moscow symphony now in progress. Rest assured, no news broadcasts will be allowed in."

He went on, "We must soon attempt to communicate, but Ivan may not speak English. I request a Russian-speaking expert be brought in at once, preferably an older man from nearer Ivan's time, and one with interviewing experience."

The Secretary of State broke in: "He's on his way."

The President turned to look at Tanner and gave him an approving nod.

"Good," said Hemming, as though to a capable subordinate, and continued, "I also request the services and advice of a professional psychologist, preferably someone familiar with the Russian, or better yet, the Soviet military mind."

The Chairman of the Joint Chiefs of Staff interjected, "I know someone like that. He's a reserve officer, now on duty with one of our strategic planning teams. Excuse me, Mr. President." He hurried from the room.

The flight chief continued, "I believe we are watching a process of exploration and adjustment to new realities. My aim is to alleviate the man's confusion, gain his trust, and convince him to put away his weapon. Adam has covered the cargo bay windows to prevent Ivan's seeing into the flight deck area. Adam will stay out of sight but will watch the bay on TV. I'm as new to this as you are, so I'll now take any suggestions."

Cooper spoke up, "Hemming, can Ivan see Tim on mid deck?"

There was an instant of ominous silence.

"Adam!" ordered Hemming. "Snap off the mid deck lights. Quickly! But don't try to cover the window. Stay out of sight."

There was another silence. Then Hemming said, "Washington, thank you. I totally forgot about the lower window."

Silence again. The TV monitor showing Tim's trussed body went dim as Adam doused the mid deck lights.

----------------------------------- 86 -----------------------------------

Andrei was a graduate of the original cosmonaut-training regimen. It assumed that much could go wrong, including emergency landings into icy wastes, deserts, or jungles. That prompted a program of survival training, severe demands in hard conditions. Not only did it teach how to cope with nature, it assumed you might land in hostile territory. As a result, training included the arts of the guerrilla warrior and the military scout. Its value began to show.

Acting automatically, Andrei moved clumsily but cautiously forward. He pressed himself close to the flat wall for cover. He knew that intelligent creatures operated this machine, and he was relieved that they hadn't seen him. Or had they? Maybe they had watched him from behind the flat wall he hugged. Beyond the lower window he could see a totally different world, one of lighted panels and equipment. He went closer, ignoring the darkened upper windows.

He would take a good look inside. He placed his right eye at the lower left window corner and slid his head to the right at a 45-degree upward angle. This allowed his right eye to look in while minimizing the area of his head that an inside observer might see. He would take a quick peek.

A glance is often more certain than a stare, especially in dim light. He recoiled in horror.

Nothing could have prepared him for the sight inside. Nothing. He could not believe what dominated the room. The view tumbled his mind with visions of savagery, inhumanity and a chilling fear. Petrified, he surmised that the creatures that manned this ship of space had captured him for sacrifice, perhaps torture. Perhaps even — he shuddered — for food. His fate might soon be that of their last unfortunate victim, a broken, blackened human male. Arms limp and extended, the creature was suspended like a charred, crucified Christ.

He steeled himself to look again, this time for details, and began to slide into position. Suddenly, all lights in the room went out. Too late! In grim anger, he thought, *They are trying to hide this barbarity! But I have seen it, and I am warned, and I will kill those who would kill me.*

The cargo bay illumination began to dim, fading to a dusk that let almost no light into the lower window. Andrei floated to the air lock door and positioned himself behind the hinges. They would have to come through that door to get at him. The door itself would be his shield. He fingered gun and knife. He would battle them at close quarters.

———————————— 87 ————————————

Tenement One could no longer see Andrei. Nor could the flight chief or Adam. The cameras in the payload bay looked rearward from the air lock wall. By going to the wall itself, Andrei had, in effect, gone behind the lens. Adam heard him collide with the wall upon arrival and heard him shortly thereafter banging around at the air lock door.

Adam called, "Houston, I've got an idea. Ivan's out of camera vision, but I think I could see him from the flight deck window. I request permission to look. The area's dark enough. I won't be seen, and I can move without noise."

When Hemming agreed, Adam floated silently to the top corner of one of the windows. "I see feet," he whispered. "Ivan's having a hard time not floating away. Damn, I need curved eyeballs for this job."

His patience paid off. He saw Andrei drift off the wall several times and pull himself back. One outward drift showed him totally, gun and knife in hands. He was rapidly learning how to move in weightlessness. Adam saw him huffing air to jet into a slow tipover for a handhold on the insulation. From there, Andrei pulled himself back toward the air lock. But first, he loosed a few feet of lashing line from the supply that Adam kept looped on belaying pins near the air lock. He cut off a short length and took it with him. Adam did not see him floating again.

"Houston, maybe you saw that action. I think he's using a line to tie himself close to the air lock door. He's carrying weapons and shows every sign of being ready to use them. I figure he's taken up a position near the door to ambush anyone leaving the air lock. This guy's looking very grim. He's not the carefree acrobat we saw earlier. I'm a little worried that he may get impatient, waiting for someone to come out. If he's as upset as he looks, he may try to break a window and shoot his way in here. I don't like the idea of a gun on board. If he puts holes in this tin can, it could end us. We've got to talk him into being peaceful. Where the hell's the psychiatrist?"

Hemming joshed him, "Don't be picky. You'll be getting a psychologist."

Adam snorted, "Send whoever owns a couch. I want this guy strapped to it."

The flight chief got serious again. "We'll let you know as soon as one arrives. Meantime, you're coming up on a sunrise and you'll have a problem with light getting into the mid deck. Do you want to turn ship or put a blackout curtain on the lower window?"

Adam considered the choices. If he worked near the window he might be seen and shot at. From that standpoint, turning the ship would be safer. However, it meant he'd have to repeatedly adjust the shuttle's attitude, pointing its belly toward the Sun. His current strategy of turning required only gross automatic adjustments to keep his belly toward earth. Doing anything different would defeat his strategy of hiding behind the tank. He thought about it.

If light got in the cockpit windows, it would behave as it does on earth, reflecting off all interior surfaces; it would penetrate to the mid deck. Tim would then be visible through the window, and so would Adam when caring for him. That had to be prevented. Who could tell what a confused, armed man might do? Adam opted for the blackout curtain. He wanted light and clear visibility in caring for Tim. He also wanted the flight surgeon to have access to all information about this patient, including constant visual impressions. Silently and carefully, working in darkness, he taped a thin, aluminized sleeping blanket over the window.

Adam worked with Hemming, gently turning up the volume for the speakers in the cargo bay. As the music of the Moscow Symphony slowly rose to flood the silver cylinder with the skipping, exuberant, pounding finale of Tchaikovsky's Symphony No. 5, the remote microphones in the payload bay picked up the alarmed voice of an atheist blurting Jesus Christ's name in Russian, not as a prayer, but as a startled, repetitive expletive.

─────────────────────── 88 ───────────────────────

Julian Kostiaskov tumbled from bed with only two hours sleep. In the private section of a sleek limousine, he listened skeptically as a Marine colonel of questionable sanity told the story of Ivan. They followed a screaming police escort to the White House. The story began to become more believable. Blue lights still flashed in his head as he entered Tenement One. He was tired, but tranquil. Composure was typical of Julian.

For 20 years he'd been chief of American interpreters in USA/UCS negotiations. It was Julian's job to convey the content of each side's position, but not the emotion. He could absorb the ultimatums, screaming, threats, and passions like a self-cleansing sponge. Although he thrived on the stress, it broke some of his people, men and women. Julian saw stress as a grindstone. When you hold people against it, some wear away; others, like good steel, get sharper. His people, like air traffic controllers, faced such stress. Some got ulcers, but others just got better and better at their work. *If only we had a test to predict.*

Julian dealt in accuracy, thoroughness, and clarity. He often became the calm eye of raging diplomatic storms among willful men who wielded ultimate weapons. Julian, however, never flapped. He hoped he would perform tonight as the cool professional in his new role of talking to the risen dead. Why not? He smiled. After all, he had talked for decades to brain dead politicians. Many of them, he believed, qualified for the famous epitaph coined by a Columbia University dean, *"Died at 50, buried at 80."*

Twenty minutes after arrival he had quit smiling. A solemn president had briefed him and his new partner, Major Yuri Beletsky. They had also seen a video of Andrei's emergence and behavior.

Yuri, the promised psychologist, had been pried from bed with little sleep, but it didn't dampen his natural exuberance. In fact, "the interruption," as he called it, prompted great personal hilarity. Yuri believed that humanity is designed to be tempted, and then frustrated after yielding.

"She was so remote, contained and inhibited," he harangued his military captor on the mad drive in from Fort Meade, "that I knew I was about to unleash the power of Niagara. Just as that beautiful dam was breaking, you arrived to ring and ring, and pound on my door, and beat on my windows. You are a force of nature! Who could hide from you? You imposed water hammer on me at the peak of hydraulic pressure. However, I do not blame you for your perverse timing. You are merely a tool of great cosmic forces.

The whole thing is fantastically funny." He repeatedly burst into loud, legitimate laughter, interspersed with, "Oh, it hurts. It hurts."

The general's aide viewed him warily. He wondered if Yuri's hobby might be to calibrate sundials at night, and he expected the next assignment to be finding a psychologist for the psychologist.

Yuri was quirky, cynical, fatalistic, and detached, and a keen observer of the human condition. He was also optimistic, gregarious, relentless, and uninhibited but structured. He expected nothing from life, but he wanted all it had to offer. All, that is, except marriage. He had the cynics' belief in the female view of a wedding ceremony: "... *an irresistible force meets an improvable object.*" Sure, he had needs, and he seldom slept alone. But nobody, ever, would be allowed to mold him.

Nothing people did surprised Yuri. Everything they did fascinated him. His special interest was their group behavior in totalitarian societies. No current nation gripped his interest as much as the UCS. His hobby was Russian history. He absorbed some of the language during visits to Russia, and during extensive debriefings of defectors. But he refused to learn the language well for fear of *feeling* Russian. He thought it would introduce subjective emotion into his objective study and analysis of behavior. Thus, he truly needed Julian's help to get through to Ivan. Julian's language skills were so good that they were called "transparent." It meant that whoever spoke through him forgot Julian was in the loop and focused on communicating.

By contrast, Dr. Yuri Beletsky was controversial. Although some top brass maligned, others lauded him. The Chairman of the Joint Chiefs, who had sent for him, was an admirer. Years earlier, when the general served as a lowly colonel in Europe, he became impressed by Yuri's accurate predictions of Kremlin behavior. He believed that Yuri understood the Russian mind. He now gave him a disturbed Russian mind, one resurrected from history, to predict and transform.

89

As the guards got closer, Byron Desault got calmer, again under his normal icy control. It and his self-esteem had crumbled in the face of the mocking disbelief from his Washington telephone contact. *That infuriating bitch! That unimaginative bimbo!* She would pay for her behavior. He would see to that. He had never before lost emotional control. Putting a good face on things, he concluded that he would learn from the incident. He knew it was already making him stronger, more controlled. He eased his car forward for inspection.

He now faced the tight security he had anticipated. He had not seen the technique before. The personnel director had created an apparent campaign for safe driving. Designed to obviate rumor, her disarming process used a lollipop in a velvet glove on an iron fist.

Normally, as hundreds of cars left at shift change the guards merely waved them out the exit gate. A few times a year, management stopped and inspected cars at random to discourage theft. All employees had, at one time or another, been through this drill. Today, however, it wasn't random; the guards stopped all cars. Susan Hoffen stood at the gate, smiling sweetly at every person in every exiting car.

"Hi," she said to the occupants. "This is an injury prevention campaign. Everyone who leaves with the safety belt buckled is eligible in a lottery for an extra day of vacation. Please buckle up and speak your name and I.D. number into the recorder." Then, she held the microphone to each occupant and watched and listened. There was laughter, and the occasional admonition for a fellow passenger to "buckle up, dummy!"

Two cars pulled out of line and tried to turn back. Guards brought the drivers to Susan at once, but she found only stolen tools and not her quarry. She sought a face that matched a screaming voice.

Byron Desault, minus mustache and sideburns, drove forward and tucked his voice into a drawling lower register. Also tucked away, stowed under his dashboard, was a disc of Andrei in the payload bay. Byron eased through, as one of the homeward bound employees. But he did not go home. Instead, he turned onto the highway and drove to the airport. He ignored the one in Houston. Blurring his trail, he went to Washington via Dallas.

90

With a great bear hug, smiles, back thumping, and a champagne toast, Dmitri Yemetov welcomed Marshal Vasili Ogrov to Moscow. By comparison with his victory dance with Gerasimov, the Marshal appeared restrained, modest, and properly military. He smiled in appreciation of his achievement and its recognition. He startled when Stepka Yakunin hugged him, for she was rumored hostile to men. Ogrov considered that a benefit. It kept things even. What man could be attracted to this cold, ambitious machine? Relaxed in his joy, he hugged her in return and forgave himself hypocrisy.

The Premier said, quietly, "Comrade Marshal, you have done your country a great service. Unfortunately, what you have achieved cannot be made public. This is why."

He handed Ogrov the official press release, ordering, "Read only the cover story. The rest is validation in depth. You may keep the entire package."

While Ogrov read, an aide entered the room and handed the Premier a note. Yementov nodded, flashed an open hand to indicate five minutes and turned to Ogrov.

"I do not understand," said Ogrov.

"Well, you see," purred Yemetov, "we are not claiming we hit the shuttle, but just our Falcon. Their tank got hit, of course, because they left it behind. We want no adverse publicity from killing the Americans. We shot only our own spacecraft and their dead metal. Now, the Americans are boxed in. They must explain why they did not heed our public warnings, but instead defiantly left their men at the target. Their other choice is to invent some reason, perhaps an ocean crash, for the loss of their men and their shuttle."

"I do not understand."

The Premier oozed on. "Vasili, Vasili, we are projecting an image of concern for humanity. We must try to present the American leaders as people who are unconcerned and uncaring about their astronauts. We must say the Americans told us they had put our satellite back and flown away. We must make it that they lied about leaving. When we fired, we did so with complete trust that they had told the truth and departed."

Ogrov was dug in on the issue. "Why?"

With his arm around the Marshal, Yemetov cooed, "So that the American leaders will be publicly to blame for the deaths of their astronauts, you see. Not us."

"Are you saying we had no right to fire, even though they defied our ultimatum?"

"As the Americans say, Vasili, we are playing it that way. It's wiser. The most that can be charged against us is poor timing, poor communications, or an accident."

He now switched to vodka, pouring for all three of them. "It is very important we handle it this way because of what I soon wish to achieve in the United Nations. Therefore, we will be making no public identification of who was involved in the attack, including you. You are a public figure, Vasili, famous for your rocket defense planning. It is important that foreign diplomats or journalists not see you for several months. You might be questioned."

Yemetov did not want to take any chances with the press, given Ogrov's notorious bluntness. "It is enough, Comrade Marshal, that we know what you did for the motherland. You have always been a man who did his duty and never bragged about it. We merely formalize your own behavior by this tactic. And now, as a gesture of appreciation, here is the key to my own dacha. You have earned a real vacation."

The Premier and the Minister of Information allowed only chitchat for the closing minutes as they walked Ogrov out to meet the escort who would fly with him to the Black Sea resort.

As they reentered the room, another door opened and a short, square man came in. Pleasantries done, Yemetov asked, "What's so urgent?"

The square man replied, "Comrade Yemetov, we have been watching the ruptured American tank with radar and, through an occasional hole in the clouds, with visual telescopes. We have discovered that it is presenting the same face to the earth at all stages in its orbit." The man was Lt. General Fyodor Lubinin, Director of Space Flight Operations.

He explained the unnaturalness of the tank's behavior, and concluded, "So you see, Comrade President, I recommend that we send cosmonauts at once to investigate. I do not recommend any kind of observation satellite. If we discover that the American astronauts have survived and are hiding in their shuttle behind the tank, and they are controlling its behavior for camouflage, we must take immediate action. I am against another effort with any of our anti-satellite weapons. American luck or skill has already frustrated us twice. I want my men to be right there, on the scene, to finish this job! I regret that this information on probable survival was only slowly accumulated over the last 24 hours. However, I have a ship nearly ready for our space station supply flight. The crew can be diverted to confront the Americans. I request your permission to do that."

Yemetov stared at him long before speaking. "Comrade General, I feel like a pendulum. You specialists are whipping me back and forth. Ogrov just left here, claiming destruction of the shuttle. Now, you are here, claiming the opposite. If you did your work down here on earth, I would agree that you should go and look for your enemy behind your chosen tree. However, you want me to spend millions of rubles so you can look behind a tree in space, so to speak. I must think about this. Get me more proof. Pictures! An intercepted conversation! Bring me proof I can understand."

—————————————————— 91 ——————————————————

"I am opening tonight's broadcast with an appeal for someone in the audience to phone me and explain what the USA and the UCS are really doing in space at this very moment! Will someone call in and tell our listeners why both countries are lying to us, or at least hiding information, about their activities? Our lines are open."

The speaker had the improbable name of John Dough. He was the originator, producer, commentator, interviewer, and star of *Space Week,* the popular, nationally syndicated TV program. During a long engineering career at Nastran, his hobby had been writing and speaking about space to the public. For years, in the Speakers' Bureau, he explained space exploration in schools, at service clubs and science fairs, in radio and TV interviews, and on call-in talk shows. He acquired a convincing stage presence, and an ease at the microphone. He took these skills into retirement, working as a science reporter.

John Dough knew the space business intimately. He could talk to anyone, in any line of work at any level, place or time. He was famous for checking and rechecking, always listening patiently to people's ideas and viewpoints. He had been such an advocate of space exploration his wife asked, "Why don't you focus on space news for a living?" That started a conversation that lasted hours. Along the way, she said, "You're as good as the people I see hosting programs like *Wall Street Week* and *Congress Week* and *Business Week."* That very night they designed the basic format of his show. A week later he sold the idea to the local TV station. In three months it went national.

His show always had solid, factual information, stemming from his vast experience and his constant research about space activities worldwide. But its most attractive ingredient was John's directness and integrity. If he said something, you wanted to believe it because you believed in him. He developed a legion of followers who saw space as a holy cause. To scores of thousands, space was the Final Frontier, the logical next arena for venture and adventure, now that the Old West had disappeared. They believed that space exploration and eventual settlement in space would help to keep America from decay.

Many space purists regarded space development as the next step in the evolution of mankind. In their crusade, anyone delaying the process was interfering with divine intent. They challenged anyone who tried to play politics with space, and they inspired and guided whistle-blowers. Space purists provided John with anonymous calls, or with envelopes slipped under the door. Startling stories had sprung from these tips, sometimes leading to jail terms for space contract fraud. John's tenacity for digging into such leads earned him a justified reputation as a top investigative reporter.

Several times during today's broadcast he repeated the call for someone to please tell the truth about Russian and American activity. "The reporters of the world," he said, "have been ignored, avoided and misled by Moscow and Washington. I've just read you the Kremlin's press release. I regard it as lies and deception. The White House refuses to comment. No one will say where the space shuttle Olympia is right now or what it is doing. More and more people are getting hysterical in Europe, and here at home, because they think that a huge vessel circling earth may contain space aliens. Our elected representatives are irresponsible in not refuting the rumors."

On a scholarship, young John had gone north to MIT, adding a Boston dash to his South Carolina charm. "Precision with a drawl," someone said of his technical briefing sessions. Lots of true dolts, watching his public science explanations, felt fuzzygood about what they heard, thinking they understood the subject as the friendly, comforting tones of the rumbling bass voice rolled into their ears. He mesmerized with explanations such as, "When this little old gyroscope gets spinning real good, it just has a mind of its own, and it wants its way, and it won't change. And that's just fine, because we always know where it's aimed and we can steer off of that fixed foundation, and we can navigate all the way to another planet." Heads would nod in eager agreement.

John's persuasiveness was on full throttle tonight. "Listen to me! I believe that some of you know what is happening. You know. Yes, you do! I am talking now to you. I want you to tell me what is going on. You owe that to your fellow citizens. We will not have a democratic, free and open society if we allow Washington to behave like Moscow. You must speak up. Tell it privately to *me*. To John, your friend. Tell me, where is the shuttle Olympia? Why did internal security suddenly tighten up at the Johnson Space Center today?

"Tonight, I am broadcasting from Houston. I came here because some of the Nastran brass were scheduled for interview on this very show. But, all of a sudden, everybody begged off and didn't even send a replacement. Why? Who will tell me? I'm staying in town and will continue my broadcasts from here until I find out. I'll stay here until you reach me with the facts. This story will be broken right here, in this city! You can be the one to break it. Get a pencil and paper. Here comes my hotel and room number. Here comes my phone number and my fax number. Here comes a post office box number that I opened today. Here comes my e-mail address. Call me or write me or come to see me. It's your country. It's your freedom. Don't let them take either away from you!"

The message nourished one person's antagonism for Nastran. In a locker

room near Mission Control a disgruntled technician was going off shift —
and she carried a disc for John.

────────────── 92 ──────────────

Yuri and Julian liked each other, perhaps verifying that opposites attract.
Each sucked up information like a vacuum and then, with pertinent
questions, hunted for more.

Yuri confessed: "I understand Russian far better than I let on. I overhear
much more that way, you see. I tell you this so you'll know that I'll be
closely following what's said if he agrees to talk with you."

They studied information on the early Soviet space program and
refreshed themselves on its history. They could see Andrei's uniform
insignia and assumed he was from the Soviet Air Force, the source of
most cosmonauts. They could not decipher his rumpled, embroidered
nameplate.

"Listen," said Yuri, "we don't know what mental or physical condition
this guy's in. He probably injected himself with some hibernant chemical.
He's been immersed in that gas, whatever it is, for decades. He's been hit
by cosmic radiation all that time. He's far, far older than he looks, and
we don't know what's happened in the aging process. It's possible, even,
that he's hungry. And, based on those free-floating gymnastics he did,
pleasure can distract him and break his focus. Maybe he thinks he's a kid
again. It's going to be tough to analyze him because we have too many
unknowns. There's no precedent for all this, and it's very, very complex. So
let's simplify our puzzle, and just treat him with true dignity. We'll assume
he's normal, but bewildered and a little forgetful. I feel like that when I
wake up in a strange place. It takes a while to regroup. And remember, this
guy's been asleep for decades. What would happen to the memory, even if
he simply *slept* that long?"

The flight chief did much of their briefing. He impressed Yuri as a
take-charge guy, and that made Yuri cautious about how they would work
together.

"Flight," Yuri said, "I know you're in charge of this mission. No contest.
But I'm in charge of this sub-mission. I'll need and want things done,
maybe urgently. At times, there'll probably be no time for questions. Can
you work for me?"

There was a silence. Then, Hemming's voice came through, flat and
slow. "The answer is 'yes.' However, if I see a threat to the ship from

this man's behavior, the answer will immediately become 'no,' and maybe without any warning to you. Also, if the timetable calls for a spacecraft operation, the answer will be 'no.' In that case, of course, I will tell you in advance. If I can."

Yuri agreed to the terms.

Ken went on, "I understand your concern. You know that I made the decision to pipe Russian music to him. That may have been a mistake. His reaction was reflexive and sounded furious. It may, however, have alerted us to a hair trigger potential for violence."

Yuri said, "Yeah, I know you did that. It's justification for why I want you out of the loop. What did you expect? You're dangerous. Nobody, but nobody, would hit even a normal man, just waking up, with a crappy piece like Tchaikovsky's 5th."

There was a bewildered silence in Houston and Tenement One. It broke when Hemming's composure crumpled. He started to laugh. Not able to stop, he rose and tottered for the men's room, jerkily waving in a replacement. Ken had just learned how tired he was; and that he liked and trusted Yuri Beletsky.

93

Grigory Taksis kept himself well insulated from subordinates and sources as part of Moscow's strategy for keeping the Ambassador clean and clear, in case underlings got caught in espionage. When they did, he could say to American officials, "I did not know this was going on."

Half the embassy staff consisted of espionage specialists nominally assigned to normal administrative duties. All had specific assignments to pry out American economic, industrial, and military information. Their duties did not include active sabotage, but a few had been trained to disable communications centers or key production facilities if the need arose. All reported to Ambassador Taksis' second in command.

This man's visible duties matched those of the base commander of a military site; he provided all services and facilities to make the embassy function. He would be the highest-level fall guy to be recalled to Moscow in a spy scandal. He knew everybody in the embassy and everything going on. Byron would not get past this man or his people for direct contact with the Ambassador.

Taksis and Byron had never met. The contact in Virginia repeatedly told him never, ever, to deal directly with anyone in the embassy. Byron did not know of the espionage structure in the embassy. He knew only that the Ambassador was in charge and was therefore the person to see. He knew, too, that he would never again, under any circumstances, deal through his demeaning bitch contact. In his innocence of the Byzantine inner workings of the embassy, he phoned and asked to speak with the Ambassador's appointments secretary. Fortunately, this person had so much contact with the outside world that censoring or pre-screening calls would have been overwhelming, so security surveillance didn't apply.

Byron got through. He had found the one narrow gap in the security screen. He learned later that the secretary was Peter Taksis, the Ambassador's nephew, an astute intellectual who was dedicated to his uncle's career.

"Please write these names down and show them to the Ambassador. My name is Byron Desault. My code name is 'Gagarin.' I have just arrived at Dulles International Airport. Please interrupt whatever the Ambassador is doing and tell him I am on my way to see him right now about Olympia."

Peter, blessed with good judgment, said, quickly, "Stay on the phone. Do not move." He put Byron on hold and entered the Ambassador's office.

"This man is now holding on the phone."

The Ambassador read the note, blanched and said, "This is preposterous! He is not allowed to contact the Embassy. He can't come here! But the idiot is jumping the chain, so something must be wrong. We must take the chance and see him. Peter, you know that I can't go to him; that would be too conspicuous. You must do it. Take him to my home and wait for me."

Peter started for the door, stopped and asked, "Do you have any objection if I use the motorcycle? It's the best way to shake the FBI tail."

"That thing is not a motorcycle. It is a murdercycle. It will kill both of you! Do what you want, but be careful."

—————————————— 94 ——————————————

"Still there, Gagarin? Good. Listen carefully. I will come to get you on a Harley Davidson motorcycle. You will be riding on the back, hanging on, so you must carry no luggage. Put it all in a coin locker. What? You have none? Well, good. Now, listen: I will be wearing a red, white, and blue helmet. Be at the east front of the Metro subway station at ground level in twenty minutes. Any questions?"

Byron hung on tight, with his head sideways against Peter's back. He shut his eyes in fright as they changed lanes, jumped curbs, reversed direction on divided highways, cut across medians, and sometimes ran cross-country until they dropped off curbs onto totally different roads. Peter was a master at shaking a tail.

Only a helicopter could have followed their progress without detection. One did, aided by altitude, sound-suppressed rotors, and long-range binoculars. The FBI agents who watched the embassy and photographed its visitors had radioed Peter's direction and description the moment his motorcycle roared away. They knew who Peter was. However, no one knew his passenger. They became very interested.

Byron felt diminished amid the elegant furniture, rugs, chairs, drapes, and liquors in the den of the Ambassador's sumptuous home. Taksis used the setting for an imperious scolding of the wayward bumpkin. Byron smarted from the fiery, degrading rebuke he got for breaching security. He began to fight back. He challenged Taksis to prescribe an alternate means for getting through to him. He demanded time to explain his message. Taksis rebuffed him until rage died. Then, in a lightning reversal, the man became the smooth Ambassador again, offering sociability, comfort, and spirits.

"We will play your home movies" he said, in stiff cordiality, "but first, we will salute your assumed good intentions."

The Ambassador's repetitive toast ritual with the fine crystal put Byron deep into his third vodka martini. The effect let him ignore the man's condescending hospitality and focus instead on narrating the video. Byron resented the Ambassador's playing the cosmopolite for the Texas yokel. Two minutes later, the roles reversed. Taksis, now the yahoo, a technology rube, ogled the video and trembled. Vodka sloshed onto his splendid trousers. As the tape played on, the distinguished ambassador looked less and less distinguished. He gaped like a child watching magic. The vodka glass fell from his limp hand and bounced on the rug. Byron loved it. Ten minutes later, in a breaking voice, Taksis called for a replay.

"This time, Mr. Desault, please narrate more slowly."

They saw Andrei emerge from Falcon, within Olympia. After the fourth showing, Taksis evolved into suspicion. His interrogation continued for hours, alternately condemning Desault as a double agent and reluctantly accepting him for his true role. Byron successfully refuted all accusations that the video was a clever special effects film. Peter, analytical and very well informed, balanced out the ambassador's agitation. *My nephew is brilliant,* thought Grigory, as he heard Peter weave a believable tapestry from three prime intelligence sources: the recent public activities and statements, the contents of the disc, and the events neither country could or would explain to the media.

Finally, Taksis said, "Mr. Desault, you will be staying here until Moscow authenticates your movie and gives you instructions. I am sending this disk over on the next possible flight."

Byron protested. His chief concern was not to overstay his two-day break before returning to work. "I've got to get a confirmed seat on a particular plane or I'll miss my shift and raise questions. We must not blow my cover."

Peter calmed him, "Relax! Untraceable tickets will be delivered here early tomorrow."

Grigory spoke on the scrambler phone to Moscow. His urgency impressed two higher levels in the chain. His third audience was the Premier. As he told his implausible story, Taksis staked his career on its validity. Yemetov agreed to see the disc immediately upon its arrival.

Yemetov hung up the phone and made notes for a while. Then he sent for the air force historian. He also ordered an urgent search for several of the oldest living cosmonauts. "Get them from wherever they are and bring them here, even if they have to be carried in!" Most of the hero cosmonauts had been granted the cherished license to own a home in Moscow. Their proximity would help speed the roundup.

Then Yemetov's aide had a brilliant idea for an even swifter response. He would go to the Life Extension Institute. He knew that some cosmonauts, consistent with their dedication to service and country, had volunteered for experiments on how to lengthen the life span. They followed prescribed diets, exercise, and lifestyle regimens. The research progress was slow, but promising. Scores of the Institute's volunteers were well past the 100-year mark but still ambulatory and functional.

95

American equipment hummed expectantly as it waited to play the prized package arriving in the noisy helicopter settling within the Kremlin walls. Ambassador Taksis had rushed Byron's disc onto an Aeroflot hypersonic airliner in a diplomatic pouch. It got aboard just before starting its two-hour flight to Moscow from Virginia.

In Yemetov's briefing room, records and photos from historical files covered the massive conference room table. He moved around and around the table, staring alternately at the exhibits and at his guest. He controlled his impatience by a slow, deliberate pacing that matched the careful, measured questions he was asking the old man. Deference was essential. He was dealing with Leonid Malyshev, thrice decorated Hero of the Soviet Union. He had been a cosmonaut cadet at the time of Andrei Borodin's flight. He had later flown twice to the moon, orbited Mars, and become Director of Cosmonaut Training, from which he retired.

"Comrade Premier," interrupted the wheezing Malyshev, "you have asked me interminable questions about Borodin. I have picked him out of scores of old pictures and movies for you. I am ill. I belong back in bed. I am tired. But I am not too tired to be curious. Your emphasis on this man has an unstated purpose. You know, as I do, that he did not go on his last flight alone. Yet you focus on him as though he were Charles Lindbergh. In truth, I was less impressed with Borodin than I was with his companion. In exchange for my inconvenience tonight, and for whatever service I am rendering to you at this hour, please tell me why this man is of interest to us after all our years of imposed silence."

"Leonid, my friend, you are as sharp as ever. Forgive me for not mentioning that you are now involved in a campaign to right a wrong. This crew was never honored for its sacrifice. We are considering such honor. It is necessary to capture the facts and to accurately identify the crew. You are helping enormously. We merely started with Borodin. I will need you later to identify his companion and provide facts there as well. I should have been more considerate. You must be exhausted. I'm sorry. I will not keep you much longer. Only one thing remains. We have discovered film scenes that may be pertinent. They show a person who may be Borodin. We need you to stay for this one last identification."

Yemetov sat and took the old man's hands caressingly and ran his fingers over their cold, silky gnarls; it felt like touching candles. "Will you do it for me?" he pleaded, gazing earnestly into the rheumy eyes.

The old man withdrew his hands with sudden strength. He smelled evil again, as he had on entering the building. Strange, he thought, why only the environments of man seem sinister. Those of other creatures seemed merely fearsome, awesome, dangerous, or squalid. Sinister seemed to require morality, with its option for evil. He found little morality among politicians. Men like Yemetov had always disgusted him. At his age, he felt the freedom to be frank.

"I will do it for my country."

"Please rest. I will return in a few moments." Yemetov was unruffled. He left the room in response to an aide's signal that the movie could begin. Watching intently, he saw the saga of Andrei in the payload bay. Energetic and commanding, Yemetov had begun the viewing with his usual pacing.

That slowed and finally stopped. He sank wearily into a seat and watched the silent film again.

Lubinin broke the silence. "Could it be true?"

Yemetov, recovering, bounded to the disk player, saying, "That's what Malyshev and the others will tell us." He froze the video on a close-up view of Borodin and brought the old man in.

"Do you know this person?"

"No, I do not."

"You mean you have never seen that face before?"

"That's not what you asked me. Certainly I have seen it before. We have spent some hours looking at it."

"Then why do you say you don't know this man?"

Malyshev laughed, "That is a lookalike. Granted, it is a perfect copy. But this young man is appearing in a beautiful, modern, high-density television image. We had nothing of the sort when my crews were his age."

Yemetov flicked the movie along, then froze the scene.

"Is the uniform accurate?"

Malyshev stared. His heart accelerated. A dread and chill descended upon him. He felt the palpitations begin. Commanding himself to an imperious calm he announced, "If you want my cooperation, you must show me all of this movie."

Yemetov, in a desperate need for confirmation or refutation, consented. He ran the video from the start. Several times the old man cried out, "It cannot be." He passed the last few minutes in silence. When the lights came on, the reason became clear: he, himself, had passed.

Fyodor Lubinin began to weep. He had trained under Malyshev in the man's last active years. The impact felt like losing a grandfather. Yemetov rang for help and some guards appeared. "This visitor has had a heart attack. Please take him to a doctor." He signaled to his aide, "Bring in the other gentlemen one at a time."

The ancient cosmonauts each entered with rigid dignity, striving for soldierly carriage while tottering, poking with a cane, or hovering over the cursed walker. They fought for the military bearing appropriate to the honor of a personal interview with the Premier. Inwardly cursing the inching progress, Yemetov greeted and seated each arrival. He thought of dentists. He wished he had multiple disc players in multiple rooms so he could whip from one completed client to the next prepared and waiting.

Yemetov handed the old cosmonauts photos and asked them separately, "Who is this?" Each of the three old men promptly said, "Andrei Borodin." He did not show them the video and probably prevented throwing them into shock. Their answers convinced him. His imagination wrote an incredible, compelling story: Borodin was alive, preserved in youth, in

the Americans' hands; the Americans hid behind the ruptured tank in a
damaged shuttle; the Americans held the key to suspended animation.

Yemetov stared out the window in a thundering silence. Finally,
composed, he turned to Lubinin.

"Launch your cosmonauts as soon as possible."

96

"First, we'll set the mood," said Yuri. "Then you'll do your stuff." Julian
nodded. Yuri gave the go-ahead to a musician at the Marine Barracks.
The bandsman put down the phone and played a disk of old martial
music by Soviet military bands. The output went to Houston. From a
subliminal level, Hemming raised the volume slowly until it barely entered
the audible range for humans. With close concentration, it could be heard.
The volume stayed at that level for a half hour. Then, it was increased little
by little.

Andrei, poised by the air-lock hatch, had subsided from the excitement
of the Tchaikovsky concert. It had given him the first grip on reality in his
bizarre new circumstances. Its start, in the eerie silence, had startled and
bewildered him. But then, as it went on, with an announcer occasionally
introducing other works, he had reveled in his first active link with home.
Now, questions nagged him. Who or what had sent the music to him?
From where did it come? Why, and how? It had stopped as mysteriously
as it had started, and he was again enduring hours of stillness.

Now and then, he found himself moving rhythmically, either tapping
the air with his foot or clapping a hand on his thigh. Several times he
deliberately stopped, only to see the movement start up again as though
synchronized with some rhythm. He listened intently. At times he heard
nothing, and at others, he thought he heard music, military music. Parades,
ceremonies and graduations flooded his mind. Memories of years of
military drill welled up. His mind filled with the great patriotic music
he had shout-sung with the other young lions in training camps. He could
hear the music clearly now, and he began singing softly to his national
anthem.

It all began to make some sense to Andrei as he listened to the familiar
procedure, as though from Falcon, his own spacecraft. First came the wake-
up call from flight headquarters. Julian's voice, as the ground controller,
came through in a mixture of authority, cheerfulness, and worry. It faded
in and out, riding on manufactured static.

"Come in, Falcon. I repeat. This is Flight Operations, comrade. Good morning, Falcon! Why do you not answer? Hello? Either one of you may answer. This is Flight Operations. Please respond."

Andrei, a mixture of discipline, conditioning and adrenaline, shouted, "Baikonur, this is Falcon. We hear you! We hear you! Come in, please."

The ground controller's voice rose in excitement, "Hello! Hello! Who is speaking? Identify yourself. Come in, please."

Andrei shouted, trying to add energy to his broadcast. "This is Borodin speaking! Baikonur, can you hear me? This is Andrei Borodin!"

Static bursts greeted him, but then came a perfectly clear voice saying, as though offstage, "I thought I heard something, Comrade General, but if I did, it has faded away. I must have been mistaken."

A gruffer voice said, "Follow every lead. You must keep trying every half hour. Those two must be rescued unharmed. I will be in my quarters. Call me the moment you get anything."

Andrei shouted for a while longer, then stopped and looked at his watch. It was not working. The sweep hand was stationary. The date was four days past his launch date. He should have been down to earth by now. Mysteries rode in on mysteries. Puzzled, he wound the watch and set the alarm for a half hour.

Andrei had drifted into camera range and Tenement One had seen it all. Amid the tense faces, two smiled happily. Yuri Beletsky turned to Julian Kostiakov and said, "Bingo."

Julian, grinning with mischief, said, "The behaviorists would be proud of you."

97

John Dough prided himself on his personal touch with the public. He often phoned those who wrote to him, questioning or debating their views. He answered much of his fan mail, and he personally read it all. He also opened the mail, every item. In a deliberate policy decision, he had begun this technique for keeping the common touch. His wife wanted it stopped. She had been permanently unnerved years ago by a failed letter bomb that fizzled before their eyes on the kitchen table. She felt that John, investigative and contentious, could always be someone's target. John recognized the mail bomb possibility, but he would not assign that risk to others. She remonstrated with greater frequency as he became more famous.

His answer, a measure of his integrity, said, "Still no, dammit! I'll not allow some minimum wage kid to get maimed because lunatics object to what I do or think! If I'm the provocateur, I should run the risk."

The risk, of course, varied. Politicians and executives imprisoned for space-associated crimes swore vengeance. His occasional feature, a retrospective called, "R.I.P., Lest We Forget," kept their deeds alive as a warning to others. The "RIP" meant "Revelation, Investigation, Prosecution." Other types, including psychotic cranks, also considered him dangerous; many wrote him diatribes every week. John suspected that some of the authors could tip from fanaticism into assault behavior.

One nature cult, the Congress-haranguing DUST (Don't Underwrite Space Transportation), opposed human migration off the planet. Another, the publicly shy, acronym-stretching EARNESS (Earth; Never Space Settlements), opposed his encouragement of space habitats.

Using TV, John poked at popular wisdom just as roughly as Mencken had done in the *Baltimore Sun* a century or so before. When John questioned the location of Heaven, he enraged religious fundamentalists. To John, it was not clear that Heaven was "up there." His logic said that humans, with Biblical exceptions, couldn't enter Heaven while wearing the flesh of this world. The manned landings on the moon, therefore, had led him to say that Heaven's boundary had to start beyond the moon.

When the first explorers circled Mars, John speculated that their presence had moved Heaven's boundary farther out. He broadcast some listeners' letters that objected to this idea, and then publicly chastised the writers in his rumbling drawl, "Don't demean the Creator by implying that we are separated from Her by mere distance. It ain't that simple."

He knew he was pushing rage buttons. Incoherent screamers phoning the show had to be screened out. Now and then, he'd let one be heard on the air. He felt that their ranting proved his points. But because of them, and the other angries, he wore what he called his "mail mail." The full-sleeve jacket wasn't actually chain mail, but the sturdy stuff of bulletproof vests. So were the gloves. A full-face shield completed the costume.

"Color me paranoid," he told his wife, adding, in his fondness for alliteration, "I'm a proud paranoid, properly providing protective precautions."

She left, knowing he wouldn't open the mail with anyone nearby. We become what we are by centimeters or crisis. Either way, behavior evolves. John had evolved into a communications warrior, constantly at risk, armored and equipped. He stroked his tiny portable sensor around the mailbox, sniffing for harmful content. It showed an apparent OK for chemicals. His second device recorded no biological surprise such as anthrax. An observer would think John's rite peculiar, but it made total sense to John. He fully expected a vengeful virus or blast would someday come. "Maybe from this very package," he mumbled, lifting the first bulk item.

It proved more explosive than anything he could have imagined. It propelled him seven miles high at six hundred miles an hour. It sent him to Washington, for a "See Me First!" meeting with a pleading Frank Cole. Such was the power of the videodisc from the aggrieved technician in Mission Control. John had promised the space boss he would not broadcast the video prior to talking with the President.

Not a bad situation for a li'l ole country boy, thought John, grinning into his bourbon in the comfort of first class, both courtesy of Nastran. He smiled in recollection of the disc copy in his hotel's safe, boxed securely with a xerox copy of the technician's anonymous letter of explanation. He had an historical scoop shaping up. His mood was comforting, professional.

Slowly, the historical aspect stopped his congratulatory musing. How could it possibly be? Get serious, John! A man rejuvenated from another century!? Was someone perpetrating a great hoax? If so, why? He had asked himself these questions before using threats to pry Cole out of session with the President. The evidence had lured him on, despite his doubts about the reincarnation he'd seen on the video. He subdued those doubts in the fierce, demanding announcement he made to Cole: "The White House subterfuge is over. I have the facts!"

Cole had crumpled, pleaded that national security was involved, swore him to secrecy, and arranged this luxurious, immediate flight to Washington.

A voice interrupted. "This is the captain. If those of you at the right side windows will look down and slightly aft, you will see a rare sight."

John saw nothing but the slightly rolling, endless expanse of continuous, white clouds. Then he noticed a thin, lengthy, fuzzy line skipping over the undulant, cottony blanket. It raced along with them.

The pilot said, "That is our condensation trail, a cloud in itself, casting its shadow on another cloud."

After a silence, he added, "You are seeing the ethereal projecting the intangible on the ephemeral. You are privileged. Enjoy."

John gaped at the thin, leaping, relentless spear in pursuit below. Perhaps he had evidence as insubstantial as this obscure, fluctuating line. His evidence, itself an image in motion, was also conjured. Angry with the lyrical pilot for causing doubts to resurface, John set his jaw and accepted the phantasms of truth to be truth itself. Why not believe the unbelievable when it gave him such huge leverage with the White House? The answer convinced him that the unbelievable was really happening. He hugged the disk strapped under his shirt, and he planned how to use it in his next ultimatum.

─────────────── 98 ───────────────

Yuri played Andrei as carefully as a trout on a weak line. His strategy was designed to tighten Andrei into an intense desire to break through to his ground controllers.

"The more he wants it, the more he'll accept a breakthrough without questions. He'll be achieving *his* goal, not ours."

Yuri contrived four attempts at communication, deliberately mixing static, clarity, confusion, failure and the hope for yet another try in another half hour. On the fifth try, Julian began shouting, "Get the General! I'm getting the frequency! I hear him! It's Borodin, for sure. I know how he sounds."

A stern authority link was established. A crisp, commanding voice, that of "General Anton Tyutchev" empowered Andrei to answer questions, but to ask none.

"Congratulations, Comrade. Your courage has insured your survival. From now on, your cooperation will ensure your rescue. Communication is difficult, and we may be cut off again at any time. You will therefore provide me with information as rapidly as possible. Get your mission log from the capsule and bring it to where you are now."

In the next hour, Andrei silently positioned each page of the log before the camera lens. Houston made hard copy photos from the screens and sent them to Washington. Energetic interpreters provided Yuri with English versions of each page. The story emerged. Yuri drew from the log the hard facts of being marooned, of isolation without resources or hope, and, finally, resignation. He gathered the story tenderly, verifying the historical event of the first humans stranded in space.

Julian, as "The General," provided Andrei with a compression of events, explanation, and instruction designed to be overwhelming. Andrei heard a version of history, of his location, and of his forthcoming duties. He knew now that years had passed since he had gassed his capsule and pressed the hypodermic needle into his arm. This accounted for some of the new names and voices from ground control. Desperately, he broke in, "What year is it?"

Prepared for this, Julian sighed heavily, "Ah, comrade, I would trade places with you. How I would love to do that! You will return to us young and famous. During your absence, I have aged." Another sigh. Then, abruptly, sternly, "Major, do not remind me of my age again! You will learn what you need to know upon your return. Pay attention to your briefing!"

Andrei was told of an American offer to rescue his spacecraft. He discovered that the United States had the only vehicle in existence that could do the job. He learned of the injury to the American crewman, and of damage to their shuttle. "These brave men, sent to rescue you, are now themselves stuck in orbit," said General Tyutchev. "You will do all in your power to help them repair their ship and get all of you back to earth and home. Is that understood?" Andrei fairly shouted agreement. Duty was duty at any time, he reasoned, but now it was also the key to a thousand questions, to rescue, to a homecoming, and to fame.

"Close the safety latch on your gun and stick it in your pocket! You must not look threatening or hostile to the American crew."

He was told to go to the lower window as his first introduction to the Americans. Adam cleared away the shade and moved out of sight. Helpless Tim was visible. The General explained Tim's battering by the heat shield.

"I assign you to care for this man," said the General. "It will allow the commander to focus on repairs to the ship. This man's injuries may require that his metabolism be suspended until you land and he can get professional medical care. Do you have any hibernation fluid left over to administer to him?" Andrei said yes.

Adam was introduced. Andrei went to the upper windows for this meeting and peered in. Behind the smiling commander he saw illuminated panels of instruments and controls. In the ruptured Russian that Tim had joked about, Adam said his halting piece. "Welcome, Andrei, to my ship. I wish to show it to you."

Andrei was awed. This man from the future would teach him this machine from the future. It was incredible.

"I am honored," he said, in heavily accented English of a halting, but conversational quality.

"Perhaps we should start with our first meal together," Adam said. "I will let you in now."

Andrei suddenly realized he had a greater need. The first abdominal rumblings from his earlier gymnastics had accelerated toward pain.

"Commander MacGregor," he said, "I must very soon move my bowels."

Adam replied, "You can do that in here. While I am opening the air lock, you may wish to put your gun back in your spacecraft. For safety, we do not have weapons aboard."

Andrei did not head for his capsule. He hesitated. Yuri, watching and listening, absorbed this first potential for trouble and whispered into Julian's ear, "An order! Reassure him!"

At once, the General's voice broke in, "Major Borodin! You have been given a choice. Use it. You are in a strange new situation. Retain your gun if you wish. When you feel more at ease, put the damned thing away. It has no place on a spacecraft. Now, go to the toilet. Report to me as soon as you are finished. You are to begin an orientation on how to help this ship to land. You will take your instructions from the Americans. Do you understand?"

"Yes, Comrade General."

99

The Ambassador's garage door rose and the motorcycle moved out fast with Peter and Byron aboard. Even faster, a zoom lens camera in a nearby high rise window got their picture. The FBI had missed this visitor on his way into the Taksis home, but now they had a photo. The clandestine efforts that marked his entry also marked him as important.

Unfortunately, their helicopter had landed to refuel. Alerted by radio, a south-position cyclist swung in to track them. Peter wove through traffic, heading for the heart of the city. He controlled speed cleverly, making himself the last to cross intersections as the light changed. Then, relying on diplomatic immunity to dismiss a brutal traffic fine, he went two blocks against one-way traffic. At Metro Central, Byron slipped off and vanished into the multi-layered subway crossroads.

Spotting the solo rider, the pursuit biker radioed an assumption that the passenger was taking the subway back to Dulles Airport. A fax machine in airport security began stuttering out Byron's picture. Experienced watchers, armed with the photos, took position.

An hour later, the embassy chauffeur entered the garage. The door rose leisurely. The limousine, exuding privacy and power, flowed to the front entrance and parked. The chauffeur opened the rear door and stood, waiting. Ambassador Taksis emerged, halted on the portico to talk with two men, bade them good-bye and made for the limousine. Entering the dim, quiet comfort behind the smoked glass, he placed his feet carefully to avoid stepping on Byron Desault. The limousine headed into the city. No one followed as Taksis headed for a known appointment at the State Department.

The limousine detoured. It went to Metro Central and stopped. Byron stepped out, trotted swiftly down the escalator, and zipped through the turnstile, courtesy of a supplied fare card. He surfaced in Maryland. Peter had booked him on a flight from Baltimore. Byron's double, meanwhile, had exited the subway at DuPont Circle to improve his French at an import movie. Byron had neatly outmaneuvered the security professionals in the nation's capital. He would not be so fortunate with an amateur in the provinces.

100

Prowling and thinking, Susan Hoffen still smarted from her group's teleconference tongue lashing by Frank Cole for failure of Houston security to detect and stop espionage. Apparently, someone had made a bootleg video of events in Mission Control and smuggled it out to a reporter. Perhaps it was done for money, perhaps to harm Nastran. Whatever the motive, Cole wanted no more leaks.

Susan blamed herself. She had not been swift enough to capture the man who used the hallway pay phone to call an outside contact. She continued furious at herself for not being able to match the caller's face to a voice she knew. Nearing fifty-five, she worried that short-term memory was declining with age. Her teen-aged son showed that the young aren't sensitive to declines in capability.

"Mom, don't worry, it could be an asset sometimes."

"Oh, sure. Like when!?"

"Well, like extra fun at Easter. You could hide your own Easter eggs." She smiled at the image and then shuddered at the prospect.

Susan believed the illicit video had been sent by the pay phone caller she'd overheard, but she knew instinctively that he had not been talking to a reporter. There would have been cooperation. Reporters knew the importance of getting the facts and not prejudging. No, she realized, the caller had been shouting at a transmitter of information, not a user. And that transmitter didn't want to be bothered with the "science fiction" that the screaming caller denied. Russian astronauts arising from the dead in space, for God's sake! The caller had offered headlines for the *Universal Inquirer,* and nothing more. The whole thing on videotape, he had said! Who could believe it? No wonder the man's contact was skeptical and implied drunkenness. But now it no longer seemed like science fiction. Frank Cole's anger gave credence to something bizarre.

Susan did not know about a second violator. She focused on finding a man who could leave a workstation in the fifth hour of an eight-hour shift and wander to a pay phone. He needed access to Mission Control, to communications links with the shuttle, to TV recording capability, and to privacy in which to make his video copy. Susan's persistent, unorthodox sleuthing yielded four names. One, a female, was obviously not involved. Or was she? Had she made the video and relayed it to the hysterical phone caller? Susan decided to concentrate on the men, and she began with Byron

Desault's locker, the first of four she would open and inspect. His schedule said he would arrive to start his shift in four hours. She picked his lock in the empty room.

Byron returned from Washington with hours to spare. He decided to report in early, get into his uniform, and gather what gossip he could in the cafeteria. Unobtrusive by nature and practice, he arrived at his locker silently. Susan, busy reading a crypto message that should have been destroyed, was feeling excitement and achievement when she also felt a violent arm circle her neck, ram her chin up and clamp off her breathing. She couldn't match the power that pinned her. She stamped hard to crush his instep and got him. He winced and swore. Tall, he spread his legs wide, making her other strikes fall short in a waste of fading energy.

She drew her gun from its holster on the Sam Browne belt, a Texas affectation. He made no effort to stop her, knowing that the guards carried guns for appearance only and that they often got kidded about their visibly empty revolvers. Byron had looked at her gun, thinking to use it as a club to break her head before he stored her body temporarily atop the overhead utility pipes. He felt the muzzle go against his leg. He heard the futile clicking as she pulled the trigger and the hammer fell on empty chambers. He shifted, thinking she would next try to swing it back and club his genitals. She didn't.

Frank Cole's scalding teleconference had tightened security seriously during Byron's absence. Management now allowed loaded guns as self-defense for the guards in their increased probing and patrols. However, to avoid alarm among employees, the new policy dictated no change in appearance and applied it with two rules. The first rule made one bullet the limit in a loaded gun. The second rule specified its chamber location. That insured non-visibility, but also insured that firing off a real bullet had to be a contemplated, deliberate act. The bullet's designated position was chamber One, in line with the barrel, and not evident.

Susan desperately plodded on in the last act of her life. In the silence of the locker room, with his ear at her mouth, Byron heard her harsh expulsions and the tiny screeches of throttled air. He heard the gun clicks go on, at longer intervals, as his victim's strength died. The sixth click never sounded. Instead, there was a great boom and a crush of pain as his tibia top and kneecap flew off in splintery clumps of sodden scarlet.

—————————————— **101** ——————————————

Adam started Andrei's education with the waste collection system. Held by foot restraints and seat belt, Andrei achieved what he gleefully described as "a delightful defecation."

Cooper said aside to Benson, "I was expecting 70-year old radioactive rocks."

Benson, studying him, concluded that Cooper had internalized the miraculous, unbelievable events, and gotten back to normal faster than anyone present. Quick adjustment to extraordinary events seemed routine among highly technical people. Cooper had apparently already accepted as fact a Soviet achievement of suspended animation. With the astonishment over, he simply waited for a scientific explanation of the miracle.

To Andrei, multiple miracles lay all about, in a ship beyond belief. For the moment, however, totally fascinated by the toilet, he bedeviled Adam for information on its workings. He got an engineering description of how the sealed system's airflow carried solid waste to storage for later analysis in earth labs. "We open the chamber to space," said Adam, "and get a vacuum-dried product to take home. Now, let's move on. We have much to cover."

Yuri commented to Julian about Andrei's sustained interest in "going potty" but couldn't assign it a simple psychological meaning because it was so entwined in technical interest. "This guy isn't easy to get to know," he told Julian. "He's like a kid one minute, plain and likeable, but complex and ominous the next."

Julian asked, "Any pathology?"

Yuri pondered. "Yeah, I think we're looking at a paranoia that's simultaneously aggressive and manipulable. Fortunately the brilliant team of you and me is doing the manipulating. But we'll have to watch our step. At root, the guy is unpredictable, and he could be dangerous, even unarmed. As soon as we dare, I want that gun locked away."

Adam intended to give Andrei a swift explanation of all major items, but Andrei's probing inquiries threatened to bog down the process. "Major, I am very, very tired," Adam finally said. "Make notes of your questions and hold them for later. We'll eventually go over everything many, many more times, especially flight skills. You and I may have to land this thing as a team. We're damaged and we don't really know how badly." Adam picked up the pace, turning the briefing into a familiarization tour. At its end, he said, "Now, let's look at the damage the heat shield did."

In the payload bay, Adam looked at the Soviet capsule and reflected on Andrei's consistent disinterest and silence about the woman crewmember. Realizing that Andrei might be full of pain or guilt at her loss, Adam kept silent. Perhaps, he reasoned, it hurts so much that he's driven the memory from his mind; or maybe his memory was damaged by radiation during the decades in orbit. Resolving not to think about it, Adam bent to his task. Together, they moved the heat shield aside, anchored it anew, and cleared away the shuttle's insulation. They found a severed fiber optics cable bundle, designed to carry signals to the elevon. This control surface acts like a combination of elevator and aileron, regulating pitch and roll when the shuttle reenters the atmosphere and begins to fly as an aircraft.

Adam wished now for the simplicity and reliability of the primitive, direct, rod and cable connections of ancient airplanes. Space and airline flight had long since graduated to "fly by wire" systems. He couldn't splice the cable's hair-like fibers, so repair was impossible up here.

Adam described the trouble to Houston. "I've still got the backup control. I can fly home on that."

Hemming didn't hesitate. "Negative," he said. "The backup is now primary and has no alternate for failure in reentry. I don't want you starting home crippled unless the flight surgeon wants Tim down at once."

Dr. Nanterre opted for flight safety and the continued healing of Tim in neutral gravity. Hemming ordered a stay in orbit to make repairs while Adam and Andrei continued to care for Tim. He promised the earliest possible flight for delivering the replacement part.

"You've got a month of supplies," he told Adam, "but we should have a supply flight to you in about a week. Now, why don't you get some rest? Give Andrei a nose cone headset so we and he and Baikonur can talk without keeping you awake. OK with you, Andrei? Or do you want to sleep, too?"

"I am too excited to sleep!" He wanted very much to talk, learn and understand. Adam, taking his cues from Houston, played the host. He didn't know how to get the sleep he needed unless he showed as much trust in Andrei as Houston did. *I don't want a stranger with a gun on my ship!*

But Houston was continuing its silence on that subject. Exhausted, Adam teetered between Houston's judgment and his own natural caution. He'd been ordered to get some sleep. If he fought sleep, it would happen anyway; and when he finally did doze off, he'd have the same situation that worried him.

As a caution, he split communications. Andrei would speak on AG-2, an air to ground channel, while Adam kept AG-1. That would let Houston proceed with Andrei's orientation while still able to wake up Adam. He clipped the little radio to his clothes and set the switch position to transmit and receive. He smiled tiredly on realizing that he would transmit snores.

Andrei watched Adam's preparations for bed, admiring the Spartan plainness of the sleep system. Adam entered a bag floating from a bulkhead. He donned the cap and nose cone for communicating, put on a sleeping mask, pulled up the internal tab on the full-length zipper, mumbled goodnight, and promptly started snoring. Andrei responded to Adam's goodnight and then anxiously prepared to don the nose cone communications helmet. His mind panted for the answers to some desperate questions.

Why did I survive and my partner did not? Will I stay alive? How old am I? Where will the Americans take me? How did my country and America come to such comradeship and cooperation? His head buzzed with the questions that General Tyutchev had ordered him to withhold.

He never donned the helmet. On raising it to his head, he looked up. Above him hung the roof windows of the flight deck. What he saw outside froze him into a tingling, quivering mass of patriotism, pride, and awe. A great ship of space sat there. Massive. Unmoving. Emblazoned with the red star of his country. Beneath the name "Eagle," he saw windows from which two men in space suits watched him. They took off their helmets and smiled. He hardly breathed as the mutual staring dragged on. The men conferred with each other, repeatedly looking at him and then down at something the size of a poster board one held in his lap. One man smiled. He reversed the poster board and held it up on display. Andrei gasped. He was looking at a large picture of his own face. Smiling again, both men pointed to him, to the picture, and back to him, nodding in affirmation of the identity check. The second man's hands began to move gracefully. Andrei's eyes began to mist as they spoke to him slowly in the sign language he had been taught so long ago.

"Comrade Major Borodin! We are honored to meet such a great space pioneer. And we are privileged: we have been chosen to help you escape from the Americans."

General Fyodor Lubinin's men had arrived.

102

Hemming kept calling Andrei to respond. He couldn't be heard because Andrei had not donned his helmet. Hemming turned to the TV monitor and saw the helmet drifting lazily, moved by random air currents. He also saw Andrei. The cosmonaut, a study in concentration, made bizarre motions. He alternated between periods of immobility and intricate hand movements, always staring intently at the roof windows. At times, his moves turned swift and jerky, as with irate gestures. When Hemming switched to zoom cameras that could show Andrei's features, the coming and going of anger was obvious. He did not know that Andrei stood deep in debate with the cosmonauts. At one point, Andrei mimicked sleep. Then he drew his revolver and waved it toward the ceiling. He broke the weapon and spun the cylinder so that the bullets showed in the chambers. He emptied the bullets into his palm and held the open hand toward the ceiling. He reloaded and pocketed the gun. He patted the pocket, pointed to his chest, and nodded his head determinedly. Yuri began to think that Andrei was telling someone that he had the means to take care of himself, that he was in charge.

Breaking into the murmurs of concern and puzzlement in Tenement One, Yuri said, "The guy's doing dumb show! He's acting to an audience."

Then, to Houston he yelled, "Hemming! Is he facing into one of your cameras? Play acting, maybe? "

Hemming replied, "He's simply facing the roof windows."

"Then he believes he has someone to talk with outside that window." Yuri groaned within, imagining a hallucination mingled with megalomania, and worrying about the power and control implications of the gun display.

The President spoke, "Tell us more, Dr. Beletsky." Yuri plunged on, "I believe we're watching a man acting out an intense imaginary conversation. Andrei has just asked a question, and in a very disputatious manner. He wants somebody to tell him why an American commander would trust him enough to go to sleep and leave him armed and free to move about."

Yuri had it right. Andrei didn't buy the cosmonauts' story. The conversational pantomime went on. Andrei, who became more voluble as old skills returned, signed non-stop for minutes at a stretch. In time, his energy flagged as he tried to cope with two people signaling to him. Enduring, they answered all his questions, some for a second and third time. Their persistence wore at him. Slowly, he began to accept their hijacking tale. *A renewed Cold War!*

His years of Soviet indoctrination undid him. He yielded to their authority, arguments, and blandishments. His heart gave up the prospect of trust and cooperation, and his ego abandoned thoughts of flying home in the incredible shuttle. Substitution began; instead, he reasoned, he would go home in a proud vessel of his own country's fleet. And he would do it with a captured American crew. Ancient drums and bugle calls began to sound in his brain. Watching carefully, he received instructions on what to do. He repeated some, feeding them back in a mixture of playacting, mime, and his ancient dactylology.

Yuri suddenly shouted, "Hemming, that guy's talking about opening the bay doors to let somebody in! He seems to be hallucinating. If he tries it, can you stop it?"

Flat calm, Hemming said, "No. And I hope he doesn't try. The air lock doors are open. All air will leave the cabin as well as the bay. This guy may be sleepwalking some weird dream. That could get dangerous. I'd better wake up Adam."

Andrei astounded them by two actions that even Yuri had not been able to decipher from the pantomime. He went swiftly to the nearest audio terminal unit and turned off the system. These units made crew intercommunications possible, receiving and relaying talk by wire or radio from the voice activated microphones. Houston could no longer give Adam a wake up call. Then, Andrei approached Adam with a spare sleeping bag. He unhooked the lower snub line of Adam's bag, slid on the new bag, zipped its full length shut, and smiled at the sight of Adam tightly ensconced in a bag within a bag, with the outer bag zipped shut behind his head. Andrei locked the zipper shut with wire from a tool kit. He punctured the bag's edge, threaded wire through it and the zipper tab, and twisted the sturdy wire ends together with pliers. Adam stirred restlessly, mumbled unrecognizable thoughts, and slept on, sealed in. Andrei signed to the cosmonauts that he had neutralized the commander in the equivalent of a two-layered, full-length straitjacket.

103

John Dough penetrated the curtain of press silence easily. He did not need to invoke an ultimatum; his leverage was too great. No one dared deny him access to the unfolding facts, once they saw his video of the action aboard Olympia. John not only had the story's key elements, but he could broadcast video copies if the White House did not cooperate.

John agreed to withhold broadcast in the interests of national security and astronaut safety. That earned him a full briefing from Frank Cole and Ron Engle. They showed him additional video and answered his questions. They took him into Tenement One. The President nodded him a welcome. Ron Engle sat beside Dough and whispered commentary as Andrei bagged the shuttle commander.

Art Cooper came back into the room, pale and hesitant, without his normal insouciance. An amalgam of open shame and fury, he went directly to the President and handed him two sheets of printout.

"Mr. President," he said, clearing repeated chokes, "the first sheet lay undelivered, at a level of my own command, for hours. We do not yet know why. I have no excuses, Sir."

It said that a Russian spacecraft, apparently crewed, had been launched into Olympia's current orbit. The second sheet announced that the same vessel had rendezvoused with Olympia.

"When the second message came in, it sent us looking for the first. We found the first had been filed away in error," said Cooper, in confessional embarrassment. His team had been victimized by an ancient law of paper shuffling: *The crucial memorandum will be snared in the out basket by the paperclip of the overlying correspondence and go to file.*

The President spoke to Mission Control, describing Cooper's delayed intelligence on the arrival of cosmonauts. Finally, he said, "This may explain Major Borodin's behavior. Is there any way to see what's outside, near the shuttle?"

Hemming responded, "Only if the payload bay doors are open, Mr. President, and if the visitors happen to be in line of sight of the cameras."

Yuri broke in, "Ken, it's clear now that Andrei was actually having a hand signal conversation through the roof window with visitors. I believe he has received orders to take over the shuttle and let them in. Tying up the commander was the first step."

The President said, "It seems so. Now, Ken, what are their options?" Everyone watched Hemming, large on the split screen. He was writing on a clip pad. The screen's other half showed Andrei searching through instruction manuals, probably for the bay doors' instructions.

Ken spoke. "First option. If Andrei succeeds in opening the cargo doors without first closing the air lock, the Russians will come aboard and find everyone dead of anoxia. They will be able to take corpses to their craft and go home. They will be able to acquire all the remaining fluid used for suspended animation. They will not be able to take the Falcon vessel; it's too big.

"Second option. If Andrei knew how to let them in safely, the cosmonauts could put everyone in space suits and effect a rescue. All would return to earth alive in the Russian ship. Here, too, they would get the remaining fluid."

"Thank you. Our side doesn't have much choice, does it?" The President was silent in several moments of agonized thought. Then the nobler part of his nature showed, although the Communists would have called it pragmatism. "I believe we're obliged to save lives. You have my permission to instruct Major Borodin on how to open the cargo bay doors properly for rescue to occur."

His great gamble was over. The Kremlin had won. And they had won big, in a game whose original prize and purpose now looked insignificant. He visualized the propaganda. Negative headlines flashed in his mind:

"Russian scientists achieve suspended animation! Cosmonaut returns from decades of sleep! American hijacking attempt foiled! Hijackers captured!"

Finally, a positive headline dawned on him: "Tim reaches earth and proper medical care." It made him feel better while bitter.

Ken's voice reestablished reality, "I wish I could follow your orders, Mr. President, but Andrei cannot hear me, nor was he instructed on receiving computer messages. I will send a fax message. However, he probably won't hear it coming in on a laser printer. We'll just have to hope he passes nearby and sees it. Otherwise, I have no way to communicate with him. We must simply hope he does things right."

104

Cooper, intent on redeeming himself, broached an idea to Benson. He got two responses, one objective and one political.

"Art," said Benson, "your idea seems to be the only hope we have left. And you know how this President hates to lose. Go tell him. If it works, maybe you'll get to keep your job."

"Let's hope so. The only other job I'm trained to do is speech therapy for parrots."

He moved off and found Sisco. "Mr. President," he said, "we still have communication to Tim Carver. Why don't we talk to him and see if . . . ?"

The President, grasping the idea at once, gripped his arm in a quick, quelling gesture, stopping him in mid sentence. Enthused, Sisco turned and shouted at the screens, "Hemming! Put the flight surgeon on at once!"

Sisco asked for, and got, a clinical summary of Tim's treatment. Dr. Nanterre equivocated in his evaluation of Tim's condition.

"All vital signs have improved. If I saw those readings without any background, I would not know the patient had been injured. However, I am getting no responses from him, except for an occasional yes when I ask if he hears me. No, I cannot tell you if he can understand what's said to him. For hours I have been talking *at* him, meaning not *with* him. I've played him tapes of the mission, over and over, in hopes of stirring embedded memories of purpose and identity. Everything that's happened has been compressed and we've played selections into his earphones repeatedly. We can tell that he sleeps a lot, but when he's not asleep, we believe he's alert."

"Can you hook things up so that I can speak directly to him?"

Hemming and Nanterre agreed that it could and should be done. The technicians arranged the link.

"Mr. President, your line is ready."

"Never mind, Ken. It's too late. He's no longer on the line. Look at your screen."

---------------------------------- 105 ----------------------------------

After days of hanging in coma, Tim awoke. In a groggy awareness, feigning stupor, he fought to reconstruct memory and the ability to think.

I am one damned mess, whoever I am.

His struggle turned a corner of understanding in a subtle switchover. One minute he needed training wheels and the next he didn't. His instincts told him not to let it show. Shrewdly, he let time pass to gain strength and information. He had listened for days, in torpor, to the flight surgeon, live or on tape, iterating identity and striving to bring him back to awareness and will.

Nanterre's soothing voice had told him repeatedly of developments almost beyond belief. However, Tim accepted the outrageous idea of suspended animation because the living proof stood beside him on Olympia. He could not accept the idea of an American vessel under the control of foreign forces.

He feigned sleep, but slyly watched Andrei come and go. Andrei had been nurturing him, and Tim dimly knew this. Now, Andrei squeezed water for him and Tim swallowed, eyes slit, face slack. He saw Andrei's gun bulging from a pocket. It meant trouble. This man from the past, from a hostile society, was either breaking the rules or he was making the rules. Tim intended to find out.

He saw Andrei wandering about, referring to instruction manuals and reading nameplates on controls. The shuttle felt alien, eerily quiet after days of voices. Now and then machinery started up, did its work, and subsided. Tim shammed sleep as Andrei paused near him for several minutes, apparently listening to the regular breathing. Shortly after, Tim heard the clanging of someone in clumsy passage through the air lock. That couldn't be Adam; he could slip through like an eel. Andrei must have bumped his way into the cargo bay. Warily, Tim arched until he could see out the window. He watched.

Andrei went to Falcon and took the uncomfortable bulk of the revolver from his pocket. He tucked it into a fold on the empty seat. He looked long and longingly at his crewmate. The fluid had not worked for her. Perhaps the injection dose had been enough to kill her. His heart quickened with a new possibility. Perhaps their equal injections had been just right for his greater bulk. Maybe, even though her dose had been too much, it wasn't enough to kill. Maybe her awakening was merely delayed. He choked a moan of hope and moved on to his new job of learning about the bay doors. He started to study the mechanisms under the insulation blankets.

Tim, relying on Andrei's concentration, left his prison of rope hyperbola. He dimly recalled struggling earlier to get free. What had been the problem? It was simple now. He merely slid out of his shorts and left them strung on the lines. Nude, he moved like a tropical island diver, floating in a spacecraft flooded by the clearest sea. A glance through the bay window confirmed Andrei's preoccupation with the manuals. Rapidly, Tim headed for the toilet. The whispering entreaties of nature had turned to roaring commands. He obeyed. Afterwards, he found Adam in a bag cocoon. *An enemy has the shuttle!* Tim went looking for the pliers, intent on freeing his trussed commander. A reflection from above made him look up. He saw Eagle and its people. The cosmonauts gawked at his nakedness, at a creature from Eden, a multi-millennial jumper to this high tech setting. Tim gaped back, beginning to understand. The cosmonauts already understood. They had only one way to warn Andrei. The Eagle pilot gently rammed his ship into Olympia.

Tim grasped the purpose. Andrei would rush back. Tim could no longer feign coma. Andrei would be told about him. Andrei might arrive armed, but even unarmed he'd be dangerous. Tim felt too weak to grapple. He had one prospect. It meant a race. He zoomed to the air lock and slammed the inner door just before Andrei arrived. They did not see each other. Tim flew to the flight deck window and saw Andrei moving away, pulling headlong over the insulation, headed for Falcon, headed for the gun. He had to be stopped. Tim rapped rapidly on the window with his Naval Academy ring. *Finally useful,* he thought. Andrei slowed and looked back. The sight of Tim stunned and stopped him. Tim, looking out the window, and smiling his friendliest, beckoned Andrei back. All the while, he threw switches and took controls off safety locks.

Andrei ignored the beckoning invitation. As he turned again for Falcon, he flinched from three loud, sharp, metallic, clacking sounds behind him. He turned and saw several holding clamps clattering loosely at the base of a bulky mass. He heard hissing bursts of gas. Mesmerized, he watched the bulk rise and begin to fly. It lifted delicately from its anchoring base and hovered in midbay for an instant. Then it glided swiftly down the center, apparently to pass him. He sensed the mass of the thing and shrank to let it pass, marveling at its maneuverability. It stopped abruptly, alongside him. Stunned and startled by the noises and braked momentum, Andrei hovered apprehensively.

He could see ice forming on the thrusters' exhaust and he rightly assumed it used liquid air. Suddenly, in a move he could not evade, the thing shot laterally and slowed, colliding with him gently, then relentlessly pressing him toward the starboard wall. It drove him into the insulation, pinning him firmly, spread-eagled. Tim was grateful he had not left the Lead Ass Dummy behind in orbit. The maxim came again: *"Waste not, want not."*

106

A new spacecraft darted aloft, trailing smoke, flame, and thunder. Plunging into low-lying clouds, it flash-illuminated their undersides and vanished as a fading glow. Launched from the Kagoshima Space Center on the island of Kyushu, it was owned by Asahi Shimbun, the Japanese news colossus. Like John Dough, the Japanese news gatherers had grown impatient with Russian and American silence and deception. They, too, had decided to break through the secrecy.

Following its first satellite launch in 1970, the Japanese space program was financially starved and politically ignored for years. Some of its scarce budget went to buy off local fishermen who said the roar of rockets annoyed their prey and reduced their catch. The apologetic rocketeers had to limit launches to a 45-day period in winter and another in summer, skirting the fishing seasons. Slowly, however, the space muscle grew. Japan sent a pair of probes to Halley's Comet in 1986, when the mighty Americans could not afford the trip. In 1990, with its Muses-A spacecraft, it became the third nation to orbit the moon.

The Japanese, smelling profits, entered space business in a big way. They sold launch services, manufactured communications satellites, leased room on their spacecraft to other countries, and built world-class space instruments. In orbiting laboratories, they manufactured new products that captured the major share of the global market for space-derived materials such as metals, ceramics, and pharmaceuticals. They also created a unique satellite to do investigative journalism. Called Peeker One, it was inspired by Asahi Shimbun's frustration with early Communist behavior.

In the 1980's, the USSR tried to hide its Chernobyl nuclear power plant catastrophe that contaminated large areas of Russia and threatened Europe. Explicit pictures from defense satellites disproved Soviet lies about the disaster's location and scope. The media, however, had to buy grosser images from America's *Landsat* and France's *Spot* spacecraft. Broadcasters featured the photos in energy-equated color, explained by experts. The facts forced the Kremlin to tell the truth about the catastrophe.

The world media could no longer tolerate that only national governments had the power to peer deeply into closed societies and pry out hidden information. They concluded that recent advances in technology gave them the muscle to create an alternative. Media empires in major countries decided to buy and fly their own quick-launch, remotely controlled observation satellites. Only the Japanese followed through, creating Peeker One.

Japanese scientists believed the hulk in the sky to be the external tank of the American shuttle as it might look after an explosion. Japanese media sent Peeker One to find out. They, too, had noticed that one side of the hulk always faced earth. They, too, speculated on the whereabouts of the shuttle itself. They wondered if the smooth, symmetrical projections past the ragged outline of the blown-out tank might be parts of the still-attached shuttle.

As General Lubinin's men had done, Peeker One floated in from behind and above, unseen. This time, however, the North American Perimeter Command had tracked it to rendezvous. So did the Kremlin, without knowing its purpose. Washington however, did know, informed by sources that worked with Japanese space companies. President Sisco realized that the little satellite would blow his cover. He begged the Japanese Prime Minister to stop Asahi Shimbun from doing a broadcast until it could coincide with an American press conference. The newspaper refused its government's request, saying that the public would see images within the hour but warned that it would be sooner if the government tried to stop the broadcast.

An ambivalent Sisco spoke to the Secretary of State. "Arnold, I don't know whether to be pleased or upset. I'm pleased because Tim has neutralized Major Borodin, so now we stand a chance of getting Falcon down here. Also, we'll probably get the needed time for repairs because I don't think the Communists will attack while the Japanese media is watching and broadcasting. On the other hand, I'm upset because we now have to hold a premature press conference. Given this Peeker One quirk, I have no alternative. So, I've decided to tell the public everything that's happened, the entire business, unbelievable as it has become."

He turned to the task team. "Listen up, people! It's time to earn your money. Arnold, I want you to chair preparation of the press statement. Do this by the book. Pull a team together. Use my conference room. Don't allow any leaks! I want a consensus statement in three hours."

To the press secretary, he said, "Greg, schedule a press conference and national broadcast for 9:00 tonight, local time. I want to hit both coasts at once. I will make a statement but will not take questions."

———————————————— 107 ————————————————

Tim watched Andrei's struggles for a while. He learned, quickly, what a strong and clever opponent he confronted, as Andrei finally stopped thrashing, feigned a faint, and hung limp. Tim relaxed the jet thruster to conserve fuel. Andrei, with a sudden surge, his back buried deep in insulation, pushed against the LAD in the equivalent of a weightlifter's bench press. Triceps bulging, he overcame both the LAD's enormous inertia and the diminished, fizzing jet that Tim had set to keep him pinned. Andrei suddenly stopped pressing and, in the gap he'd created, scrambled sideways to freedom. Tim, a virtuoso of controls, would, at his best, have played Andrei like a hooked trout. In his impeded condition, he barely recaptured his quarry. Yet his solution was swift and automatic: he shifted maintenance jets to press the mass continuously against the wall of insulation and rolled the LAD to overtake and pin Andrei again. This time, he kept a heavy jet pressure, depressing the major into insulation.

Tim floated swiftly through the air lock, took rope from the toolbox, and moved to tie up Andrei. He began a time-and-supply race, needing to be done before the LAD'S air pressure fell too low to keep his prey pinned. Repeatedly, Tim tried to lasso Andrei's powerful arms. On one attempt, Andrei grabbed the rope and yanked. Tim, holding the rope loops too short around thumb crotch and left elbow, flew toward the clutching hand. He narrowly escaped being seized. In his weakened condition, he dared not let that happen. Driven by events, confusion, and fear, Andrei had the power and speed of the crazed. An acrid tide of sweat flooded his struggling body. The best Tim could do he did; he corralled Andrei's ankles and drew them together for a tight tie. It left him weary.

Tim reflected. He *had* to succeed, with the fate of Olympia and the mission at stake, but he felt his strength fading. Andrei's throttled anger and furious eyes foretold what would happen if he broke loose. Tim went to Falcon to remove the gun. He didn't want it available if the major suddenly escaped again. Then too he might need it for protection. He might have to wound Andrei or kill him; and there was no other weapon. As he seized the revolver, he saw the woman for the first time. He'd heard about her. He stared. Her lidded gaze watched eternity. He felt obscene, flying about naked before this waxen female. Anxious now about the LAD's diminishing air pressure and his own weakening condition, he hit upon a plan. He glided into the crew cabin, stuffed the gun and two items he needed into a medical ditty bag, and went back to Andrei.

"I heard you, so I know you speak English," he said. "I don't want to harm you, so do as I say." He tossed Andrei the middle of the rope. "Put your wrists together and wind this rope around them five times." Andrei spat at him, fury amplified by the memory of being made the fool by this man whose injuries he had tended, this faker he had thought hurt and ill.

"I take no orders from you," he roared.

I'd better put this guy away right now. Tim reached for his apparatus. Hovering half hidden behind the LAD, he took a camera from the ditty bag and set it for automatic repeat. With a swift motion, he lifted it from behind the LAD and triggered the shutter as he clamped his eyes shut. Andrei went blind momentarily from the sudden, brilliant and repetitive flashes. Unseen, Tim dropped below the LAD, avoiding the icy discharge from the pinning jet. From the ditty bag, he took a factory-filled syringe. He stuck the needle deep into Andrei's thigh and pressed the plunger all the way. Slowly, Andrei's kicking stopped. Tim had no idea how long the sedative would last. He hadn't taken time to read the medical instructions, but he knew at least that he hadn't given a lethal dose.

He sped to the cabin and shut off the LAD's jets. Returning, he pinioned Andrei. He tied the man's wrists, with the arms bent up behind. Tim led the rope around Andrei's neck in a noose. If Andrei tried to lower his arms, the loop would start to choke him. Tim drifted him to Falcon, positioned him athwart the door seat, feet protruding, and tied him down. To conserve the LAD's fuel, he moved it manually back to its base, using a few snubbed controlling ropes, and he locked it down again. Then he went to gather the drifting and dispersed manuals and drawings that Andrei had abandoned when the cosmonauts nudged Eagle into Olympia. He was unfocused, easily distracted, and not thinking clearly. He should have gone to free Adam.

108

Adam awoke refreshed. Like Flight Chief Hemming, he could go without sleep for days and still perform well. He needed only the chance to nap a few hours, every so often. For him, sleeping in the space environment speeded rejuvenation. No mattress, waterbed or hammock on Earth could compare with the comfort of levitated sleep. He thought it could benefit the world's insomniacs.

"There's a market for it, Tim, if only we could package it!"

They had discussed how earth-bound expressions took on literal meanings in space. "Drifting off to sleep" was an apt term for snoozing in a satellite — where the sleeper needs a tether. "Sleeping like a baby" was a reality when the free-floating body, totally relaxed, tended toward a fetal curl.

Starting to stretch, Adam found his movements restricted. His sleeping bag enclosed him more cozily than ever. In fact, it felt confining. He looked down at the bag. It didn't belong to him. Slowly, he came to understand that he was in his own bag within another bag. Was Tim up and about, playing practical jokes? Perhaps he was fooling around to relax Andrei. *Had things calmed down that much?* Well, he'd go along with the gag. He certainly wouldn't bawl Tim out in front of a guest. But, of course, he couldn't just wait here until they came back to release him. Instead, he would get out of both bags quietly and go surprise them. He zipped his own open and reached ahead for the outer bag's inside zipper toggle. It was not there.

Adam shrugged out of his own bag and worked it down past his feet. Taking a little chafing at the neck, he turned himself within the second bag until he reversed and faced its zipper. He tried pulling it down. He felt and traced the wire, determining its purpose. He had been deliberately locked in. *Unacceptable!*

Immobilizing the commander, when an emergency could arise at any time, was irresponsible. He would give Tim a strong dressing-down for such a caper. He began flexing the wire, hoping to heat it to the point of fatigue and breakage. It did not yield, even though the heat burned his fingers. He stopped trying and started thinking. In a few minutes, he had the answer. These bags could be opened from either end of the zipper. Andrei had not seen the second tab. He had pulled one up tight and wired it shut. The other tab stayed at the bottom end of the bag. Adam, losing skin, swiveled and pulled his head through the bag's tightly wired top. His ears and nose bled from the forced passage, but he got totally inside the bag. He crouched, grasped the lower internal tab, and moved it upward. The bag zipped open. He slipped out.

109

Some of the silent watchers in Mission Control began shouting in alarm. Neither Tim nor Adam could hear their warnings in a ship still radio silent. Adam wondered about the silence. He wondered why Houston hadn't raised hell when they saw him being wired into the sleeping bag. Starting for the communications panel to check the switch settings, he diverted for a moment to look into the cargo bay. He stiffened in shock, immobile. A cry of warning choked in his throat, then burst forth. Tim heard the shout of alarm come through the air lock. He spun quickly, puzzled. The move saved him. The blow that would have broken his skull fell instead on his shoulder. Someone collided with him, body striking body, and head knocking head. Dazed, he grappled instinctively with his assailant. Somewhere, he heard a woman's staccato screaming, an unending siren of horror.

Andrei had arrived like an avenging projectile. Strands of cut rope hung from wrist and ankle. He had launched himself in silent fury from Falcon's door. But for Tim's reflex move, he'd have killed him quickly. Now he had to battle. Andrei did not want to shoot. A bullet could damage the vessel he planned to capture. Holding a large gun by the barrel, he swung the butt again and again at Tim's head. The weakened Tim, fighting for life, dodged repeatedly, and then used one hand to catch the gun arm by the wrist, stopping the blows.

Experienced at moving in weightlessness, Tim grasped Andrei's suit at the waist and pulled him forward. The incoming groin met Tim's outgoing knee. Andrei cried out, fighting groggily in a haze of pain. Tim's grip pulled Andrei downward while a fist of clenched thunder rose in an uppercut, snapping Andrei's head back. Tim tried for a kill, his only chance against the powerful cosmonaut. His free hand caught Andrei by the back of the neck and yanked. The incoming face met Tim's lowered, butting head. Bone crunched and blood flew. Barely conscious, nose broken, Andrei reached up, took the gun with his free hand, pressed it to Tim's head and fired. In a flash of light and pain Tim sagged, and his mind plunged through darkening strata to final black.

The deadly struggle, swift as a catfight, ended in a soaking red fumulus. Blood spurting from Tim sent him twisting and floating about, his face a florid mash of flesh and bone. Soaked with his own and Tim's gore, Andrei hovered, savage and unreasoning. He saw the woman in Falcon's hatch, gasping and sobbing and still screaming, "Nyet! Nyet!" This sight and its sound of criticism and disloyalty reverberated in his battered head. It broke his last link to rationality. Abruptly, she too became the enemy. Sighting wildly, he shot at her. She cried out, grasping her arm. Blood ran between her fingers. She swung Falcon's door and ducked behind it as a shield. She backed through the doorway and latched the hatch shut.

Adam, hurrying to Tim's rescue with a hammer, was struggling from the air lock when he saw Tim killed and Andrei shoot the screaming woman. In the stillness after the gunshots, Andrei heard Adam moving. Enraged beyond reason, he turned and fired at him. He missed. One bullet ricocheted off the air lock door. Another, against million to one odds, plowed through the port side insulation and struck a major fiber optics bundle, including the backup for elevon control.

Adam, retreating, locked the door and flew to the upper bay windows. Andrei spotted him and fired again, piercing a precise hole in the special glass.

He's mad, thought Adam. *God knows what damage these bullets are doing. I have to dump this maniac!*

In a cold rage, he threw the switch to activate the bay doors. He turned the rheostat to high-speed opening, and quickly taped the bullet hole as air began to whistle out.

Andrei heard an abrupt, booming noise as the emergency release vents in the cargo bay rocked open. That dropped most of the air pressure that would otherwise have flung and twisted the opening doors like cardboard. The sudden decompression made his skull push back against a bursting brain. He screamed from the pain between his ears.

The clamp bands withdrew, allowing the doors to open without damage. The bay's residual air rushed out of the rapidly widening crack of the great doors. Gasping and swelling, Andrei moved with the air as it became wind, accelerating into vacuum. Moisture welled up to join the sweat boiling off his skin. The flash evaporation savagely chilled his body toward its swift transition to an ice block fossil.

The gases boiling from his blood made him cry out in the agony of the bends. His cries rang unheard in the airless void. His torment was short lived in the few seconds of consciousness possible in total vacuum. Then it ended, and he swept into the mute vastness of space, colliding with Tim for a last time. In the glaring sunlight, his sodden uniform flared a brilliant, splotchy crimson, rapidly fading as the blood's oxygen vaporized. The Russian and American bodies, in gyre from the first air currents, slowly danced and pirouetted to eternity in the darkness of the cosmos. Receding from the cargo bay lights, they winked out, the nude Tim first.

——————————— **110** ———————————

Immediately upon arrival, Peeker One sent back images to Suzy Arai, the director of newscasting in Tokyo. This imaginative, but cautious, woman realized that either Olympia or Eagle might try to destroy Peeker One. A chess player, Suzy Arai decided to defend against this. Within the hour she set up a live feed to all domestic and international TV networks. Her technicians showed both spacecraft at once on a split screen. Neither one could move to launch an attack without being seen as committing an unprovoked, hostile action.

Her flight controller, Toyo Akiya, skillfully stayed away from line of sight through windows, keeping the presence of Peeker One invisible to either vessel. Twice, he darted into position to photograph spacecraft names and insignia for positive identification. Japanese space reporters gave expert, running commentary about the incredible scene. Mrs. Arai had a global scoop on her hands, and she had let the world know it through a bottom caption in several languages. It gave the name of her company. She had prepared the commercial message before liftoff. The action was typical of her country's long-range thinking. There was no reason that the act of giving should not also be self-serving. Her grandfather had taught her that concept. He, a trade diplomat, had persuaded his government that part of the huge reparations Japan owed to Korea for World War II occupation should be paid in cars and trucks. Cleverly, it set up a market for decades of replacement parts.

"Pan along the cargo doors," she directed, "and get all the marking and numbers on the body and rudder." Toyo did so until she suddenly called out, "Stop! The doors are moving!"

As the doors opened wide, the world saw the unbelievable results of the battle in the bay. Suzy did not flinch from close-ups, including Tim's nudity, the mutual carnage, the death struggles of Andrei, and the balletic disappearance of the dwindling enemies. Every nation saw live coverage.

In Moscow, Premier Yemetov turned away from the screen in anxiety and bewilderment. "Reopen the Hot Line!"

In Tenement One, an ashen Simon Sisco, who had seen Tim killed, wiped at his eyes and said, "Try the Hot Line again."

PART 7

YLENA

111

She stirred in dark depths, a cycling cicada, and began breaking free. She moved, as through a clinging ooze, to loose an ancient grip. With the darkness turning murky, she struggled in a seeming liquid toward a dawning light. Swimming now, she stroked upward, farther and faster, toward light and air. Above all, air! The powerful strokes pulled her on, but in futile vigor. She could not make the surface! She knew it. Yet she could not stop. Her nature demanded struggle to the end. She would absolutely not inhale. To breathe would be to yield. Her mind drove some biological lock that throttled her windpipe and shut out the flood of drowning. Soon, she knew, would come weakness and then the faint to oblivion.

It never happened. Ylena's eyes opened. Her throat opened. Air rushed. Sweet, sweet air! Heaving and gasping, she stopped her stroking arms, no longer in the drowning water. She was in Falcon! Trembling and shivering, she awakened from a desperate nightmare in the deepest sleep of her life. A syringe swayed wildly on its needle stuck in her arm. A torrent of memories swamped her mind. She endured none of Andrei's bewilderment upon awakening. Everything was clear. They had become marooned. Andrei had produced the revolvers and handed one to her. In extremis, they would count to three, and shoot together, each with a gun at the other's temple. They would exit this life simultaneously.

Even if one wilted, a shot by the other would convulse the survivor's hand and cause its gun to fire. Neither would be left to retch in a slaughter-splattered box, stripped of the nerve to shoot, as might happen with your own gun to your own head.

Stranded in space, they talked about the mutual suicide. Then followed a long, quiet, deliberation. Finally, she stored her gun.

"Let us not do this," she said. "Let us, instead, inject my father's liquid. He promised it would be painless, and probably pleasant, and might let us buy time until a rescue. If it doesn't work, we will then consider the guns."

He agreed. He seemed never to disagree anymore. His behavior in the early weeks of training had been very disagreeable, but not lately. The change had worried her. Was Andrei, like so many other men in the program, becoming enamored? The likelihood dismayed Ylena. Her intent and goal was achievement, not ensorcellment. She regarded symptoms of ardor as distracting and disconcerting.

She and Andrei had followed the instructions from her father. She removed the equipment he had put in her personal bag. She taped a flat solar-cell panel to face out one of the windows and ran its wires to a tiny black box that she then hooked to the radio antenna. She did not know that this piece of wizardry would become the source of the "uscom" signal. They taped a solar panel into every window. Andrei ran their wires to the cabin heaters; at least they would not be frozen solid in their sleep. He then set Falcon into slow rotation to insure that each panel saw sunlight and generated its share of power. This barbecue mode also distributed solar heat evenly on Falcon's skin. Finally, Ylena mixed the chemicals that would fill the cabin with the darkness and haze of a gas that prepared lungs for hibernation.

Then, each loaded a syringe with her father's liquid, and, in the dimming light, injected. After that, while simply waiting, she reached to shake hands good-bye with Andrei. He took her hand, but not to shake. He continued to hold it, pressing it to his lips as they fell gently into sleep.

Now, awake in the future, she turned her head and saw two startling changes: Andrei was not in his seat, and the hatch door was open. Through the hatch opening she could see walls, equipment, and lights. When she noticed Andrei's trussed body on the floor, his bound feet projecting out of the hatch, she got out her gun. Uneasy in the strange new setting she moved carefully.

Guarding against unknown risks, she took the weapon off its safety. Her survival knife quickly cut Andrei's wrists free. Slyly, she cut the tethering and ankle bonds. Was he alive? She checked and heard shallow breathing. She whispered to him as wakefulness returned.

Andrei heard the familiar voice warning, "Do not move. You were tied up. Do not move. I have cut you free. Do not move. Whoever tied you may be watching. Do not move."

The litany went on. It prepared him for a return to consciousness. He arrived warily. Only his eyelids moved, opening. She put her ear to his lips. In a confessional murmur, he began a halting, military briefing on what had happened to him. Ylena smiled tolerantly as the mad fantasy unfolded. Suddenly she stopped smiling and became a believer, stunned by a reality. A powerful, naked, young black man floated into view, busily gathering floating sheets of paper and stuffing them into a canvas bag. He headed their way.

She sat immobile, watching through eyelashes, hoping to imitate her previous condition. Tim looked in. He failed to notice the cut ropes. The woman had his full attention. She sat as before, a statue, belted to a seat, still sphinx-like, still with hooded gaze fixed on infinity. But there was a difference, a radiance. The waxen beauty now had coloration. "Amazing," said Tim, aloud. "Maybe this one will wake up, too."

Still unfocused about priorities and duties, Tim continued his cleanup, acting out the tidiness compulsions drummed into him by the ancient needs of life at sea, the practical mandate for meticulous, sanitary order where thousands lived together in the tight confines of ships. The sequence was always clear: disorder, dirt, disease, defeat. A sick crew could not fight its ship. With the fastidiousness born of a naval education, Tim reached into Falcon and retrieved two drifting sheets of diagrams.

Andrei had been watching, also under lidded eyes. He almost attacked as the American reached in above him in his puzzling activity of tidying up. Surely, the man had a hundred more important things to do. As Tim left, Andrei looked to Ylena and signaled for the gun. He slowly sat, trying hard to hold his projecting feet from moving. His head lifted to where he could watch the departing Tim. A moment of opportunity arose.

Swiftly, Andrei rose up, eyes narrowed in malice. Placing his feet on the hatch edge, he took the gun by the barrel like a striking weapon, steadied himself and dived at Tim with weapon raised to club his victim. Ylena heard a man's warning shout. It had to be the other American she had been told about. She saw Tim turn in alarm; and she watched Andrei's deadly swipe break open the naked man's shoulder. *Why is he trying to kill him?* Andrei had a gun. He could threaten, then control. Yet, he kept clubbing, tearing skin from defending arms, drawing blood.

Ylena screamed at him to stop. The gun fired, taking off part of the man's face and skull. She screamed on in horror and disbelief. In one swift motion, with no stop for appraisal, Andrei turned toward her and fired. Blood ran down her arm. Her crewmate was insane, gone mad! He would kill her. She backed into the hatch, slammed the door, and latched it shut. Through a porthole, she saw him turn toward the wall with the windows. She saw the other American behind the glass. She saw him duck as Andrei aimed and fired.

Then, the incredible happened. The entire top of the silver cylinder began to split down its length. Papers flew to the widening crack, and the mist of red blood moved through it. The heavier masses of Andrei and the American slowly floated to the same opening, accelerating as they moved. Suddenly, in awe, she knew she was looking at stars, looking into space, and she watched with caught breath as the slowly expanding bodies vanished into the void.

Everything Andrei had told her now rang true. They had indeed slept long. Time had indeed passed. Great ships of space had been built. The rivalry of their countries had continued. She had been captured by an American vessel. Or could she, should she, think of it instead as "rescued?" Her father had spoken of rescue. Her father! *Oh, God! Is he even alive?* The advances in technology she saw all around her could not have come swiftly.

How many years had passed? She had been 25 when Falcon launched. How old had she become? She looked at her skin, her hands. She saw no clues to aging. She cried out in anguish and confusion. She sobbed for the dead Andrei, and for the American, and for all the deluded men who hate and fight and kill their fellow humans. Barbarity was a pitiful legacy to take to the stars. Sitting in the future, she shuddered for the future.

112

Fury, nausea, and remorse overwhelmed Adam. In tears and moaning, he watched Tim's battered body leave the bay.

"Why did I sleep? Oh, God, why?" he groaned.

The Crisis Management Team heard him clearly. Benson turned to Beletsky. "Yuri, you may have another patient."

The psychologist, oscillating his hand, said, "On that, I give you a definite *maybe*. This guy's very, very strong."

Even as he spoke, Adam's soul groped for the balm of assimilation. His trembling mind met his need, envisioning trumpets and thunder and heavenly choirs. A warrior had fallen in combat. Through streaming tears, Adam saw the welkin sunder and the first Valkyries swoop in through roiling clouds. Under silent wings, hovering and protective, they took Tim up tenderly and judged him bravest of the brave. More of the beautiful, supernatural maidens arrived, flying in their triune squadrons. Like Hamlet's "flights of angels," they bore him gently to his rest.

Adam, covering his face at the horror of the cargo bay, had recoiled in an agony of failure. Now, dazed and envisioning the clarion fanfare, he stared numbly through the gates of his fingers at a hazy, brilliant glory. This was fitting! Tim was no carcass tumbling off like road kill. No, he was rising, rising to Valhalla! This day, his wounds would be healed. This day he would feast with the valiant. They would shout lustral incantations, beat swords on shields, and pound out his rousing welcome down a gauntlet of honor. He would live on, forever, in the great hall of the warriors.

Adam's clumsy, elegiac, poignant vision was the best that the remains of his poetic nature could provide. His very core strove desperately to encompass the tragedy. After that, perhaps, the compartment called duty could function. The old trio trooped in his mind: duty, honor, and country. He choked on the latter. How often it had come to mean nothing more than politics. He was here because of politics, maybe even bad politics. Who could tell good politics from bad? Yet, once wrapped in the flag, politics, for Adam, became patriotism. Time and place, those whims of birth, shape our patriotism and nationalism. He understood that very clearly. American Germans who killed German Germans in two world wars proved the point. But all he had left to relieve his anguish was patriotism, obligation, or whatever we might call a man's covenant with his country. Struggling to overcome horror, grief, and despair, Adam willed himself to duty, to action.

He came alert under healing waves of curiosity. *Who is this woman? Why is she here? Is her wound fatal?*

113

The Hot Line blistered from traffic. Yemetov and Sisco dealt directly in working out a joint communiqué. Gregory Taksis helped, tied by a secure splice to his embassy, and thence to Moscow through an encrypted satellite link. While the Hot Line was vital for agreement on the written word of the communiqué, the phone line was vital to interpretation and verification. Taksis used it to describe what he had seen happen on Olympia.

"Yes, Comrade Premier," he said, "Our man tied up the American commander and killed the pilot. He then shot at the commander, who had broken free, but who was unarmed and had no defense or recourse but to eject Borodin into space. Sisco connected Houston right to the embassy, and he played and explained the TV record to me. I have seen it all, including the Japanese broadcast that picked up the ejection of the two bodies into space. You saw that yourself! No, comrade, it could not have been staged. It is all fact and it is still unfolding. The woman has awakened. She, too, was shot by Borodin. She has locked herself in Falcon. There is limited air in there. We do not know how long she can last. If you wish verification, I will bring the General here."

He was referring to the espionage officer who functioned as executive officer of the embassy. Yemetov said that was not necessary, but he did wish to open an encrypted satellite TV line as soon as possible, so he could see the claimed trammeling of Adam and the murder of Tim. The President gave Taksis approval for the TV showing.

Sisco proposed the outline for a joint communiqué and sent his version. Yemetov responded with a variation. The Hot Line exchanges began to resemble a tennis volley.

The President said, "I am willing to congratulate and compliment the Soviet Union and the United Communist States publicly for a magnificent science achievement in suspended animation. However, you must indicate that your wake-up experiment, and therefore the cosmonauts' lives, became at risk because your Falcon spacecraft did not respond to your signal to return to earth. You must explain that your ship's electronic equipment had aged and become inoperative. At that point, you asked us to retrieve Falcon with our space shuttle."

Yemetov agreed. "This can be an example of international cooperation in the exploration of space. However, you must destroy the film of Borodin's attacks on Olympia's crew."

"But how do we explain the killings?" asked Sisco.

"Simple. Explain that your pilot was not rational, because of his injury. Our cosmonaut was not rational because he thought he was defending his ship against capture. They fought. Our man won. But your commander had no weapon of defense and had to eject him when attacked."

Sisco agreed. "I understand. Let's go on. The United States will say that one person from each country is still alive, that we will repair and land Olympia, and that your crew member and Falcon will be returned to you."

"Nyet! You will land Olympia at our Baikonur spacedrome. We will remove our property and our citizen. Then we will return Olympia and Commander MacGregor to you."

"Impossible! You introduce great hazard. There is too much risk in landing at a strange site. Also, our laws forbid placing shuttle technology in your hands, even temporarily."

"I am flexible, Comrade Sisco. You must be flexible, too. I offer you a different option instead: you will land Olympia in a neutral nation that will assume control of all property and persons. They will return what is yours to you and ours to us."

"I cannot agree. Safety is primary. The pilot is dead. The commander is alone. He needs every advantage. He must land at a site that is familiar, properly equipped, and with sufficient runway space to overshoot, yet roll to a halt. Remember, the shuttle is still a glider. It gets only one chance to land."

"President Sisco, you make a convincing case. I agree. However, because of the delicate medical nature of the suspended animation experiment, our doctors must be the first persons aboard so that they can provide immediate care. They will treat our cosmonaut and take her at once to the Hibernation Studies Clinic in Moscow. You must allow our jet to be waiting at the landing site."

Sisco concluded, "Your jet may be present and your doctors may go aboard, but I cannot promise they will be the first to go aboard Olympia. The conditions at landing may require emergency crews to board at once." Yemetov agreed, and Sisco told Adam.

The thrust and parry of bargaining sought the grand prize, the hibernation fluid. The Russians had the upper hand, due to a crucial bit of knowledge: they knew that the Americans believed the early Soviets had invented a hibernation fluid. The Americans wanted to get their hands on whatever remained.

However, the Americans did not know that the Russians had none of the fluid, nor that they not only wanted it desperately but would act dangerously to keep it from the Americans. Washington, in its offer to congratulate Moscow for a science coup, was assuming that the Russians had conducted a suspended animation experiment. It assumed that they had created and used the formula. Only the unorthodox Cooper sensed an inconsistency.

"Why didn't they bust a gut to get those hibernators back?"

Benson considered and said, "Art, they still don't have a shuttle. How could they possibly do it?"

"By paying for it, for God's sake! Nastran does jobs like that for a price. They brought back that German crystal growth factory last year! I tell you, Mike, the Russians intended to let their cosmonauts spin in and burn up. Their own people, merely hibernating! Why? Why? Just ask yourself! Did they sense a failure? Did they want to avoid bad publicity? That could have been avoided. Easily. Don't you see? Falcon could have been trucked back by us and turned over to them unopened."

He rolled on, "They could have justified it as removing space debris. Lots of decades ago! Or, at any time, they could merely say they had proprietary experiments aboard. Capitalists would understand that. We understand when the Germans and the Japanese do it on the space station. The Russians have a great achievement here, but there's every sign they were willing to let it be destroyed. I tell you, again, Mike, something's fishy as hell."

———————————— 114 ————————————

Eagle moved to Olympia's front windows and flashed lights into the cockpit to get Adam's attention. In rough sign language and a waving of hand held microphones, a cosmonaut signaled a wish to talk. Adam found their frequency. They offered help and asked to come aboard. He declined and set off to restore communications with Houston. He did not realize that the Eagle commander had pulled off a clever distraction.

Unknown to Adam, and courtesy of Peeker One, the world watched a daring cosmonaut, riding a maneuvering unit, leave a port on Eagle's hidden side and fly into Olympia's cargo bay. There he hand signaled Ylena to put on her helmet and depressure Falcon so the door could be opened. He would then toss in the compressed air bottle and new hard suit he carried. She would then close and latch the door and pressurize her cabin with air from the bottle. He reminded her that she would soon need the fresh air or die. Once Falcon was pressurized again, she would remove her ancient suit and don the new one. After that, she could open the door with impunity to the vacuum of space. He continued signaling.

"It will be a swift depressure and repressure. Your existing suit will protect you during the short opening of the hatch. You can dress quickly in the new suit and leave with me."

She had seen the effects of vacuum during Andrei's death throes. Cautious and questioning, she caused delay. From the corner of his eye, Adam saw Hemming on the TV screen waving frantically and pointing to a TV monitor in Mission Control. It showed Olympia's cargo bay. Someone in a space suit was out there. Adam whirled and looked. A cosmonaut! The Eagle commander had pulled a masterful diversion. Adam shot to the rear control panel and punched the controls to close the huge doors.

Quick and skilled, the cosmonaut jetted for the opening.

He would have made it, but for an inspiration Adam later thought came from the grave. It seemed as though Tim whispered to him, "Rotate the ship." He moved Olympia while the bay doors closed. The spin was slow because the shuttle was pressed against the tank hulk. But it was unexpected, and that made the difference.

The long opening was narrowing, but now it shifted. Flying hard, the frustrated cosmonaut could not vector anew in time. He crashed into one of the clamshell doors, cushioned by the insulation. The doors closed and trapped him in the cargo bay. Peeker One broadcast the action worldwide. Suzy Arai went into reruns, weaving advertising for Japanese products into the feed.

The clamor for an explanation became irresistible. Moscow and Washington responded within the hour, simultaneously releasing the joint communiqué. Neither, however, would take questions. Neither had independent answers. They had to work out what to say about the latest events generated by the people in the sky. The confrontation in space meshed poorly with the cooperative harmony of the announcement. John Dough feverishly made notes for the greatest story of his life.

Fighting mad, Adam resolved to confront the cosmonaut trickery in his own way. He switched off all remaining communications with Houston. The woman's life depended on having no interference with his next steps. He tuned his radio close to the frequencies the Russians normally used, and he hunted about. He knew there was radio talk going on, for he could see the cosmonaut in the bay speaking, undoubtedly to his commander in Eagle. Adam hit upon their channel; he listened to language too swift for his skill level. He broke in, identifying himself in halting Russian and in English.

"You know of the joint communiqué?"

"We do," said the Eagle commander.

"You and I are obligated to get Falcon and the woman to a landing in California."

"We understand."

"Your country wants her back alive."

"That was our mission when you interfered."

"You deliberately misunderstand. You know that she and Falcon are to return together."

"What is it you want?"

"I have no air left to repressure the bay. You must convince her that she can wear her old suit, open the hatch and take in the air tank and the new suit."

"We have tried. She is frightened, and does not believe us."

"Tell her she will soon use up her air and die in Falcon."

"We did."

"Tell her I said your method will work. She should look to me. I will signal my agreement."

The trapped cosmonaut cut in. "What will be the good of this? You have us locked here in the bay. She and I will simply die in our suits when our air runs out."

"No. Your job is to get her into the suit."

"And if I don't do what you say . . . ?"

"Your air will expire. I will watch you die in my cargo bay."

"That will also kill her."

"That is up to you. My orders are to bring her back with her spacecraft for shipment to your country. That can be either dead or alive. I intend to follow those orders. Your refusal to cooperate will cause her death."

His stone-hard words triggered bargaining. "What happens to *me* if I cooperate?"

"I will open the doors and you may return to Eagle."

"How can I trust you?"

"We are on TV. Everyone knows what is happening. I could not explain your death if she lived. But if she dies, I can easily explain why I let *you* die! I suggest you get persuasive with her. Even now, she may be getting faint."

---------------- 115 ----------------

The cargo bay was remarkably clean after the blood bath. *More like a blood shower,* thought Adam, groggy with grief. Here and there, drops rested on surfaces, drawn by the tiny gravity attraction. The escaping air had carried most of the blood mist and the globules away. He worried now about other air. The reanimated woman couldn't live long on the air in Falcon. Now and then, he could see her through a window. He expected she would soon nod off to final sleep. Why couldn't that guy from Eagle convince her to don the hard suit?

Getting anxious, Adam wondered if he should put on his experimental hard suit and go into the bay to help explain. *Better not, better not.* It would mean a tricky routine with doors, and a jammed-tight complicated passage back through the air lock with her. *Besides, why would she pay attention to me if I go out there? How could I communicate any better? And how can I trust that tricky bastard from Eagle not to start another takeover? Maybe the two of them would turn on me. Oh, Lord, is it even possible that they're both playing me along to get me out there? What is it they're saying in that sign language? What do I know about her? Even if she's not a fanatical Communist, she may be as nutty as Andrei after all the years up here getting her brain sloshed by radiation.* He stopped debating with himself. He decided against going. Instead, he called the cosmonaut.

"What is your name?"

"Major Gennady Kuznets."

"Listen, Major, she may need encouragement from both of us. I'd like to try communicating with her."

"I've told her your advice, but she laughs. She thinks I've made it up to strengthen my own case."

"Does she speak English?"

"Yes."

"And she knows Morse code?"

"Certainly."

"Tell her I said I will talk to her in that way."

"I will do it."

"Who is she? Her name?"

"Captain Ylena Valena of the Soviet Air Force."

The man rapped on a window to get Ylena's attention and then signaled swiftly, pointing to Adam at the wall window. Adam extinguished all the lights in the bay. After a moment, they began flashing on and off, slowly, in a careful signal series from Adam. It lasted for several minutes.

Major Kuznets spoke, "She understands, but she wants to know why she should believe you."

She and Adam looked at each other across the airless void. He stayed silent, thinking hard. Finally, he put out all lights on Olympia. In the most profound darkness, time passed in utter silence. He clocked five minutes on his glow watch.

Then, using only a flashlight in the window, he blinked, "That was death. If you believe in life, believe in me."

To resemble dawn and the rebirth of hope, he brought the bay lights up slowly, changing from dark, to dim, to pale, to bright.

"You melodramatic humbug," he mumbled.

Tenement One had been reading the Morse code. Yuri turned to Julian and whispered, "Who's the psychologist around here, anyway? What the hell do they need me for? She's got to say yes. Just got to. This guy is too much."

Ylena decided. She beat on the port window to tell Kuznets. He did not respond. She rapped hard with her knife to get his attention. When he did not respond, her impatience burst into distraught laughter, as she finally realized no sound could reach him in the vacuum.

Adam saw the action and said, "The lady wants to talk to you."

The Major turned. After more hand sign conversation, he said, "She is willing."

Adam spoke, "As you tell her what to do by signs, say out loud what you are telling her. That will allow me to confirm your instructions so that I can tell her we both agree."

He made notes of Kuznets' slow interpretation as the hand signaling droned on. At the end, he flashed her a message.

"Captain Valena," Adam began, "nod yes if the following message is what he told you and if you understand it all."

She nodded for him to begin and he started Morse signaling. At the end, she nodded yes.

Adam instructed Kuznets, "When she has the new suit and has closed her hatch door, I will open the bay doors. You may then leave. I'd appreciate it if you would gather up all the food and water you can spare and come back and leave it all near the air lock."

The startled major said, "I will have to ask my commander."

The voice of Eagle's Commander broke in, "It will be as you ask, Commander MacGregor. The lady's first meal will be from her native land."

Adam said a thank you and smiled to himself at this Russian gallant. The more supplies he gave away, the sooner Eagle would have to go home.

---------------------------- 116 ----------------------------

Ylena moved rapidly, her doubts assuaged. She donned gloves and
helmet, suiting up fully. She tested the suit by venting Falcon slowly to
a half atmosphere. The suit began to balloon. Kuznets watched through
the porthole, nodding approval. More slowly, she vented Falcon to full
vacuum. Struggling, she opened the hatch. As the little remaining air
hissed out, her ancient suit did not burst, and she gave a prayer of thanks.

She moved back to make room for the incoming air tank and the rigid
suit. Kuznets worked frantically, in dread that her ancient suit might sunder
at any moment. Kuznets held up the air tank and showed the stopcock
control for bleeding it rapidly. He shoved it just inside and slammed the
door. She latched the door clamps and turned at once to the tank, releasing
compressed air. It soon equated to that within her suit, reducing it from
a semi-balloon to a garment once again. At that point, she turned off the
stopcock.

Breathing freely once more, Ylena undressed in her cramped confines.
She flattened and rolled her old suit for compact stowage and put it away.
Then she turned to the hard suit. It took all her suppleness to warp and twist
into this marvel. It was basically a container, functioning like a small room.
Rigid, it would not balloon in vacuum. The air inside the suit would stay
at the pressure of the room where it was donned. Its cleverly articulated
joints allowed freedom of movement. She rotated the helmet shut and
experimented with the air supply and temperature controls, poised to tear
off the helmet if suffocation started. All went well.

She moved, as in a late, heavy pregnancy, trading time for skill, adapting
to the new bulk. Kuznets, who had moved away in unnecessary modesty
during the suit change, came back to the porthole. Turned away from
Adam, he appeared immobile. Up front, however, he resumed hand signals.

His message said, "I will leave, but will wait just outside the huge doors.
Pull yourself up the door wall to the rim and I will fly you to Eagle for a
return home. Bring all remaining hibernation fluid."

He waited for an answer. He got none, either by hand or expression.
His instructions evinced no acknowledgement, response or clue. Through
Falcon's glass window, and the two faceplates, he could see the vivid
eyes, an astonishing bright jade green, speckled with tourmaline, fixed
impassively upon him. He had once before met such a gaze. In a zoo, he
had unwittingly locked eyes with a caged panther and been fixed in a cold,
timeless, unblinking appraisal.

The hypnotic abeyance snapped as a movement of the bay doors caught
his eye.

"Time to go, Major!"

"Yes," said the chilled Kuznets, "and I will return with the promised supplies."

He sailed off through the widening slit and tacked left. Outside, however, he doubled back, hovering just beyond the lip of the great door.

Ylena depressured Falcon and entered the bay. She moved along the wall toward the air lock. Kuznets, seeing her approach, anticipated her joining him. He had a long wait. Ylena began a wary pattern of movement, an eye on the door gap. The sheer floating freedom captured her as it had Andrei, and it did so in a condition of greater need. She was like a child denying a recent catastrophe, anxious to wall off a memory of horror and fear. She began a diversion of weightless play. The reprieve from her overwhelming circumstances became pure joy.

She pushed from wall to wall, cautiously at first, and then gamboling with a gymnast's verve. She spun, twirled, and tumbled, in an ecstasy of release. Adam caught occasional, whirling views of a huge smile. He imagined boisterous, delighted, gratified laughter in the helmet. His body bent and twisted in the sympathetic movement of coach with athlete. He found himself chuckling, and with good reason. His deadly bluff with the Eagle crew had succeeded. And now he saw a gleeful, weightless dance by a hippopotamus ballerina, on the most unlikely stage, with the universe as backdrop. Smiling, he turned and reopened communication with Houston.

Hemming's shouting voice restored reality, "Olympia, close your doors at once!"

Peeker One had shown Hemming what Adam could not see.

117

Ylena, breathless from cavorting, settled at the door edge, holding on, looking outward. She felt again as a child, resting from spirited freedom, peering over a fence. Above her, in the infinite freedom of the cosmos, the unwavering, hard, bright stars burned. Among them she saw Eagle, its own bright red star calling, rousing memories and yearnings. Suddenly, the red star contrasted harshly with the others. It became an omen, refuting freedom. Meanings engulfed her, tearing about in a swirl of family, country, fantasies, hopes, truth, lies, and realities. They settled in a layered mix, and hardened into an answer: her father's answer.

Kuznets pulled himself toward her, along the lip, reaching. She recoiled. He crept on. She ducked below the rim. He straddled it, reaching for her as the door began moving to shut. He stretched and grabbed, got her and held, dragging. She put a foot against his body and pushed. It broke the grip. He shot, tumbling, into the void, skillfully reorienting himself with jet puffs. Ylena's kick reaction impelled her inward. She bounced off the bay floor and ricocheted toward the shrinking gap between the doors, headed for open space. Adam beat the window, shouting "No, no, no!"

Ylena's diversion into levitated romping had built a rudimentary skill for weightless movement. She called on it, lengthening her body as she rebounded outward. Crosswise to the bay length, hands overhead, she passed through the door gap. Her fingers caught the door edge and held, forcing a gymnast's giant swing. It arced her full body to a frontal crash against the convex exterior of the closing door. The rebound swung her in a reverse arc toward a rapidly narrowing opening, now smaller than her length. Adam frantically reached for the reversing switch, but stopped. It was too late.

Childhood lessons prevailed. Ylena's years of gymnastics had engrained basic movements. Training, instinct, and thought merged as she swept in the reverse arc that would slam her hinder knee into the outside of the opposing, closing clamshell door. But she crouched. This shortened her in the giant swing, and, like raising the grandfather clock's pendulum weight, it speeded her sweep. She curved through the pinching gap and arced to a cushioned crash in the concave insulation. As the sky squeezed away above her, she started eagerly for the air lock, waving to Adam. Relieved. Beaming. Exultant. Free!

118

Peeker One's constant gaze showed Olympia and Eagle, bright and inert, on dedicated screens in Mission Control and Tenement One. For hours it beamed boring images. Once, Suzy Arai decided to take a chance that inaction and boredom would continue, and she authorized an excursion to show the shuttle's blasted external tank. Later, narrators explained these scenes repeatedly on replay. Their non-technical speech unintentionally demeaned the remarkable achievements of engineering. Silence would have been better — the images alone told a compelling story of power and destruction. Peeker One's controller, brilliantly minimizing fuel use, poked in and about, doing a Cook's Tour of the blasted, inch-thick metal sections, where once slept the latent fury of hydrogen.

Peeker One returned to do its numb staring at Olympia and Eagle. Just then the bay doors began to open.

"Whooeee!" said Cooper, "Back in the nick of time. Suzy just missed getting her ass in a sling!"

Hemming heard the comment and grinned in spite of his perplexity about why Adam had broken off communications after trapping the cosmonaut. On the Peeker One screen he saw the doors open and watched Kuznets emerge, veering slowly toward Eagle. As he watched Kuznets, something about the man's body language, even through the rigid suit, alarmed him. Kuznets' movements and intentions seemed to turn from helpful and hesitant, to furtive, even menacing. Suddenly, Hemming understood. Grabbing the microphone, and hoping to get through, he shouted, "Olympia, close your doors at once!" He got no response because Adam was just ending the silent-movie showdown with Kuznets.

While Hemming continued shouting repetitions, Adam restored the voice circuit and heard the message. Hemming saw Adam dash to close the bay doors. Then, helpless, he agonized through Ylena's struggle with the cosmonaut and her incredible escape. When she headed for the air lock with a triumphant wave, he imagined wind-blown pennants, and crowds cheering, and that he heard Olympic trumpets over his own whispered, "World Class."

119

Overtime reigned. During the deceptive "practice rollouts" before Olympia's launch, most of the planned maintenance and improvement work had turned chaotic for the other California-based shuttles. The disrupted schedules toppled once again as Hemming's promised supply-and-repair rescue flight for Olympia took precedence. The orderly flight manifests and sequences suffered because Nastran didn't have enough shuttles to keep up with contracted launches. The total shuttle inventory had grown to a fleet of three on each coast. There they specialized in the orbits that could be flown from each location. On occasion, one would change coasts to help with peak business. This costly practice had to be justified by a net profit.

The turnaround time for successive flights was lengthy. Tests, inspections, repairs, upgrades, and engine changeouts added to the months between flights. The public did not understand. People thought of the shuttles as they did commercial airliners. They didn't realize that every new shuttle model that appeared was an experimental aircraft-cum-spacecraft.

The point was made in the complex troubles now grounding the West Fleet. The USS Odyssey could not reach full thrust on one of its main engines in preflight tests, and the USS Constitution was leaking hydrogen somewhere deep in her piping. No one could predict a date for successful repairs. No one saw how to mount a rescue flight to Olympia within the week or two that Hemming had promised.

Nastran's fleet managers flew into Washington and conferred with Frank Cole through the night. Technically ingenious and imaginative, they solved the quick-launch problem several times in the brainstorm sessions. But in the challenge sessions, the same solutions died under attack. Cole, frustrated, kept his composure, rolling in his mind the adage: *For every complex question, there is someone with a simple answer — probably wrong.*

Use of the Spaceplane appeared impracticable. That growing fleet had gone wholly commercial to help boost the nation's export earnings. The Spaceplane went into orbit, of course, but was configured only to speed around the world, reenter, and deliver cargo to a target airport. Hard cash had turned it into a vehicle that did not stop and dwell in space. Its ability to make large amounts of money by carrying passengers or urgent freight had specialized it early. It had become for the U.S. a 21st-century version of its 19th-century clipper ships.

The clipper ships had not driven all other vessels off the seas. However, the Spaceplane had nearly done the equivalent in aviation with its monopoly on flying cross-ocean, or cross-hemisphere. The point-to-point vehicle could get from any airdrome on earth to any other within two hours. It rode above weather, needing only takeoff and landing clearances, but not one vehicle of that fleet currently had the features needed for orbital rendezvous and rescue.

President Ronald Reagan, in proposing its construction, had called it the "Orient Express." He could hardly have been more prophetic. It carried hundreds of thousands of people a year, taking them to heights and views previously the province of astronauts. The result was an unexpected bonus for the "greens" of society. Just one flight made a passenger an environmentalist. Each saw the closed system and the self-contained nature of the fragile earth. All the scientific results from the Earth Observing Satellite System finally got widespread acceptance. The ecological caretaker movement flowered, perhaps just in time, for no one knew how close humanity had come to a point of irreversibility in polluting the oceans and atmosphere. As one zealot put it, "We treated the earth as though we had a spare in the trunk."

Cole got treated as just another swimmer in this think tank. He thought of his college years in water polo. If you had the ball, the opposition swam right over you. At least in water polo only the other team sank you. Here anybody would do it if your idea couldn't keep you afloat. When he explored the limits of using an East Fleet shuttle for a northerly launch out of Florida, they swamped him with facts about the inclination limit of 65 degrees from the equator. Olympia flew in a near-polar orbit of 85 degrees. A chase shuttle launched into that orbit from Florida would have to fly over dense population areas of the United States and Canada. Possibilities of a crash on launch ruled that out.

Someone proposed to launch an East Fleet shuttle that would circle earth and land on the West Coast, as had been done sometimes with the early shuttles.

"Then," he said, "we'd have a tested, functioning vehicle ready in California to fly into polar orbit."

Only pieces of this idea lay around the room when the Murder Board ended its battering. The speaker had overlooked the length of flight preparation time for the Florida launch and the even longer inspection and preparation for a subsequent California launch, assuming that absolutely nothing went wrong on the flight to the east to get around to the west. The minimum time that the most gracious critic would concede to the idea was five weeks for readiness to launch toward Olympia.

Though depressed about the results, Cole was gleeful about the process. He knew the value of generating competition in the marketplace of ideas. He encouraged his people to speak up. He often wished all his staff had independent incomes so that none would be hostage to a paycheck. All *were* hostage, however, so Cole complimented himself for their openness. He attributed their spunk and spirit to his personal selections in hiring his mixed-gender crew, " . . . fearing neither man nor beast nor me."

The group finally reached consensus. Gulping a bit, Cole fought to swallow the bitter bubble of their practicality. They handed him a ghastly, demeaning recommendation of good logic and terrible taste. They advised him to hire a Russian vehicle for the supply and repair rescue. The argument said the Russians are as hungry for hard currency today as in the late 1900's when they pioneered by selling rides to orbit for foreign journalists. Back then, they had also rented out launch-day advertising space, emblazoned down the length of rockets, for European wines, shoes, and perfumes, and Japanese disposable diapers.

Self-inflicted on their proud space program, these indignities had given some economic analysts early hints of impending bankruptcy in the Soviet empire. The continuing Russian need for money jump-started a new travel industry in 2001 when they flew a wealthy American to orbit for $20 million, making Dennis Tito the first space tourist. Nowadays, Russia also offered another routine service, reliable trucking to orbit at very competitive prices.

Following their boorish, bungled attempt to kidnap Ylena, they could hardly refuse, under humanitarian pressure, to cooperate in a repair and rescue mission. Cole's staff even had a suggestion on how to proceed. President Sisco had only to tell the media he intended to ask the Russians for rescue collaboration, wait for the news to reach Yemetov, and then call to make the official request. How could the Premier refuse?

When Cole reluctantly relayed the group's advice, he was astounded by Sisco's response.

"I agree. Start your engineers at once on identifying all of the incompatibilities between our equipment and theirs. Make anything you'll need for the transfer of fuel, water, air, gases, food, and whatever . . . "

The President had spoken and was moving away.

Cole pursued, fidgeting. "You mean you'll actually ask?!"

The President turned. "What? Oh, sure, Frank. The answer is yes. Of course. And I'm rather glad for the chance. I'm going to enjoy it. Tell your people I'm grateful for the idea. Very creative of them. Now you go work the engineering and logistics, while I unleash a little public opinion."

120

When Ylena entered the air lock and secured the outer door, Adam pressured the little passage. When it matched the cabin's pressure, he opened the inner door, braced himself and reached. Ylena took the proffered hand. Adam drew her toward him. She floated free of the cylinder, rose to his level, let go, and came to attention. Then, in the tradition of boarding a vessel, she snappily saluted her host. The huge suit hid her condition of being at attention. She might as well have straightened to stiffness in another room. Belatedly, she realized this, feeling foolish.

Something else was happening. By letting go, to free her hand for saluting, she had parted from Adam before dumping energy; inertia kept her moving. When the snap of saluting set her body to turning and rotating, the "welcome aboard" ceremony took antic form. Her face, set in the bubble of the huge helmet, was intent and serious with the ritual requirements of arrival etiquette. Their eyes met at an odd and changing angle. The eyes locked, and, tracking to their corners, bulged white, as her bulky suit, in a slow tumble, floated its rigid occupant sedately past, to a resting place, face up, on the ceiling. Adam heard the faint, shrieking laughter of tension snapped. The suit, like a baffled robot, buried its globular head in its hands, convulsing.

121

At Sisco's request, the leaders communicated again. He had turned the screws of public opinion hard on Yemetov, pleading humanitarian need and the temporary incapacitation of the U.S. shuttle fleet. Yemetov, feeling dumped on, came back bargaining like a merchant. He had not been satisfied with how the last talks ended. He had been bested on where Olympia would land, and on the subsequent procedures. *That bastard put me in a box last time.* Now, handed a negotiating crowbar, he intended to pry open the landing arrangements issue. The Hot Line chattered his response.

"President Sisco, I sympathize with your dilemma. I also appreciate the kind statements you made to the world media about Communist space prowess and our reliability. Thank you."

"You're very welcome. It's settled, then? You will arrange for one of your ships to fly the needed supplies to Olympia?"

"We will consider the request; however, my medical advisers tell me it is essential for our resurrected cosmonaut to return to earth in the manner we had planned at her launch so long ago."

"Oh? Please explain what you mean."

"Certainly. Before the American interference with our experiment, we would have been able to signal a command for reentry of our spaceship, Falcon. That would have returned both of our young people to us alive, still in suspended animation, in their sealed capsule. Follow me?"

"Not quite."

"It's really rather simple. The United States, in the interest of science, must help us restore as much of the experiment protocol as possible. We will explain to the media, of course, that you are cooperating in reestablishing everything that can possibly be salvaged from our original hopes for the medical trial of the hibernation fluid. We will laud the way that you are cooperating in an objective gathering of physiological data."

"I still don't know what you want us to do."

"We want our experiment and our courageous volunteer restored to the essential, intended, original conditions of the experiment. When Olympia lands, Captain Ylena Valena is to arrive on earth sealed within the Falcon spacecraft. However, as a concession to her sensitivities, we will not require a second use of the special cabin gas for breathing, nor any further use of the suspended animation fluid. We wish merely that she be alive and breathing, but within the sealed Falcon spacecraft. This was our original intention, an intention that was prevented by the intervention of your astronauts. Our medical specialists will be in attendance at landing, as will our transport equipment."

"I'm beginning to understand what you are up to."

"Regardless, she must remain in Falcon. Your crane will lift it from Olympia's payload bay and load it aboard our cargo plane for an immediate flight to our Hibernation Studies Clinic. There, it will be opened in a controlled environment in a sealed chamber, as we try to preserve whatever we can of the original conditions and integrity of the experiment."

"This all seems rather extreme, Premier Yemetov. Falcon's seal has already been broken, and Ms. Valena will have been in a normal atmosphere for days, perhaps weeks, by the time Olympia lands. I see no reason to stick her in a container and have her whisked away. We would certainly wish to honor her here in America for a while."

"President Sisco, I know the disdain, imprecision, and lack of foresight which is so widespread in the United States concerning science. I hope that the boorish, luddite behavior of your citizens has not infected you."

"Premier Yemetov, I cannot agree with your gross diagnosis, nor do I see what it has to do with the situation."

"You will. We have both seen historical evidence of the compromises to science, and perhaps the dangers to humanity, in the offhanded approach American culture takes to controlled experiments. Surely, you have viewed TV reruns of the Apollo 11 spacecraft parachuting into the ocean after the first walk on the moon?"

"Indeed I have. A proud moment for humanity."

"It could have been a disastrous moment for humanity. Remember, President Sisco, how your three astronauts entered a sealed container on the aircraft carrier, for a long quarantine?"

"Of course. That was a reasonable precaution."

"Do you remember, however, that first they walked across the flight deck and only then did they enter that container? And that only then was it sealed?"

"I do. Helicopters lifted them from the sea and to a welcome on the carrier by President Nixon."

"Exactly. It was an unconscionable action by the United States."

"I do not understand you."

"Think, President Sisco! Think. The United States put those men in quarantine in case they had brought back some plague that could decimate life on earth."

"Again, that was a reasonable precaution."

"I agree. But think it through. The United States used inadequate precautions for preventing contamination by the first material to come from another world. Moon dust was all over their equipment and suits. It was in the return capsule. Yet you opened that vehicle to the atmosphere of our earth, while it floated in a warm saline solution, the southern ocean. A setting like that could have cultured a dangerous life form."

"Are you saying that Ms. Valena will be contagious?"

"She is *not* Ms. Valena! She is Captain Valena. You have called her Ms. twice. She is not a civilian. She is an officer in a military unit. She is still carrying out her orders. She is a vital part of a carefully designed experiment."

"Are you telling me Captain Valena will be contagious?"

"I am not! But just in case you are not missing my point deliberately, I *am* telling you that the United States must stop interfering with the structure of our research. If you do not, I will publicly compare your current, irresponsible attitude toward our experiment with your reckless behavior of the past. I will point out that nothing has changed. I believe the world will side with me when I tell the media that we will help with the rescue only if you publicly agree to our medical procedures."

"Premier Yemetov, for someone who is reaching back into history so far to make a point, you certainly have a short memory. Remember, your own automated digger brought back the first soil specimens from Mars. We had to twist your predecessor's arm to get him to put that soil in quarantine with volunteers on Space Station Freedom. He wanted to parachute the stuff onto the Siberian steppes. And that was soil from a planet with an atmosphere! My God, man, the comparison's illogical. The moon was arid, sterile, a total vacuum incapable of supporting life. You'll impress nobody."

"Well, Mr. President, perhaps we can tell the media something that really is impressive. Suppose we announce an embarrassment to match your own? Suppose we claim that our entire rocket fleet is also temporarily inoperable. Who could dispute our statement? How unfortunate. Then where would you turn? Who would fly your needed supplies to Olympia? Do you understand me? I am tired of playing this game with you. You know my terms. What is your answer?"

"Premier Yemetov, I will call you back soon. I must think about this."

—————————————— 122 ——————————————

The Secretary of State paced, musing. Finally, he stopped and said, "I see no way out of this, Mr. President. They could have staged a great outrage, publicly damning us for what they'd have called our 'unauthorized, presumptuous interruption of a vital and delicate experiment.' That alone would have gotten them international sympathy. They didn't think of it early enough, and we've given some plausible reasons for our actions, so we didn't get pilloried, thank God. People have assumed that we just didn't know any better. But this is different! Vastly different. We must not be seen as the nation that deliberately decides to interfere with a justified request for cooperation on an experiment. In addition, this is medical research, and you're going to look like the villain who's willing to risk that young woman's health or life."

Benson disagreed. "There's still a way out. Yemetov thinks he can tell her what to do. The decision is not really up to him, or even to us. It's up to that young woman. So, I suggest that we should agree to the Russian terms and say it publicly. Let Yemetov make the announcement, so it starts out as his initiative. In a week or so, when Olympia's ready to fly home, we'll put the question right to her. Maybe Yuri can tell us how to turn her into a refusenik! Then, we'll have a great public case for political asylum. Remember, she's already been seen on Peeker TV breaking away from the guy that grabbed her."

"I like it," said the President, "but we must keep their side from sweet talking her into wanting to go home. I'll have to prohibit communications with her."

Yuri broke in, "With all due respect, Mr. President, if you try that, you'll get your head handed to you. You must not appear as the callous capitalist who controls her communications. That girl needs to talk with any remaining family or friends. To the public, it's going to be like the return of hostages or prisoners of war. The whole globe will want to go hand in hand with this young woman on a vicarious emotional binge. They'll want to cry with her and laugh with her and have orgies of nostalgia for her vanished world. That'll range from bathos to pathos, but the interest and empathy will be more intense than anything we've ever seen. Just remember, nearly all of her world has vanished. She's facing what normal people fear most: she's all alone."

The President nodded, "You're right, Yuri. Absolutely right. I should have thought of that. I guess the public will think that anyone who is not with her is against her. But why can't we restrict her communications to family and friends, if any are still alive, and keep government officials out of the loop?"

Yuri spoke slowly, "You're dealing with an unprecedented event. Captain Valena will need to talk with anyone who can help her reestablish contact with society and today's reality. Only the Russians have the social links she needs, so we'll have to work with them. Only *they* will be able to find and produce the people she wants to see and talk with. We'll have to work with them to meet her needs for very private communications, for consolation, and for professional assistance. If you want to be excoriated by every mother and father and woman alive, just try depriving her of access to psychiatric help. Even though she'll have to deal with one of their discredited state quacks, the world will believe she would be understood best by a psychiatrist from her own society. And, you guess what? I'd probably agree with that! But just for starters."

When the meeting ended, Sisco sent Yemetov a message of agreement, with no strings attached.

123

Adam twisted his hook-lock shoe into one of the floor's foot restraints. Reaching up, he took Ylena by the hand and drew her down from the ceiling. Balancing on the high wire of extreme emotional stress, she stood poised for a fall into somber shock or into a protective, denying laughter. The latter won. She felt the high spirits of battle and victory, and of achieving her father's goal of escape. Adrenaline helped overcome her embarrassment about the fiasco of the boarding ceremony and made it seem comical. Round tears of release and stress stood on her cheeks. Some floated off and bumped against the faceplate. Occasionally, when she started to shout something to Adam, in what sounded to him like English, she collapsed into laughter again.

His visitor's untimely joviality was infectious. Adam found himself smiling in return, and he was glad of it. They both needed some release after a drumfire of shocks. She especially, he thought, needed respite. Not only had she seen savage battle and two deaths and been shot, but she had lost a friend, maybe a husband. Besides all that, she was shipwrecked, somewhere in time. In addition, despite her apparently joyful choice of Olympia versus Eagle, she was in a sense in enemy hands.

He held up two velcro straps for her to see; he used them to bind her shoes to the deck. The bulky foreign suit, now stabilized, leisurely straightened up. The right arm once again came up in salute. It came slowly, ever so slowly. She intended there would be no snappy movements that would spin her out of control this time. Ylena, taking command of herself, was engaged in a forlorn, second attempt to do the right thing, to do that right thing right, and to regain dignity.

Adam misinterpreted. He thought she was prolonging the arrival ritual into travesty, into a superb burlesque. Stress seeks solace, but sometimes in impulsive, irrational ways.

Severely stressed, Adam thought Ylena's actions hilarious, more so because he saw them as deliberate drollery and a mockery of protocol. He marveled at her extraordinary sense of humor and at the remarkably balanced personality that this implied, given the bewilderment, tragedy, and fear of the last few hours. She had laughed merrily at the botched welcome. Now it became his turn, in a chortle of released stress, as he looked at the pantomime of a salute.

He was struck on the ear, as Ylena hit him hard in anger. She had come to him in hope, and trust and relief, abandoning everything familiar. She had sensed strength and security in this man and all he represented. She had volunteered her future to what seemed a warrior philosopher of freedom, not to some boisterous, derisive giber. She had been wrong! This taunting boor would not laugh at her! Adam saw flaming eyes immediately precede the coruscating lights from her blow. This woman who had waved cheerfully in her voluntary trip to the air lock was attacking him! She had gone from elation to fury in mere minutes.

The roundhouse punch carried through and toppled him in an arc. Feet anchored to the floor, he rebounded, bobbing upright like a punching dummy. He rose, only to meet another blow from the hard suit. He blocked it with a forearm, but it sent him twisting off in another arc. The reaction had set Ylena to a similar pivoting motion. When they collided upright Adam threw his arms around the suit and hugged. Locked and rooted, they swiftly braced to a halt.

Ylena, struggling, alternated between long, staccato, intake sobs, and yelling insults.

He shouted, "I'm sorry. I'm really sorry." He patted the suit consolingly, as though calming an oak. It felt stupid. He rapped on her faceplate to signify removal, took hold of the helmet, rotated it off, lifted it free, and let go. It hovered like a crown in coronation. He crouched, trying to meet her averted eyes. The furious, sobbing figure, awash in the big suit, did not respond.

He kept murmuring, "Please don't be angry."

The distressed sobbing continued. Her classmates would never have believed this scene possible, not from the woman of eternal cheer, energy and resolution. Ylena, feeling exhausted, confused, and humiliated, fought for emotional control. This quavering, compulsive gasping was not for her!

It began to slow. It finally stopped, leaving her in charge of herself again. Now she could deal with the American. He seemed genuinely apologetic. *Perhaps I've misunderstood his behavior.* She wondered if she had been overly friendly. No matter. From here on her relations with him would be quite formal.

Her swiftly gathering composure suddenly vanished. It disintegrated with the start of obstinate, clacking hiccups. This ultimate interference with communication and dignity tickled her keen sense of the ridiculous. Frustrated and finally overwhelmed, she dissolved into a resigned amusement. Adam's spirits rose as he heard the accepting, periodically punctuated chuckling. He had learned his lesson well, however, and he resolutely presented an unsmiling face of concern. He struggled to keep it that way, but, as the hiccups continued, he found himself yielding, with mouth corners straining to twitch. Another social crisis loomed.

A voice spoke and saved him. "Olympia, Houston. The flight surgeon wants you. The visitor's wound needs treating. Come in, please."

124

Yuri Beletsky coordinated with his Russian counterparts in designing Ylena's emotional adjustment as a time traveler. He had control of all means for communicating directly with Olympia, and thus with Ylena. It allowed him to deny access by any person, or to any procedure, he deemed harmful. His tough protection made some of the Russian psycho-manipulators break down in frustration when he overruled their plans.

One screamed at him, "How dare you contradict me, Beletsky? Do you not know that I am the Chairman of...?"

Yuri interrupted the pompous doctor, "Stop! Just damned stop!"

Then, in a calm voice, Yuri went on, "Don't call me Beletsky. Call me Doctor. That's D-O-C-T-O-R. Do you understand? It's 'Doctor' to you, Doctor."

They could not grasp the concept of the man. He was an independent practitioner, not employed by the state, living by his wits and prospering as a consultant. When they finally categorized him, they could accept him. As a mad genius, his views could be considered. Until then, his lack of organizational title and status made *him* unacceptable and, therefore, his *ideas* as well.

They finally absorbed the lesson he beat into them: the person was a patient. They learned to treat Ylena as just that, a patient, and not as a tool of the state.

Then he taught them the futility of hidden agendas. "Not that you guys are any good at subtlety. While you're supposedly creeping up on her, your machinery is grinding out loud, and your parts are hanging out and clanking on the ground. We can hear you coming a mile off. You're no good at it, so stop trying. Play things straight or I'll cut off your access."

Eventually, they reached several agreements about Ylena's needs and care. First, she could have unlimited time to talk with any friend or relative still alive, and with any minister of her choice. Second, she needed an update of the history she had slept through. Third, she could have private sessions with any medical doctors she chose.

Ylena cried a lot at the start. Her past had vanished. Walking down the road of life, she had stopped and turned around to find behind her only a steep, yawning cliff shrouded in fog. Father, friends, teachers, and classmates ... all gone. She asked for information about their passing. With successive photos of class reunions, she traced people she knew. She tracked them through fattening, fading, and disappearance. She came to understand Time's Law: *Everybody Vanishes.* She got whatever obituaries she asked for. She spoke on closed circuit TV with several people purported to be nieces or nephews. They had been brought in at her request, in her desperate search for a link. The cherubs she used to know had vanished. Strangers stared back at her blankly, some from wheel chairs. There was mutual non-recognition. Most had been brought from old age homes.

Once, screaming in an agony of realization, Ylena threw herself on Adam, hugging hard, trembling and crying out, "It cannot be! I cannot be twenty five and all are dead!" Swallowing and choking, she sobbed, "Oh, Commander, it cannot be!"

Stoic Adam, unequipped for consolation, could only rock her gently. He murmured an awkward "There, there," to the young ancient in his arms, while he tried to do the math on whether he was soothing the equivalent of his great-grandmother or merely his grandmother.

She worried about being able to adjust to modern life, saying one day, "Commander, I do not know if I will be able to change and catch up."

"Don't try to change anything. You're just fine as you are. Let the world adjust to you. Besides, you may not have to change if the right changes occur around you."

"I do not understand."

"Well, mountains look like islands if the sea rises."

"That is change! They are now islands."

"No way!" he said. "They're still what they were. The mountain stayed true to itself. Only the surroundings are different. Take a lesson."

Neither country tried to debrief Ylena. Although each had a thousand questions about the Falcon mission, Yuri would allow no interrogations. His design for mental health kept the start of Ylena's adjustment dedicated to emotional wringout and recovery. Facts sometimes emerged from her emotional ramblings. One involved her father. The news of his death upset Ylena more than any other loss. Her mother had died in childbirth, so her father had functioned as both parents. Sorrow cramped her heart at the thought of his high hopes for her. Yuri wanted her to come to grips with the father's loss first, and most importantly. He instructed Adam to encourage her to speak of the man openly and often.

As Ylena praised the love and brilliance of her father, a multitalented scientist, it became clear that he had hated the Soviet system. He wanted success in her space flight aboard Falcon because it would make her famous and permit foreign travel. There, her father said to her, she could escape.

"But I am happy here," she told him.

He brushed the idea aside as the outlook of a young innocent. "You will understand when you are older."

She sobbed again to Adam, crying out, "Older? Oh, God, if he could see how old I am now!"

Ylena told of her father's passion for her to defect after a successful space flight.

"And what if I get stuck in orbit?" she teased him.

"Even so, I will make sure that you have an opportunity to live in freedom."

She remembered his feverish experiments, in his home laboratory, on the blood from hibernators. He sought what he believed had to exist: a common ingredient among bears, squirrels, woodchucks, reptiles, the dormouse, and all creatures of long sleep in winter. He had even probed the cases of successful quasi-hibernation, or months-long rest, through famine winters, among Russian peasants.

He was thorough and relentless, but the traditional paths led nowhere. She could see his daily disappointment. One day, however, she found him disposing of the blood samples, emptying the no-longer-needed jars down the drain, and laughing happily.

"I found it! I found it! I found it!" he shouted and sang. "It's not in the blood! It has nothing to do with the blood. The secret's in the tissue cell itself!"

Enlightened, he had gone off on a totally independent research track, eventually synthesizing a hibernation fluid. He called it Americanol, " . . . in honor of your future home."

Once in possession of the fluid, he planned the other technical means for her escape.

"The rest is easy," he confided. "It requires merely tapping the engineering talent."

This he was able to do in his role of Chief Scientist at the Lenin Medical Engineering Center. There, he had access to experts in magnetism, solar cells, mechanics, electronics, computers, anesthesiology, chronology and radio, and to the fabricators of his exotic devices.

"You have three possible fates on your flight," he told Ylena. "First, you may die upon launch or reentry, in which case I cannot help you. Second, you may land successfully and become famous. In that case you will not need my help, for you can defect while traveling in other countries as a celebrity. Third, you may get stuck in orbit, in which case I can help you. What I mean is, this fluid and these devices can help you."

He described the materials and equipment he had secretly developed for her flight.

"Your signals for help will be made only over the United States. We have merged timing and the geography of the earth's magnetic field so that your broadcasts will be triggered only over America, and only at specific times. I have scheduled your signals to coincide with the great day that freedom began in the United States. I want the Americans to notice this, to realize that you are honoring their day and their successful revolution. It will show that you are one of them in spirit. They will want to make you welcome. It may take a while, but the Americans will one day come for you in a great ship of space.

"Do not smile like that. There *will* be great ships of space! That kind of progress is inevitable. History shows it happened with ships of the sea, so I expect no less of space. Knowing that the Americans will one day come for you, I will be able to die happy, even if you are stranded on this flight."

This insight electrified Tenement One. They suddenly realized that the USSR, and now the UCS, never knew about the suspended animation experiment! No wonder their UCS political establishment behaved so irrationally. The Communist hierarchy wanted the hibernation fluid as desperately as the Americans.

When President Sisco learned these facts, he called the Crisis Management Team to urgent session.

───────────────── 125 ─────────────────

Cooper turned to Yuri and said, "Poor Adam! How do you think he's really coping?"

"What's running through that quirky mind of yours now?"

"Well, the more I see of Ylena, the more I understand why Ben Franklin advocated affairs with older women."

"My professional diagnosis of you," said Yuri, "is expressed best by the Latin adjective 'kinky.' Also, your thinking is sloppy. Franklin didn't mean an age-mixture like Ylena's, but just straight age. And, speaking of age, how are you enjoying adolescence?"

The banter triggered Yuri into new thoughts for protecting Ylena. She already confronted an avalanche of stress. He didn't want gossip added. How soon would the news hounds start speculating about relations between a man and a woman confined alone? He began to think about rules of behavior and appearance for public consumption. He was in this frame of mind when Adam asked for a personal session.

On a secure link, he complained to Yuri about having others hear Ylena's private thoughts and see her grief and shock. Yuri saw a problem starting. *He's getting protective.* He gave an abrupt answer.

"First, Commander, I don't tell you how to fly the shuttle. Second, if she talks, it helps. If you listen, it helps. But I've got to listen, too, because, believe it or not, I've been trained to help. Now, you do everything you can to draw her out."

Adam subsided, realizing he had flared because he felt like a guardian. This battered, young/old woman had suddenly come under his care. He admired her actions and qualities — her spunk in punching him, the cheerful good humor in her harrowing circumstances, the lightning response to the bay door emergency, and the gritty ignoring of her wound's pain. He had first felt compassion stir while he dressed her injury.

The bullet's kerf was about a half-inch wide, and of shallow depth, running for nearly five inches between her elbow and shoulder. The flight surgeon guided Adam in dissolving dried blood that bonded her shirt to her skin, and then in binding the wound. Afterwards, Adam gave her fresh, oversized clothes, provided a meal, recited red-faced instructions for the toilet, and announced an order to sleep.

He got an unexpected reaction. "Sleep!? You are the funny man. You are making a joke, no? If no, you are not understand. Yes, I am exhaust, and I feel wobble. But I am not for sleep. I have just sleep my life away."

Then she astonished him. "Besides, sleeping here is not for recommending. Look what happened when you went to bed. Enough is enough."

Adam gaped in stunned delight. Yuri, tickled by the drollery, clapped his hands in satisfaction.

"Marvelous, marvelous," he chuckled. "She'll normalize them both within the hour."

He was wrong. During that hour, at her insistence, the "healing" talks with the UCS began. So did the grieving. It mounted as she mined her past for family and friends, but found only bones. She felt more like a freak with each passing day, the unnaturalness of her resurrection somehow making her feel no longer human. She was the lost child of the cosmos, wandering about in time.

Yuri believed you can endure almost anything if you can write about it. He convinced Ylena to keep a diary. "Every day, write what you do and your impressions. Write what you think and how you feel. Past or present. Prose or poetry. Doesn't matter. Just write."

After a week of pouring her heart through her pen, she showed him a poem and said, "I am too much anger." Its title said, "Communism." He read:

> *Beliefs they sold*
> *Whose roots took hold*
> *On lies they told*
> *To us when we were children*
>
> *Are past their crest*
> *And fail each test*
> *As we with zest*
> *Let later insights kill them*

"Good. Let it out. Keep writing," was all Yuri could say, gaping startled by the quality of her written English over her spoken, and by how his mind assigned her poem angry titles of Race, Sex, Politics, Religion from his own life.

When Greg Gandary cut in on another circuit to ask if Ylena would say something during the President's press conference, her answer was prompt, relieved and eager.

"Yes, I would like say hello to American people!"

The doleful pall in Olympia rolled off like fog as an excited Ylena danced around Adam for ideas on what she should say. Yuri smiled. Her desire for social contact told him he was looking at a healthy organism with an instinct for self-healing.

Cooper grunted, "Ever see anybody so mission-oriented?"

Benson disagreed. "Maybe she's mission-dependent."

Yuri pondered this exchange, speculating on the nature and strength of Ylena's resolve. He would have life and death evidence before the flight ended.

126

Olympia's crew compartment was enormous compared with Falcon's confines. Ylena felt it was like a small house in space. She relished the sheer joy of movement, whether floating about exuberantly, or exercising. She was strict about her workouts, made into a believer by Doctor Nanterre's astonishing descriptions of how extended weightlessness degrades the body. At the time of her launch, scientists knew little about the lurking hazards of life in orbit. But hibernation had apparently suspended the harmful, complex processes, allowing her to awaken intact. Now, however, weightlessness put her at risk of muscle atrophy, especially of the heart. This muscle would actually shrink in size without the demands of gravity.

The mass of all muscles would decline, of course, but it would be most notable in the useless legs. Her red blood cell production would fall and the cells themselves would become distorted and ragged, leaving their normal disk shape. Urination would carry off calcium and cause progressive bone loss.

"We are toothpick structures," said Nanterre, "and we can't function on thinner toothpicks."

He described how medicine had learned that the bone loss rate in space is about half a percent per month without exercise. If not for their gravity substitute, Mars-bound explorers would arrive debilitated. With fragile bones, no one would be able to exit the spacecraft or to stand - even in Mars' lesser gravity field. This, she and Adam realized, was probably the reason both their countries wanted the hibernation fluid.

Exercise was an antidote on the shuttle, but Adam wished he had the experimental G-berths of Space Station Freedom. Designed to accommodate four at a time, the spinning wheel simulated gravity, with each person's feet outward, as in a personal spoke. Crewmembers learned to sleep standing up, as horses do. Or they got their gravity ration while otherwise occupied; some used the gravity spokes as a library.

Ylena loved Olympia's huge windows. She spent hours at a stretch watching the earth roll by.

"How many people does earth house now?" she asked Adam.

"Seven billion, and counting. Mainly lawyers."

"Is this the modern humor, to joke on a distinguished profession?"

"It's no joke to me. America has too many lawyers."

"To have many lawyers is a good thing. You are lucky. They will defend your rights. If is seven billion people in the world, and counting more coming, there will be too little room, and too little food, and much need to control everyone. More and more rules. No rights. In my country the lawyers are, I mean say were, expensive and few. You could not afford one to protect you from the state."

"In my country, they are the state. Our congress is 85% lawyers."

"Why should that be upset you?"

"Hell, I'd be upset if even 20% of our Congress came from *any* single source. It wouldn't matter if they were engineers, or economists, or teachers, or electricians. Whatever! We're too diversified a nation to be so heavily represented by one group."

"But your people choose them!"

"Who else is there to choose from? Who else can get time off from the job to run for office? Who else can have a job waiting if they don't get reelected?"

"You mean to be in your Congress is not a service to your country?"

"What?"

"Is not your job held for your return from your Congress?"

"Nope! But that sounds like a great idea. I hope you become Americanski citizenski. You could do our thinking some good. However! Even that idea would have limited attraction. Imagine the obsolescence of a doctor or a scientist after just a few years away! I think that's why we have only three technical people in a Congress of 700."

"Then system will continue as is!"

"Well," he drawled, "I fight it where I can. I never vote for an attorney if there's a capable opponent who isn't one. I also never vote for a man if there's a capable woman opponent."

"What is wrong with the man?"

"Again, too much representation by one group. In addition, I don't trust male-dominated politics. It needs a balance from women. Male politicians have a lot of hidden agendas. The ones I know are driven by ego, power, and money. I find women to be more nurturing of the nation's needs. Those I know seem to think of the country as 'family.' I think it helps produce a more humane society."

"You give us too much credit."

"I wouldn't say that. I happen to think that men are born savages and women are born civilized."

And so it went, as the weeks passed in training, study, grieving, healing, orientation, language skills, entertainment, and exercise. She got hooked on TV soap operas, saw through their repetitive ooze in a week, and quit. Agog, she gaped and winced through six professional wrestling matches, passed judgment and quit. American football had her begging for old and new clips of highlights. To her, the game swung back and forth "between trench war and blitzkrieg." And she added, "You may be right on the savages!" Then she discovered basketball and the sleight-of-hand flying dunkers.

"They are giants doing ballet!" she cried at first sight. "They all belong in the Bolshoi."

Every day, Yuri sent her a few space-related cartoons and jokes. She was rapidly catching up on modern humor. She posted her favorites on the crew cabin walls. She repeated jokes she did not understand, wondering what made them funny.

"Why did the first restaurant on the moon fail?"

"I don't know."

"No atmosphere."

When he laughed, she said, "Why is that funny? Explain me."

She was interested in discussing all manner of subjects with Adam, but especially his views on religion, history, philosophy, family and friendship. She seemed to speak faster every day and to spend less time groping for words. Her English was improving. Still, she felt it a hard language to learn, and regarded it as imprecise.

"When you told me on your boyhood," she said, giving an example, "You told of an uncle. You said he was 'uncle.' It does not say if he is brother of your mother or brother of your father. Why do you not have a word for each?"

"That was Uncle Frank, my father's brother."

"It does not tell me who he is brother."

"You mean you want a specific word to distinguish my father's brother from my mother's brother? Like a title?"

"Not title. Just precise word. He could be 'muncle,' for being of your mother. No?"

"And 'funcle' for my Uncle Frank! Oh, boy! We'd better stay up here a few more months. America needs time to get ready for you! Is that the way you tell them apart in the Russian language?"

"No. We say 'dyadya,' only one word, same as you. It does not distinguish father from mother."

"Then why are you complaining about English?"

"Because I am expecting more. Your country is so good at making the acronyms, like laser, and maser, and radar. You could do it easy."

"You're babbling. I think you've been up here too long."

She sometimes chattered on and on, as though a deluge of inanities would flood away the threatening facts of what, and where, and when she was. Yuri told him she was trying to insulate her vulnerability.

When they got around to talk of love and family, she learned about the car crash. Their conversations told her how Adam lived and spent his time. She knew he was not searching for a woman to start another family. What that implied made her heart go out to him. She felt herself in the presence of a monumental sorrow that would forever lament an irreplaceable loss.

She had it partly right. She knew an old Russian saying that losing a loved one in death is sad, but losing a loved one in life is tragic. She did not know that the proverb applied doubly to Adam, where both losses had occurred, close together. Knowing little or nothing about the woman in the car crash, she presumed harmony in the marriage. She had no understanding of the complexity of his loss.

127

"Standing room only," said the electronic signs at Simon Sisco's press conference. The United States had agreed to face the media first. That gave Moscow a full day to adjust before Premier Yemetov, too, would brave the questioning. Sisco fought for and got an important concession from Moscow: they allowed Ambassador Taksis to participate. That would help show solidarity, and put the best face on the situation. So would the location.

"This place was a good idea, Greg," said Sisco, as he peeked out at the audience.

Gandary had chosen to use the Interplanetary Geographic Society's auditorium. As press secretary, he scrambled to provide every possible advantage for the President's public events. This setting emphasized the exploratory and cooperative nature of space activities. As neutral ground, Greg hoped, the site might help minimize embarrassing questions about the hostile actions in space between the two countries.

The President began with a review. He described his plan to use America's new shuttle capability in a peacemaking gesture to relieve international tension. He wanted to take the derelict Falcon spacecraft from orbit for delivery to Moscow as a gift. Yes, the Kremlin had misunderstood for a while, and there had been a short confrontation. After that, the nations communicated intensively, and cooperated actively. Yes, the UCS had sent a salvo of missiles near the shuttle. Ambassador Taksis would soon explain its purpose.

Most of the Crisis Management Team sat on the stage behind the President. Occasionally, he would call on a team member to answer a technical question. When asked why the Russians had waited decades without deciding to retrieve Falcon, Sisco willingly turned the microphone over to Taksis.

The Ambassador was ice cold in defense. "It was the plan. We are patient. We do not rush our experiments. Next question."

He went on, explaining his country's initial misunderstanding of American intentions. Once that was cleared up, he said, there was cooperation.

"The missile salvo? Why, that was a signal of celebration, very much like a 21-gun salute. It honored Olympia's successful rendezvous and rescue of Falcon. It was a ceremonial display, a spectacle. That's why we launched at night, so it could be seen."

Except for this response, he gave blunt and cryptic answers. No, he knew nothing about rumors of Russian missiles damaging Space Station Freedom.

"An errant rocket is always possible, but if there are no accusations, we will not bother to investigate."

Greg Gandary was astounded that the journalists didn't nail Taksis' lies to the wall. "He's getting away with it!"

The President grunted, "More holes than a Russian condom."

The questions moved on: What about the lethal attack by Andrei on Tim? In a demonstration of oily respect for the reporters, Taksis became conciliatory and puzzled. "Who knew that the American astronauts would create atmospheric pressure in the cargo bay before we could give them safety instructions for landing? Who knew they would cause Falcon to open and awaken our people prematurely, causing their confusion and defensive reaction?"

Therefore, he could not explain Andrei's attack on Tim. No, the UCS doctors did not believe that long exposure to space would make a person dangerously psychotic.

Unpredictably, he began a deliberate, chiding harangue of the media. He berated their representatives for fault finding, for impugning character, for trying to create troubles between partners, and for looking to the past. The audience seemed paralyzed as he raved on.

"Perhaps this is your worst problem," he ranted. "You are stuck in reverse, ignoring the future. You are disregarding the important news! You are blind to our revolutionary achievement. A person from the past has been revived! No nation in the history of the world ever accomplished such a feat. But you wish to wallow in the shallows of politics. I say shame! Let us move on. Why do you not focus on the miracle of this Communist woman? I mean 'focus' literally. Would you like to see her on television? Who would like that? Would you? Right now!?"

From the stunned crowd came a few replies of yes. Then, as the implication set in, the calls became shouts that synchronized into a demanding, rhythmic clamor.

Taksis signaled for quiet and boomed, "Very well, then! It shall be! Mr. President, show them the heroine of the United Communist States, Captain Ylena Valena, of the Soviet Air Force!"

Greg Gandary, choking on his rage, cried into the tumult, "Oh, that sneaky, rotten bastard! How did he find out?"

Taksis had somehow learned of, or anticipated, plans for the surprise broadcast from Olympia. Greg had worked on it all through the night, obtaining medical clearances, getting Ylena's agreement ("Yes, I would like say hello to American people."), and arranging technical timing and equipment. He had labored long and hard, carefully crafting the words and meanings in Sisco's preamble to the broadcast. Now, the remarkable event he had sculpted lay smashed to shards, appearing as a Communist achievement, with the President of the United States cast as a roustabout assigned to throw a switch.

128

Greg Gandary believed in the politician's motto: *Don't get mad, get even.* He practiced it now with Grigory Taksis, alerting a technician to disable the man's microphone. He enjoyed the twitching carnival of expressions this caused on the normally poker face. Cueing in the TV, Gandary brought the giant screen to life for the press. Choosing his scenes from a bank of monitors, he first displayed a shot from Peeker One, showing Olympia buttoned up. Then he showed Falcon, with its open hatch. He segued into the shuttle cabin, building suspense, steadying on the flight panel.

"Go out there!" he prompted Sisco, nudging him to the microphone with the cue, "And say Adam is the only appropriate person to introduce her."

Sisco, equally piqued, adopted the theme. "Ladies and gentlemen," he thundered, "Ambassador Taksis is not the person to be introducing our heroine!"

He paused for dramatic effect. The suddenly silent audience shifted uneasily. Out among the TV billion viewers, many started at the rebuke.

He went on, all at once conciliatory and humble. "Nor am I the appropriate person to present her to you!" Pause.

"No! No one here is entitled to do that." He looked around. "All that we can do is to bid her welcome to our age and to life among us." Short pause. "Why? Because Ms. Ylena Valena no longer represents any particular society. She represents all of earth!"

Another pause. "Who, then, should it be? I think we all realize that no one on earth has the right to introduce this heroine, this planet's time-traveling guest, this world's remarkable revenant from generations ago!"

There was relieved applause.

"And so, we turn to someone who is not on earth. She will be presented to you by the person who rescued her: Commander Adam MacGregor!"

Adam's face filled the huge screen, momentarily stunned.

"Not fair!" said Cooper as applause resumed.

John Dough disagreed. "Don't worry about it. Remember, he was a test pilot. You can throw anything at those guys."

He was right. Adam, waving off the applause, broke his creased face into new creases with a huge, winning grin. "Thanks, but I just did a *job*. This lady did *history!*"

Audiences roared and clapped. As the tumult settled down, Adam said, "Here to speak her thoughts is Ms. Ylena Valena."

There was no applause or motion, only silence and awed expectation.

Deep in Tenement One, appraising the absolute silence, the irreverent Cooper tilted his head and whispered to Yuri, "You could hear a mouse peein' on cotton!" Yuri elbowed him in the ribs.

The camera widened beyond Adam, to include both him and Ylena, then zoomed in on her alone. The screen filled with an unlined face, somewhat puffed from the extra blood no longer pulled to the legs by gravity. It made her features slightly oriental, a setting appropriate for the jade eyes. Silent, she gazed long and thoughtfully at half the people of the world. In breath-held gaping, they stared back, entranced. Ylena began to speak, very slowly.

"I am talking at you in English and say thank you, America, for kind things you have done me since my new life. Some day, I hope I can tell you I am happy for being woke up, and say thank you for that, too. Not yet. It may be, later. You understand, yes? Right now, there is all confusion to me.

"My home is gone. All is new. Everyone by home is new. I find true everywhere. Everyone on whole earth is new to me. All the old people are gone. Everyone I know is gone. I am alone. It is a hard thing."

Around the globe, people reached to touch or hold. Translators choked up. Tears flowed on the planet and in space. Ylena's tears, swelling beyond the size of her pupils, stood round at her eyes. She paused, put out her lower lip and huffed upward. The huge drops, gigantic on the screen, rose away, undulating.

Her voice held steady. "Commander Adam says that I will make new friends. He is right. All my first life I did that. But kept old friends, too.

Always there to comfort. Now, no more. It is feeling very lonely. From my big emptiness I will preach you my lesson: Love each other while you can."

The lucid green eyes, gentle now, pulsed with a compassion, knowledge, and understanding that captured, embraced, and warmed the world. They underwent a gripping change in the following silence, slowly growing luminous and lively, fired by Ylena's vigorous spirit. Finally, flashing the message of regeneration, they matched her words.

"My other life is finished. I must prepare coming to you. Commander Adam will teach me his ship so I can help get us home on earth. It will mean much work. We will succeed. Then I can say you hello again, back down on ground. Then we will talk. Thank you for being interest in me. Now, I must tell you good-bye."

She waved farewell. The screen went dark. Reporters who should have been taking notes had been immobilized, watching and listening. The stunned silence finally broke. In an eruption of frustration and recrimination, the bedazzled journalists clamored for more. They had all assumed there would be a question period.

Gandary worked to restore calm. "Quiet! Be patient! Ms. Valena does not know our ways. I will contact Olympia with your request."

His voice circuit got no farther than Houston. Ken Hemming refused to put the call through to Olympia.

"Greg, she's now a member of the crew. The flight surgeon won't allow any more stress. In fact, he's the one who scheduled her shutdown. Want to talk with him?"

Greg said yes. Bill Nanterre came on. He was a rock on the issue. The best Greg could arrange was a question and answer session with the doctor. The media questions got so clinical, both physically and psychologically, that Greg was unexpectedly glad Ylena was *not* involved. Now he understood the wisdom of the doctor's precautions on stress.

Afterward, Nanterre warned him, "You get those morons to agree on rules for decency and courtesy in talking with that brave woman or I'll keep an indefinite medical moratorium on any more TV appearances."

——————————— 129 ———————————

President Sisco finished a second playing of Ylena's conversation with Adam and asked, "Are we agreed?"

Heads nodded around the room. All on the Crisis Management Team believed the flight of Falcon had not been an official medical experiment for suspended animation. They had no reason to disbelieve what Ylena had told Adam about her father's private research.

"This means," said Sisco, "the Russians are as anxious as we are to get hold of that fluid. We can expect them to try almost anything to acquire what remains. I expect them to call in 'The Watchers' on this one. They'll make us do an inventory at the landing site."

He was referring to the UN team of impartial observers that gathered facts on international disputes. Chosen from the ranks of eminent jurists in all member nations, the team had developed a legendary reputation for objectivity. Their reports had more believers than the sworn word of any political leader. They had been enormously successful in keeping elections honest and in finding out which countries had nascent clandestine biological, chemical, or nuclear warfare capabilities.

"I intend to have some of that fluid," growled Sisco. "It does not belong to the Kremlin! In fact, it was developed, we now see, in hostility to the purposes of the old USSR."

He was working to convince himself. He had the decent man's need for a rationale when planning deceit.

"Indeed," he went on, "it was meant to provide benefit to the United States! It was not made by or for the USSR. A private party made it, Dr. Valena. He did it for another private party, his daughter, so that she could get to this country. We may assume that she would bring all she owned with her. However, I don't want to take any chances on the whims of Captain Ylena. That's too uncertain when you recall the behavior of her shipmate."

He paused and paced about. "So, the very least I will do is to have Commander MacGregor acquire half the remaining amount from Falcon and refrigerate it for study and replication by our chemists."

Sensitive to process, the Secretary of State shifted uneasily. "Are you implying that the Russians don't know how much original material there was and won't know if we retain some?"

Sisco beamed slyly. "Right! There's the value of our hearing her conversations with Adam. Her father didn't know how much would be needed to suspend two people. Nor did he know how long suspension would last. He must have thought there might be a wake-up and the need to inject again, perhaps several times. So the supply was ample. We know that, but the Russians don't! That's our little secret until she talks to them about the fluid. *If* she ever talks to them about the fluid! So far we've been able to control the topics very well. There's a static maker assigned to foul the voice circuit if that topic arises.

"Let's sum up the options possible. First, Captain Valena may defect to us. In that case, everything becomes simple. We merely deny there was any fluid left, and we tell her to avoid that subject. Second, we may put a look-alike in place of the fluid. The medical people are making a list of onboard liquids as we speak; we may choose from that inventory. Third, we retain half the fluid and give them the other half as though it were the full remainder. Fourth, we publicly say how much fluid remains and openly offer the Kremlin half. We will look enormously fair handed if we do that, don't you think?"

The press secretary spoke up, "No, Mr. President, I don't. Not if Captain Valena chooses to return to her home! In that case, all of her property will have to go with her. The Watchers would see to it."

Sisco smiled. "Keen. I like your clarity. Let's get some more discussion." He turned to an easel pad and keynoted the four options. When people's positions hardened and conversation started circling, Sisco stopped the talk and announced his conclusion.

"We will retain half and leave the remainder behind. The sealed Falcon will be craned into the Russian cargo plane. The Russians will at once open Falcon and discover the supply. They will have no way of knowing if that is the total. If Captain Valena defects, we keep it all. Any questions?"

Frank Cole spoke. "We've got an operating problem. The fluid's still in Falcon. There's no air in the payload bay. If Adam goes out there to make the tap, outside a locked air lock, he leaves her, a possibly hostile officer, alone in the control room. Remember, there are still cosmonauts standing by up there in Eagle. What if she doesn't let him back in? Suppose his air runs out? When he's dead, she opens the bay doors, and Major Kuznets comes back. She suits up, they take the fluid, they fly to Eagle, and they fly away home."

"Solutions?" said Sisco, looking around the room.

Mike Benson said, "Frank, would that problem go away if you had air in the bay?"

Cole thought for a moment. "Sure. With that, Adam could keep the air lock open and come and go as he chose. He could even tap the fluid while she's asleep."

"OK. So what you need is some air tanks to go up on the Russians' delivery flight you're chartering."

Cole winced. He was still smarting over Nastran's crippled fleet. Then he smiled a very devilish smile.

"I like it. We'll get them to carry the very thing we need to pirate the very thing they want. You're a master of intrigue, Dr. Benson."

Cole went on, "The Russians are refusing to let any of our astronauts fly up along with our equipment and supplies. They want freedom of action, maybe even to grab the fluid and leave Captain Valena behind for whatever can be worked out later. Adam will have to monitor the deliveries into the air lock itself, with the bay doors ready to slam shut and coop up any cosmonaut who heads for Falcon to steal what it contains."

The President came in decisively. "That's it, then. Work it out, Frank. Thank you all for your help. Let's break."

On exit, they found the Marine guard confronting John Dough, who was trying to look into the room.

"What's going on? Why wasn't I invited?"

────────────────── 130 ──────────────────

Ylena had unwittingly taken the world by storm. Armies of attorneys researched the limits of liability for implying her endorsement of products. Any magazine with her picture on the cover sold out swiftly. Journalists descended on Moscow to research her childhood, photograph her early home, interview anybody from the neighborhood, broadcast from her college dorm room, visit her military training bases, and invade the space museums for retrospectives on early flight equipment.

Every TV network had its documentary on the world's new sweetheart. Her face seemed ubiquitous, appearing on Tshirts, beach towels, billboards, posters, coffee cups, and wall plates, in addition to the deluge from product advertising, newspapers, magazines, and television. Tanzania issued a stamp bearing her features.

Dormant charlatans bloomed like desert flowers after a rain. Pushers of eternal youth, they tapped that universal human addiction. They capitalized on dreams, selling hopes of no wrinkles, no cellulite, no sags or bags. Every cosmetics producer contrived a link to Ylena, hinting at powers in the product that would create similar beauty and preservation. Lotions and potions and creams and soaps appeared in new packages, bearing her picture.

Creative advertising worked overtime, producing an early benefit for one pill pusher in the diet industry. Its ad theme became "You can be leaner than Ylena." Pronounced specially, it rhymed. TV ads said it slowly and seductively, against a background of stars.

One travel agency, suggesting space itself as the panacea, took deposits from aspiring immigrants to future space cities. Ylena's face appeared even in industrial catalogs, allied to technical products. The *New Yorker* wrote drolly of a radar equipment ad that mentioned "The face that launched a thousand blips." Squads of journalists dug for her background, tastes, style, and interests.

The sensationalist tabloids blasted the Russians' reticence, and their inability or unwillingness to provide information, with "WHAT IS MOSCOW HIDING?" headlines. Ylena was their darling, the lost child of the cosmos. Sentimentality sold. It was temporary, but was a welcome relief as it displaced the daily tabloid drivel, including a healthy Hitler seen by astronomers on an asteroid.

High style modeling agencies elbowed for access to a possible contract. The agents for stage and screen scurried by phone or plane to question Moscow. "Can she sing? Dance? Did she study ballet? Can your government contract her for a film with us? Why not? It means big bucks! Western currency! Isn't she your property?"

Customers swamped libraries for James Hilton's old classic, *Lost Horizon*. Happy publishers sold every copy they could roll off their presses. Journalists compared Lo-Tsen with Ylena. Each woman had a preserving aerie, one in Shangri La, and the other in a spaceship. Each was young, yet old. The coolly delicate Manchu was contrasted with the cheerful and caring Ylena. One left a preserving valley, headed outside to rapid aging. The other would leave a preserving sky, headed home to glory.

The "Ylena Look" sprouted. Auburn wigs took on value. Hairdressers dyed, and redheads poured on HairGro. Factories worked around the clock to meet the contact lens demand. Eskimo women with inserted green eyes smiled into mirrors. Jewelry of military bracelets and pendants boomed. Paris was first with the new fashions in clothing. Its baggy, survival look was snapped up. Ylena dolls appeared. Some, on springs, jiggled happily in auto rear windows. Others, cute little cuddlies for beddy-bye, sparked shopper frenzy in stores with limited supply.

TV evangelists took Ylena to their well-dressed bosoms. "She of the angelic face and heavenly mystery," one dubbed her. They viewed her as the redeemable product of a regime of atheists. She was the living proof of the second chance promised by the Scriptures. The doctrine of forgiveness was being made evident in the heavens. Ylena had done the first half of the job; she had been reborn physically. Now she could do the other half, she could become reborn spiritually.

"We can make that woman's rebirth happen! We can do it by our prayers. We can even *watch* as it happens! It has been set out for our edification and inspiration, right up there on the Lord's great stage. Now, friends, I am asking Nastran for time to speak with her personally, to speed the process. The broadcast time will be expensive, so remember to send your contribution. Meanwhile, we'll keep her in your mind by vigil display right here." The channel's normally dark periods carried Ylena's smiling face and continuous organ music.

Popular music took a turn. Sentimentality returned. Composers and lyricists banged out paeans to Ylena that included: *"Forever with you,"* *"You've come back to me,"* *"Now we can start over,"* *"I look up to you,"* *"Doll in the sky,"* and *"Why not go 'round with me?"* They told of love renewed, love without end, heavenly love, and love forever young. Some daring composers tied the lyrics to thumping energy. They got nowhere. The mood was not for harsh energy, but for happiness, joy, romance, and mystery. One odious product arose from the cigarette years of the 20th century. Its ancient lyrics sang, *"You've come a long way, baby."*

Paralleling Ylena's resurrection, *Green Eyes*, a mid-1900's song, became the hit of hits. Radio beamed its reborn, joyful beat constantly, and people walked in sync with its hummed rhythms. The old melody intrigued all ages. Puzzled teenagers marveled, wondering how any music so fresh could come from the quaint people of the dark ages. Ylena, foot-locked, hugged herself, smiling happily and swaying to the marvelously foolish rewording dedicated to her:

> *Oh, cool and flashing Green Eyes,*
> *No longer need the stars rise . . .*
> *For you are shining brightly*
> *And Heaven now means you.*
>
> *Your gaze from far above me*
> *Sees in the hot heart of me*
> *The need to stop and love me . . .*
> *'Cause I'm in orbit, too.*

She had captured the world. She was a growth industry. Bill Nanterre fueled it unknowingly. His medical moratorium caused global deprivation. Ylena's isolation added remoteness to her basic mystery. Social historians understood, remembering the intense public interest stirred by the inaccessibility and reclusiveness of the early film star, femme fatale Greta Garbo.

Cards, letters, and gifts poured in for Ylena. The White House set up a special communications unit in a warehouse. Within a week, their effort to organize and respond fell well behind.

The flight surgeon got some calls from presidential aides, apparently acting on their own. They pleaded an inability to get the government's work done due to the continuing deluge of public demand for access to Ylena. Why not another TV session? Why not a "real" press interview? Why not now? Veiled threats came from veiled men.

Nanterre told one such caller, "Don't ask again! Being independent is one of the reasons I became a doctor. I'm not hostage to anuses like you."

That's a medical term. I can find work anywhere. If you try pressure, I'll hold my own press conference on politics versus medicine, and I'll name you, and I'll quit in public."

He held Ylena out of circulation for nearly a month. Then, he and Yuri agreed that her overall condition would allow her to make another TV broadcast. When she agreed, they began to plan the rules.

--------------------- 131 ---------------------

The crammed weeks flew on. Adam daily administered Houston's flight training program for Ylena. It was interspersed with Yuri's psychological adjustment program. The schedule called for staggered periods of play, exercise, movies, technical study, ship maintenance, earth gazing, private reflection, medical sessions, phone talks, and updates on world history.

Ylena told Adam she was not surprised that the old USSR had come unglued. Only permanent force could contain the diverse, hostile, ethnic, and religious groups that Stalin had subsumed. Even within groups, she said, there was often a widespread, thwarting meanness. It would work against allowing success to happen to a neighbor, even if you, too, were also doing better. She recited an ancient story to illustrate.

"God spoke to a man one day and said 'You may have any wish. My only condition is your neighbor will get same, but doubled. What is your wish?' The man thought long and said, 'I wish to be blind in one eye'."

"Ugh! Nice neighbors. No wonder communism failed."

"Do not form too bad impression! We have much better peasant tales from old days. I will tell you stories."

In their leisure time, she spun the fables, and it annoyed him that, aside from Rip Van Winkle and a few others, his culture had little to match the Russian lode of lore and myth. "Well," he told her, "I hope we'll have more than scanty offerings when we too are an ancient country."

Her stories amazed him with their recurring theme of magic and witchcraft. Wondrous talking animals — whether firebirds, friendly wolves, wise bears, cunning foxes, or airborne horses — conferred supernatural powers on humans, usually on the poor and the good. The virtues of truth, honesty, and diligence were rewarded. Peasant lads, granted sudden wealth, rose to marry Tsars' daughters. Equivalents of Cinderella were discovered by princes and lived happily ever after. Heroes could fly or be instantly transported wherever they chose.

Ylena's tales always had happy endings: a love attained, a youth gaining wisdom, a lost child restored to parents, wealth achieved, or hunger forever banished by a bottomless, refilling pot or basket. The folktales, he realized, sprang from the hopelessness and desperation of marginal existence. They came from the dreams, wishes, and aspirations of generations of peasantry, impoverished, close to the soil and its creatures, in a bitter climate, with little or no hope of betterment, travel, or escape.

Through the fantasy of her stories, Ylena partly satisfied her own need for escape from her shocks and fears. Adam was proving to be a good listener and good company. She particularly enjoyed her radio talks with American women astronauts. The Russians still had no female cosmonauts, having changed policy after the first few historic flights of women in the mid-1900s.

In 1976, General Andrian Nikolayev expressed their frozen macho mentality. Saying the job was "too dangerous and demanding," he went on to clarify: "We love our women very much, and we spare them as much as possible."

"He didn't remember The War!" Ylena said. Proudly, she told her women astronaut friends that, in the 1940's, the Soviets had regiments of female fighter pilots who fought, and triumphed or died, flying Yaks against male Nazis in Messerschmitts. One, Lilya Litviak, shot down 15 enemy aircraft. Nazi soldiers feared the squadrons of women bomber pilots called "the night witches" for their darkness assaults on ground forces. All told, the women pilots flew more than 30,000 combat missions.

The Communist policy change on women in space startled and disappointed Ylena. She remembered the highlight days of Valentina Tereshkova's flight. The policy amused the American women astronauts. They thought it quaint that some man should make decisions for them on what was too dangerous or demanding.

Ylena's conversations with the women, group or singular, achieved much that Yuri hoped for. They gave Ylena role models. She was bonding to the women astronauts in a sorority of the skies. She could feel her confidence rising. She became convinced she could master the new technology, and she worked at it strenuously.

Making Ylena competent was important to Houston. Much would be riding on her if Adam became ill or injured and she had to maintain Olympia until Nastran could send up replacement astronauts. But the scenario of a long maintenance period wasn't the worst. Houston saw a more disquieting prospect: the shuttle repaired, an emergency need to return to earth, and Adam sick or disabled. Who would fly it home? The Russians had refused to transport even one shuttle astronaut on the charter supply flight.

Adam taught well and Ylena learned well. He found her smart, patient, persevering, and thorough, with excellent reflexes. She was rapidly reclaiming her bright and serene personality. Adam trained and drilled and tested her relentlessly, but she came up for more.

He worried about the intensity of her exercising. It gobbled oxygen faster than did his own regimen. Flight Surgeon Nanterre was making a tradeoff between Olympia's limited oxygen supply and Ylena's need to prevent the strength decline that occurs in minimal gravity. He let her have her way, a vigorous, exuberant way. Perhaps, he recognized, she instinctively knew her body's needs. The doctor knew the well-established requirements for female astronauts, but this woman was fresh from a condition never calibrated. So she rowed, skipped, skied, and stretched the bungee cords as she willed.

She and Adam continued to talk at length at the end of each workday. Following an "evening" meal, they would sit in the flight chairs of the darkened cockpit for a short night and marvel at the mysterious, fiery universe around them.

Adam sometimes saw their sky as a punctured canopy leaking brightness from elsewhere. Innumerable points of light ran a span of colors from intensely bright to dubious dim, hinting at a brilliant source beyond. In firm prediction and clocked precision the stellar furnaces wheeled relentlessly into view. Adam lived in a state of continuous awe. And yet, the boredom of training crept in. He began to think we can be awed and bored at the same time because we are meant to be up and doing, not totally gaping. He wondered if he would be bored while awed in heaven should he get there. With a wry chuckle he pondered this as a reason for fallen angels.

Slowly, he came to prize the quiet times together. It vexed him to think they would end on landing; he would miss them sorely. Suffering premature nostalgia, he smiled at his personal turnabout, realizing he no longer wanted this mission ended quickly.

They talked more often of their past, their views, and their hopes. Adam described their sessions as "our cosmic conversations, 'way up here, jest a'sittin' and a'rockin' on the highest front porch in the universe."

They counted the ever-present forest fires, watched the jagged legs of lightning sprint miles along the cloud tops, marveled at the bluish green of the dancing aurora, tracked meteorites from first glow through dying burn, searched for ship lights on the dark oceans, and pondered the dramas in the twinkling cities. Nearby hung the silvery, refulgent moon, serene and majestic. Below, the south polar cap winced under its ice-fanged winds. Above, in a sky of absolute black, the stark, fat stars stared and the moon watched silently. It was glorious and sublime, immersing kindred souls communing.

The place and the person drew him out. Adam, grown quite fond of his young ward, gradually eddied into a type of domestic bliss. She spoke about her childhood life, of savage winters, and of the warm drowsy murmur of summer days. She lived her early years in a golden, happy world that included vacations to a seaside dacha where she splashed in the sluggish dwarf waves of the Caspian shore. She seemed to know every Russian fairy tale. She told him more old country stories, and they laughed at clever Russian proverbs. Now and then she sang a folk song or translated a poem. No, she knew no Russian poems about space. Adam suggested that poems about space had come after her time but were rare even at this late date. She wondered why, and he floated his father's answer.

His dad, an astronomer with the old NASA, had pity and abuse for the inflexibility of poets. His father felt that poets simply wouldn't take the time or make the effort to master the terminology or the concepts of space travel. Some poets said it involved too much machinery and too little humanity. Yet the ingredients for epic poetry were at hand. Mythology was equaled or exceeded. Man rose toward the sun on a column of fire. Automatic birds took wingless flight through the dust of creation to explore other worlds. Some meteors that lit the skies bore humans home. Men fell for days toward earth. Freezing voyagers struggled home aboard damaged vessels, arriving ablaze. But from the poets there was silence.

"My dad wrote space poems while very young. He was only fourteen when he wrote the poem I like most."

When she said, "Tell me," it flowed from him like breath.

"Well, Dad had a mind that saw romance in a pile of organized metal flying past Pluto. He loved space exploration and what it represented. He knew every NASA program, every launch vehicle. At fourteen, back in the 1970's, he used his savings to pay for a school bus trip to the launch of Voyager II. It was starting off on what they called The Grand Tour of the outer planets. The engineers played interplanetary billiards, making bank shots from planet to planet by careful timing and steering. They used planetary gravity to redirect Voyager, year after year, from one planet to the next and the next. Dad saw Voyager as a scout, seeking out the path for people. The poem says what he felt at launch. When I was a teenager, I found it in his desk. I used to say it at night, going to sleep."

Eyes closed, she whispered, "Say it."

"Well, Dad called it *'Voyager Departing'*. It went like this:

Vessel of our wrung thought,
Night sweat, misting pride . . .
Launched to Heaven's sea,
With Time itself your tide . . .

Speak to us from solar storms!
Scout our path to goals.
Spy the cosmic macerators;
Chart celestial shoals . . .

That course and armor
We may gauge . . .
To launch another age,
When ships take flesh."

Adam blanched from his wistful reverie, suddenly chagrined. He had forgotten that the camera was still on for Yuri's needs.

"It's a kid's poem," he explained self-consciously.

"Oh, how I wish I had written it! Is what I feel. Is hard to believe he could write that even before he went to space."

Adam shook his head in vicarious disappointment, saying, "No. He never flew. That was sad, because flight was his dream. He wanted to be a scientist astronaut but hadn't the health."

Ylena touched his hand in consolation. "He flew. He flew where we really fly, in the mind."

Adam did not draw away, as he had from so many of their touchings in work or accident. As their ship flew on, lost in the wonders, he raised her hand, pressed it to his lips in a chivalrous gesture, and gently gave it back. In silence, he left his seat and went to his sleep station. Ylena, yielding to an enveloping lassitude, an overwhelming desire to hover and dream, basked on in warm, pensive musing. She had not expected to feel happy in her bizarre circumstances, but she was. She had already found a friend, a most courteous friend. Adam's gallanting brought her pleasant memories of home and her travels. His gesture, his lips on her hand, had seemed quite natural at the moment, yet now it did not. She wondered if it was a custom in America. In Europe it was a gallantry directed mainly to married women. She stirred uneasily, speculating drowsily that it might mean something different in America. Starting to awaken, she felt alarmed confusion at the glad swelling of her heart as a tremor warmed her loins.

— 132 —

Adam couldn't see Eagle through a window. It hovered behind Olympia. He imagined that her crew had orders to prevent Olympia from leaving, if that ever became possible. He relied on relayed images from Peeker One to watch the Russian craft. Otherwise, he disliked the prying Japanese machine. The thing had become an oriental paparazzo, buzzing about and invading privacy without notice, courtesy or consideration. Sometimes, forgetful of its presence, Adam awoke, stretched, and scratched his parts. And the world knew. He felt like a baseball player, caught crude in the outfield.

Aptly named, Peeker often stared for hours into his flight deck. Sometimes, the thing seemed gone, but if he looked closely he would find its lenses, snug in a window corner, keeping watch. Broadcasters tried to explain what was going on inside Olympia. Their comments were often incomprehensible or wrong, making the public angry and impatient. Needing knowledge and accuracy, the networks hired former astronauts with resonant voices. At attractive hourly rates they provided the public with some knowledgeable, 'round-the-clock chatter. They liked Peeker One; it helped overcome the social quarantine Nanterre had imposed on Ylena. At least, it let the public see she was up and about, and on the emotional mend.

Yuri liked the Peeker for two reasons. First, it boosted Ylena's ego and confidence to be "on stage." This gave her a continuous flow of adrenaline that stimulated performance and recovery. Second, the Peeker's constant watching delayed the dreaded romantic linkup he anticipated. He expected that to appear first in the tabloids at the supermarket checkout counters. Those rags would soon claim Ylena was pregnant with a goateed, radioactive fetus toothily cannibalizing her uterus, all due to quick-kilt MacGregor. Yuri's rules never allowed both of them off camera together.

When the chartered Russian spacecraft arrived, Peeker One let Adam see Hawk dock with Eagle. He had been following the Russian radio conversations, with Ylena giving him rapid translation. After docking, the radio talk stopped as the cosmonaut leaders apparently met personally in one of the united ships. They did not respond to his radio calls. After twelve hours, Adam got a call from them. It was time to transfer materials, they said. Houston had chosen distinctive wrappers for all supplies so that no substitutes could creep in. The flight directors had fought Administrator Cole against allowing delivery into the air lock. Cole had laughingly called Hemming "properly paranoid," but had given him the point. Delivery would occur in the open bay, away from the air lock door.

The transfers began routinely enough. A bulky cosmonaut jetted over from Hawk and placed his package on the bay deck. As he started home, another carrier left Hawk. A third carrier appeared, and then a fourth. Each methodically delivered and returned for more.

John Dough had interviewed and exposed every known kind of con man. His memory tingled. With Gandary's permission, he spoke to Houston.

"Mr. Hemming, aren't those awfully small loads each man is moving? Could they, should they, be carrying more at a time?"

Hemming said, "There's no weight, only mass to get moving and then stop. Sure, they could each carry more. Why do you ask? We've got so many deliverymen that the job's about done."

John Dough, still tickled by instincts, said, "Well, that's what bothers me. They put a fleet of guys out there and then dragged out the process. Why such small loads? Why so many people?"

"Out with it, John!"

"We're watching a conveyor belt. Dull. Routine. Boring. I sense an old trick. I think they're setting you up with a lulling pattern. I think they're going to pull something."

Even as he spoke, Eagle broke away from Hawk and rose out of the view from Peeker One. The Japanese operator turned his craft to follow whatever Eagle intended. Houston and Tenement One lost all sight of Hawk and the outside cosmonauts.

"Close the bay doors!" cried Hemming.

Adam spun from the bay windows to the door controls.

"Suzy!" screamed Hemming into the Tokyo circuit. "Suzy! Turn it back! Make Peeker look back!"

Peeker One spun and focused. It showed the bay doors closing, with two men riding the starboard door as it moved, legs astride its mating edge. Skilled and swift, they assembled a sturdy skeleton from pivoted bundles of snap bars. A four-foot, open, box girder cube took shape. Undoubtedly of special steel, it would hold the doors open more than enough for cosmonaut traffic. Striking that metal frame would surely damage Olympia's hinges and warp her doors, making flight back home impossible. Adam braked the doors to a kiss contact with the four-foot barrier.

One side of the box frame had parallel rectangular projections sticking out like lips. These had been slid about two feet over the starboard door's edge, gripping like a dog's mouth on a frisbee. Four cosmonauts squeezed through the slot of open doors, entered the bay, and moved toward Falcon.

—————————————— 133 ——————————————

Hemming remembered one of Tim's maneuvers. Flat voiced, deadly calm, he spoke, "Olympia, this is Houston."

Adam took Hemming's instructions with mounting excitement and savage satisfaction. A few moments later, the clamps holding the Lead Ass Dummy flew open. The four men in the bay heard nothing in the vacuum of space as Adam played the LAD's jets. Like a grim, cosmic bowler he flung the LAD ponderously into their ranks, striking and scattering three like duckpins. The fourth, only nudged, dodged away into a tight space between Falcon and the bay wall. His companions floated unconscious in the bay. Adam, seeing the LAD'S low fuel readings, abandoned pursuit of the remaining cosmonaut and positioned the LAD under the box frame barrier.

He opened the bay doors a few feet and moved the LAD upward to push the barrier away. The monolithic surfaces of the LAD could not hook to the barrier and drag it free. The frame box had been designed well. Instead of pivoting free, it began to merely bend at the base of its deep clamp on the door edge. Adam realized he could not push or batter it loose. He worked carefully to avoid warping the door or its closure edge. Fortunately, the gripping lips of the box had been shoved on at a point where they straddled one of the door's bracing beams. Only this support allowed him to get any results at all. He had to be satisfied with the LAD's success in bending some of the box out of the way.

He brought the doors closer together. The frame box, now bent somewhat up and outward, still blocked the doors, but only as a bent box, as a wedge. The opening had been reduced to two feet. At least no one in a space suit could get in or out. Adam now had four cosmonauts trapped within the bay. In mute frustration, he saw the LAD run out of fuel. The uninjured cosmonaut saw this, too, as the condensation sputtered to a spritzing fizzle. He emerged confidently from his niche and went directly to Falcon. He spoke rapidly in Russian to his commander back in Hawk. Ylena, although saddened by the Russian casualties, spoke in outrage against their attempt to steal her father's property. The fluid did not belong to the State.

"He will find it soon, commander. It is not his! He cannot take! We must stop them! He told his leader suit up and come. He will hand it through slot. After that, he said, you will no longer have reason for trap. Then he will do your soft side, so you will let him take injured comrades home for medicine."

Adam decided to make the man's job tougher. He carefully rotated Olympia to put the bay in shadow. Then he darkened the bay to pitch black. The cosmonaut produced a flashlight and kept on searching. Adam sighed and put the lights back on.

Suzy Arai smiled in relief. Lights helped the view from Peeker One as it poked and watched along the door gap. The Peeker had broadcast the entire action to the world.

134

With the constant, ubiquitous, commercial imagination of the Japanese, Suzy Arai grasped an opportunity. She spoke to Hemming on Nastran's special link to Tokyo. Although happy to be part of the Houston network, she knew it would now be the wrong circuit for describing an idea.

"Mr. Hemming, I wish you to give me three commercial phone numbers. I must speak with you privately, and at once. I will call you on one of them."

Ken asked no questions, ready for help from any quarter. He sent an aide running off to nearby offices for some desk phone numbers. Suzy, meanwhile, spoke intensively with Joji Asaki, her current Peeker pilot, a virtuoso of remote manipulation. A slow grin lit Joji's intent face as he talked with Suzy. His eyes twinkled. He made a little growling noise, like a beast expecting meat.

"Ah! Yes. I can. Thank you for the opportunity!"

Hemming took Suzy's commercial call from Tokyo and listened to a proposal from this international entrepreneur. What she proposed would benefit her employer, herself, and her country, but it would violate diplomatic procedures. Ken had to hear the proposal twice before he could believe that she really wanted him to take the deal to President Sisco.

"I will trust your President's word. If he agrees, have him call me on the Nastran circuit and repeat the telephone number we are now using. Then I will act immediately."

On a secure circuit, Hemming described the proposal. There was a long silence before Sisco said, "We seem to have no other options left and we're out of time. Give me the lady's number."

Hemming linked them, and Sisco spoke the phone number signal. Hemming then called Adam saying, "Stand by the bay door controls. Be ready to operate on my instructions."

Adam took position. He heard the cosmonaut who was searching in Falcon radio jubilantly to Hawk, "I found a needle. A hypodermic! I will seek others."

From Hawk came the response, "Excellent! I am entering the air lock now. I will be right there."

On the TV screen, Adam watched as Peeker One did a full scan of the vicinity, viewing Eagle and Hawk. Neither had a crewmember outside. Then Peeker One took a position near the girder cube. One last look into the bay confirmed that the cosmonaut was still busy ransacking Falcon. Peeker One settled onto the outer skin of the bay door.

The Peeker view screen now showed a blurred surface. As the incredible zoom lens focused, the surface began to clear and finally became a horizontal bar across the screen. Had it carried numbers, they'd have been readable. Peeker pressed against the bar, the perimeter piece of the box clamp's upper lip. Suzy intended to push the girder box off its lip grip on the edge of Olympia's door!

"We're ready," said Suzy

Hemming said, "Olympia, open bay doors three feet." Adam complied. Joji, swift, sure, and skillful, nevertheless worked feverishly. He might be the cleverest satellite operator in existence, but he realized that, at any moment, the uninjured cosmonaut might come up and attack Peeker or at least hold the barrier in place.

The barrier box slid back a few inches, then tilted sideways and jammed. Only by pushing in the exact center could Peeker have moved it back smoothly and without binding. That central point proved hard to find on the now distorted box. He slid Peeker left and pushed again. The bar straightened. Joji slid Peeker toward the middle and goosed thrust. Peeker's shadow visor, projecting beyond the lenses by half a foot, became the bearing surface. It began to buckle under the pressure. Joji had to prevent damage to the lenses. He rolled Peeker 90 degrees and began to take the bar's pressure on the other two sides of the shadow cap. The barrier moved back some more.

It had been driven half way off its clamping grip when a warning call rang out from an alert observer in the returned Eagle. The trapped cosmonaut heard the strange alarm. It came at an untimely moment for him, causing confusion. He had just found a second syringe and backed out of Falcon, holding both aloft triumphantly. He parked them in midair and looked around alertly.

"I see nothing. Calm down. What is the matter?"

The Eagle observer told him to get to the barrier at once. The LAD, still sitting overhead, blocked his view. Fortunately, he did not go straight up over the LAD to see the problem. Instead, he jetted down the bay, stopped, turned, and saw, in panorama, the undoing of his trickery. The barrier was nearly unseated from its grip on the door. For his purposes, he should have gone outside, through the gap, now even wider than the box had made it. Instead, he jetted straight ahead, colliding with the LAD, and grasping for the barrier box. It was just beyond his reach and still being loosened. As he stretched his grasp, he saw it yield suddenly and slide off the door completely. The abrupt end of resistance caused Peeker to spurt straight ahead into space; the barrier went tumbling off at an angle. Before Hemming even began his shout to shut the doors, Adam had them closing.

The trapped cosmonaut made an offensive gesture. Then, deliberately, he moved back near Falcon and obtained the two syringes. Even more deliberately, he came toward the bay windows. Locating the TV camera lenses, he positioned himself before them.

Suzy called, "We're back."

The screen showed the returned Peeker's view. Moving along the door's mating edge, it was like a newshound sniffing.

"Can you open up a crack?" she asked. "I think we've earned the right to a look inside."

Hemming told Adam, "It's up to you."

Adam made a one-foot opening. Peeker One looked in. The shade cap was compressed nearly flat all around. Fortunately, the lenses had not suffered and still sent quality pictures. It now showed to a global audience the behavior of a man in a fit of pique. Even his bulky space suit seemed to radiate rage. He made the offensive gesture again. Then in a universally understood action, he squirted the fluid of suspended animation from the syringes until they emptied.

In the clearest kind of sign language it said, "If we can't have it, neither can you!"

Suzy Arai became ill, choking. Her inspired bargaining had been futile. In exchange for using Peeker One to remove the door barrier, President Sisco had agreed that the U.S. would share the fluid with her country.

Through the door gap, Ylena saw the final cosmonaut from Hawk arriving. Adam closed the bay doors completely. The newcomer radioed to his captive shipmate, "Come to the spot where you had placed the barrier." The inside man did so. Positioned just above the LAD, he said, "I'm right there." The outside man said, "I'm right above you. Wait."

Peeker watched him. On the screen, Adam saw the outside cosmonaut wrestling mightily with the door edge. He had gripped it securely with one hand and was pushing his other arm downward. Looking from the bay windows, Adam saw the man's gloved hand appear inside the bay. Determined and powerful, the cosmonaut leader had worked his arm through the compression of the rubber faces of the door seal.

"Now," he radioed to his crewmate, "hand me the fluid." The captive cosmonaut pounded his fists in fury and frustration on the hard surface of the LAD.

135

Moscow moved quickly to disavow the actions of the Hawk and Eagle crews. For reasons unknown, said the UCS Ministry of Truth, the crews had acted on their own. Naturally, they would be immediately returned to earth and disciplined. For compassionate reasons, of course, the ministry demanded that the U.S. release the three battered men for return to their ships. Any delay could worsen their injuries and perhaps exhaust the men's dwindling supply of air.

Adam had already begun to make Moscow's wishes come true. He did not ask anyone's permission. He saw the casualties as patriotic men who had obeyed their orders. He might have been sent on such a mission himself. Speaking to the Russian commanders, Adam arranged for retrieval and rescue. There is a brotherhood of the cosmos, but he also wanted no dead bodies cluttering his vessel and complicating the mission. He and Peeker watched every movement as new cosmonauts flew their injured brothers back to their ships.

On Ylena's advice, Adam required the cosmonauts to gather the syringes and place them back in Falcon. He confirmed that they had moved all the promised supplies and equipment to Olympia. When the last cosmonaut left, Adam closed the bay doors.

He tilted Olympia to watch the Russian ships depart. His hand rose slowly in a silent salute to daring and capable men. He felt a concert-hall moment, like the hypnotic hush before pent up applause. *Close,* he thought. *Very close.*

He and Ylena donned hard suits. Bulky and clumsy, they went through the air lock together and set to work. As a priority action, they secured the new high-pressure air tanks, hooked them into the ship's piping system, and began to pressurize the bay. They took selected items of food and equipment back to the cabin. Then they separated, as required by Yuri, for a well-deserved sleep. When they awoke, the cargo bay would be a shirtsleeve area. Adam, bedding down on the flight deck, broke out laughing when he suddenly noticed Peeker One watching him through the windshield.

"Number One Peeker Paparazzo!" he cried jovially. He waved to it as to a friend. Pest or not, it had certainly proved to be his ally today. A warm peace wafted him to sleep.

As a concession to Suzy, President Sisco personally ordered Ken to rig a temporary TV feed from Olympia. It gave Suzy an exclusive, as the sole public broadcaster of internal action on Olympia. In addition, Sisco called and talked with her, thanking her profusely for her idea and action in turning Peeker One into a pusher. They commiserated over the mutual loss to their countries from the stupid, barbaric discarding of the fluid by the angry cosmonaut. Sisco was glad that he had not spoken on the videophone. Suzy might have been able to see his smile as he wondered how many liters Ylena had hidden away somewhere.

136

In Bern, a computer cycled through the calendar and lined up its daily person-check assignment. For decades, with Swiss dependability, a clerk had surfaced every recorded person's name and compared it against the news from scores of countries. Progress in technology had relegated this search job to a machine, saving work hours and increasing profit. That made the officers of Bern Bank Ltd. happy. The bank, through its service subsidiary, *Time & Again,* did a lot of time-critical tracking functions for the wealthy and the weird.

Time & Again conveyed money, property, and messages on given occurrences or dates, to persons, or to schools, hospitals, foundations, and other organizations. Most of the contracts for the search service contained a condition that would trigger action. For example, money was waiting to be dispensed when children reached a given age, despised in-laws divorced, or if daughters left the convent. Awards, offered by the philanthropic and the peculiar, lay waiting for "first-ever" achievements, including a substitute for sight, a height-limited lawn grass, and the regrowth of a limb. The pool of purposes reflected human nature from affection to vengeance. Dr. Mikhail Valena owned one of the private contracts.

His payment for service of indefinite length took all the money he owned and could borrow. A friend in the American Embassy converted the money to high-denomination U.S. bills, easily hidden, easily carried. That ruled out the counterfeit money, all too prevalent in Moscow. The interest on his balance in the account would pay for service forever. The bank's contracting officer had wondered about the purpose of searching news headlines, for one Ylena Valena, across scores of generations. With the legendary Swiss business privity, however, he put the question out of his mind.

Ylena's father had made the contract during a science meeting. Kremlin authorities had nearly cancelled his trip to Switzerland. They knew of his initial distress over his daughter's fate. They did not understand an evident recurrence years later. After all, he had borne with great composure the initial, secret news that she had been marooned. However, five years later, he began to show anguish. Dr. Valena had always been a reliable, stable party member. Yet, in pain, on travel, he might publicize his loss. They debated whether to let him travel. Eventually, they realized that he could tell the hidden story to a western reporter right there on the streets of Moscow, just as readily as he could in Lucerne. They allowed him to go. No one ever suspected the true cause of his torment.

The bank's computer signaled success: a headline match for the name Ylena Valena. The clerk opened a deposit box and took out a large, bulky envelope, sealed, and marked #1. From it, he removed a single sheet and another sealed envelope, marked #2. The sheet was titled "Instructions." The first line said, "Time is of the essence." The second line read, "The enclosed envelope, marked #2, must be conveyed immediately and confidentially to Ylena Valena, Captain, Soviet Air Force, USSR, serving as copilot on the spacecraft Falcon. It is vital that Captain Valena receive the message while she is in space. It must be conveyed before she returns to earth!

"One of the Bern Bank officers shall serve as urgent courier and is to personally place the envelope, still sealed, into the hand of the chief of the space program of the United States. The courier must then validate that the envelope is opened and its message is actually transmitted to Captain Valena, in space. The full balance of the account shall become the property of Bern Bank upon successful accomplishment and documentation of this mission. If the message is not received by Captain Valena while she is in orbit, the account balance shall become the property of the International Red Cross."

The maintenance cost of the *Time & Again* account had been a huge amount to Mikhail Valena. It equaled petty cash to Bern Bank. But Ylena's obvious existence instantly made the account important. The woman existed! And in space, as predicted! Her face appeared everywhere, in print and broadcast.

The contract, instructions, and sealed envelope from Dr. Valena flew up the Bern Bank hierarchy. From the tip of his economic mountain, astride trillions in cold cash, a financial genius deliberated. The woman and the mission fascinated Stephan Maurier. His bank had been given an urgent task in an unprecedented setting. He could sense no hoax. He decided to deliver this message personally.

In Maurier's rarefied world, the way to find the chief of the space program of the United States was to ask the person's boss, the American President.

When Maurier phoned, Simon Sisco, now splitting his time between the Oval Office and Tenement One, took the call at once. He listened to the mysterious new development, spellbound and apprehensive.

"Your representative should talk with Dr. Frank Cole," he said at last. "And he is here with me. What! You're coming in person? You! Well, I'm impressed. When will I see you, Stephan? This afternoon! Excellent. The tilter will be waiting for you."

The banker arrived at Dulles International Airport and changed to the President's aircraft for the five-minute flight to the White House lawn. He delighted in the changes his enormous investments in the tilter concept had made in air travel. Its helicopter type blades lifted the craft to height and then the rotors tilted forward to become propellers that drove the winged plane several hundred miles per hour.

Nowadays, it was a mean little town that didn't have a tiltrotor air pad. The tilters gave people accessibility to cities not readily available since the days of bus service. Traditional, mixed-traffic airports had vanished or become sites for continental or intercontinental flights. Washington's airport, so long a dangerous place for big jets, had become a hub for tilters.

Flying over the cleaner, quieter city, Maurier reflected happily on how long it had taken the authorities to see the inevitable. The delays had allowed him time to buy up land in key places globally, for the tiltrotor air hubs. He ranked the tilter project as the most enjoyable among dozens that had made him wealthy. Also, he took great satisfaction from conceiving the vision of this great social improvement and then making it happen.

Maurier, a man mad for a better future had little future remaining. He resented nearing the end of life. It shouldn't be happening when he still had scores of projects ahead. He had postponed them all to make this grotesque trip. At age 91, he was on his way to court an older woman. She had something he wanted. Perhaps he could romance her with nostalgia. They could get together and talk about old times. Who knew what might happen? He had always been a convincing salesman. How could she deny him just a little? Just a small sample of the fluid that preserved her would be enough for his researchers to duplicate. Then, he, too, could move into the future.

137

Benson, on hearing that the President would bring Maurier into

Tenement One, commented to Cooper, "You picked the right name for this place. How crowded is it going to get in here?"

Cooper responded, "It's a non-problem. You know as well as I do the guy's a banker. They don't stay in tenements."

Benson smiled. The irreverent Cooper had been a helpful tension breaker in crises over these many weeks. But, neither of them could see any possible connection between this banker and the Olympia rescue effort.

The President clarified the mystery with an introduction of Maurier and an explanation of his mission.

"Everything that happens here is classified. You will all be witnesses that I have placed no preconditions or impediments in the way of the bank's execution of its contract. We are to assist in the transmission of a message from a father to his daughter. Mr. Maurier, as agent for the bank, will witness the act of transmission, and its confidentiality, in keeping with the rights of privacy between parent and child. Our security services have checked all aspects of authenticity. The message is probably a farewell. Dr. Valena died of cancer six months after he contracted with the Bern Bank.

"Only our own Dr. Beletsky has any reservations. Yuri is concerned about negative reminders at this time in Ylena's recovery. The rest of us are operating on the premise that her father knew her personality better than any of us. He chose this method to communicate with her, and he specifically requested delivery while she is still in orbit. This may be a congratulatory message; or it may be one to boost courage and morale as his daughter prepares for a new life, among new people, in a new century. Does anyone here besides Yuri see any reason we should not fax this message?"

Benson's instincts made him edgy. "Why, Mr. President, don't we have you and Yuri and a few other advisers see what it says before we send it?"

Maurier at once raised his cane, like a sword. He stood, a commanding presence. "Please understand, gentlemen, that the terms of the contract with Bern Bank do not allow that. Therefore, you would give us no choice but to wait until the young woman returns to earth and then deliver the letter to her personally, still sealed. That alternative, of delivery after a return to earth, is what her father specifically proscribed."

Sisco looked around. "Anyone else?" he asked.

Benson persisted. "Mr. President, think about it. Nobody could send a fax to spacecraft when Dr. Valena prepared this message. To me that says he was prepared to have it seen by other people or it could not have been sent. I submit to you, sir, that the respect we are showing for privacy exceeds what the father himself ever had in mind."

Maurier again stood, saying, "Our psychologist friend can tell you of the strong desire for privacy in emotion or intimacy. Dr. Valena would undoubtedly request the opportunity for confidential communication with his daughter. In print, that would be your fax transmission. In conversation, that would be a secure voice line to his daughter. You would, no doubt, honor a dying father's request and provide that service. Do I understand correctly that you do provide such private links, on a routine basis, for your astronauts to talk with their spouses on earth?"

Sisco looked around again. After a silence, he said, "Very well. Stephan, you may proceed."

The banker handed the envelope to Frank Cole, saying, "You are the head of the space program of the United States, as our contract requires. You are the appropriate recipient of this envelope. Will you please allow me to witness its opening and your transmission?"

Cole agreed. He accepted and opened the envelope. It contained hand written pages in the Cyrillic alphabet. Cole placed them in the fax machine and told the communications officer to stand by for transmission.

In an unexpected move, the President led Maurier to a console chair and sat beside him, calling up Hemming.

"Ken, put me through to Ms. Valena."

When she came on the screen, Sisco chatted genially with her for a few moments and then explained that he had learned of a message from her father. He gave some background on Maurier and then said, "He is here and wishes to speak with you."

The banker came on, smooth, courtly, and ingratiating. His first statement, delivered in French, was a compliment: "Please tell me, mademoiselle, in which language it would be most comfortable for you to speak."

"I will do the English! Please tell me everything on father."

The Crisis Team got more comfortable. They would understand the language.

When Maurier finished, Ylena felt she had found a new friend and a protector. It astonished her that this man of wealth and power, this embodiment of a top capitalist exploiter, would have any interest in her and give her any of his time.

"Contracts are sacred," he had said, "and family contracts are the most sacred of all. I hope that in the mere performance of our duties we have been of help as well as service to you."

Ylena was awed. "When I get to earth, I hope you will let me come to see you and to thank you in the face."

"My child," whispered Maurier, "I would be honored. Now, let us send your father's letter. I bid you good-bye so you may read it in peace and privacy."

Ylena blurted joyfully, "Oh, no. Do not go. There may be things he writes me that I can tell you. You remind me of him much."

Benson bent to Yuri, saying softly, "Feeling queasy?"

Yuri nodded, responding, "He's working very hard at inter-generation seduction. I wonder why?"

When Adam confirmed receipt of legible copies, Maurier fed the original into a shredder. Ylena, elated, took the first page from the fax machine. Her beaming smile slowly faded into a face of puzzlement.

Maurier came in swiftly, "Is anything wrong, mademoiselle?"

Ylena shrugged and gave a nervous laugh. "It is his writing," she said. "My father starts, 'My darling daughter,' and then he says, 'You know I never meant for you to do manual labor, but ... ' and he stops making sense. From here on, is mush. Oh! Let me see the other sheets that come!"

With that, she took the others from the machine and quickly scanned their content. "It is all mystery," she said. Abruptly, she brightened, with a rippling laugh and a mock smack of a palm on her forehead.

"It is his game! He is playing. He is reaching back from where he is, just to make me laugh and happy." She dissolved into tears, but went on in a choked voice.

"Oh, Mr. Maurier, this is a fun we had with secret messages when I was a little girl. I know what he is doing. He is thoughtful, like you, and he is making me to be absorbed in breaking his code. He will not leave me time to mope sad. Breaking code will be like working with him again. I thank you again, more, for bringing me his letter."

The President concluded the transmission in a caring, diplomatic manner, thanked all for their presence and contributions, and began to escort Maurier back to the Oval Office.

Maurier, however, asked for the rest room, and waved Sisco back with, "It is a one man job, as you say here." He went off alone.

Taking advantage of the respite, Sisco went straight to where Benson stood with Yuri. "Gentlemen," he said, "I hope we don't come to regret my decision to overrule you. I'm not having second thoughts, but I am having second intuitions. I've got a delayed gut feeling that we need to know what's in the letter. Ask Ylena after she decodes. If she won't cooperate, get a look at the sheets by TV. They say that gentlemen don't read other people's mail, but I'm suddenly alarmed and ready to make an exception. Maybe I just made a big mistake. Mike, I want your people at CIB to break that code. Yuri, help the cryptographers in any way you can. Now, do either of you have any other thoughts before we part?"

Yuri nodded. "You are objective enough for me to say, Mr. President, that I hope you will think about and try to find out why Stephan Maurier is so anxious for personal contact with our guest, and why he worked so hard to set it up."

Sisco stared, astonished. His mind churned. They watched his visage move slowly toward disapproval. They sensed it was not for them. Had he been used? If so, for what? He rocked a fist in the opposite palm.

"Thank you," he said, and turned for the door.

———————————— 138 ————————————

Repair began. It pleased Adam to see Ylena as ready to generate a sweat in work as in exercise. She had been unable to break the code, and she used labor to work off frustration. They wore masks while they cut away insulation. A vacuum hose minimized dust. They finally peeled off a long strip of insulation, a foot wide, from below the hinges of the port door. With the wiring harness exposed, they could now replace some damaged fiber optics.

Color-coding in the wiring harness helped identify copper wire from end to end. So did the neat parallel runs. However, it was quite different with the hair-like strands of fiber optics. There was no possibility that they could do fiber optics splicing; that took special training and special tools. Their job thus became one of removing the old and installing the totally new optics cable. It wasn't easy to get ready to install the new wires. At each passage through a girder, a factory-installed anti-abrasion, cushioning guide held the cable tightly. Adam tired quickly from lunging to jerk the old damaged wiring through each girder's clamp.

Ylena was puzzled. "Commander Adam, I heard you say to Houston your plan to cut the crap away. You have cut away only insulation. Is old fiber wire also the crap?"

Adam grinned and gave a sanitized definition of crap.

"Is still a good question," she huffed.

"What do you mean?"

"I am meaning, you are pulling, not cutting. Why not do your idea? You work very hard in pulling. Instead, do your plan. Cut crap away."

Interested, he said, "Show me what you mean."

At one of the girders she pointed and said, "Here. Snip wire crap on each side, up close. Then hammer hollow plug out. Is not that the plan you made in your mind?"

She had concluded that the replacement control wire wouldn't pass through the existing tight guides, even after Adam had pulled the tunnels empty. The originals came as a tight fit from the factory. Adam would eventually need a larger hole for threading wire through each girder.

He swallowed, grinning sheepishly. "No, my diplomatic mechanical genius, it is not. But it's a helluva lot better than what I *have* been doing So, let's try it your way. I think my hernia has a hernia."

She liked his sense of humor. She told him so in one of their front-porch sessions.

"Well, I'm glad of that. Thanks. Flying airplanes is very serious, so it helps to have a lighter side; and flying's where I got started. Space flight is funnier, though."

"How is that?"

"I forgot. You haven't been around to see the changes. But you've seen the space cartoons and jokes that Yuri sends up. They originate in every society because people fear things they don't understand, and so they joke about things they fear. It helps get the worry level down."

"You mean people fear space?"

"Oh, I guess it isn't space itself. Maybe it's just what might come out of space. Say, some alien intelligence. There's a great cartoon about creatures from a flying saucer standing in a fuel station in front of a pump. They all look just like the pump, you see, and one of them is ordering the pump, 'Get your finger out of your ear and take me to your leader!' "

"That is very funny! I would like to get many more. Is much more?"

"Oh, sure. You'll be sorry, though. You'll get tons."

"I will need tons to laugh against so much change since my flight. A long time makes much change. When I was a little girl we said, 'What goes up must come down.' Was true, but now no. Now, could go into orbit."

"Yup. Space travel changed a lot of thinking. In my teens I had a car I'd tinker with to get the most miles per gallon. Now I fly a spacecraft that can go farther on a gallon of fuel than any vehicle ever invented. Millions of miles to the gallon are routine. It's almost like perpetual motion once you get up here."

"Is a hard idea to catch; like this Olympia ship is a moon."

"I'll go you one better. Did you ever consider the idea that Station Freedom is a location? No? Well, think about it. Let's accept the idea that space is a place. No, really! It is! Just as a lake is a place. And an island in the lake is a place. Now, think of Freedom as an island in the sea of space. Compare it to Malta, sitting in the Mediterranean."

"It does not compute," she said, quoting one of his idioms. "Malta does not move."

"Well, yes. Of course! You're right. Station Freedom keeps moving! So think of it as a moving island. That makes it a moving location, but we always know where it is! And we can go there."

"Why would we want go there? It was my hope to go moon."

"Because we can do things nearby on the station that can't be done anywhere else. Some of it lets us make money, like manufacturing specialty items. But mainly we go there so that we can look up, for astronomy, and look down to keep watch on how the whole earth's behaving. I shouldn't have to jog your memory on this; your own country has had a space station longer than anybody."

"Is not my country!" she snapped. "And we had no space stations in my time! I am not responsible for knowing things done when I sleep!"

"Hey, relax! I keep forgetting. Everything about you is too fantastic for me."

"Do not tell me is too fantastic!" she said, clipping out the words. " Is easy for you. I am from your own history books. You are meeting only one new person. Just me! But I am meeting many. Too many. Too fast. I am the one who face fantasy. Everywhere!"

"Ylena, I apologize. I'm a little too callous."

"OK. I accept. Is not a harm. Is more harm to be always agree and be boring. I cannot stand boring. That is why I would rather take chance and go to moon than be on space station."

He understood completely. In her was the same urge that drove him in his quest of onward and outward. Even average citizens, America's vicarious pioneers, seemed similarly driven. Their determination was well expressed by Robert Frost:

> We will not be put off the final goal
> We have it hidden in us to attain.
> Not, though we have to seize Earth by the pole
> And, tired of aimless circling in one place,
> Steer straight off after something into space.

When he recited this for her, she said, "He is wise about people. He would understand me. I would go today to Mars if I could. I am impatient. But you are patient, and your country is patient. Why are you not going to Mars again?"

"That takes a little explanation. We went to Mars with twin ships. One was American. The other was international, with a United Nations' flag and crew. Both broke down and neither would have gotten back if the crews had not cannibalized vital twin parts, taking from both to make one useable ship. The landing on Mars went fine, and so did the ascent to rendezvous for going home. But they did the landings with specialty vehicles, just transfer buses that had one-use lifetimes. What nearly killed the overall mission was the longtime use of machinery on the big ships.

Everything had to run without fail. Halfway back, after nearly two years of operation, equipment began breaking down."

"Did they not fly formation?"

"Absolutely. Outbound and inbound. In fact, after the first equipment crisis, they lashed the two ships together and made one the prime driver. Each had become a warehouse of spare parts. That's the way they limped home to Station Freedom for quarantine."

She fidgeted. "So? You do not say why you do not go back."

"Oh, we'll be going! But we're going to be better prepared. We're taking a lesson from the sea. Ships and their equipment got better and more reliable very slowly. Remember, early sailing was done close to shore. We're doing something like that with our space sailing, so to speak. We're sort of hanging around our planetary shoreline nowadays, focusing on space stations and the moon. We're pushing hard to extend the lifetimes and reliability of equipment and materials. Then we'll go."

"I would go right now," she whispered.

He knew there would never be a shortage of spacefarers, neither men nor women. He believed completely that there would be no turning back from space, as there was no turning back from the sea. The spirit of adventure guarantees it. The pattern was set on the oceans of earth. There will be some differences, of course, but the human response will be the same. We will dare the unknown, the dangerous, and the new. When there is need we will invent, as we created a technology for the sea. When there is risk we will face it, with the courage of the early mariners.

We may, however, need strength beyond theirs, for space could prove crueler than the sea. The new mariners will face new tests in the new ocean. They, too, will make great voyages of discovery, but without the prospect of finding other humans. Instead, they will face the new reality of unremitting, unprecedented, utter loneliness. The first to know this condition was Astronaut Michael Collins. While his companions of Apollo XI walked on the moon, he circled the lifeless, alien planet. No human had ever been so far away, alone.

The great trial for the new mariners may not be the hostility of space, but its vast indifference. In the cosmic void, some will die, unseen at awesome distances, while yet seeing the pinpoint light of home. They may die even as they talk with loved ones back on the space shoreline. The human spirit will be sorely tried. But it will make us press on. It is in our nature to explore, to fill in the map, to push back the infinite. Adam felt that Tennyson said it best, *To follow knowledge like a sinking star. To strive, to seek, to find, and not to yield."*

Many of the science fiction predictions of his youth had come true. The driving force, as described by author Ray Bradbury, came to mind.

He recalled snippets: *"The universe has come alive through us, and we go in search of ourselves. It will be a terrifying struggle; the human agony that must go into it is immeasurable. But how can we expect less agony from our own future than we have known in our past. The important thing is that the race is on the move . . . "*

"Now!" shouted Ylena.

"What?!" His head jerked around from his musing.

"I told you before: 'I would go right now'! You do not listen."

He smiled gently. "You're right. I know you would. But first, you need more training. Now back to the grind!"

Ylena's flight training continued. Adam coached her on maneuvering Olympia locally after he backed away from the tank hulk. She was soon to do practice runs on lining up for reentry. Her physical and emotional health had peaked. Dr. Nanterre pronounced her so fit that her upcoming TV broadcast could be an actual press conference. He gave her the choice of doing another monologue or of taking questions in a TV interview session. She never hesitated: "We will do press conference! I am study full time up here to answer Commander Adam's questions. Much 'homework.' Will be relief to do questions with no homework."

139

A code of conduct had been worked out with journalists. Even Nanterre agreed that their questions, submitted in advance, had improved to the level of dignity. Both he and Yuri wanted to avoid pitching Ylena into any kind of trauma. The reporters had agreed not to badger her about decisions, such as going back to Russia. They had also made taboo any questions about age, bodily functions, religion, politics, and any mention of her childhood friends or of the tragic Andrei.

Hemming told Ylena that under no circumstances should she refer to the remaining supply of the suspended animation fluid; nor should she even hint the hibernation fluid originally came from her father.

Her counselors needn't have worried. Ylena, holding TV court, could do no wrong. Men saw in her their secret fantasies; women saw hope for enduring youth and beauty. A goddess to some, she was at least an historical figure, a charming and lovely beauty from another age. This child-elder had seen Stalin, had walked in the world of Einstein, and had breathed the wafted dust of Hiroshima.

From fields and rooftops, millions of people scanned the night skies, working from public announcements of orbit timing. An aspect of the messianic-mother was in their gaping, and in their entreaties, when people saw her star twinkling across the heavens. Children frazzled their parents with tearful pleas to delay bedtime; they wanted to wave and dance and call to the transiting beacon of "The Time Lady in the Sky."

As the interview went on, Ylena became less a curiosity and more a personality in her own right. Her eyes and countenance flashed between inquiry and certainty. She shone and dimmed as naturally as sunlight on a cloud-scudded sea, ranging from ingenuousness to babushka wisdom. She could arrest, intrigue, and transfix the most blase'. She was direct and frank. Not knowing something, she said so. Having an opinion, she gave it. The press clamored for her views on fashion, music, love, food and movie stars (reruns soared).

She steered among the snares adroitly, perhaps innocently. Once, challenged on an opinion about fashion, she defused a looming contention with, "It is only what I believe. I am entitle. You may believe better. More muscle to you!"

The disarming charm captured everyone. Her sense of humor told Yuri reams about how far and fast she had progressed. When asked if she still suffered from the loneliness mentioned in her last TV talk, Ylena laughed. "I think no. Commander Adam made me humor. He said true loneliness is to be college roommate with electrical engineer. Was twice funny, because was my own study!"

She could talk without babbling, and she laughed easily. The relaxed and invigorating session ended all too suddenly. Nanterre had rationed it to an hour. It ended dramatically. Every person in the interview hall stood and applauded, including the camera crews. The last view of their orbiting celebrity showed Ylena cheerfully applauding back in the Russian manner. Then she returned to her major problem, decoding her father's letter and its incredible message.

140

When Adam reported no progress in deciphering the letter, Sisco told him to offer Ylena confidential help from Washington.

She declined, laughing, "No, no. You would make my departed father into Lenin!"

"I don't understand."

"Oh," she teased, "is just a Moscow expression."

"That doesn't tell me anything."

"Use imagination."

"That makes my head hurt. So tell me."

"Pay attention. Lenin was a revolutionary. What does revolutionary do? He makes revolutions. You see? No? Really, no? Well, revolution is a turning. You have an American saying about someone turning over in his grave?"

"Yeah, we do; and we have harsher things to say about dumb jokes. But maybe I'll forgive you."

"Only part was joke. Getting help on his code would very disappoint my father. I must not give up."

Yuri beamed upon hearing her joke about her own seriousness. *Stabilizing faster and faster.*

Turning to Benson, he said, "She's not going to let anybody get near that message until she figures it out. She's appalled at the thought of quitting."

Frank Cole drew Benson aside. "Mike, we've got lenses up there that let us zoom in the TV on any instrument that needs watching. Sisco wants the information in that letter. If I film it, can your guys crack it?"

Benson flinched from a dart of conscience. Eavesdropping on this woman seemed obscene. For the first time in his spying career he thought, *God, but I hate this.* To Cole he said, "Yeah. If anybody on the planet can decipher it, my people can. Do what you have to do and so will I."

During Ylena's sleep time, Adam used the muffled microphone to get routine directions from Hemming. Technicians gave him assigned locations for placing several kinds of work, just to keep lines of sight clear for the cameras. No one told him the real reason for the repositionings because he might refuse. Benson had noticed Adam's growing fondness for Ylena.

It worked well. Sneaky focus over Ylena's shoulder by the zoom cameras saw and captured parts of her father's letter. The powerful CIB code busters toiled without rest, churning combinations from her letter, but, like Ylena, they got nowhere. Benson knew she was no cryptographer, so the design of her father's cipher simply had to be unsophisticated and direct. These often became Benson's most difficult assignments because of their base in information known only to the sender and receiver. Such codes gave his experts migraines. Ylena's message was too short for his people to set up arbitrary, rotating assignments of letters for the message units in hopes of hitting on a pattern.

Had she been at home on earth, Benson would have bet money on the method involved. The code had to be based on each letter writer's having a copy of the same edition of the same book. The apparent gibberish could then become meaningful. For example, the seven units of "IXD23AV," could be code that meant the ninth Chapter, 4th page, 2nd paragraph, 3rd line, first word, fifth character. That would yield one alphabetical letter. And in Cyrillic, to boot! Even with the needed key, there would be a long, laborious flipping of pages in the decoding book.

Benson had correctly deduced the procedure used by father and daughter. Their common base had been *The Cossacks,* the first blossoming forth of the youthful Leo Tolstoy's genius. The thin, lyrical novel had made translation rapid. Benson's suspicion could, of course, do him no good. He needed the key, a copy of his own. Ylena's nosey college classmates had been similarly deprived and they had never been able to fathom her coded letters from home. Some had actually slipped into her room, copied pages in her absence, and gone off to work hard at decoding. To no avail.

At home, Ylena and her father had hotly debated many topics, including politics and the ways in which humans should be governed. He believed that tyranny could be prevented only by a healthy social pluralism, where factions contend vigorously and keep one another in check. This was treasonous doctrine in the Soviet system. He believed that the purpose of rulers is to protect and encourage the creative talents of citizens. Anything less would only foster mediocrity and lead to decay. Away at college, she had greatly missed their provocative sessions. That started their coded correspondence.

Now, with no access to *The Cossacks,* Ylena could not divine her father's current cipher process. Nor could she imagine why he had sent the letter in code at all. Habit, perhaps, from venting his raging political apostasy? Or was he saying to her an intensely personal good-bye? Poised with her papers at the navigation table, she rolled her shoulders, trying to soften the locking, hurting knots of tension.

"You don't look very happy," said Adam.

"The puzzle is causing a neck headache."

"Would a rub help?"

"Only the fool drinks when he *needs* a drink!"

"No, no," he laughed. "A rub's not a drink. Besides, we're not allowed any liquor up here. I meant a shoulder massage. They're great for taking out the tension before an exam."

"Hiee! We did same. Oh, a good comfort! Yes, I accept."

It took some improvising to get ready. Ylena used the navigation table to provide a base for resisting pressure. With shoe locks hooked, and waist bent, her torso lay face down across the narrow foldaway table, held to it by her encircling arms drawn firm with elastic as wrist cuffs. For Adam, the ungainly, tethered result triggered an inadvertent memory from driving in Los Angeles traffic. A passing bumper sticker read, "It's been so long since I had sex, I can't remember who gets tied up." He flinched, instantly uneasy. He thought he had his lid clamped tight. It became clear that he wasn't keeping busy enough, just being here in orbit, marking time. He would up the pace tomorrow! Suddenly, sensing a threat to his insulation and independence, he regretted putting his hands on this woman.

He couldn't stay sorry long. As he touched the bunched shoulder muscles, drawn hard and tight, he knew he had to provide what help he could. She needed relaxation; he could feel her tensing in irregular spasms. In reality, she was heaving in mirth. He heard suppressed laughter, and then the well-earned echo of his own Navy jargon.

"This is one stupid lash-up!" she growled.

The pre-massage preparations became so elaborate, and the table rig so cumbersome, that they made her chuckle despite her tension and distress. That triggered him, and then her, and then him, until tears flowed in continuous laughter. The giddy fits eventually tapered away, leaving Yuri and Adam less worried about Ylena's peace of mind.

Ylena felt the hilarity reduce her tension. Then came rapture and relief, as Adam, braced near her head, resumed kneading. She sagged in delight as his hands wrought gentle relaxation. His sensitive fingers found the tiny knots and worked them into flaccid strands. In sync with the rhythmic, rolling pressure, her breath came in pleasured sighs, and her mind drifted to thoughts of the masseur. He was proving considerate and gentle behind his gruff barricades. He was attractive, too, this man of the stark white square head, rumbling voice, and infinite patience. He knew everything about her life but had dodged discussing his own. At least she knew he'd been married and she realized that its memory was painful. Was that marriage the reason for his resolute wariness?

With one exception he had avoided touching her during their weeks of confinement and training. Then, unexpectedly, had come this marvelous, relaxing gesture she now enjoyed. Was it just an offering to a crewmate? Did it happen because he saw her as just a comrade in need? His craggy face and its slow smile filled her mind. The most minute, warm flickers of desire began to stir in her body. This is the second time, she realized.

She quivered in sleepy resistance to her interest in a man almost twice her age. *Inappropriate!* Or was it? No, it was the other way around, she realized. Instantly, she felt herself to be The Ancient One; this man was two generations her junior. *Oh, Lord, it's so confusing. What is right? What have I become? How will he think of me?* She wanted to rise and end the stimulating contact before it might cause her to do any foolish thing. It could not be, for she had been too weary, and now, had become too slack. Her questions dwindled away and she succumbed. Ebbing into soothing rest, she slid away in pliant bliss.

A world of warmth and solace greeted her, and she dreamed of childhood, home, comfort, and the happy days of games with her father. He had teased her often, back then, as his letter teased her now, always pushing her to imagine and speculate. What could her father have been thinking? Had he changed much in the years before he wrote this letter? He sounded like another person in his uncoded, opening reference. Why did he say, "You know that I never meant for you to do manual labor, but . . . "? She certainly *did not* know that. They had never discussed the topic. It made sense, of course, because he had insured that she got a superb education that would obviate manual labor.

"Manual labor," her mind said, and kept repeating the phrase. What has that got to do with anything?

Her dreaming mind, hovering on the question for hours, finally got an answer. With a joyful shriek of insight, Ylena understood. She burst into wakefulness, crying with triumph, only to find herself wrestling with a table. Her cry and the sounds of a struggle startled Adam from his sleep in the pilot's seat. He sped to her. They collided as she exited the navigation cubicle, caroming away against lockers and bulkheads. She recovered, stabilized, and set off again, yipping and cheering. She headed for the air lock and the cargo bay. When she returned from Falcon, beaming victoriously, she held her flight manual.

Benson knew she'd found the key. He knew now the meaning of Dr. Valena's wry introductory sentence about manual labor: his daughter was going to have to labor in her manual. Unfortunately for Benson, the passage of time had made the manual into a rarity. *How can I get a copy?*

PART 8

THE SHANGRI-LA EFFECT

141

With a rusty skill that quickly oiled, Ylena powered into the decoding. Adam saw an alarming transformation: Ylena's happy interest soon degraded into a headlong, ferocious engrossment. As she worked through the pages, he saw that the uncoded letter was going to be rather short. In Ylena's cipher system, it took about three pages of code to convey one page of message. Her concentration drew his attention like a magnet. The distracting silence interrupted any attempt to spend his rest period reading. Her intensity brought back a memory. He saw his ship, descending in a lock in the Panama Canal, unable to cast off a mooring cable that began to carry the vessel's weight. He sensed that Ylena was tightening like that cable, just before it snapped.

He was about to ask if he could be of any help, when she began odd noises. They came in guttural, quavering surges. She started to tremble, her skin was pebbling, and sweat stood on her forehead.

"What is it?" he asked, placing a hand on her brow. She felt clammy cold. "I'll call the doc!"

"N-n-n-nuh-no-NO!" she said, teeth chattering. "They will want explanation. Do not."

She worked on, determinedly, wiping off blinding tears to proceed. Adam thought of an insect — seeking, scrambling, never stopping, and machine-like. Her human side told otherwise. She collapsed several times into shudders that blurred her printing, and into groans that tore his heart. Then she continued, in an obvious agony of pressing on. He watched in respectful silence, aghast at her pale horror. The relentless was confronting the hopeless.

The pencil floated away when she finished. She looked this way and that, as though seeking a path. After several failures at speech, she said, "I will be away. I need alone."

She imposed her will on her body, coordinated her movements and started for the mid deck. Breathing heavily, she stopped, pulled herself together with a strained dignity, and said to him, "Read from my father."

Then, in an eloquent mix of fear, hope, declaration, and plea, she said, "Not for anyone else. Private. Just for us. We will fight." She turned and floated slowly through the floor.

Adam read, in his labored Russian, "You are my beacon. Through the years, I have watched you twinkling by each night. My hopes for you, and the success of our plan, have been high. Now, I must conclude I have failed you. After you flew away, I came upon a problem of suspended animation and worked for years to solve it, but without success. You knew before your flight that I made a wide variety of animals enter and return from hibernation. Because we had little time, I conducted only short-term experiments. Later on, I continued the work, leaving many creatures suspended for long periods.

"Years after your launch, I began to awake the animals. Those I woke within their normal life spans resumed their lives with the attributes of their age at the time of starting suspension. If they began as puppies, they awoke and played as puppies, but only for a little while. Very soon they began a process of accelerated aging, which quickly caught them up to their true age by the calendar. A month aged them as much as a year would have. In effect, they swiftly caught up to themselves and then aged normally. After all my hopes, they lived no longer than if they had stayed awake. It seems that nature may be delayed but not foiled.

"It was even worse for the animals kept suspended beyond the normal lifetimes for their species. To my dismay, when I awoke them they at once began a much, much greater speed of aging. Oh, my dear child, it was, in fact, all very visible. Weeks brought on changes of age that equaled years of normal aging. To understand, try to remember time-compression films. Think of a flower swiftly opening its petals. It was somewhat like that, with the aging of the over-life animals. Also, the longer the hibernation period lasted beyond normal life span, the faster did their catch-up aging occur. The longest sleeper endured a very accelerated withering and went to death within hours.

"I am in anguish over what I have done to you. I pray God that whoever finds and cares for you has access by then to new medicines that may provide an answer. If you, my dear daughter, have awakened long after your normal life span, and you find that a very accelerated aging has not quickly begun, it may be due to a variable of being in space. It may be due to a factor that exists up there, like radiation. Or to something that is not there, like gravity. Or to my greatest hope, that there is some difference between humans and animals.

"If there is no medicine for you, our dream that you could enter a new life, in a new society, in a new century, will become just that, a dream. I hope that you do not have to pay a penalty for dreaming with me. I am proud of you for all you have achieved, for all of your promise, and for your great courage. I regret that your faith in me was misplaced. Please forgive me. I love you."

The original was signed with the uncoded word, "Father."

—————————————— 142 ——————————————

The purring sounds of mechanical duty hummed in Olympia, cycling the programmed tasks of sustaining life and communication. Here and there, equipment came on line, whirred, shut down, awoke again. In the semi-silence, Adam suffered from an anguish nearing nausea. He had watched Ylena's descent into deep melancholy. Now, he could hear her turbulent illness, a blend of retching and subdued keening. The lament for her father's apologetic agony was pure pain transformed to sound, quavering under her crushing disappointment and numbing fear. The threat of sudden, headlong aging and disintegration, perhaps to swift death, had abruptly quelled her hopes for a new life.

Trembling violently, Ylena envisioned the worst of her father's catastrophic scenarios. The very molecules of her body would begin churning and collapsing, desiccating to parchment as she watched with fading sight. Her sturdy spirit, straining to survive this latest shock, hunkered under the pounding blows of emotional extremes that had accumulated since her resurrection.

Adam, distraught and bewildered, called to her softly, offering solace, asking how he could help. Through the partition, through the tears and fears, came a desperate burst, "I must alone!"

He moved away, envisioning a wounded creature, burrowed deep, recovering in its den. But Ylena was *not* recovering, she was still in mortal conflict, fighting for her sanity. She was battling in the dark defiles of the soul with the personal demon that claws and burns to destroy the mind. As in a trance, she saw the hunched, vulturous form that had come to rape her mind and shred her will. The drooling obscenity exploded into screaming rushes to claw and rip in hellish frenzy. Again and again, she resisted the stinking monstrosity, gasping for the strength to fight on. At the lip of the shadowy pit of lost minds she battled for her sanity.

When all went silent, Adam debated: Should he go behind the partition? What remained of her? He had answered her plea for time and privacy. Her condition had moved him to petition Houston for a stress break. They said OK and told him to manage it at his discretion. He had dimmed all lights, except hers, and he'd silenced all speakers and microphones. Now, as he deliberated, the panel swung slowly aside, and Ylena floated into the half-lit hush. To Adam, she radiated a force. It increased like a physical pressure as she moved toward him. She looked worn, but serene, strong, assured. She wore the thin, tight smile of the barely victorious.

"I am survive. I am ready. I hope you will help. Let us talk."

They kept their backs to the windshield to frustrate Peeker, always looking. Deaf students from Gallaudet University had used the Peeker's scenes to read lips. Starting as a party joke, the interpreting had blossomed into a surreptitious, fee-paid, journalism service supporting a small stable of students on shift work for reporters. Private conversations from Olympia, and some shipboard routine that was never broadcast, appeared regularly in the media. For a while, all the earmarks of a security leak had Tenement One hopping mad. Then, a newly prosperous student talked too much through his champagne in a Georgetown bistro, and the source became known. It made the remedy clear: face away from the cockpit.

"They do not know on earth?"

"No, but Mike Benson wants me to hold your flight manual up to the TV camera one page at a time so he can make a copy."

Slowly, with the finality of a bank vault closing, she said, "He may not see. It is mine. I decide. Also, I decide what happens next to me."

Adam got edgy. "What does that mean?"

"Very sudden, very old, very fast. That may happen to me. Is already overdue. You know."

"Now, wait! Your father said it might not apply to humans."

"It applied to all the animals. Humans are animals, no? I am at risk from the aging."

"But your father said if aging hasn't started there may be some force preventing it."

"He said also maybe absence of a force. Think. He said gravity."

"Well, so he did, but what are you driving at?"

"It was near, that I lose my mind. You say 'close call,' no? But I won. It makes more strength. I can do decisions. Here is decision: I will die *how* I choose. I will choose *when* I choose."

"If you're talking suicide, I'll do everything possible to prevent it. If necessary, I'll take you back tied like a mummy."

"That is accidental funny. I may land being real mummy, wrapped up right by Commander Adam. You will get medal for foresight."

"Stop it! None of this is funny. You're talking murder, self-murder. Your last act would be murder. What are you, one of those communist atheists?"

"Do not lecture. I am follower of Christ. He did his own suicide. He made plan to die and carried it out. My church has many heroes who decided suicide and did it. If I decide suicide, I will do it."

"You're talking about martyrs! It's not the same."

"Is same. They did management of their life. This is management of my life. It is same. Do not tell me about management of my own life. And do not be upset. I will do only with good reason."

"And the reason would be sudden, catch-up aging?"

"Yes."

"But it may happen so fast you won't be able to act."

"I know. That is why you must help me find out what is true. I must know. I want no surprise that immobilize me."

"C'mon, Ylena, spit it out. Help you find out what?"

"Make gravity for me. Just a little. Maybe just a little gravity makes just a little more age. Then we know. Then you stop gravity and I am still function to make decision."

"To kill yourself?"

"What is alternative? Is better that Commander Adam kill me by gravity in reentry? You like that way? I hate such a way."

"You want a test. But suppose it shows nothing?"

"Then I go home with you."

"And take your chances on leaving space radiation? It may be beneficial. Being up here may be helping you."

"I will take chance."

"Ylena, they'll never give me permission to stress Olympia."

"Do not ask permission."

"You know, you're really wild. I had a classmate like you. He said it was easier to ask forgiveness than permission."

"Listen to classmate."

"Cut it out! We're talking my career here, not yours."

"We talk my life here, not yours. Remember, the career is one piece in your life. The life is all I have."

"You're really serious!"

"Is only way. There must be test. If you do not test, and I die of reentry gravity, they will scourge you for not try to save me. Do test. If bad result, I will television to American people and show father's message, and say you save me from bad dying. You can be hero."

"I don't want to be any damned hero."

"Then be scientist. Get fact. You want to act with no fact. Here is fact: I will suicide before I fly onto earth without test."

143

A furious Ken Hemming could not make contact with Olympia. "No, Mr. President," he told Sisco, "It is not a technical problem. I believe that Commander MacGregor has deliberately closed off all two-way communications circuits. And we are not even received by fax."

Sisco probed patiently, "What do you think is going on?"

"I'm sorry to say, sir, that I think he is doing, or wants to do, something we would forbid. The Japanese are working with us by the minute with Peeker, trying to get a clue. I wish we had those lip-reading students back on the job."

The President sighed, "It's no help. We brought one of them in here to try to pick up some clues. We finally sent her home because all their talking is done facing away from the cameras. Just what we told them to do. Ken, why do you think Adam left the TV on?"

Hemming brightened. "I believe, sir, that he wants us to know that the crew is alive and well. He wants to keep the worry down. But he's showing all the signs of preparing to do something that *he* wants to do, and to do it with no interference from us. Remember, he cut us off completely once before when he trapped Major Kuznets in the cargo bay. He wanted no interference from anybody. He intended to let that guy die there without air. He's found a way around his own nature and training. He won't disobey orders, so he makes it impossible to receive orders he doesn't want to obey."

"Tell me, Ken, what you make of what we're seeing."

"Well, sir, they've laid out and retested the hard suits. Also, they've done a lot of calculations. I've zoomed the lenses as best we can to try to read their sheets. All we can really see is some sketches that look like they're designing a tower. Now, when all this began, Mr. President, our telemetry showed that Adam started up the vacuum pump to pull the air out of the bay. He's saving it into tankage. That means he plans to open the bay doors, and that he wants to close them later and pressurize the cargo bay back to a shirtsleeve environment.

"The suits mean they're both going to be doing something in vacuum. What, I have no idea. It's certainly not to finish the repair job; the suits are too bulky and clumsy for that kind of work. It makes more sense to do repairs in a pressurized bay. Another thing, our engineers have been watching what books and manuals he's been using. One's a physics handbook. Also, he's been going over inventory lists of stuff in the bay. Finally, he's spent a lot of time on the manual for that new Canadian grappling arm. It all adds up to one big mystery. Oh, wait! Hold a minute. We have lights coming on. It's the RCS. For some reason, he's preparing to use the RCS."

It was true. Adam had energized the flight panel of the reaction control system. Choosing among the scores of small rockets that made the shuttle maneuver locally, he backed Olympia away from the shattered external tank. He had sucked 90% of the air out of the cargo bay and compressed it back to tankage. He could never get it all, and getting even a few more percent would require hours. It wasn't necessary for his purposes; he opened the cargo bay doors and let the little remaining air escape.

Peeker pounced on him at once, peering through the bay bulkhead windows. It watched his activity at the Aft Crew Station, as he activated the RMS, the remote manipulator system. This newest of the Canadian grappling arms was larger, faster, more accurate, and lighter, yet stronger, than the arms on earlier shuttles. Adam stood its 80-foot length straight up out of the cargo bay. Then, he bent the arm at its elbow and brought the hand end down to grip a support bracket, making the entire rig well braced and sturdy. The bent arm looked like a long triangle pointing up out of the cargo bay. Its elbow was the upper tip of the triangle.

Soon, two suited figures emerged from the air lock. One wore the belt and shoulder harness of the treadmill apparatus used for the mandatory daily workouts. The other figure carried the Teflon-coated, aluminum base plate on which an exercising astronaut stood to run while held down by bungee cords. From the tool and supply locker, the space walkers took an assortment of rope and snap hooks. Tethered to prevent driftaway, they moved upward on the grappling arm.

Adam placed Ylena out at the elbow of the manipulator arm and tied the treadmill base to the arm. She took a position as though standing and he rigged her harness to pull her tightly to the plate. When they were done with rigging, Ylena looked like someone standing on a board in midair, feet to the cosmos, tied upside down to the tip of a tall, thin triangle. The mysterious preparations ended. The apparatus for an incredible experiment stood ready for Adam to make a little gravity for Ylena.

144

Ylena had committed to the most momentous event of her life: to find out if she qualified already as earth-dead. She suspected that her failure to age in orbit might be due to minimal gravity, a factor that didn't exist for her father's long-suspended animals. She had been deadly serious when she threatened Adam that she would not begin atmospheric reentry alive. She could not bear the thought of being alive and aware during the possible abrupt onset of a swift, aging disintegration to extinction.

She now saw Adam in a new light. Since their talk, this stern, duty-driven man had proved to be compassionate and understanding. He had reflected long and quietly on *his* choices and their career consequences. When he made his choice, it was for *her* and her needs. Ylena understood the tyranny of training and the compulsion of command. She knew that Adam's decision repudiated responsibility and abandoned accountability.

He had decided to ignore practice and prudence. Nastran would never trust him with a command again. She understood what the penalty of grounding from flight could mean to an astronaut, and her heart ached for his coming loss. But she would not gainsay him. There was too much at stake.

Her pitiable figure, forlorn under remote, unblinking stars, hung like a futuristic St. Peter, crucified inverted. Captive on her own triangular cross, she thought of Jesus on his. She marveled at how the roles paralleled, although reversed: He, the immortal, hung upright, facing death on earth; and she, the mortal, hung inverted, facing death in the heavens.

Still, she did not feel lost and insignificant in the vast, uncaring empyrean. Instead, she felt defiant and optimistic, for she did not face her life-and-death issue alone. Adam was with her. The forecast made her giddy. Had her liking for this stranger become something deeper? She imagined again his strong fingers working her flesh, soothing her into peace. Faint tinglings began. Savoring the unfamiliar sensations, she recognized the birth of desire and heard the click of love. A cry of joy escaped her, ending in despair at the hopelessness of her fantastic situation. Adam heard her cry and turned, this man who could have been her son or grandson. She gave the sign for "no problems."

With new eyes, she watched him reenter the air lock. When he appeared, unsuited, at the cargo bay windows, she waved to him and radioed her readiness. When he vanished, she imagined his movements. He would occupy the pilot's chair, strap himself in, make a last radio checkout with her, and begin judicious maneuvering with the reaction control thrusters.

Soon she saw stars begin to move, and she knew the slow roll of the shuttle had started. They had calculated the revolutions per minute she would need, at her distance on the grappling arm, to create an inward support of one-g, earth gravity. Adam would build her slowly to that gravity pull, harnessing the force that lets us swing a bucket of water and spill none. Her feet on the treadmill board would soon think they stood on earth. Shivering in apprehensive delight, gasping as waves of exhilaration washed her mind and body, she swept past swirling stars. Quelling the thrills of her flying rapture, she forced her eyes shut and focused on her grave duty.

Concentrate! Look inside!

Searching intently for something within, and not knowing what, she spun on and on. Adam slowly increased rotational speed until it yielded the one-g force. Ylena's legs began to buckle under her new weight. She locked her knees and braced against the powerful pull she had not felt in nearly a century. She remembered her first experience with gravity's return. As a child in a full tub she had put the heels of her floating legs on the tub rim and let the water drain away. She smiled in memory of the odd sensation of great, growing weight. The tub had not been threatening, but in this setting she would have blacked out except for Adam's precautions. *"Drink it all; I want you fluid loaded."* He had also laced her into a g-suit that bound her tightly to prevent blood from draining out of her brain to pool in her legs.

Adam periodically called the time, but made no conversation; he knew that silence aided her personal scrutiny. Every fifteen minutes he asked, "Should I stop?" She declined and endured, determined to test the limits. An hour went by. An hour and a half. Her fortitude astonished him, as did her relentless will. No wonder she had been the pick of a nation.

In bone, sinew, blood, tissue, muscles, and cells, at the deepest levels, remembrances fluttered, programs stirred. Atom by atom, unknown mechanisms triggered dormant biological clocks. Long neglected, they began to tick, then to tick hurriedly. Ylena, tiring, grimly focused on the muscular effort needed for mere standing. Then, the slightest shadow of a distracting twinge crept through her concentration. *What was that!?* It had seemed like the tiniest prickle. On the scalp. It came again, stronger, but slowly died away.

Then came a different stirring, a tingling at her fingertips. *Oh, God! What is happening?* Minuscule twinges began at the ends of her toes. Slowly, the finger stings sharpened, like a leg with the thousand pinpoints of "gone to sleep." In futile instinct, she bent to see her hands. But their mystery lay deep in the huge gloves. Abruptly, the torment eased. She took a deep breath of thanks but choked on the next as an agony of internal fire coursed her arms, spreading fast. Points of pain stormed her body, a flashing and piercing torment that broke into a numbing cold as from steam turned sleet in her veins.

Staccato needles danced and pricked across her skull, became a hot itch, and then flared like slapped sunburn. In a new horror, her scalp began a writhing, as of worms on skin. Her cap shifted, the chinstrap pulling taut. She tried to reason. *Hung up on a connector?* Atop her head the agitation grew.

A fresh tremor worked in her hands. In terror she felt her fingers gently pushed away from the tips of her gloves. She tried to make a fist within the big gloves. The fingers could not turn inward. It was as though her fingernails had become too long, and caught on fabric. Sudden, conscious discernment burst through her anxious observation, springing upon her like unleashed pain. Gasping in frightened, desolate realization, she understood. Her worst fears became monstrously alive. Gravity would flay her, down through layer upon layer, reducing her to bones and hair. She was no coward, but she did not wish to die in this way.

Oh, God! Save me!

Life shrank into dread and pain as she dissolved into trembling, screaming horror. Adam heard her choking ululation of terror and despair. Then silence. Ylena had fainted. He berated himself for not having instrumented her. *What is happening?!* He fired thrusters to stop rotation. He heard the desperate wailing begin again and then change into the shrill, taut scream of the terrified, the demented.

Ylena's cap pivoted off her head. It moved on, forging past her face. A writhing mass pushed it past, filling her helmet in a monstrous, shaggy avalanche. Her screams died as she clenched chattering teeth to keep a choking, penetrating mass out of her mouth. She tore at her helmet, frantic to break in and rip away the foul, sinister slitheries encasing her gorgon head. Her world compressed into pure terror. She fainted again. Silence again. Desolation swept Adam.

145

Peeker had seen and broadcast Ylena's placement and Olympia's rotation to a puzzled world. The hired commentators had no answers, only verbal descriptions of what the viewing public could see. One commentator, an engineer turned astronaut turned retiree, made some rough calculations and estimated the "g" force on Ylena to be about that on earth. He had his answer for the mystery! He announced it to the world: Adam was conditioning Ylena for reentry to normal gravity. His pronouncement became "news" and started speculation that Olympia was getting ready to come home.

It had the public effect of turning drama into mere training. Training qualifies as dull TV. Viewers left the screen, resuming their lives, work, and entertainment. Those who stayed could see Olympia slow down, much faster than it had spun up. They saw the slumped, unmoving figure of Ylena splayed on the elbow of the giant arm.

Peeker gave them a cabin shot of Adam dressing feverishly in the big, hard suit and banging his way toward the air lock. They saw him emerge in the cargo bay, move swiftly along the manipulator arm to Ylena and take her helmet between his hands. His shouting was obvious. Peeker was up close, and the commander's desperate face was visible through his faceplate. When Peeker looked at Ylena's faceplate, it saw matted, reddish darkness. No one suspected it was hair. They watched the commander remove her fetters, and, ignoring the disarrayed equipment, float her swiftly into the air lock.

Inside, Adam stayed on the mid deck, out of view of Peeker. He tore himself out of his hard suit and shoved it through to the lower deck. He worked frantically to remove Ylena's suit. When the helmet came off, hair with blood globules billowed to engulf him. Three-foot tresses girdled her head. When he flung the mangrove masses aside, some random lengthy strands floated off and swung back, circling him like a boa.

He worked more carefully within the matted bulk, soon exposing Ylena's face. He cleared her mouth and nose. Her closed eyes sat in features of exhaustion. He gazed upon the unlined visage, on its familiar mystical loveliness. She lay unchanged, beautiful in repose, yet different in ways he could not detect. The difference spoke, somehow, of greater dignity, serenity, and maturity. She breathed erratically, now calm, now fitful.

"Thank God you're alive," he said, again and again. Suddenly remembering that they were being watched on Olympia's observational TV, Adam put his body between the camera and Ylena. In dread of her injuries, he began to remove her carefully from the suit. He rotated a glove free. The hand would not pass through the cuff lock. A pulsing blood mist blocked his view.

He spun to the TV camera, shut it off, and sprang to get the medical kit. Even with a lubricant jelly, skin tore off Ylena's hand upon coming through the cuff. Stunned, he saw the reason. Her fingernails, about seven inches long, had curved back and grown about a centimeter into her wrist.

He removed the other glove and found the right hand also mutilated. The berserk proliferation of curving keratin had savaged her in the brief moments from her first cry until Adam's full stop. Adam stared, dazed, unseeing. Her experiment was over. Stark and clear, he realized what she had discovered. The experiment had worked, and it had also failed. Gravity had accelerated Ylena's aging process. With riven mind, he wondered what to do.

So did the team in Tenement One. When they saw the hair drama, they called for a diagnosis from the flight surgeon. He would not speculate on the unbelievable, and said so. He would wait for facts.

Adam, rushing to take advantage of Ylena's unconsciousness, tied her to the 'tween decks ladder and went for cutting tools. He did not want her to awake and see the monstrous results of her centrifuge ride. Returning, he sheared her hair to shoulder length and stuffed the shorn mane into a bag. With a surgeon's saw, he cut the enormous fingernails and pulled the nail tips from her flesh, leaving short, dashed wounds. He cleansed, creamed and bandaged her wrists. The giant toenails proved equally grotesque but had not grown backward enough to penetrate her skin.

Chain saw surgery, he thought, cleaning up, vacuuming the air. Finished, he redressed her hands and feet. Earth had seen only her hair. Maybe someone with discretion had kept that image within the Nastran net. That would be all they'd get to see, he vowed. He would not allow the world to make her a freak, damn it. He considered Houston. Hell, they knew he had a casualty of sorts; he couldn't hide that. He believed that shock had put her into a coma. He prayed he was right, because that was how he intended to treat her — for shock and fear. He would soothe and console her. Houston couldn't.

He worried about his continuing gamble with his management, of shutting out his chain of command, including the President. But it had to be done! Ylena's intensely personal experiment was just that — personal! Still, Houston needed at least a view into Olympia that would show him functioning. He would give them that much, but not any capacity for communicating. They'd have a look, but not much of a look, and they'd just have to wait awhile. He lowered visibility to a pre-dawn light before turning the TV back on. Then he braced himself in foot locks and stood, hugging and rocking his battered bundle. Outrage for her father flooded him.

For the warrior, death is the constant prospect. Adam knew where it lived, just under the skin of the mind. He had seen it loom and place his name in combat lotteries. His macho society held it in check by a dark, gross humor, their personal prescription for control. His peers confronted it with the wry philosophy: *If you go on living long enough you will die.* Why fear the joke? True, it was the ultimate joke, but even that could be kidded.

For him, death was a familiar. He had seen men die variously and sometimes valorously. Very few had gone toward the unknown with the courage of this young woman. No one, man or woman, should have faced the version of death thrust upon Ylena. She had confronted the basic human question: What is to become of me? Nature had screamed the answer into her face. She got the universal answer, of course, but fate normally delivers it tick-tock to the excitable, eking it out over the years for the sake of sanity.

He raged at what fate had done to her. His reaction denied his personal philosophy that nature is neutral and fate is aimless. That contradiction upset him. Sailor Adam knew the winds are neither for you nor against you. He lived his daily life believing that whatever is beyond your control will happen at random, from hitting the lottery to smothering at Pompeii. He had once heard a roommate laugh and read aloud from Albert Einstein: *"I never think of the future — it comes soon enough."* Adam's rejoinder was:

"I always think of the future — it's the only part of time we can influence." He did not "accept fate" or credit "the Lord's will" for disaster or misery.

Adam rejected the biblical story of Job, balking at the idea of a divine hand afflicting a selected human. He wondered why a loving God would choose to distress one of its creations with special trials and suffering. He equated that paradox with the one of a Creator who gives you life and finally kills you. He lived stoically with the biblical message that we will not be tested beyond our ability to endure. But didn't that mean the outcome was predictable? If so, did that make the pain itself a purpose?

Though truly puzzled, he knew where he stood. He could not reconcile repeated harrowing intervention by a loving God. He raged against the rending misfortunes assaulting Ylena; tragedies that seemed beyond chance. He marveled anew at her fighting spirit and the incredible resilience that triumphed over shock after shock.

Trained and hardened against pain, he seemed the most unlikely person to shed tears. But now, with an anvil of despair in his chest, he sobbed. Though imbued with the credo that only wimps weep, he now wept freely for her indomitable courage and her devastation, and that she not be lost.

She began to stir, soughing sadly. He held her closer, speaking from a sandpaper throat. "You will be all right," he said, again and again. "Nothing's going to hurt you," he intoned. "I will take care of you," he whispered. His susurrus of sympathy was warm and restorative. To the ravaged, shuddering Ylena the message came as balm. Its implications reached her, became believable. In a thin, sere voice she spoke his name. Then again in half speech, half groan. Gradually, her face lifted, eyes closed.

He went silent, breathless, gazing on the strength and beauty ravaged by crushing storms of confusion, shock, and terror. She blurred, shaking from random, fading tremors. At length, her eyes opened and met his. Transfixed in fervent gaze, they held, in the silent aching lock of a separate world. There, spiraling into shrouded depths, soundlessly calling, they reached out to each other from their timed links in the chain of eternity, striving to transcend the gap, to embrace across the generations; and they were transformed.

They swept closer, circling in the swirling gloom of a Cimmerian realm that neither had ever heard of or dreamed. Only *they* were visible, manifested in their essence, without substance or form. Searching, reaching, lit by each other's auras, they struggled for contact through infinite, stygian blackness to challenge human isolation as a destiny. They exorcised separateness, nullifying its agents of distance, time, and sequence, and they spiraled softly to spiritual union, in the gasping, pulsing fusion of two souls.

—————————————— 146 ——————————————

Only Yuri grasped the enormity of what transpired, and he did it dimly, though firmly. *Oh, no. Lord, no!* he thought, as Adam and Ylena held each other, foreheads touching, trembling, in muted joy and wretchedness.

"God help them!" said Yuri, breaking the hush.

The President turned, "What's happening?"

Yuri shrugged a reply, "You won't have any trouble getting her to refuse that trip to Moscow. She'll go wherever you assign MacGregor."

Sisco groped, "You're implying romance?"

"Like you wouldn't believe!"

"Then what's all this about 'God help them'?"

Yuri choked a little, despite his breezy manner. "Well, Mr. President, those two have just hooked together two unrelated links from the chain of time. It hasn't got a chance of working out."

The practical Sisco ignored this. "But you're saying she'll refuse to take orders to go to Moscow? That she'll go wherever he wants to go?"

Yuri nodded gravely. "Guaranteed."

"That's sounds like good news," said Benson, "but you make it sound as if a little romance is bad news. I think two people who find each other are damned lucky."

Yuri shook his head, "Maybe, Mike. At best, I'd say they're lucky, but damned! These are the 'star crossed lovers' for real." He walked off, uncharacteristically subdued.

Cooper ambled along. "Wait. Wait. I don't get it. This looks like a case of the hots between two people simply stranded together, like on an island, but you're making it sound like a Greek tragedy. How come? What's happening?"

Yuri stopped and said, "Art, what was it like the first time you fell in love? Not the sex. Before the sex."

Cooper flushed. "How can I describe *that?*"

"Try."

Cooper tried, reluctant and bumbling: "It's embarrassing even to remember. It was mystical, exclusionary, possessive. I felt transported. It was adoration, almost. But that's adolescent; maybe even preadolescent."

"Right. You're not saying so, but what you're really talking about is innocence and hope and trust and basic needs and some magical things you think can never come for you again. In the wisdom of youth, you felt the incompleteness of the individual and the ferocious, unembarrassed hunger for a cure. When it happened, you were an open and defenseless kid, new and fresh and inexperienced. It happened before you got calloused and cynical, and before the onset of everybody's adolescent demon, being paranoid about possible mockery of your emotions.

"You can avoid talking about it, with me or anyone else, but you'll never forget the raw, overwhelming power of that fixated, first attraction. I'm telling you now that the *need* never goes away, and that for some people it comes again, in a mature form, very specific, and even stronger."

Cooper smiled, amused. "So we have here a renewed puppy love in the Pleiades?"

Yuri turned it on him, "Think even Taurus, if you must, Art, but this ain't bullshit!"

Chastened, Cooper grinned. "Touché," he said, "But how does all this bear on anything?"

Yuri stopped and looked at him intently. "Cooper, do you believe in 'love at first sight?'"

"Well, I think it happens to some people."

"Could it happen to a blind man?"

"No sight, no 'first sight.' "

"Well, then, how *do* the blind fall in love?"

Cooper floundered. Yuri pressed on. "In fact, Art, is it even *possible* for a blind person to fall in love? Can that happen? What would it be based on?"

Uncomfortable, Cooper said, "Is any of this relevant? I ask for a drink of water and you drown me with mother's milk from a fire hose."

Yuri sat down. "It may be relevant. Who knows? This is what I do for a living. I think about these things. That's part of the process at a time like this. I don't have answers for what's happening on Olympia. I'm simply thinking about it. This isn't like thinking in math or engineering. It's a lot of roaming, so I understand your impatience. Your questions are making me think out loud; you've become part of the process. But I can go silent, if you prefer. No problem. It's just that when I get a question, I assume it's sincere."

Cooper, perplexed, blushed slightly. "OK. OK. Sorry. I may be cynical. *May* be. But I'm sure as hell confused. So, how do the blind fit in?"

Yuri laughed, "How the hell do I know? I told you this is all just a lot of abstruse meandering. I *said* that, remember? I'm groping here and feeling ineffective, like I'm tap dancing on sand. But the behavior of the blind may explain what I'm sensing about what's going on up there in Olympia. So let me try this on you."

He leaned back, and said, "I think that because the blind have fewer clues and fewer stimuli in relationships, they work with more basic factors. They deal with bedrock stuff about people, things like character, kindness, concern, understanding, and dependability. You know what I'm talking about. You've been in their presence. When I'm with them, my self-esteem goes down. I feel they 'see' the real me, all warts and inadequacies. They deal with a person's essence, not appearances.

"The rest of us have been put upon ruthlessly, right from the cradle. We grow up bombarded by advertising and entertainment images, especially with the importance of looks. We've got a head full of crap about eyes, teeth, height, weight, legs, tits, and the distribution and balance of all that stuff. If a woman came equipped with one big udder with a lot of nipples, we'd be conditioned to swoon over that.

"And, remember, we've been trained for attraction by dress, style, movement, mannerisms, and a whole variety of body language. We're all victims of this social programming. I see through it. It's part of my business to see through it, but it's so strong that even I am a victim. Yes, me! Don't look so surprised. It drives me to chase a lot of tail. It even drives me to feel a lot of satisfaction when I catch some."

Cooper had recovered enough to challenge. "Relevance? What's the relevance?"

Yuri sat up straight, talking fast. "I'm saying we fall in love mainly by sight, by seeing. Adam and Ylena had that going for them, and it's had its effect. I'm also saying that more has been added on top of that. I'm convinced they've experienced whatever it is that bonds the blind. I believe those two people have gone where the self dwells, and met there, and intermingled. They are lodged in each other's essence. I think there's a lock between them, a union so powerful that everything else is secondary.

"I'm running on like this because I'm confused. They're doing things up there that we don't understand, and they couldn't explain. Their actions are driven by their relationship, one that I believe is beyond our ability to imagine or comprehend. We don't know what they're feeling or thinking or planning, and we therefore don't know how to handle the situation. But you've helped me to a conclusion, my lad, so here's the end of my diatribe: if what we want, or the Russians want, doesn't mesh with what those lovers want, both countries are out of luck."

—————————————— 147 ——————————————

Adam darkened ship, ignoring the rule that either he or Ylena must always be visible. Clinging, they perched near the forward windows, in deep shadow, enjoying Adam's version of sitting and rocking on history's highest front porch. Adam had switched off all manner of communications with earth, and darkened all windows against Peeker One. After shutting out the world, he had rocked and comforted her for nearly a day. In his constant, enveloping hug, Ylena felt the flow of his strength rebuild her own. He knew she needed the warm reassurance of touch, so he bonded them lightly with an elastic cord; it held them tightly against drifting apart during exhausted sleep.

To further the glory of their swift nights, Adam took down the cockpit window blackouts and tilted Olympia to maximize the view. Snug in the dark cockpit seat, they felt themselves part of the master plan, sweeping silently through the cosmos, two tiny bits of life amid the raging furnaces, cooling planets, and frigid rock. They gazed in undiminished and repetitive awe on the panorama of heaven and earth. They marveled at mysteries, and wondered in whispers.

"Before I flew," she said, "I told my father that in space we would find answers to all great questions and would be fulfilled. He just laughed and quoted your man Whitman at me."

Adam stiffened, electrified. "Whitman? Walt Whitman!? Did your father mention 'Leaves of Grass,' maybe?"

Ylena, startled by his hardened body, answered, "Yes, it was 'Grass' in title. Why?"

Adam held her away, stretching the bonding cord, and stared at her, perplexed. "This is getting spooky! Listen. My own father had the same outlook. He said our human nature demands exploring space. He said it is impossible for us not to go, because we are insatiably curious. Now get this — he told me that Whitman said it best, and he read it to me. It may be the wildest coincidence, but I think you and I were being shaped with the same thought. Tell me! We'll compare."

They surfaced their dim bits and pieces of memory. They shined them up and pieced them together from the two languages.

"Unbelievable!" said Adam.

They had resurrected: *This day before dawn I ascended a hill and looked at the crowded heaven, and I said to my spirit, 'When we become the enfolders of those orbs and the pleasure and knowledge of every thing in them, shall we be filled and satisfied then?' And my spirit said 'No, we level that lift to pass and continue beyond.'"*

They sat stunned by the implications of their discovery: an enigmatic, comparable tutelage. Was there meaning in the apparently accidental, but fateful convergence of their lives despite generations, governments, and geography? Trembling, they held each other in tender, reverent exultation, daring to think they could harvest love from the bleak fields of their hopeless happiness.

In the darkened cabin, their own radiance, a seeming glow under flesh, drew them as moth to flame. As they burned in solemn, joyous merge, a searing light seemed to fuse their yearning souls in love and understanding, dimming the faint, pinpoint lucency of Heaven's starry beacons and the reflected glory of the earth and moon.

148

"Around the time of your press conferences, the libraries had a big run on an old book called *Lost Horizon*. Remember that?"

"Yes," said Ylena. "Why are you ask?"

"I are ask," he teased, "because you remind me of the heroine's dilemma. If she left the beautiful place called Shangri La, she would age rapidly."

"Is a fiction! I am in real story in different beautiful place with no name. You should get brush to paint 'Shangri La' on my Falcon ship."

He played along. "A third name? Two names are enough."

"No. I want 'Shangri La.' That is good name for place I must stay or age quick."

"We called it 'Ivan' before I came up here."

"You are like commuter. You say, 'Good-bye! I will take shuttle to Ivan,' and you go to work."

"Yeah," he said, "In a way we're like commuters these days. We come and go quite often. But I never thought I'd be taking a shuttle to Shangri La."

"Find paint," she commanded. "We will rename Falcon and have christening."

He glowed with joy at the humor and energy of this fantastically adaptable woman. She seemed incapable of continued despair. His mood ended as she returned to planning.

"We must decide next step," she said.

Adam had been mulling over their options, getting ready to talk. "Well, you survived the experiment. I think we ought to start there. What did we learn?"

"Gravity will kill me," she said calmly.

"Wrong!"

"How is wrong?

"It started to age you, not kill you. It might have stopped."

"I could not even begin disagree with you less."

"You talk funny."

"I am lucky am alive to talk any kind of way. Trust to me: I was rushing to rot and die. You do not know what was happening on me. You do not know. *I know.* I was becoming babushka. What woman has such old age as me? Empress Dowager, maybe! I could feel wrinkles grow! I have conclude gravity started to kill me. No debates. It *will* kill me. But I give you one point: It did not starting kill me right away."

"By my clock, about an hour and thirty minutes. And then it seemed to explode and begin to eat you up pretty fast. What do you make of that?"

"That I could go to gravity for short times and get away again before I am to age."

"Want to try it again, say, for an hour?"

"I am laughing! Now we have two crazies up here. Why do I laugh on such serious matter? Because is a maniac idea! I take no such chance. Suppose it is start earlier next time?! Already I am five years older. Look here. Look. Rugose hands; rugose cheeks!"

"Ylena, stop it. Your face is as smooth as a baby's bottom. But, pucker up. We'll test for rugose lips."

"Enough! Time for laugh and kiss is over. I give away no more years!"

"OK. OK! All business. So be it."

"Do not dismiss with 'So be it.' You are not take age problem serious."

"Ylena, that's not true. Everybody takes aging seriously. We must all make our peace with age. I've made mine."

"This should be interest! I make war with age. How you make peace?

"It's all in how you look at it. I think of declining capabilities, declining powers. We must adjust to that. We start life with powers, and they grow, but, finally, we end up powerless."

"It is harder for woman, the aging."

"Oh, come on! 'Harder for a woman.' Where do you get that idea?"

"Your own words. Power, you say. Power is answer. You are a man. You mature with muscle power. We mature with procreative power. Is our core."

"So? So we both lose power. Time clobbers us equally."

"Is not true. Time takes *our* power sooner. Sooner than men, we lose essence of what we are. Is easier for the man when he look ahead to aging."

"Just because you say so doesn't mean it's true."

"Think. When the man age, he lose physical power, but he is busy, busy, busy to replace with other powers. Money. Title. Authority. It is his life plan."

"You really mystify me. How did anybody as young as you develop all this home-spun wisdom?"

"I have been much time up here. Do you think I spent all sleeping?"

"If you're not going to be serious . . . !"

"OK. I am very serious. I know gravity is enemy of youth. I give away no more years! None!"

"Ylena, I'm sorry I suggested it. No second spin. OK? Now, for God's sake, let's move on. Let's talk about what we know for sure. All we have is one data point. We know that after ninety minutes you trigger. I'm trying to figure out how we can build a future on that little fact. Only one thing comes to mind. If the timing stays constant at ninety minutes, you could live in one part of a space habitat and make trips to the gravity parts."

"What is 'habitat' meaning?"

"A place in space where people could live their entire lives. We have none nowadays. They will come in the future. I'll describe them later."

"Is the Station Freedom a habitat?"

"No. It's a laboratory and a work site. People live there, but they go back and forth to earth. I've been thinking about it. You could live there while the medics try to find you a cure."

"You said just me to live there. You would not be there?"

"Well, of course not. They wouldn't let me live there just because I love you. In fact, they'll throw me out of the astronaut corps if we get down alive."

"They must give us a little something! They must let me say to you that I will go with you anywhere, that your people will be my people, as our Bible says. I do not want the life on Freedom with just your visits."

"Visits! Forget about visits! They'll never even let me into a space suit again, never mind a shuttle up to Freedom!"

"If could be permission, would you live at Freedom?"

"If you were there."

"How to get there from here?"

"By a very complicated transfer. Freedom's orbit is almost at right angles to ours. They'd have to come up and get us with a specially rigged shuttle, with a whole cargo bay full of extra fuel. It's too expensive to even think about. Forget it."

"I will not forget it! I am famous artifact. Do not you forget! I can get prime time speech time to United Nations. I will ask everyone, everywhere, help us live together. That would be good heat on your President, yes? He will have to offer you a life on Freedom."

"Ylena, for God's sake, let's move on. That option is impossible. I'm sorry to say that all the others I can think of are also impossible. I've run through them all."

"Me, too! Number One is leave Olympia for your astronauts take home. We do needle injection and reentry unconscious in my Falcon. We burn up together, and no pain. But you are fussy on suicide."

"Number two is land Olympia and fast switch to new shuttle to space station Freedom. But I am fussy on the quick aging. I think it could not be fly down and back up in ninety minutes. If we try this Number Two, I will carry gun. Ha! Maybe curving fingernail can pull trigger!"

"Stop it! Stop that kind of talk! I never met a woman with such a gruesome sense of humor."

"You are suicide sissy! OK, OK. I move along. Number Three is for UN convincing your President send shuttle and fly us over to Station Freedom.

"Number Four! Needle injection and stay up here in Olympia until people from habitats to come and wake us for living with them. No? Why no? Wait! Wait! Now I understand! Olympia would not last long in too low orbit. You are shaking head. Wrong answer? Hmmmmmm. Wait! I know. Olympia must not be our tomb, but must be return to service. Your country needs. OK.

"Last one. Number Five. I sleep here in Falcon. You take shuttle home. You come back. Bring full fuel for move us to live at Station Freedom. I keep all hibernation fluid up here. Your President would come quick for that, you bet, before the UCS come and take it. Oops. I forgot about them. This is bad idea. I have no more ideas. You have Number Six?"

"No, Ylena, you've hit them all. Ah, me. How to choose, how to choose? Every choice says we're facing the end, and that's upsetting. I don't want my time with you to end. You seem adjusted to it, with all your talk about suicide. You've got to stop talking suicide so glibly. I'm trained to push on, and maybe die, but not to stop action and deliberately arrange to die."

"I've even got strong hesitations about injecting and staying up here. That, itself, may be suicide. Suppose we are never found? Suppose the solar panels fail and we become blocks of ice? Suppose the fluid wears off and we wake up with no more fluid to restart the hibernation? Suppose we wake up among future people and I go berserk like Andrei? We don't know what caused that, you know. Suppose another injection has that same kind of effect on you? And what if we wake up and the extra time has triggered something that starts us into instant aging?

"Commander Adam is afraid."

He reflected long before answering. His philosophy about courage and fear was complex, simultaneously stern and forgiving. He believed several things. He knew that in confronting identical circumstances, you could be courageous one day and fearful the next. He knew that repeated exposure to a frightening situation might build confidence that can control fear. He knew that some fears are phobias, permanent and disabling.

He believed, also, that courage is selective, and is seldom universal in any one person. Some men he knew had no fear of any living thing, but they cringed at heights, or fire, or confining spaces. He knew others who feared none of these, but froze facing a snake. Some would break down in the face of certain death, as before a firing squad. That, changing nothing, seemed a stupid time to break. Adam didn't think he would do that. In one way, he was anxious for death. His father's legacy of impatient curiosity was the cause; he had a thousand questions that could not be answered in this world. Adam felt that anyone who has no death wish has no curiosity.

Finally, he spoke. "Yes. You are right."

"Is what you call crap. You are not coward. I have seen."

"It may be worse than cowardice; maybe selfishness. Maybe both."

"Both? Fear and selfishness together? How can it be?"

"Simple. I'm afraid I'm going to lose you."

149

Peeker needed more than starlight. It poked and peered at the windows, trying to do its job but seeing nothing in the darkened shuttle. A frustrated Suzy Arai cursed Peeker's designers for omitting a headlight.

Ylena sighed, "I am love that machine."

"Yeah, it's almost a personality."

"It saved us, like a good friend. Must it really die?"

"Now, now! Remember, one test of friendship is whether the friend would give his life for you. If we do things right, we'll see that this little Peeker paparazzo meets the test."

She shuddered a little and changed the subject. "You promised explanation about habitat. I hope you did not make it up for cheer me up."

"Trust me. Habitats will happen some day. They will grow to become huge colonies at the Lagrangian points, especially L-5."

"You must tell me explain."

"Sorry. I don't know how much you already know."

"Assume empty."

"Well, in the 1700's, Joseph Lagrange calculated that at several locations in space an object would be attracted equally by earth, sun, and moon. That means it would remain balanced at such a spot indefinitely. That's a Lagrangian point. One is very stable. That's L-5. Engineers plan to use free energy from the sun to smelt ore on the moon and produce metals, ceramics and glass to construct the habitats. They plan a ballista to fling parts to L-5 and catch them in giant nets."

"Is another fantasy. But what will habitat look like?"

"They'll be hollow and they'll rotate. People who wish to live in gravity will stand against the inside of the shell. That will be the ground under their feet. Those who wish less gravity can live closer to the center. A closed system like the earth itself is possible, using the right plants and some carefully selected animals for food. For milk, goats are recommended. We can make it all happen if we apply time, will, and money. Everything else is available. We learned the facts after your time, but the lunar soil is 40% oxygen, 20% is silicon and over 30% is metals such as iron, titanium, magnesium, and aluminum. I think you call it aluminium. The whole idea is just civil engineering on a large scale."

"You are predicting new worlds?"

Adam hesitated. "Not soon. At first they will be construction sites. But the habitats will evolve like Model I, Model II, Model III. Every one that's built will be capable of building others. And groups of them, uniting their efforts, will be able to build something of enormous size. Theoretically, it's possible for millions of people to live at L-5. A hollow satellite the size of the moon is possible. Even one much smaller than that could have lakes and trees and crops pressed against the inside of the spinning shell. Who knows?"

"You think some people will want to live in shell?"

"Oh, sure. Lots of people have signed up already. It's especially attractive to special groups. Each habitat could be unique and be alien to others, dedicated to a cult, a religion, or a form of government. Some people might choose to spend their entire lives off earth for psychic or philosophic reasons."

"I am overwhelm. Cannot imagine."

He laughed. "Sure you can." he said. "Imagine the first person to go to sea. It was probably somebody carried off on a fallen tree. So that tree became the first boat. Compare that with the floating cities we know as ocean liners. Could the guy on that log have possibly imagined vessels with thousands of passengers? Or, take the Wright brothers, flying one man, out in the weather, on canvas and sticks. Compare that with the hundreds of people watching movies and eating dinner in a modern airliner.

"Let's make it closer to home for you. Imagine the little tank that took Yuri Gagarin into space. Got it in mind? Good. Now let a couple of hundred years go by in your mind and describe what will have developed in space. Hard to do, isn't it? So don't rule anything out. Including space cities."

He was speechifying again, he realized. Normally laconic, he'd become almost verbose in trying to stretch her mind to the future. Her normally open mind was now clogged by apprehension; it limited foresight. He had once told her: "Listen up! I'll give you an argument for your blindness: Schopenhauer said, *'Every man takes the limit of his own vision for the limits of the world.'* That applies to you."

"I know quotation well. Long ago. Long before you. You bet. Down in high school. Don't preach me! I hear you do not even do philosophy in your high schools. And do not shout. I am reopening my brain. It is slow."

He had felt ashamed.

------------------------------ 150 ------------------------------

On the far horizon Adam saw the first hint of the swift dawn. Peeker, now more visible in silhouette, lay like a pup at the ankles of the windshield.

"Sometimes that thing seems like a pet," said Adam.

"It is my good companion. Must it really die?"

"Ylena. Stop. You know it's necessary. We can't have either your government or mine watching. Somebody might have an angry reaction and do something stupid, like shoot at us again."

He gave her a reassuring hug. "Ready?"

She nodded.

They suited up again, still not communicating to Houston. As they headed out, he switched off the cargo bay's TV cameras. He wanted no witnesses to his crime.

A crime it is, he thought.

They exited the air lock, assembled their gear and went through the previous pattern of strapping Ylena to the triangular point of the grappling arm. Adam headed back to the air lock as he had done on Ylena's first whirling ride. Ylena waved at Peeker, and it moved closer. She smiled and began to say things. Here was a chance for lip reading.

The interpretation ran roughly, "You are my little space pet. So cute. Always here. Always friendly. I feel like hug you for how good you were in defend us. You are my big watchdog. I wish could pat you and cuddle you." She prattled on.

Toyo Akiya could not resist. Ignoring the zoom lens and profile shots, he moved into touching range for his close-up. He captured brilliant scenes.

Ylena patted and stroked Peeker, causing some image jitters. Peeker's gyros called for compensating forces, and its little jets promptly nulled the vibrations. Peeker, silently huffing, behaved like a huge, panting, happy pup. Ylena hated her part in this scheme. Her location, deliberately chosen, let her look down into the cargo bay. A frontal view of her face required Peeker to take a position between her and Olympia, looking outward toward space.

Thanks to Ylena, Peeker had little peripheral vision. Adam, on a long tether, came up behind it undetected. He floated lightly, pulling himself delicately along Peeker's length as Ylena held its camera end by imaginary ears and cooed and smiled and played kissy-kissy into the lens of her pet.

Her fondling of Peeker masked the disturbances that Adam made to its equilibrium. The lens saw her eyes brim tears and her lips tremble from their smile. This machine had become her inanimate intimate, like the cuddly wooly bear of her nursery. Affection for a mechanical species seemed quite natural to a woman bereft of every childhood friendship and cast into a new, alien setting. While saying a sincerely emotional good-bye into the great optical eye, she remained peripherally aware of Adam's location and readiness. Disciplined, she maintained eye contact with the lens and would never end that lock until her assignment ended.

Adam understood Peeker's generic design. It grouped the radio, electronics, gyros, and computer brain close behind the front-end cameras, to minimize the wiring harness. Three feet back from the lenses, he straddled Peeker and locked his ankles in a scissors hold. Leaning forward, he put his left arm around the body and held on. His right hand held Andrei's gun.

He had considered how to disable Peeker so that it could not watch the next steps in his plan. Opening a panel and ripping out its wires was impractical. The thing would never let him get close enough, for long enough, to back out a score of panel rim screws. He had considered poking holes in thruster nozzles so that Peeker could no longer be precisely navigated. He gave up that idea, realizing it might remain grossly steerable and be able to keep seeing. He could not allow that. He had to blind it. He had considered shooting out the lens, but Peeker's masters would see him in the act. He concluded that the only sure way to blind it was a kill.

Aiming carefully, so that no transiting bullet would hit his encircling arm, he placed the revolver where he believed the computer brain would be. In a calculated risk, he fired. He did not know if his bullet would penetrate the unknown metal. If it ricocheted, it might hit him or Ylena. A cracked helmet or a torn suit could be catastrophic.

The bullet penetrated. It did not exit the other side. Encouraged, Adam fired again and again. For each shot, he moved the gun back a few inches down the machine's trunk, hoping to destroy a vital part or circuit. The revolver's kick set his mount to bucking about at random. Peeker's jets spurted furiously, trying to stabilize the camera on its view of Ylena. Revolver kick and jet thrusts added up to a wild ride, nearly throwing Adam.

Just as he fired his last bullet, he and Peeker whipped to the end of his tether. He was forcefully snapped back, losing his grip. Peeker went pinwheeling away into space, not only blind, but dead, with no jets trying to stabilize. Adam didn't know how very successful his surreptitious assault had been. Earth screens had simply gone blank on the first shot. The failure remained a mystery. He had made the cleanest, neatest, and most efficient kill that anyone could want. The very last TV scene, showing Ylena's friendly smile, had simply cut off to darkness without bucking or distortion. Ylena hadn't faltered on screen, although she hated taking part in the mechanical equivalent of a murder. Now, off camera, she no longer had to act. She sobbed in loss. Another familiar something had been taken from her.

151

The absence of Peeker gave them a novel sense of privacy, but left both with a nagging sense of loss. Ylena had been right in saying it had seemed like a friend. They missed the mechanical creature that had seemed to live and work with them, and had protected and saved them. Saved them for each other.

"It was part of our little family," she said, one day.

Adam stayed silent on the subject, but he privately agreed. Ridiculous as it might seem, the robot had been company for them. Its loss magnified the fact of their lonely, stranded condition. His tension abruptly found voice.

"Anything that happens to our benefit will have to be of our own doing."

"I don't understand," she said, taken by surprise.

"We are wanted by two governments," he went on. "They have their own interests in mind. We will be no more than tools in achieving those interests. No matter what we decide, if it serves their interests to separate us, they won't hesitate."

"My Adam," she said, holding him. "You are my life. I could not bear parting from you. And now you say that even our best choice may be taken from us. What can we do?"

He smiled wanly. "I don't know."

"I am thinking," she said, "this is our only time together. It will not last long. It will not come again."

"I know," he said.

"There should be joy for us in our little time," she said. "Now should be our happy honeymoon. Not sad. Not fear. Come, we go off by ourselves. This is our time, the only time."

Amused and intrigued, admiring her verve, he was smiling and unresisting as she floated him to the air lock.

"Wait here," she said.

Turning back, she methodically confirmed that all means for communicating with earth had been unplugged or switched off.

His shout was unexpected. Inquisitive, he had come back.

"What are you doing?"

She blocked his way. Arms stole around him, and her brushing, pressing lips whispered, explaining. Didn't they deserve just to be with each other in what might be the last few days of their lives together? Career meant nothing, now. The anger of ambitious men on earth was of no consequence. All that mattered was to gather up whatever little happiness they could in their remaining time.

Her throbbing proximity overcame his reasoned practicality. He listened and decided. She proposed not the wrong or even daring thing to do, but simply the most important thing to do. It would be monstrously stupid to continue as the TV puppets of earthly manipulators. Why should he and Ylena keep marching, right up to the end, to orders that would, at best, take them from each other, and at worst, cause one or both to die? As Ylena spoke on, Adam felt his tensions fall away. For once, he would reduce life to a focused pursuit of happiness. *Why not?* he thought, giddy and fatuous, recalling frivolously that pursuing happiness was authorized in the Declaration of Independence.

His heartened spirit stirred, gathering to scourge anguish, to hack away Maria's dead tendrils of grief, woe, and shame. The giant boa of compulsion slowly loosed the coils around his chest. With each moment he breathed easier and freer; cares receding. Ylena's warmth melted his chill fortress, and he came forth as a child, prepared anew for the love we seek on arrival.

Parents see the magical creature that is a child slowly disappear, finally vanishing into an adult. That adult knows where the child has gone. It has not vanished. It is still present, hidden within. It may be called forth at special times and places. For Adam and Ylena, this was such a time, and this the unlikely place.

They bumped through the air lock as through a tumble barrel, laughing the laughter of release, and shedding inhibitions for the tonic of play. In the huge bay, they competed to see who could jet farther on an exhalation, but the walls always forced a tie. They tumbled and gyrated in whooping delight, making a playground of the vast chamber.

He began to show off for her, crawling and pulling himself faster and faster across floor and bulkheads, looping the interior. She cheered him on. Speed soon let him crouch and run. With more speed he was able to stand and race up the walls and across the ceiling in rapid circling. Yelping gleefully, she scrambled to join in and accelerated to a run as he passed her again and again. Coming from behind, he swept her up and ran with her as with a feather, slowing his loops as her kisses grew more fervent. Their long road from vigilance to curiosity to respect to friendship had led on to romance and passion; it ended in playfulness. When he chuckled at the memory of an airline's ad and she made him explain, she was convulsed by the burlesque of capitalist advice to fly united.

"We are Adam and Eve!" she cried. And so it seemed for this pair of wild and radiant hearts. They floated two alone, au naturel, in a cylindrical Eden, their own new world, one that preceded jealousy, sophistication, guile, hate, embarrassment, and evil. Every idea, each movement, every caress led to more affectionate and frolicsome levels, toward a universe of love and needs and truth and trust. They entered the world of the very young. In graceful levitation, they flowed together in tender, sinuous encounters of mingling moistures and caressing silences that broke in cries of love, relief, and deep joy. He was awash in astonished gratitude as her flood of love scoured the stagnant pool of his steeped celibacy.

Adam was transmuted from a redoubt to an oasis. He had allowed another human being close to him at last, and he found it right and good.

With the innocence and openness of children, they playfully experimented and discovered. To playfulness they added the maturity of passion. To passion, they added inventiveness, delightedly devising games. They tried slow glide, arms folded, soft v-docking, as though they were unaligned scissors converging, but every attempt led to a hilarious float-by miss. Their masterpiece was a weightless, linked acrobatic, with him an anchored, arched base, and her a tucked, giggling spinner. Letting go, he was squeezed playfully by the impish dervish and torqued into slow, gyral acceleration amid exuberant laughter at the frolicking, pleasured wonders of their unique world.

Like cubs, they tumbled in sport to exhaustion, and then, enfolded in a dreamy reserve, curled together in sleep. They dozed off in close embrace, zipped in snugly, and wafting slowly in the drifting air. Adam, fearing her fear's return, gathered her body close. He would soothe her with the comfort and reassurance of touch should she suddenly awake. She slept huddled against him, limp but for the trace of a smile.

Olympia whirled onward through its hurried days, silent in the sky, amid the quiet passage of the stars, its crew lost to all outside concerns, joining in mind and body in the timeless ceremony of love. They wanted nothing but their own private world, one they had wrested from mortality and infinity. That made it all the sweeter.

───────────────── 152 ─────────────────

"Fax from Olympia!" With a jubilant call, the communications technician alerted Mission Control.

Hemming hurried over and watched the message, proper and formal, silently appear. He read a statement of intent from Commander, Olympia, to Chief Flight Director, Mission Control. Repairs had been completed and tested. All equipment and cargo had been secured for landing. Onboard testing showed all systems functioning. Unless instructed otherwise, Olympia would land tomorrow at 0800 hours on the dry lake bed at Vandenburg Air Force Base in California.

The message asked for a runway recommendation. It referred to the promising weather pattern and asked for periodic updates. The technical considerations rolled on and on. Hemming noted with relief that the commander's planning was thorough and his preparation professional. Apparently, Adam's management and piloting skills operated somehow separate from his independent and erratic actions. Adam had behaved just shy of insubordinate behavior, but only because he had not refused any direct order. However, he had certainly become irresponsible.

"Don't confront him. Just get him down," Yuri told Ken.

Easy for him to say! He wasn't the one with a wayward employee in the sky! Hemming did not intend to give Adam a dressing-down in public, even if he could; that might be emotionally disruptive just prior to landing. But he did want some answers about the communications blackouts, the spinning of Olympia, and other deviations. He checked and found the voice circuits still off. Miffed, he sent a response fax. He did this privately, in his own hand. It directed Adam to restore full communications, explain their cutoffs, and describe the condition of the crew. Within minutes he got a reply, also handwritten. Adam, too, was keeping things very personal, obviously determined to take no questions about Ylena.

The fax read, "Crew capable. Full explanations later. Please proceed with preparations for reentry and landing. All telemetry and data links are activated."

"Damn and double damn!" growled Hemming. Furious, he saw himself hung out in plain sight of the whole agency as unable to control the flight he directed. *This is one astronaut who won't be flying again!* That decision hurt, because he had been one of MacGregor's admirers. He refocused his energies for the task ahead. If ground and flight systems checked out, the landing could occur tomorrow. The weather would hold its clear, windless pattern for several days. Adam had obviously been monitoring the meteorological broadcasts. He knew the vital role that weather plays in a dead stick landing. He had opted for a touchdown at 0800, wisely relying on the normally clear, calm, early-morning weather at Vandenburg.

Hemming started up the machine called organization. Preparation and landing would be cumbersome without voice communications, but, as for all potential failures, he had a contingency plan. He designed a new schedule that included a short sleep and rest period for Olympia. He wanted Adam in the best possible condition for return to earth. He realized that the extraordinary mission must have taken a heavy toll on the man, physically and emotionally. Perhaps exhaustion explained the aberrant behavior. *Forget it. The investigators will explain. Just get the ship down.*

He wished for Peeker One. It would have been helpful in the landing checkout sequence. He could have used it to do a final visual inspection of the ship. At least it had no holes in its metal skin that would let the fires of reentry invade. He recalled the early shuttles, with thousands of protective thermal tiles. Those shuttles had usually come back from flight with tiles damaged or pieces knocked off from launch or reentry.

Ken found all telemetry data from Olympia normal; and his equipment and system checkouts went well. The political activity also looked good. The White House had moved fast and effectively in getting the UN to send a team of Watchers to the desert for an objective inventory after touchdown. The Russian cargo plane taxied up to fly the Falcon to Moscow. All landing-site safety vehicles and apparatus took position. Even a crane needed to hoist Falcon out of Olympia's cargo bay had been found at a nearby Air Force base and trundled over. The public affairs people hustled up food, comfort, and communications facilities for the media. It looked like a go.

The only distress came from Adam's arbitrary behavior. He had shut off the TV cameras. Hemming couldn't visually monitor the ship. Adam had the cargo bay off screen just when Hemming wanted a view to help on a problem with the bay doors. One data channel showed Adam apparently having trouble in getting them to seal for reentry. Then that signal source, too, cut off. Adam would have to explain many things when he got home. Hemming, a practical man and an optimist, tried to find value in the forced use of the contingency plan. *This is the best kind of drill. This is the real thing.* He hated it.

153

Bill Nanterre had no trouble convening the top physiologists from Houston's hospitals and universities. To them, Ylena gleamed as a treasury of professional mysteries. At Benson's insistence, Nanterre sequestered them like a jury. One who objected was excluded. The rest were sworn to secrecy and given all videos and records from Olympia, as well as full histories on Ylena and Adam. Every book or lab record the team wanted was brought in. Special phones allowed consultation with any specialist or experimenter in the world.

Mysteries finally yielded to the assembled brains, and they agreed on a report. It had the gist of truth. The medical team penned a compliment to President Sisco for allowing Ylena to receive her father's coded message.

"The young woman would have died, otherwise. We believe that the letter from her father warned her. We believe it prompted an experiment in artificial gravity. Your Commander MacGregor deserves commendation for forthright action in carrying out that test. We believe that the imposition of an equivalent to gravity produced rapid aging in the patient. We believe that a return to earth's gravity would be fatal for this woman.

"Science has an incredible opportunity. We have the ability to maintain her in orbit. We recommend that she be transshipped from Olympia to Space Station Freedom, without return to earth. We know that such an orbital transfer is difficult but also that it is not impossible. We believe the effort and cost are minuscule compared to the knowledge to be gained. In the space environment, we recommend that the National Gerontology Center establish a special laboratory dedicated to the study of this woman and her extraordinary physiology. Science has been given a unique chance to understand the very basics of the aging process."

On the third day, the medical team sent for Dr. Nanterre, briefed him quickly, and gave him their hand-written conclusions and recommendations. He stood dumbfounded, ashen.

"What's wrong, Bill? Are you all right?" one asked.

On his third dry-mouth attempt to reply, Nanterre, in a despairing whisper, said, "Olympia has left orbit, headed home."

154

During reentry, the hellish fire of atmospheric friction heats the shuttle's leading surfaces. At nearly 3000 degrees Fahrenheit, the air is stripped of electrons, creating an envelope of ionized particles. Radio waves cannot penetrate this protoplasmic barrier. In the early days of space flight this phenomenon produced about a 12-minute blackout in communications between spacecraft and ground controllers.

It was later found that a reentering spacecraft was *within* a "sheath," that the "envelope" was not closed. The ionized particles did not encircle the shuttle. Instead, they spread out somewhat like a ship's wake. When TDRS, the tracking and data relay satellite, went into service, it could be "seen" at its 22,300-mile high geosynchronous orbit from the stern of a returning shuttle. That allowed a line-of-sight radio communication to it from the shuttle, and from there to the ground. During reentry, astronauts could now talk through TDRS to ground control. Adam did not.

The original communications blackout was a natural thing, but Hemming faced an unnatural blackout. It began about two hours before landing. Adam had worked smoothly with Mission Control, acquiring and providing data, setting switches, verifying status, and starting or stopping equipment. Ylena worked closely with him, helping complete checklists and confirming his actions and conclusions. Via the only operating TV camera, they could be seen in their seats, with Adam concentrating fiercely.

Each end of the team helped make the contingency plan work well without voice contact. When the TV camera screen went dead again, all telemetry continued, as did fax reception. The bay doors tried to close, finally succeeded, and then showed themselves properly sealed. An occasional fax message came down, providing terse statements on systems and equipment, or confirming procedures.

The imperturbable Hemming was turning into a nail biter. "Why the hell is he doing this to us?" he moaned. "Gonzales," he shouted to the Gold Team leader, "do continual altitude checks on Olympia."

A fixed frequency radio signal from various points of earth bathed the shuttle as she passed overhead. Olympia's transponder received the signals and triggered an immediate broadcast of its own to earth, on another frequency. The total time for the signal and response trip told the distance.

Gonzales reported. "Flight, he's coming out of orbit and making an orderly descent." An hour before touchdown, telemetry from Olympia signaled a deorbit burn at 180 miles altitude. At 24 times the speed of sound, the shuttle dropped for home.

Half an hour later the ionized particles around Olympia began the communications blackout. All data transmission shifted to the geosynchronous relay satellite. The reaction control system shut down gradually as the aerodynamic controls began to feel enough air pressure to maneuver the big ship. Adam needed to make several S-shaped braking turns to dump Olympia's kinetic energy. This reduced the shuttle's speed and helped him avoid overshooting the runway. Finally, enough altitude remained for gliding to reach the runway and not undershoot.

Gliding is a flattering misnomer. The shuttle glides like a misshapen rock, falling on a 22-degree glide slope. Heavier than the original shuttles by half, the 130-ton ship fell at alarming speed toward the desert floor.

From 100,000 feet altitude, Olympia would be on the ground in six minutes. To prevent falling short of the runway called for skillful energy management. Undershooting would be catastrophic, piling up Olympia on a hill, or into one of the lakes along the glide path. Overshooting was infinitely preferable. The new overshoot area of hard-packed surface was a comfort. It added a margin of safety for rolling off the end of the runway in a late touchdown, or in brake failure. The Florida landing site, now four miles long, offered no such comfort. There, overshooting would end in the marshes with the alligators.

Olympia needed no margin. Her twin sonic booms rocked buildings 50 miles away as she decelerated through the sound barrier. Swishing steeply down at 300 miles an hour, Adam's giant glider flared at 1500 feet to kill speed, lower the wheels and set the final glide slope. Eight seconds later came touchdown and a normal roll to full stop. The usual cheers did not arise in Mission Control, only long sighs of relief for the end of this mission of mixed emotions and incongruities.

The convoy of safety teams and equipment sped in from upwind. Even though it had safely landed, Olympia could, for a while, be dangerous to anyone nearby. Even the smoking tires posed a threat. Working in self-contained breathing apparatus and protective suits, the technicians serviced the orbiter's thruster systems and auxiliary power units. Technicians measured temperatures and toxicities, and they roped off the sizzling hot underbelly.

A ramp drove up and backed into position under the egress hatch. The UN Watchers Team stood at its base. They would be first to enter and first to talk with the crew. The Nastran TV van pulled up, its camera turret aimed at the hatch, its transmission antenna locked on a satellite that fed the Nastran communications net. The Air Force crane lumbered up slowly. Down the runway came the Russian cargo plane. Time passed.

"Why isn't anything happening?" asked the President.

"I don't know, sir," said Hemming. "There's still no communication with Commander MacGregor, and he's made no move to open the hatch."

The President impatiently asked, "Is it safe to open up?"

Hemming said, "It is now, sir."

"Then," said Sisco, "Let us do it, for God's sake, and get in there! Let's find out what's going on. You think they're injured?"

Hemming swallowed. "We don't know, Mr. President. They avoided wearing any medical sensors. Normally, I'd be able to tell you heart beats and blood pressure."

He ordered the service team leader to open the hatch and call for the commander to come out. If a call for help were heard, the leader would send in the landing team doctor, but only after sampling acceptability of the cabin air.

Hemming desperately wanted to go home and sleep and forget this flight forever.

155

Calling into the exit hatch got no answer. The air tested fresh. The Watchers protested when a medical doctor began to enter Olympia first. They felt the obligation to see pristine circumstances and conditions. When she ignored them, two Watchers pulled her back from the hatch opening. Headstrong, she struggled, helped by two health technicians. The crowded top of the ramp began to sway, moving to topple. Several Watchers frantically grabbed the hatch rim and stabilized the platform. A forceful security captain restored order. He reestablished the negotiated priority, and the Watchers went first. After four had entered, they shouted back that Olympia's cabin was empty.

Members of the press pushed forward. The security captain ordered the guard force to link arms and hold them back. He kept a few behind the ranks to stop the cameramen from diving between legs. Some of the scrambling divers got through in their zeal to photograph empty spaces, but the guards stopped them at the ramp base.

The Watcher leader, Einer Gustafson, asked that a shuttle astronaut be sent in. Harvey Enders, a disappointed pilot candidate for this flight, trotted up the stairs. Then, unknowingly hoping to reestablish some ownership in the mission, he assumed the role of diplomat and proposed to Gustafson that Ambassador Taksis or the chief of the Russian medical team should enter next.

Gustafson taught the decisive astronaut diplomacy, saying, "Do you propose pairing your Vice President with the Ambassador or with the Medical Director?"

Enders flushed, responding, "The Vice President will make that decision, sir."

"I asked for you because I need you first," said Gustafson. "Go in."

Properly paired, the entourage packed into the shuttle cabin. It was indeed empty. Gustafson ordered the cargo bay doors opened. "Just a few feet, please," he told Enders.

Sunlight began to flood in as the doors opened slowly and laboriously in the burden of gravity. Disbelieving eyes stared into a huge, empty chamber.

Ambassador Taksis bolted onto the debarking ramp and signaled urgently to the pilot of the Russian cargo plane. Its rear ramp promptly fell. Thirty Russian soldiers, machine pistols at the ready, poured down the ramp and trotted into an outward facing ring around Olympia.

Einer Gustafson deliberately legitimized the situation. Commandeering a bullhorn, he called out in Russian to the officer in charge, "Excellent dispersal, major! Hold those positions. The American guards will join you."

Turning to the Ambassador, he said, "A good move, Mr. Taksis. We must freeze the scene. Come with me."

Dragging the panicked Taksis along, he reached the security captain and said, "Place one of your men between every two soldiers. Stay there! You are jointly responsible with the Russian officer for seeing that nothing gets in or out of this area."

The guards went into position. Guns went back into holsters. He had successfully defused the threat.

"Let us now go back in and confer with the Vice President," Gustafson said to Taksis. "We seem to have a first-class mystery on our hands. We must organize a mutual investigation. It will be done with full media coverage. Signal your news chief to join us."

156

The incredible had occurred. There could be no other explanation. Adam had gambled and won. He had turned Olympia over to an experimental software program for shuttle flight control. Known as Steer I, Mark I, it had been developed to deorbit the shuttle and land it at a chosen latitude and longitude, all automatically. The Steer I system provided a hedge against flukes, such as group disease, food poisoning, or other simultaneous disability of a shuttle crew. On its first trial, and without the human presence vital for override in case of error, Steer I had performed perfectly; it brought the shuttle home to a textbook landing. Mission Control considered its performance a marvel.

In the world of politics, journalism, and diplomacy, the automatic landing didn't count as a marvel. What mattered in these realms was not how, but *why* Olympia had returned as a ghost ship. Even more intriguing, what had become of the crewmembers?

Within 24 hours, the fuming Russians ended their boycott of the United Nations. They raged before the General Assembly about the perfidy of the United States. They demanded return of their citizen, Captain Ylena Valena, their spacecraft Falcon, and any remaining hibernation fluid.

Carla Truzski publicly shamed them into joining a five-nation team of their own choosing to investigate the mystery, with full access to any person, or place or records of the United States. This, she said, would be the first demonstration of the validity of the Open Lands concept.

Billions had seen Olympia's landing sequence. Few left their screens as the drama of the empty shuttle unfolded. The chilled, night desert blazed with lights. Under Gustafson's order, technicians documented every moment and move without interruption and they fed live to all TV networks. He wanted no appearance of anything being faked or withheld.

The Russians came to realize that the frustrated and bewildered Americans had no explanation for the absence of the crew. The UN Watchers had sequestered Olympia from the moment of opening the cargo bay doors, using Russian soldiers. Nothing had been taken into or out of Olympia. Confusion reigned in Washington and Moscow.

Accompanied by the Watchers, a UN technical team began an intensive search of Olympia. Meanwhile, radar systems and hundreds of public and private telescopes scanned the skies. They were looking for Falcon because no one had definitive evidence that the ancient Soviet craft had reentered.

With its damaged heat shield, Falcon would have burned up in the atmosphere. Scientists reviewed all film and instrument records from the northern hemisphere's observatories for the early morning of landing day. Olympia's hot reentry showed up. Several streaks, obviously meteors, had been photographed. One fiery streak that partially paralleled Olympia's path became a prospect, but the math of its path proved wrong. Finally, everyone faced mystery. The observations had produced no undisputed signature of a second spacecraft reentering.

After a day of trying, Bill Nanterre got a hearing by the UN team. President Sisco had personally authorized full disclosure of the review and the conclusions of Nanterre's team of physiologists. The sobering report deflated the Russians' steaming animosity like a punctured tire. They became stymied, bewildered believers as the Watchers pounded out the evidence. They showed the TV record of Ylena's experiment, along with scenes of Adam confronting the mass of hair. The hair bag had been found earlier, discarded in a mid deck odds-and-ends net. The color scenes of the bright glory Ylena had worn now showed as bloody, matted masses, crudely cut away. Ylena's emotional plight became clear, and the world sorrowed.

A Russian scientist on the UN team proposed that rapid hair growth would be accompanied by speedy fingernail growth. This triggered a microscopic search of Olympia. One at a time, with TV watching, the investigators opened drawers and lockers for inventory. In the medical locker, along with the motorized saw, sat a ditty bag holding the large, raggedly cut sections of fingernails and toenails. Under it the Watchers found a medical equipment bag, sealed and addressed to the President of the United States.

Simon Sisco deliberated at his end of a TV conference call from Gustafson. True, the seal, and the specific addressee on the medical bag, implied privacy and only one reader, the U.S. President. The Watchers, however, insisted upon a prompt opening, right there in the desert, by the UN team, on global public TV. No other action would meet the test of openness. President Sisco considered. *God knows what will be in that bag!* What's the risk of open disclosure? Sisco knew the integrity of Chief Watcher Gustafson. He sensed the man's determination to display the contents without permission or agreement. Any attempt to stop him would show the United States using physical violence in censorship.

With the cameras now featuring him, Sisco said, "Your Honor, there is no question. You must proceed."

Gustafson broke the security seal and opened the bag, with every move clearly visible in the broadcast. The distinguished Swede removed the contents one at a time and set each on a table, announcing and describing the item aloud. The bag held the letter from Ylena's father; her flight manual; her decoded pages of her father's letter; an envelope addressed from Commander Adam MacGregor to the President; and a video from one of Olympia's cameras. Gustafson turned the bag upside down. The epaulets of a Navy commander fell out. Sisco winced.

Gustafson advised that there be no delay in opening and reading the letter. Sisco agreed. Gustafson flattened the one page letter on the table and signaled the TV camera to record its contents.

Gustafson read aloud, as a split screen showed him alongside the enlarged text of the letter. It was Adam's resignation. It spoke of a need to leave the service for urgent personal reasons that made it impossible to perform his duties as expected. He referred to Ylena as his "charge," acquired in the line of duty. The result of a return to earth would be the death of Ylena, for whom he was responsible as Mission Commander. Her forcible return would be tantamount to murder.

The world watched and listened as Gustafson read on, "With the highest confidence in the new automatic landing software, I will time-set the program to land at Vandenburg. Beforehand, Ms. Valena and I will transfer to Falcon and remain in our current high orbit. We describe our plans and hopes in a TV clip we made a few hours ago and will place in the bag with this letter. In the nature of a report, I conclude that the suspension fluid is fatally flawed. The suspicions, fears, and laboratory tests of Dr. Valena himself, her own father, have been confirmed.

"This letter is to serve as my will. I now authorize the use of all of my assets to compensate for damage, loss, and other expenses caused by me on this flight. This statement and intent supersedes any prior document I have made.

"Mr. President, I sincerely regret terminating the mission in this manner. However, our other choices require the certain death of Ms. Valena. I see no alternative but to leave the life I have known and make a bid for the future, as I do not wish to live without the woman I love."

The French member of the Watcher team nodded sympathetically. He recalled how an English king, early in the last century, had spoken similarly as he abdicated to marry an American. The shaken British establishment had seen crisis, a throne threatened by love, and brought him down. Shakespeare's tribe, of all people, had not understood. *So unnecessary,* he thought. And now a greater sacrifice had sprung from the same root. Once again, unnecessary! Misunderstanding makes love the brother of anguish or the sister of tragedy. Oh, if only these space people had been reached in time to arrange for life on Space Station Freedom! Then he smiled a sad smile. Would it have come to pass? Would the bureaucracies have understood? And made exceptions? And helped? Probably not. He recalled an adage that *"all the world loves a lover."* Fondness is one thing, however, and tolerance another. *Lovers,* he thought, *are taken seriously only after disaster.*

———————————— 157 ————————————

Gustafson, a practical idealist, believed that his role and mission could help produce and maintain world peace. He believed in the ethical tradition of the Watchers: facts and truth must out. Powerful forces in the UN still resisted the role of the Watchers. With every moment of television time, Gustafson diluted their influence, establishing precedent and entrenching the practice of on-site, objective disclosure. His broadcast promised to expose mysteries that had almost sparked space war. Now, watched by the UN General Assembly and citizens of all nations, he would use the spotlight of full publicity to end the Olympia misadventure. He pressed on, no longer seeking anyone's approval, and addressing himself only to the UN Secretary General.

"Your Excellency, this team will now continue its report. Representatives of the U.S. and the UCS verify that I am holding Exhibit Six, so tagged. This is the television disc that Commander MacGregor placed in the bag addressed to President Sisco. The technicians will now load and play it for public broadcast."

Adam appeared on the screen. In silence, he removed his Commander's insignias and placed them in a small bag.

"Mr. President, already in this bag, addressed to you, is the required letter announcing my resignation. I speak to you directly now because no document can convey my feelings and gratitude. You gave me much pride and satisfaction by endorsing me as Olympia's commander. Your support throughout the mission provided strength and confidence during some very trying circumstances.

"Also, I am speaking because a letter cannot express the enormous regret and frustration I feel for the way things turned out. This mission is ending in a way that is not advancing your hopes for world peace. Since that is why you authorized the flight in the first place, my sense of failure made me look hard for some benefit from all our efforts. Perhaps I have found one.

"Perhaps Ylena and I can serve as an example that differences can be overcome, even extreme differences such as ours. She and I were shaped by very different societies, and we came from different centuries, but we have achieved understanding and we cooperate."

He held out his hand, found Ylena's, and floated her into view. Bending, he spun her shoe into a sole lock near his own. She spoke.

"Mr. President Sisco. Hello. Commander Adam has said true. Is possible for get along together. We cooperate. Maybe that is good example. We also plan for future. You bet. That should be more good example."

The winning smile and exuberant sincerity faded into seriousness almost comical. "I know is wrong to leave the post of duty. That would be bad example. Your man does not desert, but stays on his post. Remember, you send him to bring me back. I cannot come now, so his job is not over, unless you need my corpse. Commander Adam is your protector for me for what you made happen.

"I did not take your man away. That would be more bad example. He is free will to go home, but he choose to stay with me. Is that bad example? No! You woke me, and so you owe me. Also, because his mission is at end. You gave him job to find me up here and bring me back for what you call 'show and tell.' You got from me on the TV all the 'show and tell' you could want. Now is over. You do not need him or me. You need only your Olympia ship. He has work very hard on sending back your ship. He is sure of automatic safe landing.

"Commander Adam, very early, he told to me, 'I woke you up and I will not abandon you.' You have trained a much honorable man. I am with full thanks, but what he said spoke only of a duty. Since then has come more. We are become one soul. That is reason I like best that he should stay. That is good reason we want there be a future. But I must stay in space. I must be outcast from earth, be exile. With good luck, maybe not dead exile. We will take big chances on any good idea to live together.

"He said you would say OK for me for to live on Station Freedom. That is not good idea. On your Freedom, I would be laboratory animal, feeling I must earn my way as guinea pig. Research would measure me and watch me always. Blood samples. Specimens! Like my father's dogs. No! We are to be family, I say to him. We must do better! Commander Adam will tell you our good idea. We will take chance on this other idea, not Station Freedom, to do better. You can be big help. Please listen and then be the help. Thank you. Goodbye."

Adam moved forward, filling the screen. He summarized the fateful options he and Ylena had discussed earlier. When he mentioned the possibility for living on Station Freedom, he said, "I avoided communications out of fear that a transfer to Space Station Freedom would be offered or, worse yet, be ordered. Captain Valena, for the reasons you heard, would have terminated herself rather than go. I apologize to all whose work was made more difficult by our becoming incommunicado.

"The option we've chosen poses a great risk, but may, just may, offer us the chance for a life together some day. Using the remaining fluid, we intend to enter suspended animation. We hope to be awakened when migration from earth to space habitats has matured. The fluid is of no use to either of our countries. It condemns a user to a life off-earth. No one would want that. I am the exception.

"I realize the risks, but every other option leads to sure death for one or both of us. One risk, for instance, is that we may not be revivable, if we are ever found. Or, one of us may waken and the other not. Or, we may awaken prematurely, with no rescuers. Or, I may be adversely affected, like Andrei Borodin. On the plus side, we may be awakened in an age when advances in medicine would keep us from high-speed aging if we returned to earth. That would be ideal. However, as a minimum hope, we may be awakened by people who routinely live in space and have established a civilization up here. We would hope, then, to live among them.

"We expect to remain visible by being attached to the damaged external tank. I've placed Falcon there already. You should be able to see us as a bright dot with the naked eye on clear nights. I have set all of Olympia's flight instructions on automatic and will set the cargo bay doors to close on a timer. We will move to Falcon in space suits and push Olympia away for the start of its reentry sequence. Our current high orbit should keep us up here indefinitely.

"We ask your help. Please do not come for us. Let us have our chance; give us this lease on the future. Please encourage the UN to get space migration started. Finally, I ask that you not forget about us. Please help to prevent that from happening."

From off-screen came a cry, "Adam! Wait!" Ylena floated into view, saying, "I know a way they will not forget! The nice man from Bern Bank. Remember? He will help." Facing the camera, she spoke with the assurance that she directly addressed Stephan Maurier.

He laughed quietly at her innocent assumption. He had indeed tuned in, along with most of those awake around the world. He had interrupted his board meeting for the historic drama. In a trance of tingling chill he arose, drawn toward the screen, moving mechanically, eyes fixed on the vibrant image describing his title and function malapropos to the world.

"Comrade Banker Maurier! You did great service to my father. You did great kindness to me. You brought me message that saved my life. I will never forget you. Now I bring you business! I wish your contract, like you did my father. Make your timer system to remember us this day every year, forever, until we become rescue by habitat people."

Maurier, tasting the first tears his cheeks had known in a generation, swayed slowly, murmuring, "Yes. Yes. Of course, of course . . ."

"When we awake, I will do many, what you call, endorsements, and make money. It will pay your bank."

Maurier, the man who wanted to live forever, began to smile. It grew into quiet, knowing laughter, aimed at his ignoble secret goal. *Look at these two! Headed for obvious oblivion, and preparing as for a trip!* His arm rose in an unbidden wave of farewell to the radiant, beguiling creature with such implicit faith in him. He turned to the recording secretary, bestowing upon him the first smile ever.

"Make it happen forever, Frederick, in an account for the name of Ylena MacGregor. The lady wouldn't want it any other way."

Behind him the figure waved her own farewell, saying, "If you tell about us to the future, someday someone will come."

THE END

Epilogue 1

In tiny Falcon, helmets off at last, they rested, nested tight. Leaning across the bulk of the hard suits, they lay their heads together in whispering, fond farewell. By parting they would unite, but neither wanted the conscious communion to end.

"Remember," he told her gently, "if you awake by accident, and you are frightened, breathe from this mask and give me some oxygen also. It will revive me. I will join you until we are ready to inject again."

He pointed at the syringes, filled and taped within reach on the bulkhead.

"Adam, Adam," she said, kissing the words into his ear, "you are my expert in flying *space,* but you have no hours in flying *time.* I have much experience in this, you remember. So I am senior planner. Be relax. Now, I will inject you. No, no! Not me first. You first. You are like the jealous husband, to lock your wife away. Do not worry. How do you say on your TV, 'I do not have date tonight'? Bend your head, I cannot inject through hard suit."

His laugh quieted to a smile as the fluid took hold. They had no further need for words, and they parted with only tender kisses until his fond gaze glazed and his arms floated from their bulky hug.

When he was gone, she slowly, gently, closed the lid on each infinite eye. Turning his head this way and that, she combed his hair. Carefully, she closed all his Velcro pockets and zippered pouches. Humming absently, she rubbed away the contact streaks and scrapes on his hard suit, and then on her own.

She began to tidy up the cabin, gathering the gloves, stowing his syringe, and organizing Falcon's few possessions.

She quietly combed her own hair for a long while.

Then she kissed his craggy features one last time. She set the gas timer, with no fears of any darkness ahead, but with only a sense of pervading light and bright purpose. Removing the emptied syringe from her neck, she acted on a sudden plan.

She moved with slowing motion, short now of time. From a gift box sent up by the women astronauts, she took a small kit engraved, "Sorority of the Sky." She removed a lipstick tube and printed "Shangri La" on a window.

Then, for the first time in her disciplined life, she applied a little coloring to her cheeks and lips. From this sleep, she would be awakening to love. With his firming fingers she closed her own lids. His hand to her lips, she went to join him.

EPILOGUE 2

John Dough prospered. He expanded his articles and broadcasts into a book about the Olympia mission. Full of the personal and emotional knowledge of this literate insider, it quickly became an international best seller. It told of the promising negotiations that followed the Russian's grudging return to the United Nations.

It also told of the honors and scholarship aid heaped upon Anna Schutz for her insight and tenacity in making Ylena's resurrection possible.

It even told of the subtly-staged meeting in the White House where Ambassador Taksis denied espionage. His protests ended when the President had the crippled convict, Byron Desault, brought in. Simon Sisco smiled in grim satisfaction as Taksis turned and went silently out of the room and back to Moscow.

Dough's name and fame, already national, became global. He used his additional power in an unusual way. He began a crusade. Deeply touched by Ylena's courage and Adam's selflessness, John Dough started a campaign to help ensure Ylena's wish not to be forgotten.

"They have chosen the starry way," he wrote. "They are the lover's binary. Their light, so bright in the sky, shines for us, and illuminates our hearts. As those two cherished each other, so should we cherish their memory."

A dryly-humorous colleague suggested that Dough's campaign had the battle cry: "Lovers of the world, unite!"

John Dough's rhetoric, however, was heartfelt, and rang true and forcefully around the globe. Its appeal proved irresistible. His campaign flared among the young, kindled memories in those no longer young, and enlightened the powerful on how to vote. In a unanimous first ballot approval, on an issue sponsored by Carla Truzski, the United Nations designated the Falcon spacecraft the first interplanetary historical site.

EPILOGUE 3

In early darkness, they had climbed strenuously and carefully up the hill. Now, at the lookout point, Yuri helped her onto a cragged rock. They sat in silence, joining the wind-bent arthritic trees in a patient watch of the evening sky and the frozen, crystal moon. He had never before done anything like this, spending extended time with one woman.

She was not of his race or religion. Although he considered them irrelevancies, race and religion were still the crippling hurdles for love, even in the enlightened 21st century. Under these tandem definers of social acceptance, the pressures of families and faculties had been enormous. In the storms and confrontations about his marriage, Yuri had come to understand the blinding focus of Adam MacGregor for a particular woman.

How had Adam put it, "I do not wish to live without . . ."? Yes, that was it. *Why wasn't the motivation clearer to me back then, in Olympia's time?*

"There it is!" he said, pointing upward. Embraced in partisan understanding, they stood and followed the stellar promenade of a twinkling light in stately passage south. Near them, rare at this height, a bird sprinkled the night with song. It flooded Yuri's mind with memories of Wilde's nightingale, singing of " . . . *the love that is perfected by death; the love that does not die in the tomb.*"

Above, bound for the high horizon, in the majestic arc of its vespertine vigil, they saw the lovers' vault coursing the sparkled vault beyond. Cradled by the torn folds of a battered tank, the Falcon tomb cradled a battered love. He breathed a prayer *against* the nightingale's song. He prayed that this love would not be perfected by death, but by resurrection.

About the Author

Charles Boyle retired as Educational Programs Manager for Earth Sciences at the Goddard Space Flight Center, near Washington, DC. His 32 years with the National Aeronautics and Space Administration included several at NASA Headquarters. Earlier, he worked at Esso, Western Electric, Scott Paper, U.S. Steel, and Bell Laboratories.

Boyle is the author of *Tailey Whaley*, an illustrated children's book, in which a whale, born "different," faces intolerance. His 1970's book, *Space Among Us*, described many of the emerging effects of space research on society. Boyle's writing has appeared in *Science* and *Omni* magazines, and he served as space flight editor for the *McGraw-Hill Encyclopedia of Science and Technology*. *Time Magazine quoted* from *Boyle's Other Laws*, a gathering of his aphorisms. He wrote a monthly column called "Space Appreciation" for the *Journal of Aerospace Education* and was a contributing editor to *Space World*, *Ad Astra*, and *Aviation/Space* magazines.

Boyle received a Mechanical Engineering degree from Tulane, a Masters in Business Administration from New York University, and a physics major Masters in Education from Harvard.

He served in the U.S. Maritime Service and the U.S. Navy, 1943–1947.

A scuba diver, sailboat racer, and "ancient athlete," Boyle won two gold medals in track at the 2001 National Senior Olympics. In 2004, he set a new American age group record in the USA Track & Field Masters 3000 meter racewalk.

He lives with his wife, Joan, in Annapolis, Md. They have four sons and nine grandchildren.

Also by Charles Boyle

Tailey Whaley: A Tale of a Whale with a Whale of a Tail
www.taileywhaley.com
www.whalebook.net

Space Among Us

Boyle's Other Laws
A Compendium

TridenT
PUBLISHING

Printed in the United States
62937LVS00003BA/49-69